DANGEROUS DUPLICITY

Sherry Joyce

Published by Hummingbird Flight Press

DEDICATION

To Mary Joyce, my husband Jim's sister who died in the hospital during a preventable procedure at the age of twelve from complications of Cystic Fibrosis. It was so many years ago. We were in our twenties, an age when you don't expect anyone to die. Now, having counseled many bereaved individuals through Grief Share at Holy Trinity Church in El Dorado Hills, I have gained significant insight into the challenges of dealing with parental and family grief. There are no words to explain the depths of grief for a parent who loses a child or someone who felt like he or she failed to protect their sibling. Hopefully this book will enlighten as well as remind us grief is something we all face and is the price of love. In time, one can move forward with hope.

CHAPTER 1
El Dorado Hills, California, 2011

Evan

Evan Wentworth never expected the day to end the way it started. He had the window on the driver's side partly down, enjoying the warm summer breeze and bright red crepe myrtle trees as he drove to Starbucks. "Do you want a strawberry scone?" he asked.

Ashley wiggled in her seat, with her blonde hair blowing in her face and her little arms hugging her favorite doll. "Blueberry," she said while braiding the doll's hair into pigtails like her own.

"Okay, blueberry it is."

He shut off the ignition, taking the keys with him. "I'll be right back," he said to Ashley. Normally he would not have had the police car that morning, but he had to make a stop at the police station to drop off some paperwork in the peaceful upscale town of El Dorado Hills in Northern California. Ashley begged to go along because she rarely saw her brother in uniform as much as she wanted to, and Evan enjoyed having her as a passenger since he wouldn't be on duty for another two hours. After a snack at Starbucks, he'd drive her back to his parent's home on the other side of Highway 50. For a six year-old, she was exceptionally bright, full of enthusiasm for the day when she would become a police officer herself.

He shoved the Starbucks door open with his shoulder. Evan's arms were precariously cradled to his chest, balancing scones, a Latte for himself tucked under his chin, and a juice for Ashley slouched in her car seat. He fumbled for his keys while struggling to hold the paper bags and drinks with his other hand. Focused on the car door and keys, he could not comprehend the cracking, popping sounds. What the heck? Unbelievable! Shots rang out from across the street at the bank. Evan quickly turned and dropped the carton of scones, juice and coffee, the contents now splattered on the ground. Two men with ski masks ran out of the bank. One man yelled out, while the other man ran backwards and fired shots into the bank. People screamed and ran in terror.

Evan had split seconds to think. He got in the car and started the engine. "Get down," he yelled at Ashley while he released her car seat clips.

"I don't want to," she cried, unaware of what was going on.

"Ashley, just do it now," he bellowed at her in a tone that frightened her into submission. She crouched down on the front seat, tucking her doll under her arm.

Evan called in a 211PC robbery in progress on his police radio and drove across to the scene. One gunman was running toward the far end of a large open field across from the bank. Evan opened the car door, drew his gun from his holster and took a crouched stance on the ground and yelled, "Stop where you are!"

The man kept running to the field with a large black bag slung over his shoulder.

"Stop or I'll shoot," Evan demanded.

The man did not stop, and Evan fired three shots at the robber. He watched the man flinch and grab his leg, but did not stop or drop the bag. A helicopter was circling and about to land in the field. Aghast, in the middle of chaos, Evan could not leave the car. He turned just in time to see the other robber fire at the car door—then fire at the car's rooftop, cracking the plastic lights. Bullets ricocheted in all directions. People ran for cover, while others flattened out on the sidewalk. Ashley screamed and sat up with her hands on the window. Evan yelled at her as the bullets splayed through the window, shattering the glass. Evan fired at the second advancing robber, and watched a bullet hit him in the left shoulder. The robber flinched and stumbled backward, but righted himself, turned and ran toward the open field.

The helicopter landed in the dirt creating a whirlwind cloud of dirt, weeds, and debris, making it impossible to see anything other than a wall of dust as the copter ascended upwards out of the shopping village. Apparently both robbers were on board.

Evan, unharmed by spraying bullets, looked in the front seat and saw Ashley's little body, limp as her doll, both splattered with blood. He screamed and grabbed for her, pulling her to himself and yelled, "no, no, no..." Hands shaking, he checked her pulse, which he found, but it was very weak. Ashley was barely breathing. His sweat dripped onto her face while he called for an ambulance.

On the way to nearby Mercy Hospital in Folsom, he rode in the ambulance, holding her hand, while EMT's put a drip-line into her tiny arm and an oxygen mask over her face. The sound of the siren only accentuated the pounding of his heart. Everything happened so fast and in a blur—an anxious doctor met them at emergency, transferred Ashley to a gurney and rushed her down the hall to surgery. Evan did not remember anything anyone said to him except that he was not allowed to follow her into the operating room. Time passed like a sloth moving in slow motion. His throat felt parched and his hands were clammy. He paced, unable to sit on any of the chairs in the waiting room. Evan dropped to his knees, oblivious to others in the waiting room, held his head with one hand and prayed to God—a merciful God who loved children and could save his sister's life. When the doctor appeared through the double doors, with a somber walk, downcast eyes and his surgical mask around his neck, Evan knew God had not listened that day.

In disbelief, he followed the doctor to the surgical room where Ashley had died on the table. The room closed in on him as he looked at a bloody sheet that covered her tiny body. He put his hand behind her head gently holding Ashley to his chest and broke into sobs that echoed the hallways. How would he make the necessary phone call to his parents? His little sister was dead, and it was his fault. He had no idea how many other people were injured or dead at the bank. The room began to spin and his knees went weak.

What had just happened in this small Northern California town where violence and crime barely existed?

CHAPTER 2
Three Years Later
St. Paul-de-Vence

Danielle and Evan

Danielle's woven beige espadrilles caught the edge of a cobblestone upsetting her balance. Her tote bag tumbled from her shoulder. Books and papers scattered in the wind in disarray in the middle of the street. Frustrated, she scurried and bent down to pick up the children's essays, while trying to hold on to the blue ribbons on the back of her straw hat. A gust of wind wafted her hat and it floated past her while she knelt in the street doing her best to capture every sheet of paper.

"Can I help you with those?" a man said, bending down on one knee in the street next to her, assembling papers into an orderly pile.

"Oh, thank you. I'm so sorry to be a bother," she said apologetically in English and brushed her burnished copper tendrils behind her ears.

"No bother at all," he said, smiled and extended his right hand, while carefully holding her hat in the other. "I'm Evan...Evan Wentworth."

Barely composed, and flushed, she stood up holding her books and offered him one hand, and accepted her hat with the other.

"I'm Danielle. You'd think by now I would have learned to watch where I'm going. I was looking into the café window and couldn't see over this pile of books and reports. I ought to buy a backpack instead of carrying all of this in my tote."

"Sounds like a good idea. It's easy to trip over these cobblestones. St.-Paul-de-Vence has so many narrow labyrinth-like streets and beautiful attractions to take one's mind off of walking."

"You're not from here, are you?" she said, still stacking books and papers in a tidy bundle.

"No, from New York. I'm here on vacation."

Danielle brushed dirt off the front of her white ankle-length lace skirt and shook dust out of her straw hat before putting it back on her head. Bits of dust dropped from her hat to her small-boned freckled shoulders and cascaded down her dress.

"It's a blustery day, isn't it?" she said, trying to keep the nervous conversation going. "The winds are blowing off the Mediterranean. Breezes we welcome in the summer."

Anxious to break the uncomfortable tension, he offered, "Can I buy you a cup of coffee? I don't know anyone in this town, or in France for that matter." He removed his Ray Ban sunglasses and stuck the earpiece into the pocket of his pale blue chambray shirt.

Danielle stared into his grey-blue eyes, noticing his tanned face framed by wisps of unruly wavy shoulder-length black hair. Now that she had taken the time to really look at him, she noticed the cleft in his chin, his well-defined nose, and how he towered over her. Something about him made her feel dumbstruck for the first time in her life, as if little bolts of electricity were passing between them.

"I'd love something to drink, but, let me buy it for you. It's the least I can do now that I have all of my work safely in tow."

"Wonderful," Evan said, placing his hand on the small of her back and guiding her into Café de la Place past various tables and chairs filled with locals and tourists enjoying lunch outside, their conversations punctuated with rather loud bursts of laughter.

"Bonjour, ma cherie, Danielle," Lucca, the proprietor, greeted her with affection. "I saw that you had a bit of a stumble. Are you all right?"

"I'm fine, Lucca. Just tripped over my clumsy feet not watching where I was going. I'll have an iced frappé and, oh, please, that strawberry pastry in the glass case."

Lucca nodded, "And who is this handsome stranger?"

"This is Evan. He's on holiday from New York."

"Ah, New York," Lucca said. "Such a big city and so far away. What would you like to drink?" Lucca said, while skillfully manning several other refreshment orders with deft barista skills.

"An Espresso, please," Evan requested. "And regardless of what she says, I'm paying for both orders. I want Danielle to think New Yorkers are gracious and friendly."

Danielle rolled her eyes, putting one hand on her hip and sighed. "Okay, just this once I'll let you pay."

"Sounds promising," Evan added. "This means we will be meeting again," he said, flashing a broad grin. Danielle turned her head and pretended not to hear Evan, but she caught his comment.

"Let's sit outside, but not where it's windy," Danielle said. She carefully balanced her pastry and frothy frappé on her plate, shifting her clumsy tote to her other arm, and selected a table next to a medieval stone wall flanked by a grove of olive trees that blocked the wind.

Evan pulled out a chair for her and sat down, brushing his long hair off his face. He tried not to stare at her, but he couldn't help himself. To him, she was the most enchanting creature he had ever seen. An array of freckles on her nose, and those sprinkled across her cheekbones were only part of her charm. He studied the color of her eyes and noticed they were a golden hazel, widely set apart with impossibly long eyelashes. Her lips were full and unadorned with anything but a hint of gloss. Something about her demeanor radiated both innocence and inner strength, and yet he hardly knew anything about her.

Danielle took off her hat, placed it atop her canvas tote, and put both on the ground between her feet to keep her books and papers secure. Conversation with strangers normally came easy for her, but for some reason, in this man's presence, she felt tongue-tied, at a loss for making intelligent conversation.

"What made you choose St.-Paul-de-Vence for your holiday?" she asked.

Evan studied her, considering an answer that would be honest and hopefully impressive. "I'm an art student, nearing graduation at Parsons School of Design in New York. Before graduating, and completing my final student project, I needed a break from the sweltering heat and impossible humidity in New York. Mostly, I wanted to visit the art museums here, read a good book, and walk barefoot on the beach in Cannes." He flashed a grin.

She watched his face and his calm demeanor before finding the right words. Fluent in English, her nerves often made her revert to her native French, but she carefully chose her words trying to stay composed. "Yes, I know artists enjoy the culture and history of this walled fortress, its ramparts built high upon a hill. We are famous for many artists and celebrities like Marc Chagall, who rests in peace here at the cemetery."

"And, may I ask what you do?" Evan said and gave her a warm engaging smile while taking a sip of his Espresso.

"I am a primary school teacher, with an emphasis on English, but I teach other subjects. In summer, I work with those students who struggle—how do you say, um, did not complete their studies with good grades."

"Were you teaching this afternoon?"

"No. I went to the school to pick up the final semester essays I have yet to grade, and decided to read them at home."

Evan chose his words with great care and was fearful of the answer he might receive, but he had to ask. "Do you live alone?"

Danielle glanced away, considering her reply. The sunset blazed threads across the azure sky in crimson and spun gold. She shielded her eyes with her hand to keep from squinting, thinking about how she would answer a simple question that had such a complex answer.

"No, I don't live alone." She watched Evan's forehead wrinkle into a concerned frown.

"Are you married?" As beautiful as Danielle was, he did not see a ring on her finger, but thought she might be married or in a relationship.

"No, not married," she said softly, while wistfully looking at the sunset.

"I'm delighted," he said with a deep sigh, his chest heaved upwards in relief.

"It's not what you think," she hesitated. "My father and mother are French, but my mother was raised in America. We have a large family. I'm the oldest and I live with my parents, two brothers and four sisters. One of my three brothers does not live at home."

Evan pretended not to be stunned. A young woman so lovely, still living at home with her parents and siblings, was not the answer he was anticipating. Images of a large farmhouse, chickens and animals came to mind. "I see," he said. His brow furrowed, aware he didn't see at all.

"You probably think it's strange that I still live at home, don't you?" Her voice sounded nonchalant, but also pleading.

Evan hesitated, concerned his thoughts were obvious. He did not want her to think he was judging her.

"No, I don't think it's strange at all for you to live with your family."

"I'm glad," she said, sipping the whipped cream off her frappé. "My mother, Marie, has not been well. She has congestive heart failure. My father, Gaspard, has his good days and some that are troubling because he cannot always remember certain words, and he's a bit hard of hearing. He's ten years older than my mother. It's a struggle to watch them age, but as the oldest daughter, I try to look after both of them."

Evan considered her response, realizing her life was nothing like his own spent mostly growing up as an only child. He had a sister, who died when she was six, but decided not to share the information. It still opened wounds he could not talk about.

"Your parents are blessed to have you, but what about your brothers and sisters?"

"Well," she thrummed her fingers on the tabletop. "It's complicated. Chloe, twenty-two, the closest to me in age, is a nurse at the local hospital. She's frequently on call. Lena is eighteen and has had some difficult problems that upset my parents. Amber is fourteen, still in school. Juliette just turned ten, is a handful, rebellious, but very creative."

Not wanting to pry, Evan took slow breaths, letting her ponder her thoughts.

"Do you want to know about my brothers?"

"Of course," Evan nodded. "Tell me more about them."

Danielle smiled, becoming animated. "Lucas is twenty. He works in the lavender business, and has a good job as a manager with a sizeable income. Have you seen our lavender fields?" she asked with enthusiasm.

"They defy description," he noted. "As an artist, I wanted to see flowers blooming in the fields to capture their beauty at dawn and dusk. Somehow, the splendor of blooming lavender cannot be experienced on canvas without seeing it in person."

"I agree," Danielle enthused. "The fields look different in every light, and when they are in full bloom, it's magical."

"Tell me more about your other two brothers," Evan asked.

Danielle gathered her thoughts. "Josh is twelve. He's interested in everything in the ocean and wants to be an Oceanographer. Lastly, there is Valentin, who is eight. He has trouble reading because he is—um, dyslexic, as you say in English. He mixes up his letters when he reads and writes. I try to help him as much as I can."

Evan took a deep breath, trying to assimilate the life Danielle was leading within the construct of a large family. Danielle studied his face to see if he had lost interest, but Evan was still looking directly at her…perhaps through her as if she were a window to an interesting book he wanted to read more about.

"I've told you a little about my family. Tell me about your life in New York City. Where do you live?"

"Well, it will seem odd to you, but I live alone in a two-story loft in Tribeca, an artist haven. My condo is large enough for me to do my paintings inside with canvases sprawled across the floor on top of enormous tarps. There is good lighting during the day with a view of the city."

"What do you paint?" she asked, taking a huge bite of her pastry, which caused the strawberry fruit filling to dribble to her chin. Deftly swiping her hand, she licked the remains off of her fingers.

"It's hard to describe what I paint. Some would say it's definitely contemporary."

"What does that mean...*contemporary*?" she asked, devouring the next morsel.

"That's a good question. I'm inspired to paint what I feel—forms and shapes which don't look like anything, but become an array of colors colliding into each other as an expression of an emotion."

"You mean like Picasso?" she questioned him with deep sincerity.

"No," he said. "Picasso is more Cubism."

Now confused, she did not want to seem unaware of painting styles. When it came to art, she either liked something or she didn't, but had no idea what defined good art unless it depicted something she recognized. Danielle tossed her hair off her shoulders, trying to appear composed. "I like Monet," she said. "His flowers are pretty. They don't always look exactly like flowers, but I can recognize them as flowers. Is his style contemporary?"

Not wanting to offend her, he mentally debated whether to keep this conversation about art, or perhaps change the subject. "Monet's style is considered Impressionist." He said, watching her purse her lips and wrinkle her forehead.

"I guess I've never paid much attention to the *styles* as you say. I wish I knew more," she said with utmost sincerity.

"There's a lot to learn about art," Evan stated. Without thinking, he heard the words coming out of his mouth before he could stop them. "I have a great idea. Would you be willing to go with me to some of your museums? I'd be happy to discuss the differences in artistic styles and periods."

Danielle did not expect the invitation, but realized she wanted to see Evan again. "Okay, I can go with you. Do you want me to meet you at the Maeght Foundation? I have all of these papers to grade tonight and tomorrow, but on Thursday I could meet you around ten when the museum opens. Do you know where it is on Chemin de Gardettes?"

"Yes. That's perfect," Evan added. "Or, I could pick you up at home. I have a car at the hotel."

The frown on her face let him know that she was not particularly interested in having him pick her up at home, but he didn't insist and instead let her choose. "Uh, no." She grabbed her hat and tote handle. "I have a bicycle. I'll meet you at the museum on Thursday."

Evan got up from the table, haphazardly swiping blown crumbs from her pastry off of his lap. Unsure what to do next, he went to pull out her chair, but she had already managed to untangle her belongings and was standing, looking at him. "I'm glad we met," he said. "Discussing art at the museum will be a lot of fun."

"I agree," she said with one arm folded around her tote, and the other holding on to her hat. "Au revoir, then. See you on Thursday."

He stood watching her walk down the street, wondering if she would turn around one more time to wave goodbye to him or not. She didn't. So he began the trek up the street to his hotel. He pulled out his sunglasses and put them on to shade the sunset's glare.

Despite the onslaught of tourists walking the streets, he had an uncanny feeling he was being followed. He stopped and glanced over his shoulder but noticed nothing unusual. Couples walked arm-in-arm. Artists carried canvases. A large, floppy-eared Labrador-like scraggly mutt sniffed the street for discarded morsels. A tall thin man stood with one foot braced against the gallery's façade reading a magazine and flicking cigarette ashes into the street. Tortoise shell sunglasses covered his eyes, his face shaded under a white straw hat—most likely just a tourist in a cream-colored shirt and beige linen trousers minding his own business. Evan shook his head, believing he was imagining someone following him. After all, he was traveling alone, and other than Lucca and Danielle, no one knew he was in the south of France except his girlfriend, Aurora.

Somehow, now thinking about Danielle, Evan felt lightheaded, as if his well-orchestrated life had taken an unexpected leap off a precarious cliff. He shuddered. Suddenly he realized he didn't have her phone number. What if she didn't show up on Thursday? How would he reach her? He didn't even know her last name.

Danielle walked to the end of the street and turned around to catch a glimpse of Evan, but he was already gone.

CHAPTER 3

Aurora and Evan

Evan awoke in his sumptuous bed at the hotel Le Mas De Pierre. Deep burnished gold and white geometric patterned draperies hung pulled back slightly, anchored with iron brackets flanking each side of the French doors that easily opened to the patio. Off-white glazed furniture with cabriole French legs graced the room. Comfortable wicker chairs and a table on the private patio overlooked lush green vegetation and a plethora of floral specimens. Yesterday, this room was a typical, luxury hotel accommodation. Today, the room reminded him of the fresh softness of Danielle in every way. He could imagine her sitting in one of the two comfy gold and white striped silk fabric chairs. Actually, he had a fleeting image of seeing her next to him on the bed, but he would not let his imagination go there. As much as yesterday's chance meeting had infatuated him, he knew there was a phone call he had to make before the time difference from France to New York made it impossible for him to catch his girlfriend at work.

"Hello, Aurora," he said, trying to keep his voice as normal as possible.

"Evan, darling. I've missed you. Where are you staying?"

"I'm at the Le Mas De Pierre in St. Paul."

"Is it absolutely charming? I'm jealous, you know," she said in a convivial tone, "but I know you needed a vacation."

"How's work going?" he said nervously scratching his eyebrow.

"The reception went well. I think the gallery will flourish with the rotation of art we have scheduled for the summer and fall," she said.

"How many people showed up?" Evan asked.

"Nearly two hundred. The invitations sent with the preview color brochures were a great draw. Several paintings and two sculptures sold. Charity events always bring out the best buyers in New York. Tell me what you've been doing. With the time-zone difference, I had to remind myself not to call you."

"I've been walking the streets, enjoying the art galleries here. There are so many. I can't adequately explain the charm of St.-Paul-de-Vence. It's something one has to experience— this historic city has been here since the 9th century, but officially became part of France in 1482."

"Was it an art colony at that time?" Aurora asked, then shouted orders at her secretary to send the wine glasses back to the caterer.

"No," Evan said in a louder voice, trying to be heard above her directional instructions to her staff. "It didn't become a haven for artists until the 1900's."

"You sound like a history buff instead of an artist," she joked.

"I'm both," as you know. With a tinge of guilt in his voice, he said, "I'm going to the famous Maeght Foundation tomorrow."

"What's exhibited there now?"

"Exceptional work by Chagall, Bonnard and Leger. It's an extraordinary modern art museum nestled among umbrella pines. I'd like to see the swooping cowled roofs designed by Josep Lluis Sert," he enthused, but his voice trailed off into the din of her chatter to the cleaning crew.

"I'm sorry," she said. Evan visualized her swiping her chic, razor-cut platinum blonde bangs off her forehead. "What were you saying about the museum?"

"You sound terribly distracted," Evan noted. "I was trying to tell you about the merits of the Maeght."

A loud crash of shattering glass interrupted their conversation, as her voice trailed off, momentarily. "Just use the broom in the closet, for heaven's sake," she barked.

"You want me to use a broom?" he joked.

"No, not you, silly! I'm sorry, Evan. Things are rather hectic. I have to get this all cleaned up before the gallery opens tomorrow."

He sighed, understanding her predicament. One trait he admired about her was her ability to juggle multiple priorities and run one of the best galleries in New York, but at times she did become bossy when frazzled.

"Will you call me tomorrow?" she said.

"Of course," he reluctantly consented, wondering if he would be too busy.

"Love you," Aurora said.

"Love you too," Evan acknowledged, feeling the words stick in his throat for the first time.

A pang of guilt flooded Evan's mind while he considered the conversation he just had with Aurora. Should he have told Aurora about Danielle? Perhaps. It seemed ridiculous to tell her about running into someone on the street, having coffee and talking to a stranger about art. That was not where the guilt was coming from. He tried to convince himself meeting Danielle would be nothing other than spending time with a new friend at a museum. After all, she lived here. Thinking about Danielle's smile, and the strawberry jam on her chin, he knew he was being pulled into something, and possibly someone who could complicate his life. He wasn't engaged to Aurora Banfield. They had dated on and off for years, but both of their parents expected they would get married eventually. They met in art school, and her love of art was what attracted him to her in the first place. She ran a successful gallery where he had exhibited and sold his work. It seemed like a natural fit...a comfortable fit. Why this comfort now seemed uncomfortable troubled him, but not enough to pull him away from seeing Danielle.

CHAPTER 4

Danielle

"How are you feeling today, mama?" Danielle asked while fluffing her mother's pillows up to help her breathe better.

"Good today, actually. I think I could even eat something. Perhaps dry toast and some herbal tea."

"I'm glad to hear it. I'll make you breakfast and then get you dressed for the day. The weather is warm. Would you like to sit in the garden?"

"That would be nice," Marie coughed, her chest straining and heaving to take in more oxygen from the tank sitting next to her bed. The gurgling sound in her lungs was a constant reminder of taking for granted the most basic aspect of living—breathing.

Danielle flipped on the valve in the shower to heat up the water, and returned to her mother to help her out of bed. A blessing, her mother was small-boned, barely weighing as much as her petite sister, Chloe. Danielle shut off the oxygen tank, and carefully removed the tubes, which were not critical for her mother's health, but did enhance her breathing during the night. She put her arm around her mother's back and under her arm, turning her so her feet were on the floor, and helped her to the bathroom.

Their routine, familiarly established, allowed Danielle to sit quietly on the bed for a few minutes to give her mother privacy. She glanced at her watch, noticing it was not yet 8:30. Peaceful minutes in the early morning with her mother were priceless. Most of the time Danielle would describe living with her family as a revolving door of chaos. Someone was always coming or going. Her father, Gaspard, had gone to work at his usual time leaving before 6:00 in the morning. Her sister, Chloe, was already on duty as a nurse at a hospital in Nice, where she worked the nightshift. Lena, barely eighteen, insisted on sleeping until mid-morning, a direct result of her late-night partying habits and perhaps use of recreational drugs. Juliette and Amber, full of boundless youthful energy, preferred to sleep until 9:00. Josh and Valentin were usually up and out of the house during the summer long before mid-morning. Danielle couldn't remember a time when being at home was quiet, except when everyone was sleeping.

"How was your day yesterday?" Marie shouted through the bathroom doorway.

"Rather humorous. I stumbled and lost control of my tote bag. Gusts of wind sent my books and papers onto the street in front of Café de la Place."

"You didn't fall though, did you?" her mother frowned.

"I didn't fall down, but perhaps I fell a bit another way. I met a charming young man on holiday from New York. He helped me pick up my books and papers, and then we had coffee at Café de la Place while we talked."

Her mother was silent for a moment, not sure what to say. "That's nice dear. So, you like this new man?"

Danielle heard the toilet flush, a signal to help her mother undress and take a shower. The water was exactly the right temperature, and Danielle guided her frail, naked mother into the shower, carefully placing her mother's arm on the grab bar for stability.

"I liked him right away," Danielle said. "It's hard to explain. He's terribly attractive," she laughed, while closing the shower door.

"You said he was from New York?" Marie asked, the shower water drowning out her words.

"He's an art student here on holiday."

The steam filled the bathroom fogging up the mirrors while Danielle sat on the edge of her mother's bed. As soon as she heard the shower water stop, she got up and wrapped her mother a fluffy towel, helped her dry her back, and enveloped her carefully in the terry cloth bathrobe from the back of the bathroom door. She walked her mother to a large chair by the window, and began applying a lavender-scented body cream to her mother's back.

"I'd like to wear my blue slacks today with the blue and white printed top," Marie said while slathering cream on her arms and legs.

Danielle selected fresh underwear, the other requested clothing items and matching shoes, and helped her mother dress for the day, giving her a hug and kiss on her cheek. "I'll go get your breakfast now. Would you like to eat in the kitchen or outside on the patio?"

"On the patio, since the weather is nice."

Danielle made the bed quickly, picked up the wet towels and put them in the hamper. She placed her mother's floral nightgown on her pillow, and re-hung the bathrobe on the back of the bathroom door—a ritual she considered a blessing. Caring for her mother was something she enjoyed, and never felt as if it was a burden.

"Here's your toast and tea. Can I get you anything else— perhaps a soft-boiled egg?"

"No, darling. Tea and toast are the only things I can manage right now. I'm sorry the new medication made me so sick to my stomach, but the nausea is gone today. I think my body adjusted to it."

"That's good, mama. If it does not agree with you, Chloe said she would talk to your doctor at the hospital and see if he can prescribe something else."

"Sit, sit, please, Danielle."

Danielle pulled up a patio chair, adjusted the overhead umbrella so the sun would not be in her mother's eyes, and sat down with her toast, slathered in fresh creamy butter, raspberry jam and her own cup of hot coffee.

"So, tell me more about this new young man," her mother's eyes widened while she pushed her damp auburn curls off her forehead.

"I don't know very much about him. His name is Evan— Evan Wentworth. He's graduating from an art school in New York—Parson's something, and wanted a break from his studies."

"Ah, another art student. As if we don't have enough artists in this town already. But, it is why they come here, isn't it?"

"Yes, of course, mama," Danielle said, wistfully glancing at the billowing white clouds, piled atop one another like giant exploding cotton balls. "We have exceptional museums and countless art galleries. He wants to walk barefoot on the beach in Cannes, too," she said, smiling at the thought.

"Well, it's not likely you will run into him again is it?"

"Mama, to my surprise, he asked me to go to the Maeght tomorrow."

"What?" Marie sat back abruptly in her chair, almost spilling her tea on her blue slacks.

"It's not a date, mama. He only wants to show me the kind of paintings he does in New York, since I didn't understand the description of his painting style."

Marie studied her oldest daughter, and could already tell she was in denial about her attraction to this new man. "What about Ryan?" Marie's eyes narrowed, her fingers adroitly swatting a honeybee off her empty teacup.

"Ryan is different. You know how I feel about him." Danielle's coffee cup shook and she raised her voice as if she needed to convince herself. "He's strong, determined, charming, stubborn, and a wonderful business partner for papa. We date. We have a good time with one another, but I don't know if I want to marry him. I'm only twenty-eight, and in no hurry to get married."

Marie sipped her tea, studying her daughter. Danielle was exceptionally beautiful—a mirror image of her mother when she was younger, except her daughter's hair was a lighter red. "I leave it to you, Danielle, if you do or don't want to tell Ryan you're going on a date with a stranger."

"Mama, please. It's not a date!"

"Yes, darling. It's not a date. We'll see. We'll see."

CHAPTER 5

Evan

Evan awoke early, the time zone difference made it impossible to sleep. After tossing in an unfamiliar bed, at 3:00 a.m. he decided to shower. Wafts of steam only added to his room's muggy scent because he'd forgotten to turn on the air conditioning. Slivers of moonlight beamed through the divided glass panes, creating a pattern on the floor resembling an elongated, stretched out French door. Neither hungry nor tired, he decided to don walking shorts, a comfortable tee and his running shoes, and take a drive to Cannes. No one in the lobby of the hotel seemed to think it unusual for a tourist to be up in the middle of the night, nor did the bellman object and gladly retrieved his car.

Top now folded down on his black Mercedes Coupe, his hair blew in the wind. He found the soft night air invigorating. The sea's salt spray misting in the air from the Côte d' Azure didn't resemble the familiar scents of Tribeca.

He drove the highway lost in thought until he reached Cannes. After his run on the beach, he'd have plenty of time to return to his hotel, shower again and meet Danielle. He followed the car's navigation system toward the Hotel de Ville through some of the back streets along Rue D'Antibes, until he spotted the Hotel Intercontinental, lit up at night for safety, as much as for its stunning architecture. Rare as it was, he found a parking space along Rue du Canada, put up the convertible top, locked the car, and began a light jog toward the Promenade De La Croisette. A bit of a surprise, the Promenade was filled with nightwalkers, most likely travelers from other countries unable to sleep, and residents walking a confluence of small dogs on intertwined leashes, sometimes three or more at a time.

Looking back at the Intercontinental, built in 1911 by the architect, Henri Ruhl, the Rococo-style exterior was studded with wrought-iron balconies, cornices, and two enormous twin black cupolas, said to be a model of the breasts of the notorious Belle Otero, a half-gypsy courtesan who captivated Ruhl. Evan decided Ruhl had a sense of humor.

After twenty minutes, the sound of Evan's running shoes echoed the beating of his heart, now thundering in his chest. Sweat poured down his back while he bent forward with his hands on his knees to catch his breath. He tied his hair back with a rubber band, and made his way to one of the empty benches on the Promenade. Again, he had the uncomfortable feeling of something not quite right. He looked around, watching people who seemed to be unaware of dawn breaking. People sat in the sand on the beach, smoking. Others were entangled in embraces, their movements tossing unwelcome sand onto their blankets. Women walked leisurely with their arms entwined, a sight he didn't see as often in New York where people hustled.

"Pardon, Monsieur, quelle heure est-il?" Startled, Evan wheeled around on the bench, not really understanding a word of what was said, but noticed the man was pointing at his own wrist where a watch would be, if he had one, with little stabbing motions. "Ah," Evan smiled, looked at his own watch and showed him the time at 5:45. The white-bearded elderly gentleman in a grey suit nodded, "Merci, merci," and shuffled along with his cane, tapping the pavement for support. Evan decided to keep his Tag-Hauer watch in his pocket in the future, uncertain of the potential level of crime.

He knew he had a long walk back to his car, but it would give him plenty of time to think about what he would say to Danielle, and how he would conduct the discussion about art. The Maeght has over 200,000 visitors a year, and perhaps it would be easiest to talk about Marc Chagall's 'Le Vie'. He liked Chagall, not so much for what he painted, but because he synthesized the art forms of Cubism, Symbolism, and

Fauvism, which gave rise to Surrealism. Evan knew Chagall saw his work as not the dream of one people, but of all humanity. Chagall did not try to hide his Jewish roots, but instead embraced them in vibrant color and form, often depicting village life. For an artist who learned to draw by copying images from books at the library, Evan hoped this would be interesting to Danielle.

He reached his car, clicked open the trunk, grabbed a towel and awkwardly reached under his shirt to dry his back, then stretched to dry his muscular calves and hung the towel around the back of his neck. Before sliding into the leather seat, he glanced around, just to be certain he wasn't being followed. There was no one in sight. He shook his head and decided he was being a typical tourist, afraid of his own shadow in a foreign city.

CHAPTER 6

Danielle

Danielle couldn't sleep, woke up early and made coffee. It was unusual for her not to be able to sleep, but she knew she was a little nervous about seeing Evan. She chose a powder blue skirt and floral top, shook her head in disgust, then took both clothing items off, and instead tried to find something where she would not look overtly attractive. Instead she chose dark blue capris and a pale blue tee shirt. Because of the humidity, she tied her long red tresses into a ponytail, grabbed silver hoop earrings with little blue beads strung on the curve, and flat sandals, so she wouldn't be stumbling around like a klutz. She was still embarrassed about tripping in the street, but she knew if she had not stumbled she wouldn't have met Evan.

She went out on the veranda, drinking in the scent of the jasmine and fragrant "Double-Delight" roses, a gift from one of her father's customers. Her strong coffee tasted good, doused with thick cream and two spoonfuls of sugar. A lounge chair beckoned in the fading moonlight, occupied by one of their many stray cats. It was not often that she was alone with her thoughts and rarely gave credence to her own needs. With a large family, someone always needed attention, and her mother was her self-anointed responsibility. Now sitting comfortably in the chaise, Danielle asked herself a question she frequently pondered, but was unsure she really wanted to find a different answer. *What do you want to do with the rest of your life?* The answer was always the same: *take care of my parents and siblings who depend on me.*

Fear crept into her thoughts. What if her mother got worse? What if she had to stay home and care for Marie and give up her teaching job? What about her sister, Lena? If she was using drugs, would she have to put her in a clinic? Danielle made a mental note to talk to Chloe about her fears. Other thoughts flitted in and out of her mind, and the coffee went cold. The idea of getting married and having a husband and children to care for not only seemed unlikely, but impossible. Sunrise began to break in the sky with slivers of pale yellow sending the crickets and frogs into silence. It was already time to wake her mother and begin the daily routine before meeting Evan. She stood up, took a deep breath, and refused to answer the last question she pondered: *Why am I meeting Evan today?*

CHAPTER 7

Evan

Evan stood on the walkway in front of the Foundation Maeght nervously shuffling his loafers on the pavement. He was fifteen minutes early and would have been even earlier if he hadn't reminded himself not to be so obvious. He glanced at his watch, wondering if she would be on time. It was 9:45 a.m. and they agreed to meet at 10:00. It seemed like it would be the longest fifteen minutes, so he sat down on a bench and took in the architecture of the Maeght. He promised himself he would not spew a preponderance of artistic knowledge at her. Intimidating her could be the end of their relationship, he thought, and quickly reminded himself they did not have a relationship. A one-day chance meeting did not qualify as a friendship much less a relationship.

It was now 10:15 and Danielle was nowhere in sight. He was quite certain she would show up because she sounded so enthusiastic about spending time discussing art. Deflated by 10:45, Evan chided himself for not getting her phone number—dumbest thing. Although he did not want to leave the Maeght, rejection was something he could accept. He decided what he had taken as her spontaneous personal interest in art might have been nothing more than a courtesy.

Reluctantly, shoulders stooped, Evan got up from the bench and remembered the barista who seemed to know Danielle. Perhaps Lucca would be willing to tell him where Danielle lived. It couldn't be too hard to find her farm. If he could talk to her, maybe he could convince her to trust him as a friend.

CHAPTER 8

Ryan

This was the first time the drug delivery did not go as planned. Ryan Coltrane had promised his clients a fresh supply of high-grade cocaine, for which they were willing to pay an extra five grand in cash. How was he supposed to know the client would not show up? Clients who were uber wealthy paid exorbitant fees for chartering the yacht, one of the finest in the Côte d' Azure.

Money was no object for these clients, but it was for Ryan. He had to dip into the company till to borrow money from Danielle's father's business to come up with the cash for the cocaine. Ryan charged the stated yachting charter fee, but charged the client an additional coke fee in cash, usually five grand. He paid the supplier two grand and kept three grand for himself, now a tidy sum in his vault at home along with the drugs. When the client paid him, he noted the standard charter fee in the accounting spreadsheets and reported that information to Armond, the controller.

It was easy to skim off the top, funnel the drugs from one yacht to another, stow it in the hull in a secret place, and keep it there until the clients arrived, sampled it and paid for it. In a year, Ryan had managed to stash away twenty grand.

This was the first time he'd have to front the money to the drug dealer, who would demand payment, regardless of whether the client showed up. Ryan never had a client who wanted drugs cancel a charter. The problem was he'd have to pay for the drugs himself, and go home to grab the extra cash, but he didn't have time. He decided to stop at Gaspard Yachting Charters, where he worked as Gaspard's partner, and change the computer's accounting records. He needed to modify his spreadsheets to show a default in the chartering records, because no charter had occurred tonight, borrow five grand, and put it back when he had time to get the money from his own vault at home. Risky, but it had to be done.

He brushed his sun-bleached hair out of his amber-flecked hazel eyes, and drove to Gaspard's parking lot. 2:00 in the morning was a lousy time to go to his office, but it was the only opportunity to do so when no one was around because even the cleaning crew had stayed until 1:30 in the morning. He shut the door of his silver BMW, pulled his black fleece hoodie around his shoulders and walked to the entrance of the office. He took out his card key, swiped it, and entered the hallway with a small flashlight he had taken from his glove compartment. In the darkness, with the flashlight shining small pools of light at his feet, he could see the carpeted floor in front of him and made his way down the hall toward his office.

He turned the corner and noticed a desk light was on in his office. What the—?

"Armond! Why are you in my office?"

"I know what you've been doing." Armond clenched his jaw and glared at Ryan.

Ryan controlled his voice. "Oh, yeah, what's that?"

Armond pointed a finger at Ryan. "You've been embezzling!"

"Prove it," Ryan said, his face flushed red, his palms starting to sweat.

"As financial controller of this company, I can and I will. In fact, I'm telling Gaspard first thing in the morning."

"I don't think so," Ryan bellowed.

"Watch me, you sonofabitch. Gaspard treated you so well—made you his partner, and you're nothing but a thief!"

Armond, with his stocky frame and slightly balding frizzy hair turned around and started to walk out of Ryan's office.

Ryan momentarily froze, but in the heat of the moment, walked behind Armond and grabbed him by the neck locking his arm across Armond's throat.

Armond backed into Ryan, and kicked him in the kneecap, sending both of them to the floor. Armond's head hit the glass coffee table, shattering splinters of glass across the carpet. Yachting magazines flew off the table, along with a humidor box of cigars. Both men stumbled to their feet.

Ryan punched Armond in the stomach, sending him into the wall, and knocking down a metal sculpture. The two men struggled on the carpet and fought, until Armond hit Ryan in the face, splitting his lip. Blood spattered down Ryan's hoodie. Both got up from the floor and stared at each other like two wolves unwilling to relinquish dominance, fists raised.

"I'll tell Gaspard myself," Ryan yelled.

Armond threw his hands up in the air. "I don't believe you."

"Well, believe it. It's better it comes from me."

"I'm going to the police. Assault and battery goes well with embezzlement."

"Stop it! You're being dramatic. I said I'd tell Gaspard."

Winded and exhausted, Armond breathed heavily. Sweat dripped from his forehead. He glanced down at blood spots from Ryan's lip now spattered against his chambray shirt.

"Look, I'm sorry I grabbed you. I lost my temper," Ryan pleaded. "I'm sorry I hit you."

Armond, dumbstruck and gasping, glared at him wondering what he should do next. "All right! Tell Gaspard tomorrow, or I will," he said with all the determination he could muster, and wiped the sweat off his brow. He stroked his swollen wrist, knowing it would be as black and blue as his stomach tomorrow. The door slammed, rattling the walls of glass, as Armond left.

Ryan stood there, legs shaking, dabbing at the blood on his mouth. He knew what he would have to do, and it angered him. But, he had no other choice. First, he had to knock the large glass-enclosed print of their latest luxury yacht off the wall, or he'd have no explanation for what just took place in his office.

CHAPTER 9

Danielle

Danielle was out of breath as she walked through the hotel's lobby.

"Excuse me, but can you tell me Evan Wentworth's room number?"

The hotel desk clerk looked at the copper-haired woman biting her lower lip while she stood at the registration counter as if her life depended on seeing Mr. Wentworth.

"I'm terribly sorry, Miss, but I'm not able to give out that information."

Danielle sighed, stood there and her shoulders drooped in frustration.

"But, you can call him on the house phone over by the wall," the clerk said. "There is a phone just beneath the large mirror next to the floral arrangement. I'll ring his room for you."

"Thank you so much," Danielle said, waving a grateful hand to the desk clerk as if he had just saved her life.

"Hello? Evan? It's Danielle."

"Danielle? Where are you? I wondered what happened when you didn't show up."

"I'm in your hotel lobby," she said, her voice cracking with nervousness while she chewed on the inside of her lip.

"I'll be right down," Evan said. "Give me five minutes."

He threw on a tee shirt, his jeans and grabbed his flip-flops and headed for the elevator. She was sitting in the lobby in a large, over-stuffed cordovan leather club chair that engulfed her small frame so that he could only see the top of her head.

"Danielle, this is unexpected, but I'm so glad to see you. What's wrong? You look upset."

"Evan, I'm sorry I didn't get your phone number or give you mine. I didn't know how to reach you, but then I remembered you were at this hotel." She wiped her bangs off her forehead, and heaved a sigh of exhaustion.

"Can I get you something to drink?" Evan asked.

"I can use a drink. A glass of Chablis, please."

"Great. Let's go into the bar where we can be more comfortable."

Evan sat down opposite her at a small bistro table and could see her freckles were even more prominent when her face was pale.

"I had to tell you why I couldn't meet you at the Maeght. I felt terrible about it, but Armond, who works for my father's company, did not show up for work. No one has heard a word from him."

"Is that unusual?" Evan asked, aware his detective skills were starting to resurface after a long absence.

"Yes. He's our financial controller. My father trusts him completely."

"Did your father try to contact him?"

"Of course," Danielle said, taking a sip of her wine, and then another. "My father even went to Armond's home. There was no sign of him. The front door was locked, nothing disturbed. He peered through the bedroom window and his bed was made. It was as if he never came home from work."

"That's strange," Evan said. Not sure what to say next because he didn't know Armond, so he asked. "Was he upset about anything at work?"

"I asked my father if there were any work-related problems and he shook his head. We're very worried something had happened."

"Have you contacted the police?" Evan wondered if he was intruding in their personal business.

"My father did, of course." Danielle explained. "When Armond didn't call or come to work we knew something wasn't right."

"What about his family?"

"He has a brother, Giles. We contacted Giles and Armond's parents, but they haven't seen him either."

Trying to be positive, Evan said, "I'm sure he'll turn up. Something must have happened that he had to attend to. If he is a reliable person, then he's not going to do something that will hurt his position in the company or upset your father."

"You're right, of course." Danielle began to stand up. "I should go. I know I'm bothering you with our troubles, but I didn't want you to think I wasn't interested in touring the Maeght with you. I would have enjoyed that," she said with a sigh and her eyes pleaded for his understanding.

"Maybe we can go some other time," Evan said.

"I would like that."

"Can I walk you to your car?" Evan started to help her by pulling out the chair where she sat.

"Oh, I didn't drive. I don't drive. I took a taxi."

"I'll gladly take you home. You came all this way, and it's late."

"All right," Danielle said.

"I'll be right back. Got to get my keys. Please wait here and promise me you won't disappear."

Danielle smiled for the first time since she arrived. "I'll be right here, I promise."

CHAPTER 10

Ryan

Ryan finally left Gaspard Yachting at 2:15 in the morning. The parking lot was empty and a lone streetlight cast an amber shadow. He glanced back at the card reader on the exterior of the building and knew he would have to do something about that later, but he had no time to waste now. His split lip had stopped bleeding, but hurt like hell.

He'd been so careful about dealing with clients who wanted cocaine. At first it was going to be a one-time drug deal, but then the lure of the cash was something he got caught up in. If he didn't deliver the drugs, he would lose some very high-end charters.

He shivered in his car, driving with low beams on until he reached Armond's house. Last year's company summer party was held there, and he knew exactly which house was Armond Fouquet's. There it was, a small stucco and timber home on a street with an open field adjacent to a forest and only two other houses spaced several meters away.

He shut off the engine and craned his neck to see if lights were still on in the house. They were. After the office scuffle, he hoped Armond would not have gone to bed, and in fact, Armond had left only fifteen minutes before him so he was sure he'd still be up. Ryan struggled with the inevitable. He opened the car door, got out, and stood there deciding what to do—something he didn't want to do, but what choice did he have?

He popped open the trunk and grabbed his scuba diving gloves, stuffed them in the pockets of his hoodie, and pulled the hood up over his head. Other than a black cat with one white paw prowling the street, it was eerily dark, misting slightly and biting cold. Not even a sliver of a crescent moon peered out behind the clouds to cast any light. He walked up the front stone steps, placed in an irregular garden-like pattern and knocked on the front door. He told himself this could not look like a breaking and entering scene.

Ryan heard squeaking footsteps on the hardwood floor inside the front door and took a deep breath. He heard the door unlock and waited.

"Ryan! What are you doing here?" Armond said, shocked to see his co-worker standing on his front steps in the middle of the night.

"Armond, please. I needed to come over. The whole scuffle in the office—I'm terribly upset about it."

"You should be," Armond said with a scowl, his eyes squinting for truth in Ryan's words.

"Look, we've been colleagues for sometime now, and I'd hate for this to interfere with our being able to work together."

"That depends on whether you tell Gaspard what you've done, and when you do, he'll fire you. You know that, don't you?"

"So, I'll be fired. I'll live with that."

Armond looked surprised, but relieved. "How did you get into this mess in the first place?"

"Do you mind if I sit down? If you have a beer or something, I'll tell you."

Armond turned and started to walk into the kitchen, but never got there. Ryan bolted up from his chair, scuba gloves on his hands and reached his arm around Armond's neck and tightened his hold, with his gloved fingers cutting off the artery. His other hand pinched Armond's nose closed and covered his mouth. Armond groaned and struggled, already weakened from the earlier fight, and dropped to the floor. Ryan held the chokehold until Armond stopped breathing and then snapped his neck—skills learned long ago as a black belt came back as pure reflex. No noise, no broken furniture. Now, what to do with the body?

He checked Armond's pocket and found a small keychain with several keys, his wallet and cell phone. He quickly stuffed those items into his own blue jeans. Then he picked up Armond, dead weight that he was, and hoisted him over his shoulder. The front door was unlocked, so he pushed the lever, locked it from the inside and pulled it shut. Ryan had no idea what Armond weighed, but damn, he was heavy. He stumbled with Armond on the stone steps, and Armond's body dragged to the ground. Ryan was bursting with adrenalin. Sweat dripped down the back of his neck. He popped the trunk and stuffed Armond inside, bending his knees to fit sideways into the space. He looked over his shoulder fearful someone might have seen him, but Armond's neighbors seemed to be asleep. Darkness blanketed the street and a blustery wind shook the leaves on the trees. A neighbor's dog barked in the distance, rattling Ryan's nerves.

He got into the car and started the engine. Now shaking, fractured thoughts about what to do with the body plagued him. Ryan pinched his forehead to keep a splitting headache from reaching a full-blown migraine about to blind his sight. He drove to the local village with several closed restaurants and bars. Lights off, he headed the car down the alley until he saw a dumpster.

Ryan shut off the engine, opened the trunk and looked at Armond, his chambray shirt and tan trousers splattered with blood from the earlier scuffle in the office. He glanced around and saw no one as he reached in the trunk. The stench from the alley was dank and disgusting. Fumes came up from vents in the sewers, while water from pipes dripped and trickled alongside alley crevices. Rats scrambled, nibbling at discarded food and garbage, making Ryan gag.

He lifted the dumpster's lid, with Armond's dead body hoisted over his shoulder. Just as he began to heave Armond into the trash, he noticed one foot was missing a shoe. Too late! With a soft thud, Armond landed in wasted food and sunk into heaps of discarded stinky garbage.

Ryan rushed back to the car, checked the trunk for the missing shoe. It wasn't there. "Shit!" he said out loud, "where the hell is that shoe?" He closed the trunk and took off his scuba gloves. He had to go back to Armond's home and see if he could find the missing shoe. Ryan's heart was beating in his chest like a racehorse on steroids. He shook his head in frustration. Did the shoe fall off outside Armond's house? In the house? "Crap," he said. "I can't go back into the house. It's locked. I locked the damn door."

He drove, wiping sweat off his forehead, holding his head in disbelief at his misfortune. He kept muttering, "Damn shoe, damn shoe," until he finally reached Armond's home. It was nearly four in the morning, still dark, still blustery and damp. He looked around and in the blackness of what was now a terrible night, searched the grounds and couldn't find the shoe. Furious with himself, he gritted his teeth in disbelief that he had to return to the scene of the crime. He knew the front door was locked. Would he be able to get in some other way? He went around the back of the small stone residence, and tried a window. No luck. He strained with his hands over his eyes, nose pressed against the kitchen's panes, and could see nothing on the floor. No shoe. He wiped the nose smudge off the window with his sleeve.

He felt dizzy, his headache now a raging migraine. Then he realized another mistake—the lights in Armond's house were still on. If Armond hadn't gone home tonight the lights in his home would be off. If he was mugged somewhere near the bars and restaurants, his wallet would be missing and probably his keys. A mugger would find money in the wallet, a driver's license and Armond's address, most likely thinking he could also do a robbery. Frustrated with himself, Ryan absent-mindedly remembered he had the keys.

He headed back to the car, put on the scuba gloves again, opened the front door, and looked around for the shoe. It was nowhere to be found. This time, he turned out the lights before locking the door. He'd dispose of the keys, cell phone and wallet—that would be the easy part. Other than the missing shoe, Ryan felt like he had covered his tracks well. It would probably be less than a day before they would discover the body.

Ryan headed home, doubtful he'd be able to sleep. The only thing on his mind was a stiff drink—a split lip, his migraine medication and the eventual discovery of a body with one missing shoe. Then there was the mess of shattered glass in his office, the building card reader clocking his entry to the office, the company's surveillance camera seeing him go in an out of the building shortly after Armond left, and money he would not have for the next cocaine deal.

No surprise, sleep did not come. Ryan tossed and turned, fretting about whether he'd be able to create some sort of viable explanation for his beat-up appearance when Gaspard asked him what happened. If it weren't so ludicrous, Ryan considered concocting a story about being mugged. It would explain the split lip and bruises, and he could make up a story about the appearance of the mugger, but then he'd have to put a time and place to it, and he couldn't. When and where was he mugged? He couldn't explain being mugged in a completely different village, on the same night, some distance from where Armond lived. The police would never buy it.

Ryan glanced at his bedside clock, the digital numbers clicking 5:00 a.m. He got up and decided to shower, change clothes, dump his hoodie, Armond's keys, phone and wallet in the ocean. The yacht he planned to use needed refueling—a good reason to take her out on the ocean. He grabbed a loose brick from his apartment complex backyard BBQ area, and some rope from his garage storage space. Then he wrapped the hoodie around the keys and wallet, smashed Armond's phone with his foot, put the brick inside, and tied it tightly with a rope before tossing it into a duffle bag and headed out.

Pale strands of light were breaking on the horizon with the tide going out. Yachts and other boats anchored at the marina rocked slowly in the harbor's waves. Ryan got out of the car, grabbed the duffle bag, and headed toward his company's most prized rental yacht, *Belle Chloe*, named after Gaspard and Marie DuBois's second daughter. At sixty-two meters, with six guest cabins and rooms to accommodate a full crew, she was one of the larger enviable yachts of the Mediterranean. The port in Nice was surrounded by superb Genoese-style pink and faded ochre old buildings, always captivating, always invigorating, still lined with street cafes of the Cours Saleya and beaches of Baie des Anges. The French Riviera never disappointed, except today when disposing of evidence of a murder required clandestine behavior.

"Bonjour, Ryan," Pierre, the harbormaster waved a recognizing greeting. "Looks like a calm day," he said.

"Winds have died down. Going to fill her up before taking her out," Ryan said. "Can you take me to *Belle* now?"

"Oui. Give me a minute to get the keys."

"Merci," Ryan said, trying to tilt his visor to shield his face.

"Merde," Pierre said. "What happened to you?"

Without rehearsing what he would say, Ryan created an on-the-spot alibi for yesterday's office scuffle. "I had a nasty fall at the office."

"Je ne comprends pas," Pierre said while scratching his head.

"I'm a klutz. I was carrying a plate of food from the kitchen and tripped over the glass coffee table in my office. I fell hard, knocked over a sculpture and stumbled into the wall sending a large framed picture crashing on top of me."

"Are you sure you're okay?"

"Oui, but I also have to explain all this to Gaspard who will be in disbelief when he sees the mess."

"Here we are," Pierre said, tendering Ryan to the ladder on the *Belle Chloe*.

"Thanks, Pierre. I'll let you know when I'm coming in." Ryan threw the duffle bag over his shoulder and waved goodbye. "A bientot."

The sky turned shades of crimson, rust and gold as the sun poked up over the water's horizon. After dumping the rope-tied hoodie of evidence, Ryan decided he earned a much-needed nap on deck. He started up the engine, completed a stop at the refueling station, and headed out to sea. Thoughts plagued him about how he'd get the blood out of the trunk of his car and when he would disable the surveillance system on the front of the yachting company—troubling, little annoyances not to be resolved today.

Dangerous Duplicity

At fifteen knots, the *Belle Chloe* cut through the water like the sea princess she was. Worth every penny of the twenty-million it cost to build her, taking her out never got old. He liked his own yacht, *The Southern Cross*, but this was the yacht he wanted—this was the yacht he would have someday, one way or another.

CHAPTER 11

Danielle and Evan

Evan returned with the keys to his black Mercedes Coupe. He glanced around. Where did she go?

Danielle had moved from the bistro chair and was asleep in an over-stuffed lounge chair where she seemed to disappear, her small frame sinking into the leather. She looked so tired and angelic. He hated to wake her.

"Danielle," he said softly, and lightly touched her shoulder.

"Oh, I'm so groggy," she blinked and rubbed her eyes with her hand. "I had to get off the bar stool before I fell off. I must have fallen asleep."

"I'll drive you home," he said lifting her gently out of the chair. He pulled a bit too hard and she fell into his arms now around her waist and shoulder. She stood there gazing into his eyes.

"Whoops," he said. "I guess I don't know my own strength."

Evan looked into her hazel eyes, tinged with flecks of aquamarine, and momentarily lost his thoughts. The impulse to kiss her was so overwhelming, he felt helpless and flustered. No woman had created such an intense magnetic attraction for him in a long, long time.

"Shall we go?" he asked, pulling out of the clumsy hold and guiding her to the parking garage. "You'll have to tell me how to get to your home because I don't know where you live."

Danielle gave him directions, which he tried to remember because she nodded off more than once. Evan thought about the little farm she lived on, and was a bit embarrassed by his own upper-class upbringing.

"Would you like some music?" Evan asked.

"Sure. Anything soothing is fine with me." He chose Puccini, his favorite, from a CD he picked up at the airport.

It did not take long to arrive at her home. "Is this the right gate?" he asked.

"Uh huh. Just keep going." She yawned.

Evan drove up a long driveway, lined by cypress trees and deep magenta bougainvillea. Jasmine bloomed under bushes of white and yellow roses. Although he could not see everything clearly because it was early morning, he was stunned by what he saw next. Not only was her home massive—a huge 18th century stone structure with a red clay tile roof, several levels of terraces, shuttered windows and balconies, but the driveway was flooded with several white police cars with blue stripes, lights flashing creating a chaotic scene. He was befuddled about why the police were there.

"Oh, no!" Danielle cried. "Something has happened to my mother."

Danielle leapt out of the car, and ran up the stairs, leaving Evan trailing behind.

"Mama, mama!" she cried out.

"I'm here, Danielle." Marie's voice was faint, but controlled.

Gaspard was standing on the terrace talking rapidly to four Gendarmeries.

"What happened?" Danielle asked, her anxiety now shattered her sleepy repose.

Gaspard walked over to his daughter, put his hand on her shoulder and said in a cracking voice, "Danielle, please sit down. We have some terrible news to tell you about Armond."

Danielle flinched. She tried to look into her father's eyes, but they were downcast staring at the pavement. Her chest tightened and her cold hands began to shake—bracing herself for what was to come. Evan stood behind her, one hand fidgeting in his jean pocket. He, too, felt a sense of dread for what he was about to hear. Gaspard took his daughter's shaking hands in his, and said in a low somber voice, "They found Armond today. I am grieved to tell you this, but Armond is dead."

Danielle put her hands to her mouth, muffled a gasp and shook her head in disbelief at what she was hearing. "Dead, how?" she pleaded, needing an explanation.

"We don't know," Gaspard said. "He was found in a garbage bin in an alley outside le Petite Fromage in the village. Apparently he was mugged and then killed."

Tears welled and trickled down Danielle's cheeks. She turned toward Evan, helplessly standing there. Evan held out his hand to Gaspard. " I'm terribly sorry for your loss."

"And, who are you?" Gaspard said with a furrowed forehead.

"My name is Evan Wentworth. I met Danielle a few days ago. We were going to go to the Maeght. When she didn't arrive at our agreed upon meeting time, I had no way of getting in touch with her. However, she knew where I was staying, and came to the hotel tonight to let me know why she was unable to meet me."

Gaspard nodded, but said nothing. Marie came forward and reached her hand out to Evan. "I'm Danielle's mother. She's told me about you."

"Mrs. DuBois. I'm very sorry for what you are going through," Evan said while grasping her small hand.

"Please excuse our rudeness," Gaspard said. "This is Ryan Coltrane, my business partner, Captain Claude Bouchamp, and Detectives Nichols and Wilkes."

Evan felt awkward and uncomfortable. He nodded to the Captain and detectives, then held out his hand to Ryan, whose stilted demeanor bordered on dismissive and resentful. Ryan shook Evan's hand, but it felt like obligatory etiquette, which under the circumstance, it was. Evan glanced at Ryan's face, marred by a crusted split lip with several facial bruises and wondered what had happened to him.

"I should be going," Evan suggested and struggled not to ask any probing questions. Although he had his own reasons for being in St. Paul, now was not the time to be a former cop.

Marie noticed the awkward strain between Ryan and Evan, sensing it had everything to do with Danielle. "Can I offer you a cup of coffee, Evan"?

"Thank you, but I really should be going."

"Let me walk you to your car." Danielle put her arm around Evan.

Ryan nodded toward Evan, but said nothing. Captain Bouchamp and the detectives were busy asking questions of Danielle's brother and sisters, none of whom he would meet tonight. A large wolf-like dog sat near Marie, not on guard at the moment, but his wary appearance made it obvious this was not a dog to fool with.

Danielle walked Evan down the driveway to his car. "I apologize, Evan, for all of this."

"Danielle, there's nothing for you to apologize for. I'm the one who's sorry for what you and your family are going through."

As much as Danielle tried not to cry, tears flooded out followed by a painful sob. Evan took her in his arms, and held her close as she let her emotions release. This terrible evening did not make any sense—such a terrible tragedy.

"Please tell me if there is anything I can do," Evan offered.

"Just hold me," she said, wiping the tears off her face.

Without thinking, Evan kissed her on top of her head, and did not want to let her go. "Would you call me when you can, just to let me know how things are going—and there's something I need to tell you."

"Okay," she sniffled. "I'm so upset about all of this. Armond was a good person. I'm worried about his family."

"I understand. I'm here for you, I promise." Evan said, while sliding his arms away from her body. Danielle gave Evan her phone number, turned and walked back up the driveway. He watched her from his car before starting the ignition.

Evan drove back to the hotel, unsettled by the events of the evening and considered what Danielle's father must be going through. The shock of learning an employee was murdered would be something this family would have to endure.

Hopefully, they would find out who did this. Maybe there would be some *justice*—a word he hated to use, since *justice* never prevailed in his sister's death.

Evan walked to his room, opened the door and sat on the bed, exhausted and bewildered. He checked his phone for messages, saw the black screen and realized he had turned it off. Four messages were from Aurora, whom he had completely forgot about calling. He knew she'd worry, and would probably be angry, but he was not up to a call, so he texted her instead, saying he met some friends and lost track of time. He hated lying to her, but there was no way to explain what had just happened.

CHAPTER 12

Gaspard and Ryan

Out of habit, Gaspard arrived early at the office of his yachting company. Peace and quiet often eluded him at home. His family created such clamor with everyone talking at once or bustling about—it left few precious hours to concentrate on the yachting business in his home office.

He dreaded this particular morning—a morning like no other, where he would have to tell the staff about Armond's murder. He shuddered, flipped the thick white strands of unruly hair from his forehead and rubbed the back of his neck, looking for an easy way to break the terrible news. Dressed in casual tan twill pants, and a navy and white checked sleeveless shirt, he wished he could head out to sea with clients instead of having to deal with the demise of his controller.

He heard a conversation coming from Ryan's office and wanted to discuss the best way to break the news to the staff. Gaspard walked into Ryan's office. Glass crunched under his cordovan loafers. He stared in disbelief at the broken coffee table and shattered frame of the yacht print sitting lopsided on the floor. Irritated, he waited until Ryan was off the telephone.

"What the hell happened here?" Gaspard bellowed, a dubious scowl on his face made his bulbous nose flush.

"I took a bad fall. Had no time to explain it the other night at your home."

"You fell?"

"Clumsy-ass here carried food from the microwave and missed the end of the glass table. Landed hard, split my lip and knocked over the sculpture."

Gaspard stared at his business partner and heaved a sigh, shaking his head back and forth in dismay.

"It's my fault. Take it out of my salary."

"No need for that. It was an accident."

"Sorry I smashed the yachting photo. Be careful, there's glass everywhere." Ryan pointed at the carpeting.

"I'll instruct the cleaning crew to take care of it." Gaspard groaned and sat down in a navy blue leather club chair. He tried to picture Ryan's fall—the accident that created such a mess, but he had other pressing concerns on his mind.

"I want to talk to you about having a meeting with the staff this morning—have to tell them about Armond," he said while stroking his white mustache.

"I agree." Ryan nervously rubbed the side of his nose and shuffled papers.

"Probably best we both tell everyone—call a meeting in the lunchroom and break the news. If some of the employees need to take a day or so off, I think we should let them. You agree?"

"Yeah, sure. When's the funeral?" Ryan looked up.

"Day after tomorrow," Gaspard grimaced. The stress had taken a toll on his face making him appear wan, tired and older than his 68 years.

"Do you think we should close down for a few days?" Ryan gave Gaspard a contrived empathetic glance.

"I'm good with that. New clients coming into town to rent the yacht, but that's next week. Can you manage that?" Gaspard implored.

"No problem. Do you want me to handle the accounting spreadsheets?"

"I'd appreciate that. Need to know our cash flow versus expenses."

"Okay. After the staff meeting, I'll check Armond's records on his computer. Just need his password."

"Of course," Gaspard said. "I'll email it to you."

"Thanks." Ryan nodded and managed a smile.

"I'm grateful I can rely on you," Gaspard said, and tucked his stomach paunch into his trousers as he stood up.

Ryan got up from his desk and put his hand on Gaspard's shoulder. "This is really terrible. You didn't deserve this."

"Does anyone deserve bad news?" Gaspard stared into Ryan's eyes, then lowered his head, turned and slowly walked toward the door. He left Ryan's office unaware of the sound of his shoes grinding glass deeper into the carpet.

Ryan walked around the edge of his black lacquer desk, sat in his leather chair and pursed his lips with his hands tucked under his chin in prayer position, elbows braced on his desk. A slight smirk crossed his mouth. He had wondered how he would get into Armond's computer, but now he would be given the password. This would be easier than he thought.

CHAPTER 13

Aurora and Evan

Aurora barked into the phone, agitated. "What's going on?"

"It's complicated," Evan waffled.

"What's complicated? You didn't call me for three days. I'm upset. You'd be too if you were back here in New York and the circumstances were in reverse."

"Aurora, I'm sorry. It has nothing to do with you—with us."

"I'm starting to wonder if there is an *us*. Did you meet someone?"

"Yes—I mean no. It's not what you think," Evan stammered, and felt pressure causing his temples to throb.

"What should I think? You tell me!" Aurora bellowed.

Evan stumbled around in his mind, unable to divulge what he should or should not say to Aurora.

"No, no, hang it higher. I want it three feet off the floor, dammit, at eye level," she hollered at her workers.

"How are things at the gallery?" Evan hoped to change the subject.

"Things are stressful. I'm showcasing two new artists. Their work will flank your large paintings."

"Do I know them?" Evan asked.

"No. Their work is on rotation from an art gallery in San Francisco. Let's get back to the real issue here," Aurora ranted, her voice pitching up an octave as she went on and on about relationships and the importance of honesty.

Evan set the phone down, hit the speaker button and poured himself a drink, listening to the frustration and anger in her voice, but perhaps for the first time he also heard fear. She had done nothing to deserve anything but the truth, yet he knew no matter what he said, it wouldn't come out right.

"Aurora, there's been a murder here. Someone was found dead outside of a restaurant. It has caused a flurry of commotion. Newscasters and the local police are anxious to understand how something like this could happen. "

"Did you know the person?" Aurora asked, while still shouting instructions to her display workers.

"I didn't know the man who was killed, but he's someone who worked at a yachting company."

"What does that have to do with you, and your not calling me?"

Evan gulped his drink and paused. "It's a long story. I ran into someone on the street. Her books and papers were all over the pavement. I helped her pick them up."

"Her?"

"She's a teacher—lives nearby."

"So, you did meet someone?" Aurora's voice broke with a tinge of anguish.

"The murdered person works for her father's company."

The silence was palpable. Neither of them spoke. Finally Aurora said, sounding tearful, "Do you want me to fly over there?"

"Oh, gosh, no." Evan said, and then wished he hadn't said it. "I mean, there's no reason. The police will look into it, and hopefully they'll find out who did this."

"You're not getting involved, are you?"

"No," he lied, and hated himself for having gotten into this predicament.

"You promised me when you left the police force that you'd never get involved in another crime."

"I know. I don't want to be involved with this—it just happened."

"You mean, *she* just happened."

Silence. Painful, deliberate silence.

"You're right. I met this woman, and now there's a murder in her family's business. I feel sorry for her. Perhaps there's something I can do."

"Why are you getting involved? You don't know these people."

"I've met them."

"You've met them? How?"

"It's complicated." Evan scratched the back of his head.

"Stop saying that. You're complicated. Tell me the truth."

"I *am* telling you the truth."

"Do you still love me?"

"Yes, of course."

"Are you falling in love with her?"

"Ridiculous. I just met her. I don't know."

Click. The phone went dead. Evan was not surprised Aurora hung up on him.

Saying the words "I don't know" to Aurora was painful, but somehow freeing. He didn't want to lie to her, but he knew something had happened to him that he was not going to be able to avoid—nor did he want to. He didn't know exactly what his feelings were for Danielle, but he knew he couldn't leave her alone in her grief. He wanted to do what he could to help her and her family. If that meant digging into his skeleton closet of detective skills, so be it.

CHAPTER 14

Ryan

Getting the password for Armond's computer made things easy. He was able to delete all of the original entries and modify them. In his mind, he was not stealing—borrowing money, yes. Grifting off the top, yes. Making an extra five thousand on the side here and there should not have caused such a terrible problem. Had he been careless? He wasn't sure how Armond figured it out. This worried him, but other things worried him more—like bloodstains in the trunk of his car. What to do about that? Wash it clean with bleach? Probably not thorough enough to get all the blood out of the trunk's fabric, not to mention the obvious splotches, smell and residue bleach left. What if the police questioned him and looked in his trunk? The suspicious mess of obvious DNA evidence had to be dealt with.

One option Ryan considered was getting a new car. His BMW was two years old. If he purchased a new car, there'd be a record of the vehicle transfer—and what if a new buyer bought the old BMW with the poorly scrubbed trunk full of bloodstains? Bad idea. Not getting another car. A new car's trunk would be devoid of blood, but the old car could still be traced back to him.

Befuddled, a new thought flooded his mind. At 7:00 at night he drove to the local liquor store and bought a case of cheap red wine. He drove to the marina where he knew there were several concrete abutments. It took quite awhile for most of the cars to leave the parking lot, and the harbormaster's car was one of the last to depart. The sea was rolling with whitecaps, crashing in bursts over the concrete levy. A nasty storm brewed, with dark clouds moving in rapidly. Cracks of thunder and lightning spread out over the water. He waited.

Then he put the car into reverse, slammed on the gas and backed up into the concrete abutment. He heard the bumper and trunk crunch and the sound of glass from the wine bottles shatter in his trunk. The back of his neck hurt, and no doubt he'd have a slight whiplash. He got out of the car and opened the trunk. Red wine everywhere—glass shards splayed over the felt matting. Not one bottle of wine survived. Ryan smiled at his clever thinking. Now he could take the car to the repair shop, have the trunk and back end of the car repaired, but most of all, have all the felt material inside the trunk removed and replaced. No more blood and no DNA. He wondered what this would cost him, but it was worth the money. Best of all, he'd have a rental while the repairs took place.

The storm was wild and loud. He was glad he had picked up a laser zapper earlier in the evening and drove to his office. All the lights were off. Everyone had gone home. The cleaning crew rarely arrived before 10:00 p.m. He got out of the car, grabbed the laser and walked toward the surveillance camera, pointed at it and held steady until he heard a hissing, popping sound, saw a few sparks and then a small trail of smoke—instant, clever erasure of his late night in the office with Armond. No more proof of anyone coming or going. One nicely fried surveillance system courtesy of Internet research.

Now drenched from the storm, he got back into his car, knowing he'd be late to work the next morning and would have one more dramatic scenario to explain to Gaspard who was bound to think he'd been very careless to have damaged his car. First, he supposedly fell in the office, cracked a glass coffee table, and now he'd hit the gas with the car in reverse rather than with the gear in drive. Plausible lie? Ryan knew he could live with Gaspard's disappointment over his carelessness, but at least Ryan knew he was not stupid—definitely anything but. He heaved a sigh of relief as he drove home. This would be the first night he'd sleep without plotting what he'd have to do next to cover his messy murder.

CHAPTER 15

Evan and Danielle

Evan punched in her number on his cell phone hoping she'd be at home.

"Danielle? It's Evan."

"Oh, Evan. I'm glad you called."

"I wanted to know how you're doing?"

"I'm okay, but feel drained of all energy. The funeral for Armond was yesterday."

"That must have been difficult."

"It was terrible. His brother, Giles, was there, and Armond's parents."

"I know how hard this has to be on his family."

"Everyone in my father's company was there, as well as my entire family. My father was bereft but managed to give the eulogy. I also spent time with Armond's brother and his parents trying to comfort them, but no words seemed right— none that seemed enough for the loss. My mother, Marie, is still beside herself with all of this stress and is worried about my father's health. He seems to have aged so much in the last week, and my mother has her own health issues."

"I understand," Evan said. "I was thinking you might need a change of scenery and I was wondering if I could take you to lunch?"

"That would be nice," Danielle smiled to herself, "but I have a better idea. It's been so depressing for all of us. If you are free, why don't you meet me at home tomorrow around ten in the morning? I'd like to take you out on our boat."

"You'd take *me* out?"

"Well, our family would. You can meet everyone. We've closed the company for three days out of respect for Armond.

We need time on the sea, breathing some fresh, salty air now that the storm's over. The seas are calm and expected to be that way."

"That sounds nice. I'll meet you at your home tomorrow at 10:00. Can I bring anything?"

"No, there's plenty of drinks and food on board."

"Okay. See you then."

Evan shut off his phone. Maybe tomorrow would be the right time to tell her why he was really in the Côte d' Azure. He pictured a nice sloop in his mind—something like the sailboats he'd vacationed on in Hawaii where he enjoyed sitting on the deck watching the sun go down. He wondered how her whole family fit on the boat.

CHAPTER 16

Evan

The heat and humidity bothered him, so Evan headed out early to the barbershop in town and opted for a shorter haircut. He stared at himself in the mirror and wondered why he hadn't cut his hair long ago. Aurora had encouraged the artsy-look and at the time it made sense to look like anything other than the detective he had been. Now dressed in navy shorts and a navy and white striped t-shirt he bought at the hotel's boutique, he looked less touristy. He fluffed his hair with one hand, feeling a sense of freedom he had long forgotten and drove to Danielle's home. He stopped at the iron gates and rang the buzzer.

"Yeah, who is it?"

"Evan. Evan Wentworth. Danielle asked me to come over."

Evan heard a female voice he did not recognize holler away from the phone in a rather piercing tone. "Your boyfriend is here, Danielle."

Evan rolled his eyes at the thought of being elevated to boyfriend status by someone he did not know. The buzzer on the gate clicked and the gates opened inward.

"Evan, come on up," Danielle said. "That was my impertinent sister, Lena."

Although Evan had seen Danielle's home in the dark, he was unprepared for the majestic size of their residence. He parked his car on the multi-garage bay's landing and stared up at the towering stone arches with ivy scrambling up the pillars. Several terraces were set under massive trees and wrought iron balcony railings overlooked manicured, lush gardens. Palm trees, various pine and olive trees grew in abundance.

Danielle walked part way down the steps to greet Evan, and let out a happy shriek when she saw him. "You cut your hair!" she giggled, and put her fingers on her own head pretending they were scissors, laughing. "It looks great," she said and motioned with her arm for Evan to come up to the house.

"Thanks," he said. "Too hot here for long hair."

"Come on in—I want you to meet more of my family."

The wolf-like dog stared at him, his dark black and cream face brushing up against Danielle's leg. Evan froze, unsure whether the dog was friendly, and assumed probably not.

"Oh, that's Thor. He's harmless unless he's told to attack," Danielle giggled, trying to make a joke.

"That's so comforting," Evan laughed. "What breed of dog is he?"

"An Alsatian shepherd from the Alsace region in France. We've had him since he was a pup. Weighs more than I do now."

"I would have liked him better when he was a lot smaller," Evan teased and cautiously walked past Thor, noticing his tail was barely wagging, but at least Thor was not growling at him. He followed Danielle with one eye mentally alert wishing his other eye were at the back of his head, hoping not to hear a snarl.

Evan stood in the doorway, trying not to gape at the interior. He handed her a paper bag with two bottles.

"What's this?" Danielle raised her eyebrows and stared at the paper bag.

"A little wine for the day," he said. "A red and a white—I didn't know what you preferred."

"I like it all," the intruder interrupted, swaggering barefoot into the room in very tight-fitting faded blue denim cutoffs, and a white halter tank baring her midriff. "I'm Lena," she said, shaking her purple-streaked bangs off her forehead, then tossed her glossy long black hair over her shoulder. "You must be the New Yorker," she said, pointing one finger at him as if he were the accused on trial.

"Yes, I'm from New York." Evan stood gazing at her unmistakable bellybutton piercing, large silver hooped earrings and kohl-lined eyes.

"Nice to meet you," Evan said, and started to extend his hand, but Lena turned and ignored him, shrugged her shoulders and plopped down on a beige linen sofa with a magazine of greater interest.

"Don't mind Lena," Danielle said, shaking her head in disgust in an effort to apologize for her sister's rudeness. "She's going through a difficult phase."

"No problem." Evan said eyeing the stucco finish on the walls with arches flanked with stone. Off-white stained rough-hewn beamed ceilings towered above deep russet terracotta tile floors.

"Would you like something to drink?" Danielle asked. "I'll just be a minute."

"I'm fine." Evan said, glancing around trying to take it all in.

"Follow me," Danielle suggested, and led Evan out to the terrace.

"Unbelievable!" Evan sighed as he looked at the view, the immense swimming pool on the lower level, the Esterel Hills and the Mediterranean Sea.

"It's something I never take for granted," Danielle said. "There are lots of things I don't need in life, but I have to live near the sea—it's part of my soul."

"The architecture of your home is stunning."

"Designed by Andre Svetchine, a well-known architect who built a lot of homes here and in Provence. You can lounge on the terrace while I grab a few things," Danielle said, motioning for him to sit on a huge pale blue canvas cushioned teak sofa. She quickly turned and left the terrace. "I'll be right back," her lyrical voice echoed down the hall.

Evan sat on the immense terrace, his mind in a state of confusion. When he first met Danielle, he pictured her living in a little hamlet—a farmhouse of sorts, with animals and chickens. He laughed to himself, shaking his head and almost said out loud, *Boy, did I get that wrong.* However, for someone living an extraordinary life, she did not seem affected by wealth. He closed his eyes, taking in the scents of the roses and jasmine. Birds flittered in an out of the trees, their brown and yellow bodies shimmering in the sun. Bees hummed gathering nectar. He was about to doze off, when he heard the patter of shoes on the terracotta floor.

"All set. You don't mind driving, do you?"

"No, not at all. I know you don't drive."

"Great. Lena's already left, and my parents and three of my brothers are already on the yacht."

Evan pretended not to hear the word *yacht,* but there it was—something else he had gotten quite wrong. Not a fishing boat. Not a hamlet. For once in his life, he was glad he had come from money, or he'd be far too intimidated to be spending time with this woman.

He walked to his car, opened the door for her, admiring how attractive she looked in her white shorts, and obvious bathing attire underneath a colorful knit top. She looked adorable with her hair tied back, stuck under a baseball cap of all things unexpected. He glanced at her slim tan legs, painted pink toenails and gem-studded flip-flops and tried to concentrate.

"Okay if I keep the top down?" Evan said.

"Sure. I love the wind in my face," Danielle smiled. I'll tell you how to get to the marina in Nice. It's not far."

The sun felt good on Evan's shoulders. He wanted to concentrate on spending the day with Danielle's family, but he couldn't put Armond's murder out of his detective mind. He debated about broaching the subject, but his curiosity won out.

"I meant to ask you if the police have any leads."

"We'll know more next week." Danielle said. "They want to interview the yachting crew, and the staff at work. Does that surprise you?"

"No. Makes sense. They need to do a full investigation. Sometimes it's someone closest to the victim that commits a crime," Evan said, then wished he hadn't.

"You sound familiar with all of this," Danielle frowned looking directly at him while he drove.

"I wanted to tell you, but I didn't want you thinking I was here for any other reason than to spend time with you."

"What do you mean?"

He paused and swallowed. "I used to be a cop—a detective."

"Where? In New York?"

"No, in California, actually."

"I'm shocked. I thought you were an artist?"

"I am. Art was a major career change for me."

"Why did you stop being a cop?"

It was the question he dreaded—the question that opened raw wounds of grief and anger, but he didn't want to deceive her. "I left the police force three years ago, after my sister was shot and killed."

Danielle put her fingers to her lips in disbelief. "How did it happen?" she asked in a soft tone.

Evan told her the story—the awful story of how Ashley had been shot, and how he couldn't protect her—should have protected her. Danielle listened without saying a word but was unable to control her emotions. Tears welled up in her eyes when she found out Ashley had been only six years old. Danielle's chest hurt and her stomach flipped in shock as she listened to his story, watching Evan's angst at telling her the details. Although Armond's murder and the funeral had sapped her of her usual energy, she was not yet out of tears to shed.

"Why are you telling me this now?" she sniffled, blowing her nose into a tissue she pulled from her handbag.

"It's the reason I came to the Côte. I have a lead on where one of the robbers escaped."

"But, why here?"

"Just a tip that he might be somewhere on the Riviera."

"Oh," she said, dabbing at her eye makeup. "Do you know who he is?"

"No. I'm not sure where he is, or even what he looks like."

Danielle nodded, unable to comprehend these sudden facts, but her heart went out to Evan, feeling his sorrow, while she dealt with her own. "Evan, I'm very sorry about your sister. You must have loved her very much."

"I did. She was a special light in my life, and because of me, her life was cut short. I've never been able to forgive myself."

"Are you still in touch with your parents?"

"Yes, but not as often as I should be."

"Where do they live? In New York?"

"No. They still live in Carmichael, a suburb of Sacramento. They moved there from El Dorado Hills where I worked. After Ashley's death, they couldn't stand to be in the same house and see her bedroom filled with all her dolls and toys. It was too overwhelming. My father runs a fund-management firm, and he felt he could easily work from home, so they moved."

"What are their names?" Danielle asked, lightening the conversation.

"Baxter and Kelly." He glanced at her briefly and turned his eyes back to the road. "By the way, please don't tell your family. This is my problem, and I don't want anyone else involved. Let's just have a nice day?"

"Okay," he heard her sigh, a wisp of a sound of someone slowly letting the air out of her lungs.

They drove the rest of the way in awkward silence, each searching for a safer emotional landing place where adjusting to loss was not such a burden.

Evan drove with ease, enjoying the French Riviera, aware that in the 18th century the British upper class flocked here, along with Russians and aristocrats—even Queen Victoria and King Edward VII when he was Prince of Wales. Picasso and Matisse favored Nice, as did writers Maugham and Huxley. Always a prominent yachting and cruising area, with several marinas along the coast, he wished he could stay here indefinitely—paint with abandon, in three-hundred days of sunshine—a far cry from frigid doldrum winters in New York.

"It's not much further," Danielle said, holding up her hand to shield the sun in her eyes.

"Why is the boat, I mean yacht, in Nice?" Evan asked, scratching the back of his neck.

"Um, how you say in English, proximity?—yes, proximity to clients visiting here. Nice has a very large deep-water marina for larger yachts."

"I see," Evan said, wondering just how big this yacht was going to be.

He drove along the Rue de France, past the Negresco Hotel, glancing at the tiered hillside of buildings in sunset colors of dusty pink, salmon and gold, with vivid red clay tile roofs.

"Pretty, isn't it," Danielle said, while reaching into her handbag for her sunglasses.

"I've never seen water this color before," Evan said. I could paint this on my canvas by mixing cyan and emerald green until it reflected the exact shade of the water today. I'm beginning to see why artists are captivated by this place."

"Take a right at the next light," Danielle said somewhat abruptly, pointing at the intersection. "That's the entrance to the main harbor."

"Will I be able to find a place to park?"

"Oh, sure. There's space for hundreds of cars," she noted while pulling out her cell phone. "I want to call my father and let him know we're here. He'll send someone to the dock and take us to the yacht."

Evan parked the car and started to get out.

"Wait, wait," Danielle said. "Better put up the top. Not the safest place to leave anything. Take your belongings."

He put the top up, locked it in place, and opened the trunk wishing he had put the wine in something more attractive than a paper bag—not to mention it had gotten undrinkably warm. "I'm sorry. I should have brought a cooler."

"Not to worry. We have lots of champagne, wine and anything else you want on the yacht," she said, while talking on her phone at the same time to her father. "Papa, we're here. Please send Pierre to pick us up. We'll be on the dock in ten minutes. Merci."

Evan walked towards her, wanting to put his arm around her, but it seemed too familiar and casual. She put her arm around his elbow and skipped a bit in her flip-flops. "Come on," she grinned, tugging at his arm. "This is going to be fun."

He was glad her mood lightened up, because it broke the tension and he felt less somber—less guilty for talking about his sister and bringing up such an unpleasant subject.

CHAPTER 17

Evan and Danielle

The marina was crowded, bustling with residents and tourists from all over the world. Women walked in string bikinis, either coming from the beach or heading out to bronze in the sun. As Evan passed them, the smell of coconut oil and suntan lotion wafted through the air. Seagulls dipped and swooped over a plethora of boats and yachts, more than he had ever seen in any California marina. It was not just the mere number of vessels in the harbor, but their enormous size that made him gawk. Danielle smiled at Evan as they stood on the wooden dock waiting and watching an inboard coming up to the pier. Evan thought to himself that the boat or yacht, whatever it was, seemed smaller than he expected.

"Alors! Pierre, so good to see you," Danielle said, pulling Evan as if he was slightly stuck to the ground. "This is my friend, Evan, from New York. He's going out with us today."

"Pleased to meet you," Pierre said, extending his hand. Evan shook it, feeling Pierre's calloused flesh under the knuckles and palm of his hand. Pierre guided Danielle on the boat first, and then motioned to Evan to board. He nestled into a seat next to Danielle. Pierre untwisted the rope from the cleats and got on board. Evan quickly realized this smaller boat wasn't Danielle's parent's yacht. The tender boat's engine revved up, and the bow of the boat gently lifted out of the water, creating waves that splashed on his arm. Instinctively, he put his arm around Danielle to shield her from the spray. She turned to him and flashed a grin, holding on to both of her elbows. He wished he could see her eyes behind her over-sized sunglasses.

Evan tried to take it all in and for the first time in days, he felt himself really relax. The sea was vast and magical. Cares could be left on shore and not follow you where the water met the sky. Evan noticed the boats they passed were getting larger—sailboats of all sizes, sloops, and inboard yachts. Each time they passed a yacht, he was sure it had to be Danielle's. Finally they turned toward the open sea, moving out of the harbor and there it was—a floating massive house on the sea, larger than any yacht he had ever seen. Pierre tendered the boat up to the yacht's stairs. Evan could see Gaspard waiting at the top, dressed in white slacks, and blue shirt and navy linen jacket, with a captain's cap on his white hair, making him look like an older, slightly overweight, brother of Harrison Ford.

"Welcome to *Belle Chloe*," Gaspard shouted. "I'm pleased you could join us."

Danielle scampered up the stairs, ran to her father and planted a kiss on each cheek, and then one more. He hugged his daughter tightly. "Come on," he said. "Follow me to the upper deck. Everyone's either in the pool or lounging in the sun. We have some extra bathing attire if you need it, and plenty of suntan lotion. It's easy to blister out here if you are not used to the sun." Evan nodded, wishing he had slathered on lotion with a high SPF, because his fair skin made him susceptible to burning in a hurry.

They walked along the teak floors with shining chrome side rails, up a set of stairs and then to an elevator. Evan realized the yacht had at least three decks. "Come meet everyone," Gaspard gestured toward his daughter and Evan. Danielle walked over to her mother, Marie, and gave her the same number of double cheek French kisses. Marie was smartly dressed in white slacks and a white woven knit three-quarter length sleeve tunic. A wide-brimmed beige straw hat hid much of her auburn hair tied with a printed scarf at the nape of her neck. Large white over-sized sunglasses made her face appear smaller. "Mama, you look well today. How are you feeling?" Danielle asked.

"I'm much better," she said. "The new medication is helping a great deal. I almost feel like myself." Her high cheekbones rose in a warm smile.

"You remember, Evan, mama?"

"Yes, of course. Good to see you again," she said and started to rise from her chair.

"Oh, don't get up. You look so comfortable," Evan said, air-patting his hand for her to stay put.

In the distance, Evan saw the harbormaster leave, the tender creating a nice wake as he headed back to the marina.

"I'll tell Ryan to take her out now, and will get the crew to get us all something to drink. You hungry?" Gaspard asked.

"Just thirsty," Evan said. "Maybe I'll have something to eat later."

Evan felt like he was having a surreal experience—as if he were sleepwalking in a dream and had shrunken in size. From the deck he could see Lena splashing in the pool while others were in the spa, laughing as the music blared. If the yacht was moving, Evan didn't notice it.

Danielle walked past a huge sectional sofa, a large dining table and ten sea-worthy contemporary chairs. Everything Evan looked at was either white, light bleached wood or beige, except for an impressive number of blue nautical-themed pillows and an abundance of creamy towels set out by the pool neatly rolled up in tucked bolts on lounge chairs. "Come on," she said. "Come meet my brothers."

"This is Lucas, my oldest brother, and this is Josh, all things oceanographer in the making, and my little brother, Valentin."

"Hello everybody," Evan said, waving his hand.

"Want to join us in the spa?" Lucas said.

"Maybe later," he sugggested. "Going to have something to drink first."

"Where's Chloe?" Danielle yelled to her mother.

"She had to work. Shortage at the hospital."

"You'll like my sister, Chloe," Danielle said. "She's the sensible one we all rely on. Hopefully you can meet her another time."

Danielle walked over to the pool, where Lena was dozing on a float with less of a bathing suit than was respectable, fitting for a young woman without an ounce of fat. She was exceptionally attractive despite the edgy Goth look. "You going to stay in there all day?" Danielle scoffed, pursed her lips and put one hand on her hip in frustration.

"Maybe, if I feel like it," Lena shot back, and pulled her hat over her face.

Danielle heard the shrieks and patter of small feet and turned around to find Juliette, her ten-year-old sister, running down the deck, tossing a ball for Thor. "Hey, come here a minute. There's someone I want you to meet."

Juliette scampered over, her red hair flying in the wind in every direction, Thor on her heels, tail wagging with a tennis ball in his mouth.

"This is my friend, Evan." Danielle put her arm on her sister.

"Hi, Juliette," Evan said, eyeing Thor.

Juliette ran to Evan, threw her arms around him, and starting chattering like a magpie. "Where are you from? When did you get here? What do you do? Where did you meet my sister?" And then she took a breath.

Evan laughed and told her where he met Danielle. Satisfied, Juliette dashed off with Thor, tossing the ball and giggling like a ten year old. Amber trailed off afer them.

"Sit, sit," Danielle said to Evan. "Oh, here comes Ricky, one of our crew, and he's got a full tray of drinks. There's a bar over there if there's something special that you want."

"I'll take a cold beer, if you have one," Evan nodded.

"A beer coming up," Ricky said, and went over to the bar's refrigerator.

'Danielle, what do you want?" Ricky hollered above the blaring music.

"Champagne. The colder the better."

Evan started to relax, grateful Gaspard had turned the music to a softer decibel level making conversation easier. "Have I met everyone in your family, Danielle?"

"Yes," she frowned, except for Chloe. "I wish she didn't have to work, but her nursing hours are unpredictable."

"Mind if I take my shoes off?" Evan asked.

"No, go ahead. We go barefoot around here all the time."

"I'll take you on a tour later, okay?" Danielle then took off her knit top, and dropped her shorts, as if it was the most natural thing in the world. Her bathing suit was one-piece, black and white with studded crystal gems at the front of halter ties. Every curve he had not noticed before was now on display, especially the cleavage of her ample breasts. She was small-boned, but beautifully proportioned. He felt stirrings of desire that he quickly put out of his mind.

Ricky arrived with a cold beer, a glass, and French champagne for Danielle.

Evan poured his beer in the glass, instead of drinking it out of the bottle, unsure of the decorum. Danielle took her champagne glass and said "Let's toast."

"To what? To what do you want most?" Evan challenged her.

"Someone who makes me happy and lots of kids of my own." She flashed a pensive smile.

Evan's heart sank. He clicked her glass with his, and wondered how he would tell her that he didn't want kids. It was one of the reasons he had stayed with Aurora, who suddenly flashed in his mind. She refused to have children—didn't want them and put her career first. The gallery was her *child*, and would always be. Whatever feelings he had for Danielle, now seemed to catapult him into that abyss of desperation he could not face.

Danielle reached for his hand, a gesture he did not expect and brought him back to reality.

"Everything okay?" she asked, furrowing her brow.

"Sure. Maybe we could take that tour now."

Danielle got up, noticed her mom was asleep under an umbrella. Lena was still on a float in the pool, sipping a martini with two olives. Juliette and Amber were nowhere to be seen or heard, and Danielle's brothers were sacked out on deck chairs. Thor was asleep under Gaspard's lounge chair with the tennis ball still in the side of his mouth.

"Everyone's relaxing, and I'd love to show you *Belle,"* Danielle said. She motioned for Evan to follow her to the wide circular staircase.

"I'll show you the living room first, then the indoor dining area and kitchen. An interior designer suggested vivid colors, but my mother preferred everything to have a neutral look. Our home is a bit, how do you say, rustic? Yes, rustic. Mama wanted the yacht to be modern wood, gleaming fiberglass, leather and chrome."

Evan followed Danielle around, feeling a bit like Thor, staying at her side, completely awestruck by the size of the interior rooms, the exhilaration of being on a massive luxury home on the water, complete with every amenity imaginable. The dining room held a massive lacquer table with a dozen quickly counted chairs, adjacent to the living area with an exceptionally large TV screen. The kitchen was anything but galley style. Instead it displayed a large cooking island covered in glittering white quartzite with a double sink. Sparkling chrome knobs and handles adorned gleaming off-white cabinetry, a professional six-burner range, and double-door refrigerator. A stainless wine captain was visible. Two additional cocktail bars were set up in different rooms, with seating for six or eight guests and comfortable bar-height amber leather chairs.

"I don't know what to say—it's stunning," Evan managed to croak out. He knew his parents were well off, but he had never seen wealth like this.

"Let me show you the sleeping quarters," she said, walking ahead of him in an enticing bathing suit, unaware of her own attractiveness.

"This is my parent's stateroom," she said waiving her arm in gesture toward the expansive space. Evan touched the padded walls, and noticed the custom bed, its quilted headboard with a pop-up television chest at the foot of the bed and a large sitting area with two comfortable white and beige printed fabric chairs. He followed her into the en-suite bathroom, with a sunken spa tub, sizeable shower, and two large vanity surfaces in either onyx or marble. A contemporary chandelier graced the ceiling. Matching sconces in gleaming chrome and glass adorned the vanity mirrors.

"Very nice!" he beamed, now concerned he was running out of superlative adjectives.

She continued down the hallway. He stayed close behind and noticed her perfume. It made him feel more than a bit distracted.

"Of the eight family staterooms, this is where I like to sleep," she said, pointing to a queen-sized bed covered with a pale aqua quilted silk duvet and studded pearl and crystal trimmed cream pillows. Drapes in the same silk fabric hung on the sides of the windows, and a chaise looked out of the sliding doors at the sea. "Want to see the bathroom?" she asked as a courtesy, completely unsure of what he was interested in.

Evan did not know what to say, so he followed her into the bathroom suite, only to find out they didn't both fit in the doorway at the same time. She bumped into him, got stuck and lost her balance. He braced himself on the door with his back and put one hand on her shoulder. "Sorry," he mumbled, laughing, unsure what to do with his other hand.

She stood there gazing at him, looking into those steel blue eyes unable to move forward or backward, their bodies pressed together in an awkward embrace.

And then she stood on her toes and kissed him. He didn't expect it, and let it happen, putting his hands on her bare shoulders. She stopped, looked into his eyes searching for approval, and then kissed him again, her soft full lips parted. Her hands cradled his neck while he moved his hand down her back to the top of her bathing suit, his emotions stirring an awakening passion he couldn't resist. He kissed her with fervor and desire he knew would soon embarrass him. Her skin was soft, scented by suntan lotion and warmed by the sun.

She pulled back from him, and touched the side of his cheek. "I hope you didn't mind. I'm not sure what came over me...maybe too much champagne."

"Well, I'm not going to blame it on the beer," he laughed. "I've wanted to kiss you from the first moment I met you."

"Really?" she teased him. "You mean when I nearly fell in the street?"

"No. Later when you were eating your pastry and had jam on your chin."

She rolled her eyes. "I suppose we should be getting back. Everyone will wonder what's happened to us."

"I'm hungry," Evan said. He felt his face flush from raging hormones.

"Me too. Let's go back up on the top deck."

Evan followed her up the stairs, before taking an elevator to the top deck. He glanced at her hair in a cascade down her back to where his hand had been.

Danielle walked out of the elevator first with Evan close behind and bumped into Ryan.

"Oh, I didn't know you were joining us, Ryan." Danielle said. "You remember Evan?"

"Yeah, sure," Ryan said, glaring at Evan, and then at Danielle's bathing suit. Evan caught the glance and assumed Ryan probably wondered where they had been and what they'd been up to. Evan felt a tinge of guilt.

"We're ready to have dinner," Ryan said in a curt tone, "since the weather is nice, we'll eat on deck." He forced a smile and stared at Danielle.

"Great," Evan said, putting his hands in his shorts pockets, doing his best to disguise where they had been a few minutes ago.

Danielle's family was now seated at the outdoor dining table. Candles were lit, and several bottles of wine and champagne were being passed around.

"Hello, everyone," Danielle said smiling at Evan. She was unaware of the questioning glances from her father, or the perturbed scowl from her brother, Lucas. Lena sat in a dining chair, with one leg over the armrest, sipping some frothy drink, eyeing Ryan. Marie motioned for Evan to sit opposite her at the table, while Danielle and Ryan sat on either side of her.

Gaspard sat at the head of the table and nodded toward the steward to bring the appetizers, which appeared on silver platters—all things fresh from the sea—lobster claws and chunks, oysters sprinkled with chili oil and garlic, and mussels drizzled with lemon. French bread and an assortment of fromage permeated the late afternoon air with a heady aroma. Gaspard raised his glass, filled with a hearty Bordeaux, and said "I'd like to offer a toast: To my family—you mean everything to me. To my partner, Ryan, for being here during a most difficult time. To Evan, my daughter's new friend. To health. To life." He raised his glass in the air, not clicking other glasses of each family member, but instead bowed his head instead and offered a prayer. "We thank you, Lord, for this bounty, your grace, our blessings, and your unconditional love." With a hearty laugh, Gaspard then said, "Bon appétit."

Evan glanced at Ryan, then watched Gaspard interact with his sons, Lucas, Josh, and Valentin. It was obvious how much he loved his family and cherished them. Marie shot a frustrated motherly look at Lena and said something under her breath in French, and then directed a no-nonsense demand in English at Lena. "Sit up, and take your leg off the arm rest. Manners, please!" Begrudgingly, Lena smirked, pursed her lips and put both of her legs under the table, never taking her eyes off Ryan.

Marie turned to Evan and asked him how he enjoyed the day. "It's been wonderful," he said, remembering his earlier clumsy romantic encounter with Danielle and feeling a little unsettled. "Your yacht is stunning," he commented and pulled his sunglasses out of his pocket to shield his eyes from the sun's gradual descent creating a crimson and gold ball, sitting atop the water's edge as if the earth were indeed flat. Clouds picked up all the colors from the sun, glowing strands in red, gold, and lavender. The sea was dark, with the exception of the sunset's glow on the water. Waves moved calmly in rhythm with the incoming tide and a myriad of seagulls circled the dining table hoping for discarded tidbits.

The evening air was slightly breezy, soft and invigorating. Evan relaxed and enjoyed conversing with Marie, Danielle and her family. After a hearty dinner of Coquille St. Jacques, filet mignon and green beans almondine over rice with pine nuts and pomegranate seeds, everyone enjoyed a light desert of gelato with caramel and chocolate sauce, topped with chopped cashews. Port was served last with several dessert wines. Danielle excused herself to put on warmer clothing, leaving Evan engaged in a conversation with Gaspard about how he started his company.

Ryan, although appearing professional and attentive, seemed aloof, rarely offering information about his role in the company. Evan decided he would take the risk of trying to get Ryan to talk, and removed his sunglasses now that the sun had set.

"So, Ryan, where are you from? You don't have a French accent."

Ryan leaned back further in his chair, wiped his hand across the slight scruff on his face, and stared directly into Evan's eyes.

"Cap Ferrat, recently, but born in Kentucky."

"Where did you learn the yachting business?" Evan asked with genuine interest.

"Columbia Yachts." Ryan shifted uneasily in his chair.

"Where's that?" Evan asked.

"Santa Ana, California. And you, you're the New Yorker, right?" Ryan took out a cigarette, lit it with a silver lighter and inhaled a long deep breath.

"Live in New York, but grew up in Northern California."

"Oh." Ryan flashed a look of surprise, and started picking at his thumb with his index finger. He took a long, slow drag on his cigarette, and blew it out through his mouth, tilting his head up toward the sky.

"Very impressive yacht you and Gaspard have here," Evan said, trying to keep the conversation going.

"Thanks. It's one of several. We have a diveboat and a sailboat too, in the harbor. It's part of our fleet."

"Where do you find your clients? Evan asked, sipping an Espresso.

"Internet marketing and referrals. Clients come from all over the world."

"How long have you worked with Gaspard?"

"A little over two years."

Ryan seemed edgy and didn't keep the conversation flowing so Evan changed the subject. "How's the water out here for diving?"

"You scuba?' Ryan asked, an expression of surprise flooded his face with raised eyebrows and wide-open eyes.

'Yeah. Got certified in Hawaii some years ago."

"I'll have to take you out. How long are you staying in St. Paul?"

"Probably to the end of the month. How'd you know where I was staying?" Evan asked, and then wished he hadn't been so blunt.

"Danielle told me. I asked her. You know Danielle and I date," he said in an authoritative tone, his deep voice almost sounding like a dare.

"Exclusive?" Evan probed, fully aware of the risk.

"In my mind, yes," Ryan joked, trying to assert himself. "She's still making up her mind about what she wants in life."

Evan felt that same uncomfortable tension he sensed on Danielle's portico the night of the encounter with the police. He couldn't put his finger on it, but something about Ryan's eyes—the cold, icy stare belied the words he spoke.

"Happy go to diving with you," Evan said in an attempt to be courteous.

"How 'bout tomorrow?"

"Oh! Tomorrow? Fine, sure. Where and what time?"

"Meet me at the same pier around eleven. I'll bring a smaller inboard—easier to maneuver for diving."

"Do you have extra gear on board?" Evan worried, aware he didn't possess anything more than swim trunks.

"Plenty of stuff. We take clients diving all the time."

Danielle got up from her lounge chair rubbed her eyes and walked over to her father and put the palm of her hand gently on his back with a little nudge.

"I'm getting pretty tired, "Danielle frowned. "Papa, can we go in now?"

"Yes, sure," Gaspard agreed and instructed Ryan and the crew to take *Belle* back to port.

Before they docked, Evan thanked Gaspard and Marie for their hospitality, bid his goodnights to each family member, except Lena and Ryan who were nowhere to be seen. Marie grasped Evan's hands in her own, gave him a pleasant smile and told him she was glad he could join them.

The drive home seemed longer than the drive out because traffic was heavy.

Evan glanced over at Danielle, her head tilted back on the leather seat, taking in the night air. Stars flooded the sky and the moon made a pathway across the sea.

"I'm glad you were able to be with us today," Danielle said. "I'm getting sleepy. Mind if I put my head on your shoulder?" The bucket seats made it a bit cumbersome, but she managed to snuggle into Evan.

Thoughts raced through his mind. He put one arm around her, pulling her closer to him."Ryan thinks you belong to him." Evan confessed, as if he let out a secret Ryan stated in confidence.

"That's in Ryan's mind. I like Ryan. He's smart, good-looking, and very much a major part of our company, but I'm not in love with him."

"I don't want to cause any problems," Evan said.

"Don't worry about it. Ryan is taking you scuba diving. I'm sure you'll become friends."

"I'm not certain what I think of the guy…something about him seems slightly off to me."

"Meaning?" she said in a soft, sleepy voice.

"There's tension where there shouldn't be any. I felt it when I was at your home the night the police were there about Armond's murder."

"You sound like a cop with a sixth sense instead of an artist."

"Probably right. However, gut feelings are something I pride myself on, and am usually never wrong."

"I think you're wrong about this," she said. "Ryan's been a great partner for my father."

They arrived at her home. She used her key to open the gate, and shook her head as if to shake out the cobwebs of drowsy sleep. He got out of the car, walked to her side to open the car door and helped pull her out of her seat. "Goodnight, Evan," she said and started to walk toward the gate.

"Wait," he said, shut the car door and walked closer to her. This time it was his turn. He didn't ask. He took her beautiful face in his hands and kissed her with all the emotion he had suppressed on the yacht. She yielded to him, responding, and he gently loosened his grip around her. She rubbed her eyes. He said, "You okay?" She nodded and laughed, "I can't find the ground. I think I've been swept off my feet," she giggled and tottered up the driveway with her flip-flops in one hand. Danielle stood with her knees shaking at the top of the stairs and watched him leave. She put her hand to her lips to touch them, still feeling the tingle and the tenderness of the moment.

Evan drove the rest of the way to his hotel, desperate for a cold shower, and sleep. Sleep he knew wouldn't come. He opened the door to his hotel room grateful for a chance to do nothing but think. He undressed and stood in the shower letting the water spray across his face and chest. Drying off with a fluffy towel, he put on a clean t-shirt and shorts. The comfortable bed beckoned with a morsel of decadent chocolate on the pillow, which he consumed in one gulp. With his hands behind his head on two down pillows, he thought about the day—a day full of surprises, reliving the essence of Danielle. He remembered her perfume and the scent of her suntan lotion in his mind. But, it wasn't only Danielle that was keeping him awake. He wondered who Ryan Coltrane really was.

Pleased with the free Wi-Fi in his room, he pulled his iPad out of his suitcase and wired into the Internet. He knew he could not go to sleep until he listened to the chatter in his head and paid attention to what was bugging him in his gut.

CHAPTER 18

Ryan

Who was Evan Wentworth? Pleasant enough, perhaps even likable, but everything about Evan bugged Ryan. He claimed to be an artist, but something seemed *off* and he couldn't put his finger on it. In a few hours, he'd be taking him out on his boat to scuba dive. Something he wished Evan had not accepted so readily.

Ryan sat at his desk at home and Googled *Evan Wentworth*. Professional website for Evan Wentworth, artist. Much to Ryan's surprise, Evan really was a very notable artist and one living in New York. Crazy stuff he painted—massive canvases of splattered color as if someone took a paint can and hurled it at a canvas, added three or four more colors, let them drip and called it art. "Hideous," Ryan said aloud. He wondered who would buy this crap. He scrolled around the website noticing the gallery showings, receptions, and apparent success. Thirsty, he got up went to the refrigerator, grabbed a cold beer and sat down again to do more Googling. Various links came up with several art showings and plenty of publicity.

Then, something odd caught his eye. Small heading over an interview article by a local newspaper, *Cop Turned Artist Finds His True Colors.* Ryan knocked over his beer, spilling it over his running shoes and on the floor. "Shit," he said, frustrated with the beer mess, but really throttled by the article. His throat felt dry, as if he had downed a dirty sock. What had seemed *off*, now was dead on. How in the hell did a cop, of all people, end up befriending Danielle and now this person was suddenly thrust into his life? The pit of his stomach knotted up like a large grapefruit, acidic and sour. His fingers shook, but he continued to Google. He remembered Evan said something about Northern California, and that worried him more than anything else, with good reason. "Can't be," he grumbled. "Tell me this friggen'-cop-gone-artist is not someone who was there that day—that terrible day when too many people were killed."

The Internet could be both a friend and an unsettling enemy. Ryan sat there for more than an hour, concerned his worst nightmare might start to unravel. Vessels in his head began to constrict and the brightness of his monitor blurred his vision. The onset of a migraine required immediate preventative medication. He rushed to his bedside, found two pills, downed them with water from the bathroom sink and sat down on the bed. "Get hold of yourself," he muttered, dangling his legs back and forth as if he'd lost his footing.

He reviewed the facts: First, he had changed his name. Second, after the bank heist there had been nothing in the papers for months, other than subsequent reports that the murdering thieves supposedly vanished into thin air. Third, he'd had a mask on and no one saw his identity. It had been more than three years and he'd gotten away with it. Sad thing that his brother died from a gunshot wound to the leg— infection had set in because the bullet was in there too long. Didn't plan for his brother to get shot. Didn't plan to get shot himself either, but the close-range bullet that hit him went straight through. Damn ugly scar front and back of his upper chest under his shoulder blade. Bled like a garroted pig. He shook his head, and tried to compose himself. Should he still take Evan out diving? Why not? Evan didn't know what had happened and couldn't know who he was. No possible way. Ryan downed another migraine preventative and gathered up his diving gear.

CHAPTER 19
Two Year's Ago

Kelly Wentworth entered the room holding a glass of tea. She carefully considered her words as she sat down next to her son. She stirred the ice cubes in her glass. "I can get you into art school. With my degree from Parsons and our endowments, I have considerable influence. You can't just sit on the sofa all day watching sports," she pleaded. Her voice was filled with both exasperation and compassion.

"Mom, I appreciate your intentions, but I don't have a damn bit of artistic talent."

"You'll learn, Evan. That's what art schools do—they teach and take raw, undeveloped talent and awaken it. Just try it for a semester. It'll be good for you to get out of El Dorado Hills and spend time in New York. We've loved having you here, but it's been a year of hell for all of us. Ashley's death was a devastating tragedy. I carry her with me in my heart every waking moment, but we cannot let her death define the rest of our lives. Seeing you here day after day in misery makes it harder for me, and your father wants to sell the house. We've struggled with our sorrow, but we don't blame you. It was a terrible accident. Grief can totally consume you and make you believe you will never have joy in your life again."

"Where will you move?" Evan asked. He felt upended like the last bit of stability was being removed from his life. In a flash of epiphany, he realized he had moved back to his parent's house—the house he had grown up in because it made him feel closer to Ashley. He would walk into her room and imagine her playing with her toys. It never occurred to him that the very physical things like Ashley's room and her belongings—things that kept him connected to Ashley—were the very things full of memories now so unbearable for his parents.

"Your dad and I have found a home in Carmichael. We made an offer and it has been accepted. We'll move as soon as we sell this house."

"I don't feel like I ever will be able to forgive myself," Evan said and knotted his fists together. "I still have nightmares. I can't sleep. Medication is helping, but not that much. I still feel depressed."

"Honey, you need to stop blaming yourself. We've moved forward because we have to. You are entitled to your grief and we hope you can acknowledge that it was horrible, shitty, unfair, and painful. But, nothing can bring her back, and she wouldn't want you, the brother she adored, to waste his life paying for something he could not control."

"I shouldn't have taken her in the car with me that day."

"Evan, we don't control the hour of our death. God does. We don't know his plan and we certainly don't understand his wisdom, but our faith assures us that he's with us in our sorrow and will bring us through it. None of us gets through life without pain and suffering. God helps those who help themselves and I believe he has a plan for you—a plan that includes happiness in this life." Kelly leaned forward, her blue eyes full of compassion, but her steely resolve made her seem larger than her medium-boned frame. She put her arm around Evan's shoulder and waited.

Evan dropped his head into his hands and rested his elbows on his knees. "I'm still angry, mom. I'm angry every damn day."

"Understood. So channel some of that anger onto a canvas—let your emotions out. You don't need to be a cop any more. We don't expect that, but we cannot accept your unwillingness to try something—anything new."

"Okay. Get an application. If they accept me, I'll do it, but only because of the unrelenting guilt I cannot shed. I don't see myself as an artist," Evan said shaking his head.

"Neither did I. When I went to school there, I knew I could sketch, but I had no idea of the talent I had for creating pastoral scenery or painting flowers. I learned perspective techniques, light and shading. I learned to really look at nature and copy its magic and subtle nuances like the shape of a butterfly's wings. Other art students inspired me. Once the creative side of me flourished, I started enjoying the entire artistic process. It's a wonderful kind of therapy," Kelly added, flipping her blonde wispy bangs off her forehead. "When I paint, I can't think about anything else."

The unexpected ringing of the phone broke the tension, and Kelly went into the kitchen to grab the landline. "Who? Oh, Sheriff Cosley. Just a minute—Evan's in the living room. Let me give him the phone."

"Hello?" he punched the speakerphone's button.

"How are you, Evan?"

"Not my favorite question. What's up, Bob?"

"I've gotten some unusual information that I had to share with you about the robbery that day."

Evan sat up straighter on the sofa. "Wadda' you mean unusual?"

"It's been awhile and the case has gone pretty cold, but then we got a call out of the blue—or, I should say purple."

"What?" Evan scratched his head in confusion.

"A bartender from the Purple Place in El Dorado Hills called in a tip that he thought might be helpful."

"You're kidding, right? The place where all the motorcycle riders hang?"

"Not kidding. Wait till you hear this. Apparently a week or so before the robbery, these two guys were sitting at the bar, pretty wasted doing shooters. One of the guys was asking this bartender if he knew of anyone who could pilot a helicopter."

Evan stood up and started pacing in the living room. "Did the bartender remember what the guys looked like?"

"Brief description. One guy with dark hair had a weight-lifter build. Other one had long, sandy brown hair, scruffy beard and a medium build. Both, maybe in their thirties, wearing leather jackets and biker boots."

"What makes you think these two guys had anything to do with the robbery?"

"It's not every day someone's lookin' to hire a copter pilot," Bob said. "I recall it was a military-looking copter."

"Do you think it came from Mather Field?"

"No, we checked. Had to have come from somewhere else."

Evan bit the inside of his lower lip. "Did the bartender say anything else?"

"He said the guys rode up from Southern Cal on their motorcycles." Bob cleared his throat.

"Anything else?" Evan rubbed his hands on his jeans and his anxiety took hold making his head spin—thoughts and images from that horrific day flooded back into his mind.

"They talked a lot about boats—like maybe they were racing them or something."

"Why didn't the dimwit bartender come forward before this?" Evan scoffed.

"His father was ill, so he was distracted. He said he just didn't think about it. Seeing so many people night after night, he stuck the event in the back of his mind. Apparently one day he remembered the robbery and the guys who got away in a helicopter. I don't think he's the brightest light in town, but at least he decided to come forward now with the info."

Evan's breathing became irregular and a torrent of emotions flooded through his mind. "Did the bartender get a name?"

"Said one guy's name was Jed. That's all I've got."

Thanks, Bob. I appreciate the call. Are you going to follow up on it?"

"Not sure. Case has gone cold till now. Assault weapon clips found in the field that day with no trace. Same with two people killed in the shootout at the bank. No one could add any valuable information to help identify these criminals. Not much to go on now except a physical description and a first name. Database with 'Jed' for a first name in Southern, CA has hundreds and maybe thousands of possibilities, but with no last name we have no idea where to start."

"Would the bartender talk to me?"

"Maybe. You're not on the force anymore."

"If I tell him I'm Ashley's brother, I'll get him to talk to me."

"Do you think you'll ever want to come back to the force?"

"No, Bob, can't do it. Here's your laugh for the day. I'm going to art school. My parents want to sell their house and get me the hell out of it, so I've gotta try something new."

"I've got an idea," Bob suggested. "I can get a sketch artist out to the Purple Place and see if we can put together a profile and run it in our database."

"Do it, please." Evan said. "I sure can't draw."

"I'll stay in touch. By the way, where's your school?"

"Damn cold New York in the winter. Snows there. Big Apple, Broadway and all that jazz. So not me."

"Your mother's a clever woman. She figured out how to make you miserable somewhere else."

CHAPTER 20
St. Paul-de-Vence

Evan sat on the bed in his hotel room in St. Paul, sipping vodka on ice and eating salted almonds, courtesy of the bar in his room until it ended up on his hotel bill. Despite the exceptional dinner on the *Belle Chloe*, this unsettled gnawing in his stomach about Ryan's background made him hungry. He Googled *Ryan Coltrane*. Who knew so many people had that name? He scanned and read the descriptions—a completely frustrating search. Nothing whatsoever about anyone connected with boating except what was on the Internet about Ryan as a partner at Gaspard Yachting. Evan adjusted the down pillows behind his back and wondered what he wasn't seeing. Had his detective instincts gone weak? What was he missing?

Then he remembered the phone call he had two years ago with Sheriff Cosley regarding a tip he received about two guys at the Purple Place interested in hiring a helicopter pilot. Evan recalled he had gone to the Purple Place the next day and talked with Mickey, the bartender, who was somewhat reluctant to give out any information until Evan told him who he was. Mickey had nothing helpful to add to the information Bob had given him, so it became a wasted trip, and Evan had returned home dejected. He recalled the sketch artist had no luck either, since Mickey couldn't describe facial features. That same feeling of desperation started to consume Evan and he didn't like it then, nor could he deal with it now because he didn't want to admit that he might never find out who Ashley's killer was. Frustrated, he set the laptop on the bed and closed his eyes, pondering the conversation he had with Ryan earlier in the evening. Ryan said that he had worked at a boating company in California…where was it? Santa, something. And what was the name of the yachting firm he mentioned?

Evan knew he'd had too many vodkas and his brain was fuzzy. He played the mind game his father taught him years ago when he couldn't remember something. Starting with the letter *A* he began the alphabet association. Evan let that letter mull around in his head. Nothing. Then *B*…then *C* and then he remembered Ryan had said *Columbia Yachting.* He snapped his fingers in approval of himself. Evan glanced at his watch and knew it was still possible to call Columbia Yachting in California to ask if Ryan had worked there. He Googled the yachting company, wrote down the phone number and grabbed the phone in his room to make an international call which he knew would have clearer reception than his cell phone.

"Columbia Yachting, may I help you?"

"I'm trying to locate someone who worked for you."

"Let me connect you with the manager," the woman said.

"Garrett Morgan, here. What can I do for you?"

Evan swallowed hard, "My name is Robert Coltrane, Ryan's uncle. I'm calling from France. His aunt has just passed away and we are trying to locate Ryan. He said he worked for you a couple of years ago.

"You must have the wrong company," Garrett said.

"I was sure he said he worked for Columbia Yachting."

"Well, there's never been anyone by the name of Coltrane who worked for us."

Evan felt his throat clutch, unsure of what to say next. Lying was not a skill he relied on. "My wife loved her nephew like her own son and she had left him a considerable amount of money." Evan rolled his eyes as he went on with this ruse. "My nephew talked about how much he enjoyed racing with your company."

"Racing?" Garrett's voice faltered. "Are you sure you are not talking about Jed?"

"Jed, who?"

"Jed Reddiger. He was the only person who worked for me who was ever on a racing crew."

"You said 'was'?"

"Well, he left a couple of years ago, saying he wanted a boat of his own."

"Do you know where he went?"

"No idea whatsoever. Pissed me off. Gave no notice."

"Understood. I must have gotten the wrong information and shouldn't have bothered you."

"No problem. Sorry for your loss. I hope you find who you're looking for."

Evan hung up the phone and noticed his hand was trembling.

CHAPTER 21

Evan

Evan woke up with the sun warming his pillow. Breezes slapped swaying palm tree fronds against the stucco walls of his hotel. His head ached forcing him to rub his temples in an attempt to get the post-vodka blur out of his thinking. Last night's phone call to Columbia Yachting was disconcerting. On one hand, the bartender at the Purple Place said a guy named Jed had been in the bar that night asking about hiring a helicopter pilot.

None of this had anything to do with Ryan, or did it? Jed was someone else who worked at Columbia Yachting. Evan shook his head, got out of bed and wandered to the coffee bar in his room, popped in a dark blend, added water and waited. The coffee dripped slowly into the cup as thoughts swirled through his head like the dairy creamer he just added along with a packet of sugar.

He wandered to the bathroom to shower when his landline phone rang. He set the coffee on the sink and walked to the nightstand to take the call.

"Hello?"

"Evan? It's Ryan. I have to go to the office before we go out diving today. Seems like the police are doing an office interrogation with all of us—shouldn't take long, but is there any way you can drive to Gaspard Yachting and meet me there in a couple of hours?"

"No problem. Sure. Give me the address. I'll see you there about 10.00. Okay?"

"Yeah, fine. See ya' then."

Evan glanced at the address he had written down, stuck it in his wallet and grabbed the lukewarm coffee off of the sink.

He turned on the hot water faucet and welcomed a steamy shower. As water sprayed over his head, he lathered up with a frothy shampoo and tried to sort out his conflicted thoughts. The first thing he intended to do after he towel dried was to check the Columbia Yachting Internet website to see if there were photos of the staff. Maybe a photo of this guy, Jed, would be on their web pages. Because Ryan wanted to meet him at Gaspard Yachting instead of the Nice harbor, the idea of showing up where Ryan worked in swim trunks and flip flops seemed out of the question, so he donned a pair of shorts, a clean tee, and deck shoes instead.

Hungry now, he searched the hotel refrigerator for anything edible and grabbed a chocolate nut bar. He checked the Internet for Columbia Yachting and scanned the roster of employees and found no mention of Jed Reddiger. Perhaps he could find a photo of Jed in the site's photos, but after browsing through them, all he could locate were photos of sloops and crews—faces too small to recognize, with humans bronzed by the sun and heads covered in baseball caps. Not helpful. Not what he hoped for, but then he had to consider what he expected to see: a photo of Jed, whom he did not know, or a photo of Ryan? "That's crazy," he told himself out loud. None of this made any sense, and he gritted his teeth.

Could his buried anger about Ashley's death have caused him to be suspicious of people who had nothing to do with her murder? Was the relentless search for justice that kept ripping open a scar perhaps best left alone? No! Definitely not.

He grabbed a small duffle bag, his car keys and headed out to the parking garage. The sun was white and hot. Clouds had billowed so low in the sky it looked like they had fallen and transformed themselves into mountains resting on the horizon. Jasmine fragranced the air, and he decided it would be another top-down drive up the coast to meet Ryan at work.

After a relaxing drive with local music playing on the radio, he pulled into Gaspard's parking lot, put the duffle bag in the trunk and locked the car. The stand-alone building was not what he expected—but then, nothing about this vacation had been what he expected. The architecture reminded him of a courthouse on the East Coast, with double-hung windows, rustic dark green shutters, and mossy grey stone. Two police cars were in the parking lot, and Evan felt awkward and yet curious about the investigation. He walked to the front door, noticed a card reader of some sort for which he didn't have access, but heard a buzz from the front reception desk before he grabbed the door handle.

"Hello. I'm Evan Wentworth. Ryan asked me to meet him here," he said to the middle-aged receptionist with black curly hair, bright red eyeglass frames, matching lipstick and a welcoming smile.

"Yes, Mr. Wentworth. Ryan told me you'd be arriving. Just have a seat over there by the door. Can I get you anything while you wait?"

"Uh, sure. Coffee?"

"Happy to get that for you. Cream?"

"Yes, and sugar."

"Will you be wanting to rent a yacht? We have some brochures on the coffee table."

"No. Just visiting. Ryan is taking me scuba diving today."

"Oh, well you might have to wait. The police have been here talking to the entire staff for an hour already because of the murder—oh, dear, I shouldn't have said that."

"It's okay. I know about it."

"You do? Did you know Armond?"

"No. I've met Danielle and her family."

"Terrible thing about Armond, isn't it?"

"Yes. Sounds like he was a nice man," Evan said and wondered why he was having a probing conversation with the receptionist. He mentally scolded himself for not leaving his detective skills checked at the door.

"He was. We're all pretty upset. I've gotta get back to work...name's Nicole. If you need anything else, let me know. Phone's busy. I'll get someone to get your coffee."

"Thanks, Nicole."

Nicole went back to clicking away at her keyboard and answering the phone. Evan sat there for fifteen or so minutes restless and unable to relax, too many coffees weighing on his bladder.

"Nicole, can I use your restroom?"

"Oui. Just down the hall, then turn right at the end and you will see it next to the lunchroom."

Evan got up, went through a doorway and headed down the hall past several offices with closed doors and found the restroom. He began washing his hands when he heard a conversation coming through the overhead duct vent. He ignored the conversation until he recognized Ryan's voice. Curious, he shut off the water and listened.

"How well did you know Armond?"

"We worked together, but how well do you know anyone?"

"So, that means you didn't know him well."

"I suppose that's true."

"He'd been the company controller, correct?"

"Yes, but you already know that, Detective Nichols. Is there something else you want to ask me?"

"Where were you on the night of the murder?"

"At home. I went home after work."

"And, what time was that?"

"Don't recall. Maybe around six or seven."

"What did you do that evening?"

"Can't remember. Probably read or watched TV."

"And, what did you watch?"

"Look, I have no idea what I watched. That was days ago. Probably sports."

"I've noticed slivers of glass in the carpet here in your office."

"Yes, that's from an accident I had."

"Accident?"

"Yes, I tripped over the coffee table and broke a sculpture."

"Ah, oui, oui. I've heard that before. Mind if we take carpet fiber samples?"

"Why would you want to do that?" Ryan asked, with his voice sounding pitchy and exasperated.

"We're concerned. We've talked to Gaspard and looked at the surveillance camera outside. It appears to be broken, but we're taking it along with us."

"Why? He wasn't murdered here?" Ryan said.

"Have you ever been to Armond's home?" Detective Nichols asked.

"Yes, of course."

"You're not very forthcoming, are you?"

"I'm trying to be helpful here."

"When were you at Armond's home?"

"Last summer."

"Why?"

"We had our company picnic at his home."

"So you know how to get there?"

"Yes, I just said that."

"You seem agitated, Mr. Coltrane."

"I'm not agitated. Frustrated, yes. I'm taking someone out diving this morning and I want to get going."

"Just a few more questions, if you don't mind."

Evan plastered his head against the damp wall, eavesdropping and feeling like a cad, but he couldn't help himself. He strained to listen.

"I'm going to snip those carpet fiber samples now," the detective said.

"Why? I've told you the reason glass is in the carpet."

"It's not about the glass. We've been here before and we noticed blood."

Evan nearly stopped breathing, and hoped no one would come into the restroom.

"Of course there's blood! I told you I fell and split my lip." Ryan sounded angry.

"Ah yes. I've heard that story from Gaspard."

"You don't think I had anything to do with his murder?"

Evan heard someone walking toward the restroom door, so he headed into one of the two stalls and sat down on the commode, bummed that he could not hear the rest of the conversation. Whoever came into the restroom used the urinal, washed his hands and left. Evan quickly came out of the stall, looked at the restroom door, realized there was a lock on it, and pushed the lever closed. Barely a moment after he shut the door he heard a male voice outside the door asking if he was ill, which he wasn't. He creatively lied that he'd had too many oysters and his stomach was upset.

The voice said, "Can I get you anything?"

"No, No. I'm fine—be out shortly," Evan said with conviction. "Thanks for asking."

The person who was checking on him finally decided to accept the explanation and left. Evan was frustrated he had missed part of the interrogation. He noticed a wastebasket on the floor, carefully tipped it over with the paper towels inside and stood on the basket, nearly falling over as he slammed into the wall, but braced himself on the sink with one foot to hear more of the conversation.

Detective Nichols and Ryan were no longer in the same spot in the office, because the conversation was now hard to hear, but he did hear the detective say something about a shoe—something about not finding Armond's other shoe at the murder scene. He heard Ryan ask where the shoe was found. The detective said a neighbor's dog carried it into their house having apparently found it on the lawn somewhere. He heard Ryan ask in a snide tone, "And that proves what?"

"We think the murder may have taken place at Armond's home."

Ryan and the detective must have moved to another spot in the office and the conversation became louder.

"You're saying he was killed at home?"

"We think that's what happened," the detective stated.

"And how in the world did he end up in some alley? Wasn't it a dumpster, I believe?" Ryan asked, his voice now questioning in disbelief.

"Yes, it was a dumpster. A body with one shoe missing."

"That's very strange," Ryan said. "I thought he was mugged somewhere near that restaurant.

"Perhaps," Detective Nichols added.

"If you don't have anything more, I need to be going. I have a guest waiting."

"Of course, Mr. Coltrane. Thank you for your time."

"What happens next?" Ryan asked.

"We'll talk to the rest of the staff and get back to you and Gaspard with our findings. Detective Wilkes has been with Gaspard and two other employees."

"How long will this investigation take, do you think?"

"That is the question, isn't it?"

The conversation seemed to have ended. Evan waited but couldn't hear anything more through the vent other than a door closing, so he wobbled off the wastebasket, put all the used paper towels back in the basket, rinsed his hands, unlocked the door and went back to the lobby.

"Oh, you're back, "Nicole said, her face in a contorted frown. "Are you all right? You look a bit pale."

"Too much late night drinking and some oysters that bothered me."

"Well, I hope you will be okay. We have some sparkling water here. Do you want some?"

"Ah, sure. Yes, that'll help. Thank you."

Evan sat down on the leather sofa and sipped the fizzy water. His knees felt weak and his mind was racing with information that troubled him. He had an uncanny feeling about Ryan from the moment he met him, and now he wondered if Ryan was somehow mixed up in Armond's murder. This couldn't be possible? Or could it? Worst of all, he was going out diving with this person, and suddenly he was more than wary—he was afraid.

CHAPTER 22

Ryan and Evan

Ryan spotted Evan sitting in the waiting room. "Evan, there you are. I'm sorry this investigation took so long."

"Not a problem." Evan stood.

"You look a little unsettled. Are you okay?"

"Yes. Late night drinking with too many oysters."

"Been there. Ready to go?"

"Yes, sure." Evan set down his bottle of fizz.

"Let's take my car. No reason for both of us to drive."

"Sounds good."

"Bye, Nicole. See you either later or tomorrow. Tell Gaspard to call me if he needs anything," Ryan said as he reached for the front door.

"Sure you can go diving today with an upset stomach?" Ryan asked.

"That's all behind me now," Evan managed to laugh, and noticed Ryan was chuckling as well. "I'll just grab my duffle bag out of my car, load it into yours, if that's okay?"

"Yes, plenty of room in the trunk. The diving gear is on the boat, but I've thrown some fins in the trunk I think will fit your feet since you are about my size."

"Much appreciated."

Evan got into Ryan's BMW, and wondered what the heck to talk about, except the obvious.

"So, how did the investigation go?" He glanced at Ryan.

"Went fine," Ryan said, with his chin jutted out and his hands gripping the leather steering wheel as tightly as if he was at sea on a stormy night. "Cops are annoying and doing their job, but it just upsets everyone all over again."

"I can imagine," Evan said.

"I'm sure you can," Ryan glanced at Evan.

Evan didn't know how to take that comment, so he let it go. Silence hung in the air.

Ryan rubbed his chin. "Cops think everyone's guilty until proven innocent."

Evan squirmed in his seat and wondered if Danielle mentioned to Ryan that he'd been a cop.

"Well, I'm sure no one at Gaspard's company had anything to do with Armond's murder," Evan said with his words sticking in his throat like spoiled food he wanted to upchuck.

"Of course not. Everyone liked Armond," Ryan added.

"Did you know him well?" Evan asked purposely probing.

"Not really. About as well as you know most people you work with."

Evan considered Ryan's reply and decided he was consistent, however dubious he might appear.

Ryan flipped on the radio and drove the rest of the way without talking. They arrived at the parking lot in Nice surprisingly crowded with cars on a weekday.

"Well, here we are," Ryan said. "Let's get the stuff out of the trunk, and I'll get the harbormaster to tender us to the boat."

Evan grabbed his duffle bag and a pair of large fins and watched Ryan gather up a small canvas bag and his swim fins. "You have a really clean trunk," Evan said.

"I don't usually haul diving gear around in it."

"No, I mean your trunk looks brand new."

"Good observation. It was recently redone—spilled red wine all over it."

Ryan greeted Pierre with a handshake, who waved hello to Evan. Pierre then went down the stairs to the tender and brought it around.

"Which yacht are you using today, Ryan?"

"The diveboat. She's easier to maneuver in the water."

" About how long will you be out?" Pierre asked.

"Couple of hours, depending on the water's clarity. Sometimes the currents murk things up and you can't see more than five feet in front of you, but it should be a good day since there haven't been any storms. I'll call you when we want to come in."

Ryan and Evan got into the tender, sat down and watched Pierre turn on the engine. The tender sped up creating a wake of silvery white waves. The sea air cleared Evan's head and he felt less anxious. Ryan seemed relaxed. Evan decided that he would be okay underwater as long as he didn't get too close to Ryan. After all, Pierre had just seen the two of them, and certainly Ryan wasn't going to do something where only one of them was coming back, and certainly not Ryan by himself—that was too obvious. Pierre guided the tender to an impressive inboard, gleaming on the water, the boat's wide hull in white with a blue trim stripe just under the rails. Ryan got out first, grabbed his gear and Evan followed him up a small ladder.

"You'll like this boat. She's easy in the water and the stern flips down about two feet over the water for a jump dive, so you don't need to flip off the side of the boat backwards with your tank." Ryan said.

"Are the tanks on board already?" Evan asked.

"Yes, but I have to fill them on the compressor first. They've been used before on a short dive, and I'm not sure how much oxygen is left. Follow me and I'll get you your BC, regulator and goggles."

"Using a wetsuit?" Evan asked.

"Prefer it. Water's not that cold, but if something is going to bite, you are less tasty with rubber," Ryan laughed.

"Very funny," Evan said, and realized it was the first time he'd seen Ryan in a humorous mood. It was as if he had changed personalities from a serious, grim, cautious person to someone lighthearted he'd never met before. Evan began to relax and let out a sigh of relief.

Ryan maneuvered the boat out to sea. It took about twenty minutes to find the location he wanted to dive in before he dropped anchor. Evan wiggled into his wetsuit leggings, then put on his upper body wet suit, zipped it up, and pulled down his hood. He sat on a bench and grabbed the fins that fit comfortably once the strap was adjusted.

"You look ready for diving," Ryan said, already suited as well. "Here's your BC, regulator and weight belt. I guessed at your weight—around 180?"

"Close enough."

"You want me to help you hook up your air hose to your tank?"

Not a question Evan could avoid, because it would sound suspicious if he said no, so he said the obvious, "Of course."

Evan pulled the straps secure on his buoyancy compensator. It fit surprisingly well, and Ryan put the tank on his back. Evan fastened his weight belt, and then spit on his goggles to keep them from fogging up. He put the regulator in his mouth, took the goggles off his hood and pulled them over his face. Ryan motioned for Evan to follow him to the back of the boat. Both men duck-walked with swim fins to the ledge of the boat.

Ryan said, "You ready?"

Evan dropped the regulator out of his mouth and let it dangle. "Ready. Where are we diving?" Evan wondered.

"Villefranche. Some nice shallow reefs, deep drops and gorgonians. You okay with diving down to 100 ft?"

"Yeah. Just give me a little time to adjust to the depth and clear my ears."

"Sure. I'll show you a coral cave. Been cave diving before?"

"No." Evan said, the *no* coming out as a gurgle tinged in fear.

"Here," Ryan said and startled Evan with a knife. "Strap this on your leg."

"Oh, right," Evan said, nervous again starting to sweat in his wetsuit.

"I'll take a spear gun," Ryan said, "Just in case."

"In case of what?" Evan tried to smile with his goggles tight against his upper lip making him look like he'd had an overdose of Botox.

"In case you look like fish food."

Evan spit out his regulator. "You mean shark bait, right?"

"You never know."

Evan put the regulator back into his mouth, dreading the dive.

Ryan already had his regulator in his mouth and did a hand motion to follow him as he held on to his goggles and jumped into the murky indigo water. As Evan did the same, he hit the water wondering if he would ever see blue sky again.

CHAPTER 23

Evan's Thoughts

I've been told your life flashes before your eyes when you die. I must be a complete idiot to be down here diving with a man who has made me question everything about him. Here I am in layers of murky water, brushing against schools of silver fish, following someone who might try to kill me. We dive deeper and the water clears. I've checked my submersible pressure gauge and air is flowing from my tank into my lungs. I've got to breathe slower or I will use up my air sooner than I should for this dive.

The dive down to 50 feet was easy, and now going deeper. The water has cleared and the coral breathes in shades of deep purple and lime green. I try to look at the ocean floor, grassy tufts swaying in the current, and am glad there does not seem to be any kelp. The Pacific Ocean around Monterey has beds of kelp so thick you can easily get your tank snarled in a forest of clinging vines, harbor seals and other dangers lurking in the deep. Diving is mysterious and fascinating or there would be no reason to do it. Something about moving with the current to explore our planet in the depths of the sea is impossible to explain unless you actually do it. Being able to breathe underwater with a tank is far easier than snorkeling on the surface in waves where water frequently fills your snorkel tube, lands in your mouth and forces you to blow it out.

I'm enjoying the utter peace and quiet of this dive with only my bubbles and breathing as sounds I can hear—that and Ryan's fins swooshing in front of me a good ten feet in the distance. He's hard to keep up with. Lean and muscular, he's an adept diver who has done this far more often than I have in the past couple of years.

The water is getting colder, yet it remains clear, filtered by sunlight from above. My body has warmed the water between my wetsuit and my skin and I'm not cold. I've relaxed my breathing, but it does not mean I am not nervous. I look around trying to enjoy this dive, but my mind is still racing with the information I overheard earlier in the restroom.

I pass a colorful lion fish that ignores me as if I am simply a larger fish sharing its environment with no threat. I wish I could feel the same about Ryan. Why did the detective want carpet samples with blood on them? Why were they treating Ryan as a suspect? And what was the revelation about Armond's shoe being found by the neighbor's dog? A body found a good distance away with only one shoe? And this detective telling Ryan it was possible that Armond was killed at his home? Did Ryan have something to do with Armond's murder? This doesn't make sense. No one in his right mind, who is a partner at a prestigious yachting company, kills the controller. But, why? Unless…unless it was about money.

What's happening? Ryan is so far ahead and I'm having difficulty keeping up. What the—? I kick my fins as hard as I can. Ouch, ouch, ouch, dammit, I have a leg cramp. I stop kicking and grab my calf. Ryan does not notice I'm no longer following him. I roll into a ball and hold my leg wincing in pain. My toes are spreading apart in my fin and I'm drifting away from him. I want to scream but I can't. I take out my leg knife and reach behind my vest and bang repeatedly on my tank. Clunk, clank. Ryan turns his head…thank God he sees me.

He swims toward me as I float helplessly in the opposite direction with my back sucked into an abyss and my legs out in front of me. Ryan motions for me to swim in a different direction, and I realize I'm in an undertow. I could swim if I could use both of my legs, one of which is cramping and rolling knots up my thigh in bursts of pain. He swims toward me. I can see him getting closer. I feel like I am going to black out because I've stopped breathing—not because there is not enough air, but it is a human response to fear. He's holding my arm now and stares at my mask. I point to my leg and grab it. He realizes it's a cramp and pulls me out of the current and swims across it, towing me like a sack of rocks.

I want to surface, but Ryan shakes his head and mumbles for me to bite my arm. Odd that one can actually speak with a regulator in one's mouth, but 'bite arm' was something I heard. I have to take the regulator out of my mouth to do it, and let it drop in the water. If he wanted to kill me, now would be the time to do it. He puts the regulator back in my mouth, and I gasp for breaths so quickly, I'm sure I've used up all the air in my tank.

He shakes his head and puts up one gloved finger. He drops his regulator and bites my forearm. Shit! It hurts like hell…he holds the bite, and my leg cramp relaxes. He puts the regulator back in his mouth and does a 'thumbs up' with a shoulder shrug, as if to ask if I am okay. I give him a weak 'thumbs up' and he motions to move ahead, nodding. I nod back. I'm not dead yet, but I am exhausted.

CHAPTER 24

Ryan's Thoughts

Figures. The guy's more of an artist than a cop, and I was worried, why? Not his fault he got a cramp or that he ended up in an undertow. I could've let him drift, but it would have been obvious malice. Strange having to come to his rescue. Had half a mind to take my knife and slice his air hose—just a tiny tear, but then how would I be able to explain it? As if I don't have enough to worry about. Evan's swimming along slowly, trying not to overexert his muscles now full of lactic acid. He's probably wishing he'd never come on this dive, but then, that was the idea, right? Not to kill the guy, but to scare the living crap out of him.

I needed this—an underwater escape from the shit storm on the surface that I can't figure out. Why in the hell didn't I spend more time that night looking for that damn shoe? What are the odds a neighbor's dog would find the shoe and bring it home? Probably the reason I couldn't find it that night…dog had already run off with it like a newly found toy. And what was with detective pain-in-the-ass Nichols insisting on taking carpet samples? They won't find anything but my blood.

I need to stop worrying and just breathe here underwater. Thousands of fish surround me, look at me and move in and around me. I spot an octopus slithering under a rock with his large head and bulging eyes staring at me. Huge gorgonian fan coral in every rainbow color sway with the current, shadowing a blood orange colored starfish. I feel alive down here and safe. Not at all like growing up with a drunken, abusive father who kept me in a storm cellar when we were small. If my brother pissed him off, he'd shove Ted, my older brother, in with me. We'd scream for days to no avail, and he'd eventually throw in a dead skinned mouse or squirrel for us to eat. That kind of dark I cannot tolerate. Close me up in a small dark room, and my head starts to split open.

I guess it's when the migraines started—then, or right after my brother, Ted, killed dad. Blew his brains out with a shotgun and buried the gun in the woods miles from our shanty. I should have been scared, but all I felt was relief. If Trisha hadn't left us, maybe he wouldn't have been so volatile. Kind of a crazy woman, but she gave us no mind. We weren't her kids. In a Kentucky mining town, alcohol and abuse often went together. Maybe her leaving Harry was all she could do to survive. He probably would have beaten her to death. Noticed all the bruises. After she left, didn't hear from her again. Cops never solved the murder or didn't care. Rumor had it that crazy Harry kept his kids in that cellar—the cops probably thought he had it coming and either decided it was a robbery or that we killed him, but they could never prove it.

Ted and I stole all the money we could find in Harry's blood-stained filthy jeans and dresser drawers, hopped a train out of Kentucky, slept in fields, under highway overpasses, in ditches and stole food from truck-stop markets. One day we decided to hitch a ride with a truck driver who lived in a cabin in the woods in Nebraska. He took us in, let us clean up and gave us a place to sleep in clean beds with decent food. We stayed a couple of weeks, then left when he was truckin' somewhere, hopped another freight to San Diego enlisted in the Army. Never saw the guy again…never thanked him when we left.

As I breathe my way through the fish, I feel nothing but calmness about my past. It does not exist. I check my waterproof watch and submersible pressure gauge and see that we have about a half-hour left for diving and are close to the cave. Better check on Evan, wimp that he is, to see if he can finish this dive or whether we should head back to the boat.

CHAPTER 25

Ryan

We approach the mouth of the cave with its jagged rocks and immense coral. I signal to Evan with a forward hand motion as if to proceed, but Evan shakes his head and holds up one finger in an indication to wait. No surprise. He then stops kicking and lets himself glide slowly downward toward the sandy ocean floor covered with boulders.

Evan settles down on a rock with both fins pointing outward and gently moves his arms from side to side as if he is treading water to recoup his strength. I watch in disbelief as his right foots slides off a mossy rock, settles in a crevice and now his foot is wedged between two rocks. Sand is stirred up and I can hardly see, but something is holding on to the back of his foot in his Achilles tendon. Holy shit! A rapacious moray eel has clamped on to his heel like an angry Pitt Bull terrier thrashing in the water. Blood starts to pool around Evan's foot while he frantically tries to whack the eel with his other fin to no avail. I send him a mental message to use his knife, but he's out of control. I can't use my spear gun because I'd likely hit Evan in the leg. Evan's eyes bulge inside his mask and I swim over to the snake-like behemoth and take out my leg knife and slash at the eel. Damn. I miss it. The odious eel is ruthless in the water while Evan's arms are flaying and he's kicking with his left leg in a state of panic.

The second knife stab lands into the side of the eel's head. Wounded, it releases its grip and slithers away into the deep. Evan is bleeding into the water. As divers, I can guess what he's thinking at this moment—that blood in the water draws sharks.

Evan wants to surface and starts heading up. I grab him by the legs and shake my head and point to Evan's flesh-torn wound and gurgle out the word *wait.* He glares at me as if I am trying to kill him, and the thought crosses my mind. I take out my knife and slice off a section of my wetsuit to get a wide strip of neoprene. I point to Evan's foot and motion with my hands my intent to take off the fin and put the neoprene strip under the fin strap to stop the bleeding. Evan's face looks ghostly white, but he allows me to put the temporary bandage on his heel.

I think he has calmed down, but instead he's shaking his head furiously while motioning to go up to the surface. My depth gauge indicates 90 feet and we can't rise rapidly to the surface unless we stop periodically and let our lungs adjust to the change in pressure. I nod and motion to Evan to head up and then the idiot starts to kick like he is running out of air. He's going up too fast and he's going to kill himself. Dammit. I struggle after him and grab him from the front around his calves. He kicks me in the face with his knee and knocks off my facemask, which I grab with my left hand before it sinks and manage to put it back on, but it slows me down. What's wrong with this guy? He knows better.

I swim like a person on cocaine, which I'm not, but should have been, and try to catch up. He's at least fifteen feet ahead of me. Finally, I gain on him and grab his good leg. We struggle in the water. I consider knocking him out. He's panicked and probably experiencing the toxin from the eel. "Shit!" I think to myself, "You'd better not die on me." Adrenalin is taking over and I'm raging angry. I swim around behind him and grab him around the chest, while he keeps kicking, but at least he's not kicking me. He finally stops struggling and lets me take him up to the surface with several rest stops. He's breathing normally through his regulator, but his head has slumped to the side. I check his pressure gauge and he has plenty of air. The water is getting brighter and our bubbles are rising to the surface at a steady rate properly controlled. Oddly enough at this moment it occurs to me that I have probably saved his life.

We breach the surface. I yank on his BC to inflate his vest and then do the same with mine. I spit out my regulator and let it hang in the water. Then I lift off his diving mask. "You okay?" I shout at him, no longer captive of my own thoughts in my head.

"Hell, no, I'm not okay. Isn't that obvious?" Evan bellows at me.

"You panicked down there and nearly drowned both of us."

"I know. Shoot me with your spear gun if you like, but I'm in so much damn pain I can't breathe and my leg has gone numb," Evan wails.

"You probably have hemagglutinin from the eel bite."

"What?" Evan says, gasping for air and breathing in rasps as if he was on Everest instead of in the sea.

"It's a glycoprotein that causes your red blood cells to clump."

"Terrific."

"I've gotta get you to a hospital, and there's a good chance you have the bends as well."

"Am I gonna die?"

"Doubt it. Hospital has a hyperbaric chamber. I'll get an ambulance to meet us at the dock. You have to stay here on the surface while I deflate and swim back to the boat."

'You won't leave me out here, will you?" Evan's eyes bulge.

"Of course not. It's early afternoon. Shouldn't take me more than twenty minutes to get back to the boat."

"How will you see me out here?"

"I know where this diving spot is by locating the buildings on the horizon. You'll drift some, but I'll find you. Let's see your foot."

"Why?" Evan's eyes start to close in exhaustion.

"I want to see if the neoprene patch is still in place and that you're not bleeding."

"Leg's numb—you look."

I lift the patch and peer down and the chewed flesh. "It's fine. Not bleeding. You won't be shark bait, but promise me you will relax and just float here."

"Will do. Ryan?"

"What now?"

"Nothing. Thanks…I just wanted to say thanks."

"Back soon, and just float with the current. I'll find you, I promise." I flip over and bend at the waist with my fins splashing water into to a shallow dive but deep enough to be able to move quickly in the water. Hopefully I'll get to Evan before a shark does.

CHAPTER 26

Evan's Thoughts

I'm buoyant in the water with an occasional wave cresting me up and then down again, rocking me in the sea. I have nothing to do out here but think. My face is starting to fry in the sun, and I wonder if Ryan will find me. My leg is still numb and I can't swim without causing toxins to spread throughout my bloodstream.

Not the vacation I had in mind. If I die out here, who would believe what happened? I know what the bends are, but have never been stupid enough to ascend too quickly like I did today—but then again, I've never been bitten by an eel. What a vile, ugly creature of the sea that thing is. No matter what, I'm never having eel on a Sushi menu again. My humor is not totally gone and I force a weak smile. I let my head drop back into the water, just enough so my ears fill making the water dull sounds. Here I am, helpless in the aquamarine sea staring at a glorious blue sky above filled with massive clouds, and wondering if there are sharks nearby.

This should have been a pleasant diving experience, but instead, I'm terrified, emotionally drained and alone. I doze on and off and thoughts of Aurora fill my head. Had I stayed in New York, none of this would have happened. I remember when I met her on the first day in a sketching class at Parsons. She sat down on a stool with an easel next to me. Her blonde hair was cut short with spiked wisps at the crown and at the nape of her neck so delicately curved. I recall being surprised she was barefoot during our first conversation.

"You a new art student too?" I asked feeling awkward.

"Oh, no," she laughed. "Not at all."

I remember I held out my hand and told her my name was Evan. She said she was Aurora—Aurora Banfield.

"I own an art gallery and I model for this class. It's a good way to meet new artists. And you?"

"Former cop. No talent whatsoever. Mother is an artist who graduated from here and insisted I try a new career."

"Your mother sounds like a persuasive woman," she tilted her head and flicked off a bit of lint on her black dress.

"I suppose she is," I said.

"Enjoy the class, and when you sketch me, don't think of your mother," she said with a wink.

Aurora stood up, walked to the center of the room, stepped up to the platform and dropped her dress to the floor. Her nakedness stunned me as she positioned herself atop a white table. Our professor instructed us to draw what we saw. I picked up my chalk and put it to the paper, but I couldn't move my arm. I saw her tilt her head in my direction as she adjusted her shoulders and let her breasts fall comfortably. Her legs were statuesque and her buttocks had dimples on each side of her alabaster skin. Staring at her made me breathless. I'd had a very hard year after Ashley's death, and now I was experiencing a yearning between my legs so unexpected that I had to put a towel over my lap. Of all the things I thought art school would be, I never thought it could be this enticing.

In retrospect, I'm not sure what she saw in me. I felt her power—her extreme confidence at a time when I had none. A month went by quickly and a late night class ended. I saw her walk into the supply room where she sometimes refreshed her hair and make-up. The other students had left, and the lights went off in the building. Her perfume pulled me into that room. Like her name, Aurora, she has an aura that was magnetic and electrifying. I remember she put her finger to her lips and said, "Something you want, Evan?" I replied, "No. I want everything—every inch of you."

I grabbed her and pulled her boatneck dress off her shoulders and hoisted her up on the counter. She'd didn't resist and there in that room all her nakedness became mine. I had a primal hunger repressed for way too long a period of time. I had pent up anger unleashed with a passion so intense it nearly bordered on violence. We knocked over easels, cans of paintbrushes, trays of chalk and splattered paint on the floor and ourselves. I satiated myself with her and she climaxed repeatedly, clawing at me, biting my shoulder, finding my tongue and holding my thigh while she moved unabashedly wanting more.

And that was the start of our relationship. Wild, X-rated sexual tension unleashed. She knew about my past and helped me heal from the days of dark remorse. I felt alive and interested in life again. She supported my attempts at art and encouraged me to experience emotion through canvas and paint. To my surprise, my mother was right. I had an outlet to put all my anger on canvas and threw paint at it an abandon, and more paint on top of that in different colors dripping down the canvas to the floor, swirled with brushes into shapes and forms.

When she suggested showing one of my pieces at her gallery, I balked, but she made it an exigency—a pressing necessity. Never in my life did I expect someone to see what I created, much less that anyone would appreciate it. To me, my art was nothing more than emotional color bursts, but it did make me feel free. I was no longer depressed and I knew I'd found a new purpose in life. Aurora touted me to her art patrons as the new Jackson Pollock. When the gallery lights flooded my paintings, they picked up the metallic flecks of silver and gold, and of all things unexpected, they sold.

So, here I float. The sea surrounds me and gulls fly overhead swooping with the wind. I'm filled with guilt over avoiding Aurora who I owe everything to. I'm terrified I might never see Danielle again and am worried about how I am going to tell her my concerns about Ryan. Damn. My underwater distress has led to his probably saving my life. How in the world did I become indebted to this man?

Twenty minutes seems like an eternity. I hear other boats on the water but they are too far way for me to scream for help. My body is cold despite my face being toasted. A quick pee in my wetsuit warms me up—a well-known blessing to divers since there is no other way to relieve oneself. I start to nod off again when I spot a boat coming toward me and it is getting larger and larger. I squint in the sunlight and can see the blue accents. It's Ryan! I wave my arms frantically above my head. I think he sees me. If he doesn't run me over, I will not die out here.

CHAPTER 27

Ryan and Evan

Ryan maneuvered the dive boat carefully as he approached Evan. He shut off the engine and left the bridge and headed to the boat's backdrop. He threw off his tee shirt, adjusted his swim trunks and jumped into the water next to Evan.

"How you doin'?" Ryan asked, his eyes mere slits with his brow furrowed.

"Better now that you're here. Cold, hot, crampy, tired."

"Okay, let's get you to the ladder, and I'll help you up, but I have to take your fins off first."

Ryan carefully removed the fin and neoprene strip from the injured heel, and threw that fin atop the landing area, and then yanked off the other one and did the same toss.

"Do you think you can climb the ladder yourself?" Ryan asked with concern.

"Not sure. Leg's still numb. Feel like shit."

"Okay, I'll hoist you up to the first rung and then you can pull yourself up."

Evan struggled, but managed to use his strong leg to climb onboard.

"Let me see the wound," Ryan asked.

Evan sat cross-legged on the deck and inspected the flesh wound for the first time. An ugly gash of ripped flesh.

"Not pretty," Evan gurgled trying to shake water from his mouth.

"I'm going to cut the leg off of your wetsuit so that you don't have to pull it over your heel. These damn suits fit like a second skin."

Ryan cut away the legging and helped Evan peel off the lower part of the wetsuit. Evan took off his BC, the upper suit, and weight belt and let it all drop to the deck with a clunk.

"Let's get you to one of the cabins."

"Good idea. I've gotta' lie down or I'm going to pass out."

Ryan helped Evan limp to a stateroom and put him on the bed atop the blanket.

"Thirsty?" Ryan asked.

"Like a camel on the Sahara."

"Here's a bottle of water. Drink it slowly. Make yourself comfortable, and I'll head back. Ambulance is on its way to take you to Hospital Pasteur here in Nice."

"Can you grab my duffle bag—my phone is in there and I need to make a call."

"Yeah, sure. Be right back." Ryan left.

Evan closed his eyes, grateful to be alive, but felt like someone siphoned out his blood. He waited. Minutes seemed like hours.

Ryan returned, duffle bag in hand, biceps bulging and abs tight. "Here...I'll leave it on the bed."

Evan stared at Ryan's chest and noticed two things he had not seen before, probably because he was groggy. The dragon tattoo on the upper left side of his chest was small but matched the same tattoo on opposite side of his back. He then noticed it was not only a tattoo, but also a camouflage for an unmistakable black-tinged lumpy scar—healed wounds he'd often seen from bullet holes.

"Nice tattoo. Looks like it was a nasty wound." Evan muttered, without thinking of the consequences of bringing it up.

Ryan's eyes were cold and glared at Evan. "Took a bullet in service."

Evan nodded. "Went straight through?"

"Yeah, but didn't stop me."

"I can't imagine it would."

"Ryan?"

"Yeah, what?"

"I owe you for two wetsuits."

"Don't mention it. We have plenty," and then Ryan turned and left the room.

Evan needed a bathroom. He peered around the end of the bed and spotted one, wrapped himself in the blanket and headed to the john barely able to put his injured foot on the floor. Shivers went through his shoulders and down his spine. He felt nauseous and the back of his head pounded. He braced himself on the sink waiting for relief and noticed powder of some sort on the floor next to the wastebasket. He wet his finger and had half a mind to put it into his mouth, but if it was meth or coke, he was pretty sure it would not mix well with eel toxin. He brought it to his nose and sniffed, but not enough to inhale it. Couldn't tell what it was, but it definitely was not something for baking muffins.

He opened the medicine cabinet desperate for relief from his headache. He found something that looked like Acetaminophen, or Tylenol. Maybe not good for his liver, if it was still functioning, but might help with the pain in his head. He stared in the mirror at his sunburned face and pasty white body, a pathetic combination for one who had envisioned a well-tanned body from weeks sitting on the Riviera sand with a frothy umbrella drink in hand.

Ryan full-throttled the boat's engine and the dive boat's bow lifted out of the water in a jolt, sending Evan into the bathroom wall. He braced himself and hobbled back to bed, downed the pill and started to shake from the chills. He grabbed his phone from his duffle bag and called his mother, who he knew would never forgive him if he died somewhere on the Côte d'Azur, especially when she thought he was in New York.

"Hello, Mom?"

"Evan! What a surprise. Do you know what time it is?"

"Mom, no. Didn't consider it. Listen, I've been in a diving accident in Nice."

Kelly's voice was riddled with fear Evan could hear. She fired off a string of questions in rapid succession."What happened? Where are you now? And, I knew you were in St. Paul. Aurora sent me an email. Are you going to be all right?"

"I'm sure I'll be fine. Long story, but one of the guys I went diving with is taking me to the hospital where they have a hyperbaric chamber."

"A what? Do you have polio?"

"No, Mom. It's a chamber that helps with decompression sickness."

"Evan, what are you talking about?"

"I was on a dive and I got bitten by a Moray eel, and I tried to surface too quickly. It causes joint pain and gas bubbles in the body, and…"

"I'm calling Aurora."

"No, Mom, don't."

"Why not?"

"We're not exactly on speaking terms."

"I don't care. I'm calling her and asking her to fly there. She's in New York and can get there much faster than I can from California."

"Mom, please don't call her."

"Don't argue with me, Evan! Tell me what hospital they're taking you to."

"I'm trying to remember…something with a word like *pasture* in it."

"A what? Evan, you're making me very upset."

"I don't mean to—I'm groggy. Look it up on line. It's in Nice. I'm sure you can find it."

"You call me the minute the doctor sees you and you have more information, is that clear?"

"Very. Mom? Are you still there?" Evan could hear her sobbing over the phone.

"Evan, I love you. No matter what, I love you," her voice cracked in gasps.

"I love you too, Mom. I'm not going to die. Stop worrying."

"Easy for you to say miles away from me."

"You'll call me as soon as you know something?"

"I promise." Then he heard the line go dead a few seconds before he blacked out.

CHAPTER 28

Evan and Chloe

Weird recollections are sifting through my dreamy, fuzzy mind. I'm weightless—floating. I don't know where I am. I'm watching a videostream of events I think I was part of. Perhaps I passed out and can't remember. Something about being transferred from a boat to an ambulance? The sound of sirens as we raced through the city. Was I on oxygen? No recalled conversations with doctors about my condition. Apparently I was within the window of survival because I was engulfed in some strange chamber. Odd that I remember this as if I am looking down from the clouds at an experience I had. Perhaps I'm dead. No, I don't feel dead, just airborne. Trying to analyze—snapshots of events flash past my eyes. Ah—I recall being given oxygen and then recompression in a hyperbaric chamber—that was it. Felt somewhat like being in a small submarine. My symptoms were mild, someone said. A nurse told me the bends affected my musculoskeletal and lymphatic system, causing joint pain and headaches. Underwater breathing—something slithering grabbing at my heel. An eel—that horrid thing—bit me and gave me its toxin—a complication managed with antidotes. Now, I seem to be floating in a happy place—neither on earth nor or in heaven, pleasantly weightless without worldly concern. It's interesting what the psyche does to protect you when you are in shock. You can talk to yourself in your head, and yet be mute like a person in a coma. No one seems to hear me.

"Wake up? Can you hear me? Can you open your eyes?"

I can hear her voice, but don't recognize it. Mom? No. Danielle? No. Who?

"You can wake up now. If you can hear me, squeeze my hand."

"Umm, 'lo there." I blinked my eyes into focus and see a pretty nurse reminding me of Danielle, with her auburn hair tied back at the nape of her neck.

"I'm Chloe. Danielle's sister."

"Fuzzy-headed here. I remember now. I didn't get to meet you on the yacht—the one named after you, *Belle Chloe."*

"That's right. I had to work that day. I'm sorry we have to meet like this.

How are you feeling?"

"Other-worldly and somewhat out-of-body."

"That's completely normal. You're doing fine. Let me adjust your bed upward a bit while I check your vitals."

Evan tried to raise his head, but it felt like lead. He noticed the cast on his foot, not something he expected to see.

"What's with the cast?"

"Surgery to repair your torn tendon. You'll not be walking for several weeks." She removed the blood pressure cuff.

"You serious?"

"Very. Close your mouth so I can take your temperature."

"Where am I?"

"Pasteur Hospital in Nice. It's one of the few with a hyperbaric chamber. Your heart rate is good, but we're keeping you on antibiotics for a few more days, so don't pull the drip line out of your arm."

Evan managed a complacent smile and nodded. "Can I eat something?"

"Oh, that's a good sign. Yes, some clear liquids. I'll have some soup sent up."

Chloe pulled up a chair and sat down next to Evan. He glanced into her eyes and it was like seeing another younger version of Danielle with the same spray of freckles.

"You know you gave us quite a scare," she said and patted Evan's arm.

"Didn't mean to. I'm normally pretty rational, but the underwater encounter with the eel was unexpected. The pain was so searing—I sort of lost it."

"No need to apologize. It wasn't your fault. Ryan told us you hung on out there in the sea for quite awhile alone in the water. That couldn't have been easy."

"I had no choice. Half expected a shark to bite me and pull me under."

"Well, that didn't happen and you're safe now. By the way, Danielle's been here every day to see you," she said while arranging flowers in a vase on the window ledge.

Evan frowned at her words. "How many days have I been here?"

"Four, counting today."

Evan tilted his head back in disbelief. "Has anyone else been here? I was supposed to call my mother and…"

"You mean the attractive woman from New York? I think her name is Aurora."

"She's been here?"

"Yes, sat here for hours. She's staying at a hotel in Nice not far from here."

"I have her cell number. I'll give her a call."

"By the way, the joint pain you are feeling is from the bends."

"I can feel it in my shoulders and even my elbows, but I thought it was from the extended swim and exerting muscles I hadn't used for awhile."

"It will pass. Oh, here's the cart with your soup. Want me to help you with it?" Chloe asked with a pleasant smile.

"Naw…just give me a straw. I can manage."

"I'll be back a little later," Chloe said. "Get some rest."

Evan slurped down the soup through a straw in small gulps hoping it would stay in his stomach. He no longer felt nauseated, which was a huge relief. Hospital food never tasted so good, which he attributed to being ravenous. He noticed he was in a private room where he could see the tops of trees swaying through the window. The sky was grey and fog blurred the other buildings. He continued sipping his soup and then reached for his cell phone to call his mother.

"Hey, Mom?"

"Evan! You're awake!"

"And eating, if you can believe it."

"Oh, Evan, I'm so glad to hear it. Aurora's filled me in on your condition."

"Yeah, I heard she was here, but she's not at the hospital now."

"I'm thrilled you're going to be okay, except for the cast on your ankle."

"Not happy about it, but nothing I can do except let the ankle mend."

"When you're well and back in New York, dad and I want to come visit and spend some quality time with you and Aurora."

"That sounds great, Mom. I'll let you know," Evan rubbed his forehead feeling stressed.

"You'll call me again tomorrow, won't you?" Kelly asked.

"Sure, Mom. Take care."

Evan put the phone down on his lap and rolled his eyes toward the ceiling. So Aurora was here—good grief, did she run into Danielle? How awkward was that?

He knew Aurora could be controlling—ruthless, if she needed to be to get what she wanted. If having this accident wasn't bad enough, having two women he cared about in the hospital at the same time could be a disaster. He had not sorted out his feelings for Danielle, nor had he resolved his guilt about his lack of what could be perceived as brutal honesty with Aurora and whatever his feelings were for her. He finished the rest of the soup and wished it were a vodka tonic instead to calm his nerves.

For now, he had time to think. Not about the women in his life, but about the man who saved him. The turn of events weighed heavily on his mind. He recalled the conversation he overheard at Gaspard Yachting the day the police were doing the interrogation. Very unsettling. Had the cops run the fiber samples? If Ryan was guilty of somehow being involved with Armond's murder, where was Armond's clothing? He made a mental note to find out if the clothing was still in evidence. If something happened at the office, what was it? An argument? The police suspected Armond might have been murdered at his home. However, if that were true, they no doubt checked Armond's home for fingerprints and evidence that would have confirmed someone had killed him there. The question was how? If there was a break-in, it would have been obvious, but the police hadn't mentioned anything about that.

Evan tried to adjust his position in bed and turn himself over, to no avail. The drip line wouldn't reach and his cast was elevated on a pillow. It occurred to him he was not mobile and if he couldn't get out of bed, would they bring a bedpan? Surely he wouldn't have to face Chloe with his private parts exposed. Terrible thought. New fears.

He wondered if Ryan had been to see him, and made a mental note to check with Chloe. Ryan did save his life and Evan was grateful. Maybe his suspicions about Ryan were all wrong, and Ryan was not involved with Armond's murder. He let himself doze back to sleep where no problems existed.

CHAPTER 29
Two Day's Earlier

Aurora and Danielle

She strode in the hospital lobby with the confidence of someone attending a fine banquet instead of visiting a recovering patient. Her beige linen sheath dress draped fluidly over her toned body. The scoop neckline was accentuated with pearls and crystal beads in strands of various lengths and a fluffy silk floral was pinned just below her left shoulder. Five-inch heels, strapped at her ankles, made her appear even taller. Aurora set her expensive leather clutch on the reception counter and removed her over-sized sunglasses while she flipped her wispy asymmetrical blonde bangs off her forehead. The receptionist looked up at her with wide eyes and a discerning glance. Who was this stunning woman in front of her? "May I help you?" she asked and managed a curious smile.

"I'm Aurora Banfield. I'm here to see Evan—Evan Wentworth. Can you tell me what room he's in?"

"Let me check," the receptionist peered at her computer monitor.

Aurora blinked several times, trying to adjust to the glare from the overhead fluorescent lights, so easy to detest because it gave her pale ivory skin a slight greenish cast.

"Ah, yes, he's in room 305. You can take the elevator to the third floor, turn right at the top of the stairs and continue down the long hallway. There's a lounge area fairly close to his room if you'd like to relax. Visiting hours don't begin for another forty minutes," she said with a curt smile of one who enjoyed following the rules.

Aurora pursed her lips in mock disapproval, snatched her handbag off the counter and headed for the elevator. It had been a long time since she had been in a hospital, but being here now made her remember everything terrifying she felt when she underwent a hysterectomy several years ago with subsequent radiation for fibroid tumors, one of which was not benign. Being cancer free for five years was something she did not take for granted and credited surviving Stage 2 cancer for changing her diet to plant-based organic foods.

She strutted down the hallway checking room numbers. Patients in their rooms either moaned or slept soundly, often the benefit of drugs, or were attended to by either doctors or nurses in blue, white or modern printed uniforms. Her heels clicked on the linoleum floor as she checked her bracelet watch wrapped loosely around her wrist. With thirty minutes to spare before visiting hours, she located the waiting room and noticed one exceptionally attractive young woman sitting propped up on a blue leather sofa, with one leg under her, reading a book. Aurora sat down, fiddled for a suitable magazine with photos since she couldn't read more than a few simple words of French, and only conversed in tourist pleasantries. She sat down across from the preoccupied woman with copper hair twisted atop her head. Aurora crossed her own statuesque legs and sighed in frustrated exasperation at having to wait.

"Hello," the face with the freckles said, beaming a charming grin at Aurora.

"Hello," Aurora nodded, with a weak smile intending to keep her head tilted downward to pretend to scan a magazine she could not read.

"Who are you here to see?" the woman asked Aurora, who appeared perturbed at being questioned.

"Evan…Evan Wentworth," Aurora answered in a flat tone.

"Oh! What a coincidence. Me too. He's had a rough go of it, but he'll pull through."

"So, I've heard," Aurora said with a blank expression on her face. "And you are?" Aurora asked bluntly, stiffened her back and glared at this woman.

"I'm Evan's friend—well, more than that, I hope. I'm Danielle. Danielle DuBois."

Aurora studied her momentarily. An unsettling feeling crept down her spine. In an instant, she knew *this* was the woman Evan had fallen for. Her hands felt clammy and her jaw clenched. Words were going to need to be evaluated before becoming utterances in a casual conversation.

"And you met Evan how?" Aurora stated, wishing she could pull out a cigarette from her gold case. Instead, she settled for an Altoid mint.

"Believe it or not, I literally fell at his feet. I was carrying my tote bag of books from school and tripped. The contents of my bag went sprawling and Evan happened to be there to help me pick things up."

Aurora studied her—the competition, so young, so vital, so charming.

"How nice." Aurora raised her prominent cheekbones in a stilted smile.

"You don't look like you are from here, are you?" Danielle asked. Her forehead wrinkled with a puzzled look.

"No. I'm from New York. I'm Evan's fiancé. Aurora chose her words very carefully to inflict as much damage as one could do in an instant. She watched Danielle's hands go limp and the book she was reading tumbled to her lap. Aurora was quite sure she'd been successful in her attempt to undermine her competition because Danielle's mouth was agape and her face had paled making her freckles more prominent.

"I'm sorry, what did you just say? "Danielle's mouth dropped, her voice strident in an audible gasp.

"Oh, dear. You look so stunned, but everyone knows Evan and I have been together for years. I own an art gallery in New York and helped him become famous. I'm sure he would have told you."

"Yes, he did mention the gallery, and I knew he was a successful artist...I didn't know he was engaged," Danielle said and raised a hand to her chest.

"We are so close, Evan and I. We knew eventually we would be married and saw no reason for a formal engagement ring."

Danielle shuffled in her seat. She unbent the leg she was sitting on that began to stiffen and go numb with tingling. Aurora watched her with guilty pleasure and could see she was flustered.

"Do you live here in Nice?" Aurora asked, now curious about how much information she could pry out of Danielle.

"No. I live in St.-Paul-de-Vence."

"Alone?"

"No. With my family," Danielle said with a tinge of apology in her voice.

Aurora watched closely. It was obvious Danielle was becoming unsettled, and she enjoyed watching her come undone.

To avoid a scene, Danielle began to rattle on about her life so that the tears just bordering behind her lovely eyes would not come forth. "We have a large family—several brothers and sisters. I take care of my mother who has not been well lately, but is doing better, and my father runs a yachting business," she explained without taking a breath.

"You said you dropped your books. Are you in school?" Aurora probed while stroking her beaded necklace.

"No. I'm a teacher," Danielle said and absently took out the pins in her hair to let it fall to her shoulders in a subconscious effort to look more attractive.

Aurora took out her gem-studded compact and lipstick to apply a bit more pale dusty pink. She pinched her lips together. "What do you teach?"

"English and various subjects as I am needed."

"That must be nice," Aurora noted. "Do you intend to keep teaching?"

"Well…I suppose, but some day I hope to marry and have a large family like the one I grew up in."

A nurse scurried down the hall with a cart, clanging the wheels into a door jam she misjudged. "I'll just be a minute, then you can see Evan," she spoke directly to Danielle as she entered his room.

"That's my sister, Chloe," Danielle said. "She's taken care of Evan ever since the accident."

Aurora knew she did not have much time to put a damper on this so-called relationship with Danielle and Evan. How convenient it was for Danielle to share her desire for a large family. This revelation was something she had not anticipated, but once spoken became a dangerous dagger of emotional pain she could inflict straight to the heart. "Well, I hope you get what you want someday, Danielle. I'm sure you know Evan doesn't want any children. It's why we're so perfect for one another. I can't have them, and that remains our strongest bond—well, that, and of course, his art."

Danielle's hands were shaking as she fumbled for words that stuck in her parched throat like stone pebbles piled against a log in a creek lacking sufficient water, but she forced them out anyway. "You've come along way, Aurora. Why don't you go in to see Evan. Please tell him I was here and will see him later," her faint voice broke with strained words.

"I appreciate that, Danielle."

Aurora stood, set her shoulders back on her statuesque frame as if she were carrying an inner demeanor of gloat—someone who diminished her competition like a ferret in a den who waited for its prey, pounced on it and enjoyed the kill. She grabbed her purse and headed for Evan's room without turning around to bid Danielle goodbye.

Dumbfounded, Danielle picked up her book and quickly headed for the elevator anxious to call a taxi to take her home. Although it was warm outside, Danielle shivered. She sat on a bench outside the hospital entrance overwhelmed by what just happened with Aurora. She wanted to burst into tears, but was consumed by conflicting emotions of devastation and rage. How could Evan have led her on? He had kissed her with such intensity after their day at sea on the *Belle Chloe*. It felt real… honest and certainly didn't feel like someone who was engaged to be married. She felt betrayed for having trusted him because he seemed like an honest, trustworthy guy. Tears now started to stream down her face, the sadness taking over the anger.

Images of Aurora flittered through her mind in a most unpleasant way. Danielle disliked her because Aurora was everything she wasn't—tall, beautiful, successful and engaged to Evan. What really irritated her was how direct Aurora was. Her very presence was intimidating. Besides her stunning beauty, she wondered what Evan saw in her and realized she knew nothing of their relationship in New York. It occurred to her that perhaps she really didn't know Evan at all. The taxi arrived and Danielle waved to the driver, told him her address and got in the back seat feeling blindsided.

Jealously was not an emotion she felt comfortable with, and yet, she was terribly jealous of everything about Aurora. If only she were less attractive, less tall, less a major part of Evan's success, maybe she could compete. But, what did she have to offer Evan? A school teacher with a huge family, lots of responsibility including caring for an aging parent with medical issues, and a father struggling with a recent murder of a valued employee.

On the ride home to St. Paul, Danielle wept openly, attempting to be discrete. She clenched her fists and snivled between hiccup spasms, causing the cab driver to glance more than once in his rear view mirror asking if there was anything he could do. Did she want to talk about it? No. Did someone die? No. Did she want him to stop asking questions? Yes.

She blew her nose with abandon and wanted to scream obscenities in French, which would only scare the poor driver. She slumped in her seat with her head pressed against the partly opened window. The ache in her heart was immense and she realized that not only was she in love with Evan, but learning in the most awful way from his fiancé that he did not want children was so devastating she didn't know how she would continue to see him in the hospital. The driver wove up the winding roads and arrived at her home. She quickly paid him, apologized profusely for her tears and closed the taxi door on what felt like the ending of a beautiful, however brief, chapter in her life.

CHAPTER 30

Danielle, Marie, Chloe and Lena

The house was relatively quiet, which Danielle appreciated because she couldn't deal with the normal din of chaos. Lena was outside on the patio in a lounge chair sitting backwards with ear-buds dangling down her face. Her feet air danced to her favorite music. Thor jumped off the sofa and came over to Danielle to greet her. She patted him on the head and his tail wagged in appreciation. There was only one person she wanted to talk to at a time like this, and she knocked softly on her mother's bedroom door, hoping she was not asleep.

"Mama? It's me. Are you awake?"

"Yes, honey, come in." Marie noticed her daughter's red swollen nose and blotchy skin. She knew something terrible had happened. "Oh, dear. What's wrong?"

"Everything. Absolutely everything," Danielle whimpered and dabbed her watery eyes with her fingertips unable to stop the flow of tears.

Marie motioned for her to sit on the bed and handed her several tissues.

Danielle's chest heaved as she hiccupped leaving her gasping for air at times while she unburdened her soul. Marie listened intently to the whole story, nodding her head. Before Danielle had a chance to finish, Marie sat up in bed and put her arms around her distraught daughter. She knew sometimes it was better to listen, provide comfort and not analyze. Eventually Danielle quieted and settled on the bed nestled next to her mother. Marie knew her daughter's heart was broken, not so much by love lost, but by deception. Honesty in a relationship was crucial, and she liked Evan from the moment she met him. Although she hadn't met Aurora, she now disliked her immensely. Marie also knew there was always more than one side to a story.

"Hello? What's going on in there—is everything okay?" Chloe said while knocking softly on the door.

"Chloe, please come in. Danielle and I were having a little chat."

"Danielle, you look so flushed. Something is wrong, isn't it?"

Marie encouraged Chloe to snuggle in on her other side, while Danielle agreed to proffer the same story provided her sister would get her a glass of water and some chocolate from the kitchen. Chloe agreed, and no sooner left her mother's bedroom before seeing Lena in the hall huddled against the door.

"Is mother all right? I heard crying. Is Danielle in there too?"

"Yes, apparently Danielle had a terrible day. I'm getting her some water and chocolate, because it's that kind of horrible day. Why don't you join us?"

Lena took the remaining ear-bud out letting the connection to musical nirvana trail over her shoulder. She nudged the partly opened door and took one look at Danielle and knew this was a story she did not want to miss. As much as she loved her sister, she secretly carried jealous pangs in her heart. Danielle wasn't only beautiful, smart, accomplished and sure of herself, but she also never had any difficulty getting what she worked for. Seeing her sister in distress evened life out for her. She certainly didn't wish her harm, but a little calamity seemed fair.

"Lena, do come in." Marie sat up on the bed making room for Lena and pushed the duvet to the side so Chloe would have room as well. Danielle rolled her eyes at the sudden entourage of attention, but decided a sisterhood supporting the deflated sibling warranted girl talk.

Danielle took a chocolate from the box Chloe offered, and then took two more before passing the box on to Lena.

Gaspard stuck his head in the door, saw his three daughters and Marie shaking her head at him and flipping her wrist toward the doorway to please go away. He'd seen this powwow before. He knew when a man was not wanted and might actually be in danger of having nothing of value whatsoever to add to whatever the problem was. He nodded respectfully and closed the door leaving four women to do what women did in private.

After Chloe heard the story of how Danielle met Aurora, she had little sympathy and said, "The moment I met her, I knew she was a piece of work—one of those high-maintenance drama queens."

"No kidding," said Danielle. "I think I lost my voice—my courage evaporated once I felt derailed. I didn't know what to say. I was so angry at Evan for not telling me he was engaged."

"Did you ever consider her story not to be the truth?" Marie asked.

"Why would she lie?" Danielle mumbled as she chomped on a nut-encased chocolate morsel.

"Evan told me he was very worried when he heard Aurora was coming to the hospital. He said his mother insisted Aurora visit him."

"Interesting," Lena contemplated. "Well, if his mother insisted, she must know that they are engaged."

"Maybe that had nothing to do with it," Chloe said. "Evan mentioned his mother wanted to fly all the way from California, but because of the distance and proximity, New York was much closer so she asked Aurora to fly here."

"Whatever," Lena said and reached for a rounded chocolate she knew contained a cherry.

"I don't know how I can ever face Evan again," Danielle said. "I'm so angry at him, and yes, you all probably guessed, I think I am in love with him. I didn't plan to, it just happened."

Lena crossed her legs and looked intently at her sister. "If you are in love with Evan, I'm glad. I've wanted Ryan to pay attention to me, but he's been so smitten with you, Danielle, that he doesn't really see me."

"He's too old for you," Marie said. "You need to find someone closer to your own age."

"But—mama!" Lena rolled her eyes and threw her head back in disgust.

"We should be talking about Danielle and Evan, and not your romantic illusions," Chloe snapped at Lena and passed the box of chocolates around. "Do you want to know what I think?"

"Of course," Danielle said. "You're the wise one, always level-headed. It's why you are such a competent nurse."

Chloe smiled at the compliment. "You need to talk to Evan. Confront him. Tell him how you feel, because if you don't, you are taking Aurora's word as if everything she said is true."

Danielle could no longer hold back her tears. "It's not only his engagement to Aurora that's devastating, it's because he doesn't want any children. I'm so upset. You all know what I always wanted—a family of my own, and now I've fallen in love with someone who can't or won't give me what I need."

"Why doesn't he want children?" Marie asked with raised eyebrows.

Danielle wiped streaming tears off her blotched face with the side of her palm and paused. "Because his little sister died."

"I don't understand," Marie said.

Hesitant to talk about Evan's past, because he had asked her not to do so, she risked everything. "He was a cop before he became an artist. There was a bank robbery and his little sister, I think she was six, was in the car with him and she was accidentally shot and died later that day. He blames himself."

"Well, I'll be damned," Lena said. "This is far more interesting than I ever imagined."

Marie rolled her eyes at her daughter's impertinence.

"Danielle, can I talk with you about Evan after we finish here?" Chloe whispered quietly.

"Sure."

"I have an idea," Marie said. "I've been thinking Evan's soon to be released from the hospital, but even with a walking cast, he needs time to recuperate. We have an unused guesthouse. Ask him to stay here."

"What?" Lena said with a gasp.

"Well, why should he be paying the hotel? What's he to do? Sit there all day and call room service?"

Danielle considered the idea and shook her head. "I disagree. You want me to take care of him? I'm not even sure I can talk to him!" she said with her voice going up an octave.

"Honey, do you think it was easy and I was the first woman your father fell in love with? I had to cajole your father into wanting him to be with me."

"Mother, what does that have to do with Danielle," Lena squirmed in under the duvet.

"Sometimes you have to fight for what you want. If he's really engaged to Aurora and loves her, then you need to let him go and move on with your life. But, if what she told you isn't entirely true, then you'd be giving up on someone without knowing the truth. And, I might add, true love is always worth the risk."

Danielle sat still on the bed considering her mother's suggestion. Chloe nodded in agreement and reached out a hand to Danielle. "Mama's right. You need to find out for yourself. If you don't confront him, you'll never know the truth and it will gnaw at you the rest of your life," Chloe said.

"Speaking of gnawing, I'm starved. Could we pick up a pizza?" Lena pleaded.

"I'd love it," Marie said. "Juliette and Amber covet pizza, but check with dad and your brothers too. If everyone else wants pizza, then pizza it will be."

Danielle slid off the duvet, found her shoes under the bed, slipped her feet into them and stood. "Thanks for listening. I needed all of you." She sighed, shrugged her shoulders and dropped her head in embarrassment.

"We're family. We're always here for each other no matter what," Chloe said, while she leaned over to kiss her mother before leaving the room.

"Mama—I'm sorry if I ruined your afternoon," Danielle said.

"You must never feel that way. Life is difficult, and love is often multifaceted, but you must never feel when you are hurting that you can't come to me. When you hurt, I hurt. My love for you is far greater than you can imagine. True love can overcome most obstacles."

"Did anyone ever tell you how wonderful you are? I love you so much, mama."

"As much as I love you and more."

Marie gave Danielle an embrace of comfort and sighed with deep affection for her daughter struggling with love and deception. Somehow, she hoped it would all work out, and if it didn't she couldn't accept it might be because Danielle had given up without trying. "You'll see Evan, then, tomorrow?" Marie asked trying to confirm Danielle's commitment to their plan.

"Yes, I promise. I'm going to find Chloe and see what she wants to talk to me about. I'm a little concerned and hope it's not more bad news because I'm rather fragile today, as if you didn't already know this."

"I'm sure it's nothing to worry about. I'm looking forward to pizza. Please bring me two slices and a glass of wine. I've earned it," Marie said with a wink.

Danielle left her mother's room and closed the door lightly. What a draining, impossible afternoon and evening. The television was on in the living room where her father and brother, Lucas, who lived close to the lavender business he managed, were watching soccer. Amber and Juliette were elsewhere. She waved hello and walked up the stairs to Chloe's room. Doors were open to the balcony, where Chloe sat awkwardly in a chair with her feet propped up on an ornate iron railing reading a book. "Hi. You wanted to see me about Evan?" Danielle said feeling nervous.

"Come pull up a chair out here and let's talk," Chloe said.

Danielle settled into a cushioned wicker chair with a frown on her face.

"I spent a lot of time with Evan after his surgery. We didn't talk about you, but he cringed openly when he thought you and Aurora might meet. I think he dreaded it."

"With good reason," Danielle quipped.

"But, his bigger concern is Ryan. He told me about the interrogation the police had with Ryan before he went diving. Apparently Evan overheard part of the conversation and is very concerned Ryan may have had something to do with Armond's death."

"What! Oh, I don't believe that for one minute."

"Danielle, just keep an open mind. I personally don't like Ryan, never did, and although he's done an excellent job of helping papa run the company, there is something insincere about Ryan. I never trusted him, but had no reason to substantiate my doubts."

"What did Evan say?" Danielle's mouth twisted to one side.

"He noticed some white powder on the bathroom floor of the diving boat, and was pretty sure it was either heroin or cocaine. Please don't tell papa, but if Ryan's doing drugs, maybe Armond found out."

"How could he? Armond never went out on any of our yachts or boats," Danielle tilted her head in disbelief.

"Not entirely true. Armond would go with various insurance inspectors when they were valuing the fleet and would walk the inspectors through the interiors, and that included the dive boat as well," Chloe said.

"So, what else did Evan say?"

"He was groggy at times, but he was speculating about a motive for Armond's murder and wondered if, just maybe, Ryan was running drugs and not doing drugs."

Danielle shifted in her chair, looked up at the sunset's display of amethyst and pink tinged clouds. She sat quietly pondering the possibilities and put her fingertips under her chin in an effort to hold up her head, overly burdened with the events of the day.

"I don't know what to say, "Danielle shrugged her shoulders.

"When you see Evan, talk to him regarding his concerns about Ryan. Evan's not the enemy here, and gains nothing by insinuating Ryan might be involved in a murder. He told me he'd been a detective before, so it's his nature to question things that don't make sense to him."

"Okay. I will. But, I'm feeling so exhausted right now, I can't make sense out of anything," Danielle said.

"I can hear Thor barking." Chloe glanced over the balcony railing. "They must be back with the pizza."

"Thank, God. I am stressed enough to eat the entire pizza myself."

CHAPTER 31

Danielle

Sleep eluded Danielle. She paced back and forth in her bedroom making a path in the carpeting, walked out on her balcony, sat in a chair and gazed at the brightness of the full moon casting shadows through the trees. The universe was so vast to her and she imagined the idea of being transported into space through a black hole, surrounded by galaxies of stars. It was very appealing. Any escape from these emotions would be welcome.

Not more than a month ago, her life was uneventful. She taught school. She cared for her mother in the mornings and looked after her brother, Valentin, helping him with his homework. His dyslexia was frustrating for a bright eight year old, who wanted to read music to play the piano but couldn't keep the notes in order; he reversed words when he read, and numbers were even worse for him because he was not allowed to use a calculator in school for math computations. Thirty-two became twenty-three, and columns of numbers to be added brought him to fits of dispair because it took him so much longer to complete tests in school.

But even thinking about Valentin and how he struggled could not compare with her fear about her mother's relapsing health. Although Marie's current medication kept her illness stabilized, drugs had a way of becoming ineffective as the body either adjusted or rejected the efficacy over time. As Danielle paced the floor, she realized she was purposely fretting about her family in order to avoid the confrontation with Evan in the morning. The anger she felt after meeting Aurora had faded to displeasure, to perhaps realizing and accepting she might not have any right to be in love with

Evan. She turned to her room and stood at the open French door to her balcony, letting the moonlight caress her pale skin and her tea-length white lace nightgown.

What tone and approach should she take with Evan? Should she appear nonchalant? Defeated? Upset? Calm, but inquiring? Perhaps she could find in it her heart to be compassionate, but how she'd address his relationship with Aurora was another matter. She had no idea what to say without appearing either wounded or hostile. Neither appealed to her. She thought about how regal Aurora looked compared with her own casual attire and wondered if she should cut her hair. She decided against it, because if Evan didn't like it, she could be worse off no longer being the woman he was attracted to. Shivering slightly, she closed the French doors and slithered comfortably under her blue and white Delft duvet, pulling it close to her chin. It felt like a cocoon of safety she didn't want to leave. Trying to imagine the conversation with Evan was exhausting and yet she couldn't sleep. Five slices of pizza didn't help either, making her stomach flip and growl in disapproval.

She turned on her side, snuggled into her goose down feathered pillow, punched it into a round ball and sighed. It was not just the abundance of garlic on the pizza gnawing at the lining of her stomach, it was the idea of being in love with someone who didn't want children. How would she broach that subject? She thought about what he went through with his sister's death and knew it was so devastating, enough to make Evan change careers. If he loved her, and what a big question that was, would they get married, and if they did, would he change his mind about children?

If he was adamant about not having kids, could she live without a family? Danielle clutched at her stomach, now hurting like the contents might not stay put. Everything seemed so easy a short time ago—before Armond's murder—before Evan kissed her...well, she admitted to herself that she kissed him first on the *Belle Chloe*, but he did not resist. There was comfort in knowing he kissed her with tenderness, and even more revealing was the way he followed her up the driveway that night and pulled her toward him and kissed her with such intensity she lost her balance. She closed her eyes remembering the kiss, his lips on hers, the smell of his skin, the touch of his hands on her body. Despite how angry and upset she was with him earlier in the day, she melted in those memories and let her long eyelashes close while she relived that kiss over and over until she finally fell asleep.

What only seemed like minutes turned into hours until Thor nudged himself through the slight crack in open door and jumped on her bed just after sunrise, slathering her with kisses and bringing her out of her stupor. She ruffled his hair, rubbed his ears and he flipped over on the bed so she could rub his tummy. He didn't visit her room often in the morning, but he seemed to instinctively know when she was distressed. She heard the knock on her doorframe and Chloe's familiar cheerful voice. "Want a ride to the hospital? I'm not going to be there all day, but I can take you in so you can visit with Evan, and then I can take you home."

"This is a conspiracy, isn't it?" She teased.

"Sort of. You're not getting out of talking to Evan," Chloe shouted through the door.

"I hate being the older sister who doesn't drive," Danielle said.

"You need to do something about that too. It's time you learned to drive despite the fact that you think you can bicycle most everywhere you want to go. And while you are fixing things you should have fixed long ago, please pick something attractive to wear today. I want you looking your best. No tee shirt and capris, and no flip-flops. Understood?"

"Ugh. What's wrong with the way I dress?"

"Nothing, if your intent is to look like the school teacher you are."

"I hate you," she giggled.

"Yeah, I hate you too. Now get dressed. I have to leave in twenty minutes, and you sure as hell can't bike to the hospital."

CHAPTER 32

Danielle and Evan

Chloe didn't pester Danielle on the ride to the hospital because she knew Danielle was in a somber mood with a lot on her mind. It would be a difficult day, but at least she'd succeeded in having her older sister dress for success. She glanced at Danielle in her emerald green V-necked sheath and thought she looked stunning.

If fighting fire with fire was appropriate, then Danielle was a bonfire torch. Chloe dropped Danielle at the hospital entrance and drove to her parking space. Danielle walked into the hospital lobby and the receptionist's hands froze at her computer while her mouth dropped. Danielle shook her finger at the receptionist, strutted past her and said, "Don't say a word…not one word."

Danielle took the elevator to the third floor breathing deeply, letting her chest rise and fall. She checked her lipstick, a shade darker than usual, in the elevator's mirrored panel strips and fluffed long copper-tinged locks off her shoulders letting her hair cascade down the deep V-neck at the back of her dress. No flip-flops today, but instead, open-toed sling-backed pumps with jewel-encrusted bows, courtesy of Chloe, a blessing of a sister with the same size feet.

The hallway seemed shorter, more threatening that it should be. She wished it were wider, longer and less intimidating. The door to Evan's room was open and she hoped his doctor was not there. One last deep breath before she took the plunge that would either end their relationship or, by some miracle, pave the way for understanding.

Danielle knocked to announce her arrival. Evan turned toward the opened door and dropped the book he'd been reading. It fell to the floor.

"Hello, Evan," she said placing one hand on her hip.

"Danielle! I'm so glad to see you...my God, you look fantastic."

"Thank you," she twisted her hair behind her ear, revealing a diamond stud earring. "How are you doing?" she managed a weak smile and stood awkwardly next to his bed.

"Better now. I have so much to tell you. Please sit down....pull up the chair from the corner and sit close to me."

"When do you get out of the hospital?" She sat erect with her hands in her lap.

"In another day or two. I'm so bored. Everyone's been wonderful, but being in bed all day, except for X-rays for my heel, I've been confined to this damn room. Tomorrow I get a walking cast. Just being able to be mobile will be great. I'm not one to sit still much less lie in bed all day."

"I can't imagine. I've never been a patient in a hospital," Danielle said.

"You have no idea how much I have missed you. I want to hold you, kiss you...and that perfume you're wearing—"

"We need to talk, Evan." Danielle narrowed her eyes and her demeanor changed from courteous to serious.

"It's about Aurora, isn't it?" He winced, shut his eyes and took a deep breath.

"Yes." She straightened her back in the chair in an attempt to look composed.

"First, let me say how sorry I am for not telling you about her before." Evan looked her directly in the eye.

"Go on," Danielle bit her lower lip.

"I've known Aurora for several years. We met in art school and she helped me get out of a very dark depression. I thought I was in love with her when I left New York. Coming to St. Paul was a break from final exams I still have to complete, but as you know, it was also a trip I had hoped might lead to an answer about who killed Ashley. All I had was a vague tip about the killer being in the Côte d'Azur."

"Yes, you told me about your sister, and it broke my heart that you had to go through something like that."

"I didn't plan on falling in love with you, but I think I fell in love with you the first day I met you. I was so captivated…shaken, actually, I didn't fight it."

"Didn't you think of Aurora?"

"Of course. I was consumed with guilt. Then Aurora and I had a fight on the phone. She could tell something was different and asked me point blank if I had met someone. I told her I had. She asked if I had fallen in love, but I didn't answer her."

"You didn't know or didn't want to tell her?"

"Both. There was the distance of New York seeming so far away, and everything about being here in this climate, the salty air, the scents of the flowering plants, the splendor of the sea, the day spent with you and your family on your yacht —it was so powerful, confusing and you were irresistible. Of course I had conflicted feelings. I felt guilty, but I never promised Aurora anything about our future. She assumed we would get married someday and I didn't deny it."

"But, you are engaged to her, so why wouldn't she?"

"What? Did she tell you that?" Evan's shoulders flinched. He leaned back into the pillow trying to absorb the shock.

"She did. We met in the waiting room by accident and I didn't know who she was. She had no idea who I was either until I introduced myself. Then I think she somehow knew I was the *other* woman."

"God, you look so gorgeous. I've never seen you so, I don't know, stunning."

"I'll take that as a compliment. Thanks to my sister, Chloe, she insisted I present myself as suitable competition."

Evan frowned. "Danielle, you never have to compete. You are perfect any way you want to be. To me, you are beautiful when you have no make-up on, when you are in your cut-offs and a tee shirt. I don't need dazzle to be attracted to someone."

Her eyes began to mist, but she insisted on being in control of her emotions and was not about to let Evan see her cry. "So, you are not engaged?"

"Definitely not. My parents know we don't have a formal engagement of any sort, but of course, they hoped. I have no idea what she's told her parents, but I can understand why she would have assumed we would get married. She managed my career, made me successful and gave me a new life. I'm grateful to her and love her for it, but it's not the same as wanting to be with someone for the rest of your life. I'll admit I thought I loved her until I met you. You shook my feelings to the core, and I felt like I was standing on a frozen lake's cracking ice. At first, I didn't know what to think except I was so drawn to you I wanted to be in your presence...just to talk with you, or walk beside you, or kiss you."

Danielle's misting eyes were now brimming, but she tilted her head back to keep her tears intact.

"Come here, please...please let me hold you."

She resisted, but offered him her hand. "I, uh, how do I bring this up without ruining everything?"

"Ruining things? I thought I said the honest truth. Can't you forgive me?"

"That's not it," Danielle said. I accept your explanation, however there is something I can't accept."

Fear crept across Evan's face as if he'd been slapped. "What can't you accept?"

"Aurora told me you didn't want any children and that's why you were perfect together because she couldn't have them."

"Unbelievable! That was a despicable thing to do. Yes, it is true, she can't have them because she had cancer and is unable to have children."

"It was so painful for me to hear this from her, and not from you, but we never had a discussion about how we felt about each other," Danielle said.

"I'm so sorry." He squeezed her hand tightly. "Had this diving accident not happened, I would have told you how I felt much sooner, but I didn't want to scare you away either."

"I appreciate your candor, however, something still bothers me. Do you think you can overcome your feelings about not having children?" Her words choked out like cotton balls stuck in her throat and made it hard for her to swallow.

"I don't know, Danielle. I haven't thought about it much lately, but I know how important it is to you."

"You shouldn't change for me. That wouldn't be right, and it would never work out."

"If I were going to change my beliefs, I would do it on my own. Can you give me some time to think about this?" Evan said, with conviction.

"Yes, of course. And, I have a proposition for you," Danielle said.

Evan's eyes perked up and a wide grin spread across his face.

"No, not that kind of proposition," she laughed.

"We have a guest house and I've discussed this with my mother, Chloe and Lena. We'd like you to stay in the guest house until you have to go back to New York, since your hotel bill is skyrocketing with no one in your room."

"Yeah, I thought of that when I came to and cancelled my hotel reservation. They're still holding my clothing and personal belongings, and agreed to give me a room when I'm released."

"That's nice. But, will you consider staying with me, I mean us? It's a lovely guesthouse with views. There are no stairs to contend with so you'll be able to get around. By the way, where's your car?"

"Ryan called after the accident and had someone drive the car to the parking lot here because the day we went diving, I'd left it at your yachting company."

"Has Ryan been to see you?"

"No, he hasn't, but he did call. He's busy with clients managing the yachting season at its height, plus he's also managing the controller's duties. He's really busy."

"That's true. I'd forgotten about the work centered around Armond's job."

"You know Ryan saved my life," Evan said and reached for Danielle's hand.

"I heard he had, and I'm grateful. Ryan's a good guy."

Evan was not about to ruin the mood with a contrarian opinion or to divulge his concerns about Ryan's potential drug-related activities—now was not the time, or he'd risk damaging his fragile relationship with Danielle.

"Are you going to be able to drive with a walking cast on your foot?"

"Supposedly. The doctor says it's just to stabilize my heel, but that it's mending properly."

Danielle leaned over, absently showing a bit of cleavage to pick up Evan's novel off the floor. She started to laugh. "You're reading *One Flew Over the Cuckoo's Nest*?"

"Why not?" Evan snickered.

"That's hilarious. My sister's definitely not nurse Ratched."

"Will you come by tomorrow? I wonder, since I can't drive, how I'm going to get my car to your home."

"I'll see if I can get my brother, Lucas, to come here with Chloe and then he can drive you and your car back to our house. He doesn't have to work on Saturday, so it should be okay when he's not so busy."

"There's something I want before you leave, Danielle."

"What's that?"

"I know I've fallen in love with you. I promise I'll always be honest with you." He stroked her fingers and waited for a response.

"Oh! Did you just say you loved me?" Her eyes brightened and she smiled a wide grin.

"I did, and I meant it. I didn't mean to cause you any heartache about Aurora."

"Speaking of Aurora, is she still here?"

"No," Evan said with a sigh. "She's gone back to New York where she belongs. The gallery work requires so much dedication. She can rarely take more than a few days off."

"It's been a tough week," Danielle said and looked directly into his dreamy eyes. "I feel much better about us. You have a funny look on your face. Is there anything else?"

"Come here please—I have to kiss you since I can't rip off your dress. It's not fair that you're dressed like this making a wounded man sweat. I'm saddled with a cast and can't chase you."

Danielle laughed, bent over and ran her fingers through his hair. Evan inhaled her perfume and it made him weak. Her lips parted and she kissed him just long enough to stir emotions bordering on embarrassment.

She pulled away from him, glanced at the thin bed blanket covering him and noticed a rise between his legs.

"Heavens," she fluttered her eyelashes. "Seems like I've awakened something."

"I'm injured, Danielle. I'm not dead," Evan said with a playful grin.

Danielle headed toward the door, turned and blew a kiss to him and then left.

Chloe answered her cell phone and agreed to take Danielle home, provided she would promise to let her teach her how to drive. Danielle walked past the waiting room on the 3rd floor—it no longer held the same dread it did earlier. She straightened her shoulders and felt relief, but more importantly, she had a sense of hope. Aurora had returned to New York, so she wouldn't be running into her. In fact, Aurora would no longer be part of the problem, but it was up to Evan to make it very clear to this manipulative woman that he didn't intend to marry her.

CHAPTER 33

Evan and Danielle

Getting Evan settled in the guesthouse was effortless. He was thrilled to be out of the hospital—anywhere but in antiseptic confined surroundings; this respite made him feel invigorated and almost normal again. His repaired foot was tightly wrapped in a criss-cross contraption of white tape instead of a plaster cast, so he could amble around gingerly on the injured foot by balancing with a pronged cane.

The guesthouse was not only spacious, but also had huge floor-to-ceiling glass doors that folded into the walls to open up the entire bedroom and sitting area to the outdoors. The masculine color scheme appealed to him with geometric fabrics in rust, tan and shades of blue. A large rustic armoire served as a closet, and two deep-cushioned club chairs flanked the opposite wall. A doorway led to a private bath with an open-air shower overlooking a waterfall cascading to a small pond.

With his clothes retrieved from the hotel Le Mas De Pierre, he felt blissfully comfortable in shorts and a tee shirt. He chose a chaise lounge to relax and elevated his foot. Strands of clouds wafted in the sky as if he had taken a broad paintbrush and put them there. He tilted his head back on the blue and tan canvas striped pillow headrest and took in the rays of mid-morning sunshine. The sound of melodious birds chattering provided the only music he needed to hear. The patter of feet and squeals of laughter brought him out of a Zen-like nap.

"Evan, Evan...please wake up! Would you like some oranges?" Juliette held out both hands with an orange in each one.

"Sure," Evan smiled and reached for the orange in her right hand.

"Mind if I sit with you?" Juliette said and flipped her plaited hair over her shoulder.

"Make yourself comfortable. I'll slide over and you can sit at the foot of the chaise."

"How did you hurt your foot?" She tilted her head and pouted her lips in mock suffering.

"Got bit by an eel when I was scuba diving."

"Ugh," she said and wrinkled her face into a contorted frown of disgust. "How long will you be here?"

"Not long. A week at the most." He held up his hand to shield the sun from his eyes.

"Why can't you stay longer?" her lower lip pushed out in a pout.

"I have to get back to school."

Her face reflected dismay. "You're still in school?"

Evan laughed. "Oddly enough. It's true. I'm working on my degree in Art History."

"Oh, that's right. I remember now. You're the one who paints."

"Uh huh." He peeled the orange, opened a section and took a bite then offered her the rest.

"What do you like to paint?"

"Good question." He twisted his mouth and scratched his head, trying to think of an appropriate answer for a ten year old. "Colors applied to a canvas, I guess. It's hard to explain."

"If I bring you some paper, will you draw something for me?" She snatched the last orange section.

"I'm not much at drawing. What is it you want me to draw?"

"What you see. Draw this backyard, the flowers and those hills over there and the sea. Could you put in some birds and rabbits?"

"That's a tall order. I probably wouldn't be very good at it."

Evan glanced up and saw Danielle coming toward him from the main house.

"What's going on out here?" Danielle said. "Is Juliette making a pest of herself?" Danielle flashed a teasing smile and walked toward Evan and her sister.

"No, not at all. She wants me to paint this landscape for her, as if someone who paints modern art could somehow capture this setting realistically."

"I think it's an excellent idea, Evan. You can sit out here and it will help pass the time. I'll have Chloe pick you up some paints and a canvas. Do you need an easel? What size brushes do you like? What other supplies do you need?"

"Whoa, Danielle, take a breath. I don't think it's a good idea."

"Pah-leeze," Juliette pleaded by jumping up and down like a human pogo stick.

"You're awfully hard to resist young lady," he shot her a wide grin.

"You'll do it?" she clapped her hands together.

Seeing her enthusiasm, he could hardly say no. "Okay, I'll give it a try."

"Yippee. Would you please peel this other orange?"

"Juliette, you *are* being pest. Now let Evan rest," Danielle insisted.

As quickly as Juliette, the tornado of energy, blew in, she blew out and disappeared around the back of the estate. Danielle nestled next to Evan who kissed her lightly and put his arm around her hoping for some private time. They closed their eyes in an attempt to engage in a lingering embrace when Josh tossed Thor a ball and interrupted them. The nimble dog leapt into the air and missed the ball toss that hit the chaise, bounced off Evan's head and landed in his lap. Danielle burst into applause and a fit of laughter.

"I want one too," Josh pleaded trying to mind his manners.

"One what?" Danielle wrinkled her nose.

"Juliette said Evan is making her a painting."

Danielle frowned. "You don't *make* a painting. It's not like baking a cake."

"I wanna' squid—a giant squid like in *Twenty Thousand Leagues Under the Sea*. Please make me a squid, with big tentacles and a bulging eye." His lips pouted.

"You remember, Josh, Evan? He wants to be an oceanographer."

"I surely do." He smiled and finished the last of the orange. "Seems like I'll be drawing and painting."

Josh gave a 'thumbs up' and ran off with Thor. No sooner had he left when Valentin ran across the lawn and plopped down on the patio floor with a dejected look on his face.

"What's wrong, Valentin? You look so sad."

"Everybody's getting a painting but me." He folded his little arms across his body in protest.

"If you could have anything painted that you want, what would it be?" Evan asked and leaned over and fluffed Valentin's hair.

"Thor. I want a picture of Thor," he said adamantly.

"Why do you want a picture of our dog?" Danielle asked.

"He's gonna' die someday and I wanna' remember his face. He's my best friend."

"Okay. I'll paint you a picture of Thor."

Valentin did a cartwheel and then a rolling summersault of delight before scampering away.

Evan's eyes watered. He was overwhelmed by the children's requests. Their voices and presence gave him an instantaneous stab of regret that Ashley was no longer here. Children did that to him—ripped off the scar, opened the wound and sent him to a dark place in his soul.

"You okay?" Danielle asked, sensing the mood had changed.

"I'm working on it." Evan sighed, glad Danielle could not see his insides rolling and balking at accepting little people being part of his life.

"I've got a lot of things to do today," Danielle said, and straightened out her white eyelet sundress. "Do you need anything else while I'm gone?"

"I'll be fine. I'm so relieved to be out of the hospital—this is a bit of heaven. I have you, Danielle. I don't need anything else, plus there is plenty of beer in the refrigerator."

She laughed and kissed him on the forehead. "Because tomorrow is Saturday, everyone will be gone. Mama has a doctor's appointment and Chloe will drive her. Papa is taking the boys to a soccer game, and Lena and Juliette are going to a swim event. Amber's competing and might win the competition."

"Do I sense a hint of blessed *alone* time?"

"Count on it." She winked, turned toward the path and walked to the main house.

Evan watched her walk away, and once again he'd been completely captivated by her lovely face. But, even more than the color of her eyes and the shape of her mouth, he loved her personality. She was fun, unassuming, uncomplicated and full of life. She was everything he wished he could be.

CHAPTER 34

Evan

The next morning Chloe arrived with bags of acrylic paints, brushes, a pallet knife, sponges and several canvases, a large pad of sketching paper, colored pencils and chalk. The considerate nurse also brought croissants, fromage, and a large dish of fresh framboise. Chloe happened to mention she had taught Danielle to drive, and she would be taking her official driver's exam in two days.

Before Chloe left, she explained to Evan why Danielle had resisted driving for so long, but she now accepted the fact that everyone else in the family was tired of taking responsibility for driving the younger children to events. Since Marie's health was precarious, trips to the doctor were more frequent, and with Chloe's schedule at the hospital, she was often gone in an emergency. Gaspard had agreed to purchase a car for Danielle. It's not that she hated driving so much, but riding her bicycle was a childish joy she insisted on clinging too in attempt to avoid the modern world.

Evan thanked Chloe for her thoughtfulness, and explanations. He gave her a warm hug before sending her off to a busy day of taking her mother to the doctor.

Evan surprised himself with his ability to sketch from visions in his head. What did a giant squid look like? He snuck a look on the Internet, the fountain of knowledge about most everything. He committed the image to memory, drew it free hand and enjoyed creating the tentacles with their suction cups. Shades of purple and green were slathered on the body, with a giant bulging eye staring straight at the viewer. He hoped Josh would be pleased.

Painting Thor, for Valentin, proved to be a bit more difficult, but since the fluffy family dog chose to languish at his feet expecting a morsel of Evan's chicken sandwich, he had a perfect subject to study.

The most challenging painting to create was for Juliette. It was difficult to find the right shades of green for the undulating hills, the cerulean blue color of sea, the resplendent flowering plants, and the ever-changing sky at sunset, not to mention also adding Juliette's requested birds and rabbits.

Painting did not consume all of his thoughts, and he frequently let his mind wander over so many unresolved issues. Not seeing Ryan for weeks put some distance between them, so he didn't feel the same edgy compulsion to pursue his nagging doubts about the guy. The police hadn't finished their investigation, and Evan realized he might never know if Ryan had any involvement in Armond's murder. However, before returning to New York, Evan considered the ramifications of a private conversation with Gaspard about two issues—the drugs found on the dive boat the day of the accident, and the conversation he overheard the day of the interrogation.

He was bothered by detective Nichols insistence on collecting carpet fibers where he noticed bloodstains. If it turned out to be more than Ryan's blood on the carpet, then perhaps a fight had taken place in Ryan's office, Evan speculated. Maybe the police should test Armond's clothing found in the dumpster now being held in evidence, but getting involved in this case was not his responsibility. Danielle had strong feelings about Ryan's untarnished character. Casting doubts on Ryan's innocence could cause a wedge in his relationship with Danielle, and that was the last thing he wanted, not to mention the difficulty Gaspard would have accepting the fact that his partner might be a murderer.

Despite trying to concentrate on painting, and his fleeting throughts about murder, he couldn't keep his mind off Danielle. He mixed raw umber paint with a touch of gold and thought of her eyes. Before he returned to New York, he wanted to be intimate with her, but didn't know if she would be willing to do so without some sort of commitment. The issue was not about loving her or wanting to spend the rest of his life with her, it was about her desire for a family. Having Danielle's younger siblings around, proved to be both a joy and sorrow. He liked Juliette, Josh and Valentin, but he held them at a distance with a closed door of emotions he couldn't seem to open.

He wondered if he could convince Danielle to visit him in New York while he took his final exams. Maybe she could stay at his loft in Tribeca while he was in school. On the other hand, if Aurora found out Danielle was in New York staying at his loft it could be a disaster. He grabbed a rag and wiped the sweat off his brow.

Evan was not pleased with what Aurora had said to Danielle about being engaged, not to mention his disgust when she told Danielle he didn't want to have children. He knew Aurora was possessive, and if she felt threatened, he knew she could be manipulative. However, he didn't think she would be cruel. What she had done was unforgivable, and he vowed to break off their relationship. He had no idea how ending their personal life might affect her willingness to show his work at her gallery, but in his gut he felt it would end badly. In a perfect world, he wanted to remain friends with her—continue a business relationship and have his work displayed at her gallery, but he knew it was not likely to happen. It was his source of income, and he did not want to dip into the trust fund his parents had set up for him long ago. He rubbed his face, and paint from the back of his hand streaked his nose.

Thinking about Danielle's feelings he considered getting her an engagement ring, but wanted to talk to Gaspard and Marie first. As he brush-stroked on paint, he shook his head. So many issues troubled him and made it difficult to concentrate. It occurred to him he'd fallen in love with someone he didn't really know. Maybe he shouldn't rush things. He'd go to New York, take his final exams, break off his relationship with Aurora and then try to figure out the next best step. The idea of leaving New York appealed to him. He could sell his condo and his car—that would be easy. Moving to St. Paul held considerable appeal, but where would he live and what would he do for a living? He had no idea. Asking someone to marry him when he had no source of reliable income and no means of employment was foolish.

Perhaps selling his condo and moving to St. Paul would be best, and just letting his relationship with Danielle develop. He had no idea what her political views were or what her religion was, although he was sure she believed in God. Would she want to continue to work as a teacher or have a family immediately? The pressure to resolve his conflicting feelings about having children loomed like a pervasive shroud of fog engulfing him to the point of suffocation. For now, he would paint and finish the last of the trees in the landscape. Art had always been an escape, and he longed to be able to paint or do something that he embraced rather than immerse himself in art to avoid dealing with his feelings of guilt about Ashley's death. Danielle would be home soon. They would talk. What's the worst that could happen? He had no idea, so he painted the flowers into the landscape instead as a finishing touch to something he could control.

CHAPTER 35

Evan and Danielle

Evan had the covers pulled over his head with the doors to the guest cottage slightly open. He did not hear her come in nor did he awaken at first when she slid under the covers and put her arm around his broad shoulders. She kissed the back of his neck and he stirred as if still in a dream. Her hand trailed down his spine to his hip. His eyes blinked from stupor and he realized Danielle was in bed with him. He rolled over on his side and kissed her. She returned the intensity and said "Good morning, sleepy head."

"I assume we're alone?" Evan asked with a quizzical smile while kissing her eyes and then her lips. He put his hand on her back and realized she was naked.

"Yes. Everyone's gone at least for a couple of hours. You know how it is around here, and it's rare that I'm home alone."

"I'll savor every minute of this time we have together," he said. "I'm glad you snuck in bed—I wasn't expecting this, but you do things that surprise me. I want to devour you, but I don't have any protection. I feel tacky that I, um, well…"

"Not to worry. Here's a packet for you, courtesy of a drawer in Lena's nightstand."

"I knew there was at least one thing about that girl I liked," Evan snickered.

Danielle laughed and kissed him lightly, then parted her lips. With her ample breasts compressed against his chest and her legs wrapped around his, their passion ignited.

Evan intended to explore her slowly, touching her soft skin like a rose he wanted to open one petal at a time, but her desire was so intense, matching his and soon they became lost in each other.

Drenched in sweat with the smell of plumeria fragrance in her hair, he lay next to her feeling exhausted and delirious. Having only dreamt of making love to Danielle, the reality was so much more than he imagined. He could feel how deeply she loved him—there was gentleness in her passion and a sense of wanting to please him, and he, in turn, wanted to please her more than gratify his needs. This was the difference between sex and love—an emotion he had not experienced before. He stroked her hair, kissed her forehead and said, "I love you, Danielle. I couldn't return to New York without expressing my love for you physically."

"I felt the same way, Evan, and there is no way I would send you back home without letting you know how much I loved you too, but, we have to talk, don't we?"

"Yes. I'm sure you have questions on your mind, and you want to know what will happen after I take my exams, right?"

She propped her arm up on the pillow so she could look directly into his eyes. "Exactly. I know you have a career in New York. You're a famous, successful artist, and I don't want to take that away from you."

"I'd give it up for you," Evan said and brushed her hair off her forehead.

"I wouldn't want you to. You'd resent me if I asked you to change your life. Besides, have you talked to Aurora since she left?"

"No. I'll break off my relationship with her when I get home."

"What will happen to your paintings in her gallery?"

"That's a tough question. I have no idea. He stretched out in the bed, put both arms behind his head and stared at the ceiling fan. If she no longer wants to exhibit them, I'd understand, but it's her financial loss as well as mine. She may want to rotate in another artist. If that happens, I'd have to put my work in storage."

"Could you store these paintings in your condo?"

"No. There are too many of them already cluttering my place and fifteen hanging in the gallery, some of which are quite large. Besides, I was thinking of putting my condo on the market, selling my car and moving here to St. Paul."

"What!" Danielle's face lit up. "You'd move here?"

He turned toward her. "I would. I know you can't leave your family. It's everything to you, and your mother's health is fragile. When my condo sells, I can have my things packed and shipped here, but I need to find a place to live, and I have to figure out what I want to do so I can support you."

"Is that a proposal?" Danielle's eyes widened.

"It's a promise, a commitment to you, to us, but I have to sort out my life here before I ask your father and mother for your hand in marriage."

Danielle nodded and bit her lower lip. "I know you haven't resolved your feelings about having a family—even one child—and I don't want to rush you. Can we just see how things work out when you get back?"

"That's exactly what I want," Evan said with a sigh of relief.

"Is that all you want?" Danielle said while rubbing up against him again.

"Obviously not." Evan reached for her hands and placed them above her head against the pillow.

The second time was everything he wanted it to be. She brought out tenderness in him that he had kept hidden in grief, afraid to be vulnerable.

"Do you mind if I take a shower here," Danielle said. "It will give me a reason to have wet hair as if I'd gone for a swim istead of romping in bed with you."

"Let's take one together," Evan said with a grin.

"Can you get your injured foot wet?"

"Oh, crap, no. I keep forgetting I have these bandages on."

"You stay. I'll shower."

Danielle crawled out of the bed, stepped over the duvet on the floor, and went over to his side of the mattress to toss the covers back on the bed. It was then that she noticed the tear in the condom on the floor. She bit her lower lip, said nothing and walked towards the shower.

CHAPTER 36

Evan

The next day Marie stopped by the guesthouse to chat and take a look at the three paintings. Her eyes widened while she clasped her hands together. She carefully studied each painting then turned toward Evan, who was seated, and couldn't resist bending over to give him a warm hug. "Oh, Evan, these are wonderful! The children will be so thrilled. How did you plan to present them?" she wondered.

"I hadn't thought about it." Evan raised his eyebrows.

"How about an outdoor picnic on the terrace by the pool? We could eat before sunset."

"I'd like that," Evan said.

"It's hard to believe you're leaving so soon," Marie's eyes showed a hint of sadness.

"I know. My stay here has gone so quickly."

"I see you've taken your bandages off. Does your foot feel better?"

"It's a little stiff, but it doesn't hurt. I'm so glad I don't have to use a cane any longer."

"Maybe you could leave the cane for me. I might need it in the future."

"Of course. I understand."

Marie changed the subject. "Danielle told me you must return to New York to take your final exams."

"Yes, that's true. Perhaps she's told you I'm thinking of moving to St. Paul."

"She did. I know you have to sort out a good many things before you can uproot your life there."

"I love her so much—I don't want to leave her, but I must." Evan's eyes were downcast, glancing at his feet.

"Where deep love exists, problems can be worked out if you give them time," Marie, smiled and put her hand on Evan's shoulder.

Evan nodded and reached up and put his hand on hers. "Thank you for understanding, and also for your wonderful hospitality." He stood. "I've enjoyed my stay here so much."

"It was our pleasure. Can you bring the three paintings to the picnic area?"

"Of course." He flashed a wide grin.

"We'll celebrate your last night here with grilled lamb and some cherished Taupenot-Merme wine from our cellar. I think you'll like this black cherry, tangy red."

"I'm looking forward to it." He smiled and put his arm around her shoulder. "You have a wonderful family. Everyone has been gracious and accommodating."

"Thank you, Evan." Marie turned and waved goodbye. "See you at sunset."

The rest of the day went quickly. Evan dressed for dinner in slacks and a pale gray broadcloth shirt, and packed most of his clothing except for what he would wear on the plane. The thought of leaving Danielle tomorrow was unbearable. He planned to say goodbye to her later in the evening and leave for the airport in the morning. New York would seem odd and uncomfortable—noisy and frenetic compared with the idyllic time spent in St. Paul.

The sun began to set over the sea, flaming the sky with deep reds and vidid shades of orange. The light breeze would make dining alfresco perfect. Evan tucked the three paintings under his arm and walked the stone path up to the main house. He could hear laughter in the distance as he made his way to the patio.

"Bonsoir," Gaspard said and greeted him with a warm handshake. He motioned for him to sit at the head of the table, something Evan did not expect. Lucas was at the bar opening wine while Marie, Chloe, Lena, and Danielle chattered and laughed, comfortably seated at a large table under a canopy of wisteria. Josh, Juliette, Valentin and Amber were tossing a small ball back and forth on the grassy pavilion teasing Thor who was intent on snatching it for himself.

Evan did a quick glance around the grounds and did not see Ryan, which made sense since this was a family picnic.

As soon as Josh spotted Evan, he shouted his name and dropped the ball, which Thor immediately picked up and ran with it into the bushes. "I wanna see...let me see!" Josh squealed and tugged at Evan's elbow while he held the paintings to his side. The rest of the children ran to the table and began jumping up and down with excitement.

Evan hadn't expected so much enthusiasm, and waited for everyone to be seated.

"Okay, who's first?" Evan said.

Juliette, Josh and Valentin all chorused "Me, me, me."

"Children, patience!" Marie scoffed and patted the table with her hand. "I wish my relaxed American upbringing would have produced children with more subdued French manners."

Evan, realizing he was on the spot, decided to give each child their painting, but had them shut their eyes first, and made them promise not to look.

Josh grasped the canvas in his hands as if he'd been given a box of precious gold coins.

Valentin was still jumping up and down holding his painting with his eyes shut, and everyone laughed.

"Okay. Everybody look." Evan said, with gusto, but his nerves made his voice crack.

Josh's eyes widened. He fingered the squid's tentacles and poked at the bulging eye. Valentin held up his painting of the family dog and said, "It looks just like Thor."

Juliette, the quietest of the children, glanced at her painting for the longest time before showing it to the group. "This is our home," she said. "The landscape is perfect, and you remembered to put in a rabbit and birds in the sky. The flowers are so pretty, and the sunset looks like it does right now. You're an amazing painter," she gasped. "I just love it."

Everyone clapped, and Evan was relieved to see how much the children liked his paintings. Suddenly, Josh and Valentin got up from the table and ran over to Evan, put their arms around him and said, "We love you, Evan." Juliette walked over to Evan and gave him a kiss on the cheek. "Please stay here," she said. "We don't want you to leave."

Evan's eyes brimmed with emotion he didn't expect and struggled to control. He put his arms around the three children and hugged them. In that fleeting moment feelings long repressed deep inside broke loose in his heart, and he let himself feel their love. It was as if Ashley was smiling down on him telling him to let love in. He had not hugged a small child since Ashley's death, and he was overcome with emotions of not wanting to let the children go. He wiped a tear from his eye, and was relieved to hear Danielle's voice. "You can see why Evan is so special, and now you all know why I love him so much."

Evan reached for her hand, and in that touch, he knew she understood exactly what he was feeling. He regained his composure and picked up his glass of Burgundy. "To the entire DuBois family, I thank all of you for your friendship and support. You have gone out of your way to help me when I needed it the most."

Everyone clinked glasses and joined in the salute.

Chloe, Lena and Amber cleared the dishes and went inside. Danielle sat down beside Evan and lit the candles. The children were chasing fireflies trying to catch them in glass jars. Gaspard and Lucas had moved to larger patio chairs and were engaged in a conversation about expanding the lavender business. Marie bid them all an early goodnight, apologizing for being tired from the day's activities.

"I need to steal you away to say goodbye," Evan said to Danielle. She got up and tugged at his arm. He followed her around the side of the house to the balcony overlooking the sea. The moon was rising, full and bright, casting a glow on Danielle's face and her peach sundress. He pulled her toward him and kissed her with passion he no longer had to repress, grateful for the touch of her skin and her body pressed up against his. "I'm not saying goodbye," he said.

"I won't either, " she chimed in. "Goodbyes are for when you don't expect to see someone again."

He held her tightly. "I'll call you when I get to New York and will call you every day. That's a promise."

"I start school next week, so I'll be busy. It'll help to have something to do, but I'll miss you terribly. I ache already missing you and you are still here."

"I know," he said. "I feel the same way."

"I love you with all my heart, Evan. I'm not worried about the future. I know we'll be together."

He kissed her again, and smiled. "We'll have a wonderful life."

They clung together in an embrace, neither wanting to let go, but she knew she would have to be the one to pull away. "Goodnight, my love." She put her fingers to his lips. "Sleep well," she choked out the words and tears began to trickle down her cheeks. Then she turned in the moonlight and walked toward the entrance of the house.

As Evan walked back to the guesthouse, his cell buzzed in his pocket. He glanced at his phone in the dark. It was Aurora. He sighed and shook his head. Rather than take the call, he texted her instead telling her he would be returning to New York tomorrow and he'd call her then. What could she possibly want?

CHAPTER 37

Evan and Aurora

Evan arrived at his condo, weary from travel, a delayed connecting flight and cramped legroom. The one thing he hated about flying was never feeling comfortable in his seat because of his long legs, often pushed against the seat in front of him, unless he could manage an exit aisle, not available on his flight from France.

The condo smelled musty, so he flung open windows letting in the smog and fog. Tomorrow he'd go to the post office and retrieve his held mail, which would be a hefty bin of paperwork he didn't look forward to. On-line banking had been easy to keep his bills paid while he was gone.

But today, he would do nothing—absolutely nothing but watch TV and enjoy a long backlog of taped shows and on-demand movies. He opened the refrigerator, spied two cold beers and grabbed one. No sooner had he flipped off the cap, taken one swig and kicked off his loafers, when he felt his phone buzz in his pocket.

"Now what?" he muttered in a cranky voice before answering the phone.

"Hello?" he throated it out a snippy tone.

"It's me," Aurora said. "I need you, Evan."

He held the phone and didn't know what to say. "I just got in. I'm tired, and—"

"It's back," she said in a whisper he could hardly hear. "The cancer is back."

Evan sat up on the sofa and put his beer on the coffee table. "When did you find out? Is it serious?" He rubbed his eyes with numb fingers.

"Yesterday. I'd been feeling tired and I hurt everywhere. Evan, it's in my bones, my liver and pancreas," her voice strained with fear.

"Aurora, I'm shocked. You were cancer free for years. What happened?"

"I don't know. My doctor said the cancer mutated, metastasized and came back with a vengeance."

"I'm so sorry. I want to help. What is the prognosis for treatment?" Evan asked and rubbed his eyes to push sleep away.

"There is no treatment because—"

"Because, what?" Evan raised his voice.

"It's so advanced, they have given me less than four months to live."

"What?" Evan bolted upright from the sofa and put his hand to his forehead, shaken by her words.

"They talked about a round of an exceptionally high dosage of experimental chemo and radiation, but it would only give me another month or less, and I'm not willing to go through that, not to mention all the drugs for nausea. If there is no expectation that I'd live longer than an additional month, why would I undergo tremendous pain and suffering? I'm not big on either."

"Have you had a second opinion? I mean, is there any hope?"

"Memorial Sloan Kettering Cancer Center is one of the best hospitals. My oncologist is excellent. She reviewed my case with several other colleagues, and they concur with her findings. At this stage, they respect my wishes and all recommend hospice and palliative care to make me comfortable."

"Have you told your parents?"

"Yes, I called them yesterday."

"I'm sure they are very distraught."

"Well, you know, Delfine. As a psychiatrist, her first concern was for my mental health. Dad's in shock, unable to protect his daughter from this onslaught of uncontrollable cancer cells."

Evan sighed, let his shoulders droop and took a swig of beer, unsure what to say or how to be of help.

"Can we talk tomorrow?" Aurora asked. "I want to come over. There's something I'd like to discuss with you."

Evan rubbed his forehead. "Of course. Why don't you come over around ten, but I don't have a stitch of decent food in the house, not even coffee."

"No problem. I'll bring some bagels and pick up coffee on the way."

"You sure you're up to it?

"Yes. I'm on some pretty damn good pain pills."

"I'm glad to hear that. I feel terrible about all of this and I don't want you exhausting yourself."

"I can manage bagels and coffee. It's not an art show for goodness sake."

"Okay, see you tomorrow."

Evan sat on the sofa, feeling like he'd been kicked in the chest. Even though it was warm and the end of summer, he shivered and closed the windows. He looked at the tarps on the floor splattered with paint in dark depressing colors. The sporadic glaring crimson splotches felt like an omen. Several large paintings were stacked against the walls from his previous gallery showings along with a few new ones he planned to rotate into the gallery soon. Contemplating what to do with all of this would have to wait until he talked to Aurora. His hand shook as he grabbed the chrome doorknob and opened the pantry, found a can of kidney beans and a bag of potato chips, grateful for something to eat.

He glanced towards his upstairs bedroom loft that suddenly seemed too high, with stairs too rigorous to climb. The brick walls and vaulted ceilings with skylights interspersed with overhead tubular metal heating looked like an expensive prison, instead of the place he had called home for several years.

He found a can opener, ate the beans and chips, finished the beer and grabbed the faux fur throw. Overcome with physical and emotional exhaustion, he quickly texted Danielle. *Home safe. Miss u terribly. Love u completely.* Then he pulled the faux fur throw over himself, and tried to blot out the terror he felt about Aurora's illness. He stared at the ceiling unable to come to grips with the fact that she was ill beyond hope and was going to die.

CHAPTER 38

Evan and Aurora

Evan stirred to the sound of the doorbell buzzing and momentarily did not know where he was. Out of habit he reached for the alarm clock, knocked over the empty beer bottle and righted himself on the sofa. He rubbed his scruffy face and remembered the dread he was about to face. Aurora was in the lobby. He walked barefoot to his front door and spoke into the intercom, "That you?"

Aurora said, "Of course. Were you expecting someone else?"

"No, no. Sorry. I just woke up." He shook the fog out of his head and buzzed her through the gated front lobby.

He glanced in the hallway mirror wishing he'd shaved and opened the door. He leaned against the doorframe and waited for her to get off the elevator. Her arms cradled a large bag of bagels while she balanced two cups of Starbucks coffee in each hand.

"Hey," Evan said. "Let me help you with that."

"Thanks. You look like shit," she winced and put the coffee on the kitchen table.

"Sorry. Exhausted and slept in. Long flight."

He glanced up at her face and noticed how thin she had become. She gave him a quick awkward embrace and he could feel her ribcage through her blouse.

"How are you doing?" Evan asked, unable to think of anything else to say.

"How do you think I'm doing?" she snipped at him, and rocked her head from side to side. "I'm not doing the pity party, if that's what you want to know, and I don't want to hear it from you either."

"I didn't plan to—"

Aurora chomped at her bagel, slathered with cream cheese. "God, these are good," she said. "Best part of dying, you know, is being able to eat whatever the hell you want, right?"

"Aurora, I'm so sorry. None of this is fair." Evan held his palms up and shrugged his shoulders.

"So, when's life fair, Evan?"

"I mean—"

"I know what you mean," she barked at him. "You had an affair with someone else on vacation, of all things. I got cancer. Life's not fair, Evan."

They sat in silence, each chewing a bagel, unsure of where to start.

"So, here's the thing," Aurora said, putting her bagel down to sip her coffee. "I need someone to run the gallery, Evan. It's the least you can do."

"Wait, I need to tell you—"

"Here's the way I see it," she continued. "I'll be dead in three or four months, and since you're here now, you're the only person who can manage the gallery until I either sell it or find someone else to run it."

Evan leaned back on the sofa and began to run his hand through his hair.

"Aurora, I want to help you and I'm devastated about your illness, but I have to tell you I'm not planning on staying in New York."

"What?" she gasped and put her hand to her chest.

"There's no easy way to say this, but I plan to move to St. Paul. I want to put my condo on the market."

Aurora crossed her arms and bit the side of her lip. "So, what's the hurry? Did that little redhead spread her legs and convince you to move there, as if you could possibly be as much of a success in France as you are in New York?"

"Why are you being so bitchy?" Evan snarled at her in disbelief.

"That was mean. I'm sorry." Aurora began to shake, dropped her coffee and put her hands to her head. Sounds like a wounded animal wailed out of her, followed by heart-wrenching sobs.

Evan moved closer to her on the sofa, put his arms around her and let her cry it all out.

A half-hour later she was still crying. He comforted her without saying anything and rubbed her back. A roll of toilet paper sufficed for a lack of a decent box of Kleenex. Finally, she blew her nose and wiped her eyes, now stained with mascara. Her blonde hair was disheveled, her nose rubbed raw. Suddenly, she started laughing. "Now we both look like shit," she said.

Evan managed a weak smile. "You're scared, Aurora. You're not as tough as you want people to think you are."

She nodded. "Nobody knows me like you do. We really made a good team, you and I, didn't we?"

"We did," Evan said, aware it was stated in the past tense.

"You love her, don't you?" Aurora reached out and touched his chin.

He looked into Aurora's bloodshot eyes. "Can we not talk about this right now?"

She shrugged her shoulders, stood up with a defiant anger pursed on her lips and put her hands on her boney hips.

"Move if you must, Evan, but not until I'm dead. You owe me that!"

Evan put his elbows on his knees, rubbed the sides of his head with his clammy hands and contemplated what she just said. His heart strained to find a rhythm among skipped beats from nerves. "Can you give me time to think about all of this?"

"Of course. I know you just got home and need to get settled. I have to go to the gallery this afternoon. Why don't you drop over later and we can go to dinner at Scalini Fedeli. You love their Italian food, and I can finally eat all the pasta I want."

He paused, looking at her. "Fine. I'll come by around six."

She stood, picked up her purse, kissed him on the cheek and walked out the door.

Numb, Evan sat at the kitchen table unable to move, a pain gripping his chest so tightly it felt like a heart attack.

He moved to the sofa, reclined and took deep yoga breaths. The pain in his chest subsided and he realized he was probably having a panic attack.

His cell vibrated in his pocket. He hoped it wasn't Danielle, because he didn't know how he was going to break the news to her.

"Mom?" He scratched behind his ear.

"You're home. How was your flight?"

"Long and exhausting. Cancelled connecting flights, you know, the usual."

"I'm terribly sorry about Aurora," Kelly said. "You must be devastated."

"I'm upset, mom. How did you find out she was sick. Did she call you?"

"No, her mother called me in tears. We talked for quite awhile. Delfine and Drexel intend to meet with her oncologist. They can't understand why there isn't some experimental drug that would work for Aurora's cancer. They're willing to pay anything to get her into a clinical trial. Drexel's very well connected you know, and as a banker he's financed a lot of hospitals. He's determined to find a way to save his daughter's life whatever it costs. Have you talked to her, or perhaps you've gone to see her?" Kelly pressed.

"Aurora was just here. We talked. I can't believe how thin she is. She was doing so well—free from cancer, enjoying life."

"Cancer does that. Sometimes doctors can cure it completely and it doesn't come back. In other situations it buys time. I know friends who live with cancer, but are on exorbitantly expensive, multiple medications. Some drugs work for months, even years, then stop being effective and doctors try another drug. They call it *living with cancer through experimental chemistry*. I'm sure her doctor will find a protocol that will work for Aurora."

"No, mom. She doesn't want treatment."

"What? Of course she does. You must be mistaken."

"I'm not. Please don't tell Delfine and Drexel. Aurora needs to talk to her parents and explain her choice. She said her cancer is so advanced and is in several organs. She's not willing to go through chemotherapy or any experimental clinical trial drugs. The side effects would be horrific and would only extend her life another month."

"But, doctors aren't God. There's always a miracle. There's always hope."

Evan thought of a retort, then shook his head and knew there was no point in discussing this further. "Yes, there's always hope, however, I respect her decision."

"But, you love her. Don't you want to do everything you can to save her life?"

"I'll help her, but I can't save her if she doesn't want to be saved. She doesn't want to be a lab rat."

"Evan!"

"Mom, it's not your decision."

Evan could hear Kelly sigh and he let the silence hang in the air before speaking. "Look, I will do everything I can to be here for her to help her through this."

"What can you do?"

"We're having dinner tonight. She wants me to manage the gallery while she goes into hospice for palliative care."

"Evan, I can't accept this, and I know Delfine won't either. Of course you'll manage the gallery until she's well again. It's your job to convince her to find another doctor who's willing to help her. There must be someone at Cancer Center of America, perhaps, who is willing to take her case."

"Her oncologist at Memorial Sloan is one of the best in the country."

"I'm sure that's what you think. I was hoping for a wedding some day for you and Aurora. This is so upsetting."

"I know, mom. At one point, I thought so too. But, I'm not in love with Aurora anymore."

"What? Are you saying this because she's sick?"

"Of course not. I met someone while I was in St. Paul. Remember, I was staying with Marie and Gaspard DuBois, as their guest, recuperating."

"Yes, but what does that have to do with anything?"

"Everything. I fell in love with their daughter, Danielle."

"I'm shocked. Are you sure this was not merely a summer vacation fling?"

"This is not a fling. I didn't plan to fall in love, but it happened. I thought I was in love with Aurora. She did so much to help me launch my career as an artist. But, I was fragile when I met her and needed someone to take my mind off—I can't say it to this day—Ashley, without feeling like my life was over. I couldn't forgive myself. You know this. But, I took on the role of an artist without thinking about what I really wanted. Success happened so fast and I got caught up in the glamour—the glitz of New York and the entire art scene."

"Don't you enjoy painting?"

"I thought I did. It's a long story. I'll tell you about it sometime, but not now. I have to get some rest and then dress for dinner."

"Evan?"

"Yes? What is it?"

"Don't you think you could fall back in love with Aurora if she would live?"

"Mom, no. I love her, but loving someone is not the same as being in love with a person. I loved Aurora out of gratitude and to escape reality. She was exciting and a well-known art dealer. I needed a lifeline. I owe a great deal to her and will do everything I can to help her through this. You can't ask more than that from me."

"All right, dear. I'm sorry. Just upset about everything."

"How's dad?" Evan was desperate to change the subject.

"Portfolio fund management from home suits him well. He has several clients and we enjoy living in Carmichael, closer to downtown Sacramento."

"Glad to hear it. Gotta go, mom. I'll talk with you in a few days."

Evan clicked off the phone and rubbed his fuzzy chin reminding him to shower and shave before dinner. He climbed the loft stairs, grabbed a towel and turned on the water. The hot shower felt like a physical and emotional cleansing. His major concern was not only meeting Aurora for dinner, but how in the world was he going to tell Danielle about Aurora's situation? If Aurora lived another three or maybe four months, he'd have to stay in New York.

The pit in his stomach gnawed. Panic overcame him and he stood on the towel on the floor unable to catch his breath. This couldn't be happening, but it was. He dried off, selected a lightweight summer blazer, shirt and tie, tan slacks and forced himself to get dressed. He was overdue to call Danielle, and prayed she wouldn't call him until after he'd had dinner with Aurora.

CHAPTER 39

Evan and Aurora

The taxi ride to Scalini Fedeli didn't take long and Evan planned to order a hearty entrée plus two extra meals to go since his refrigerator was still bare. The hostess greeted him and showed him to a reserved table in a quiet corner. He always enjoyed Scalini's, not only for their epicurean creations, but the cloister-vaulted ceiling reminded him of Europe. Thoughts of Danielle flittered through his mind. He ordered a dry martini to settle his nerves and assuage his guilt over having dinner in an intimate setting with Aurora. Of course, Danielle would understand once he explained the circumstances—or would she?

He glanced up, and saw Aurora being directed to his table and stood to greet her. "Hello, Aurora. The color of your dress looks wonderful on you." He gave her a soft hug and pulled out her chair.

"Thanks, Evan. It still fits and doesn't hang like a tent. I'm going to have to give all my clothing away," she said rolling her eyes at the ceiling. "However, I intend to stuff myself with calories tonight. What are you drinking?"

"Martini, dry."

"Order me one, please, and then I'd like their Hunt Country Vineyards classic hearty red with dinner. I'm fond of Hunt's DeChaunac, Rougeon and Baco Noir blended grapes. Or, you can get the Castello dei Rampolla. I like the blackberry, cedar and muscular tannins."

"Will do as soon as the waiter arrives. What do you feel like eating?"

"Pasta. Anything with shrimp and a creamy sauce."

"Do you want some fried calamari to start with?"

"Yes, and make sure they bring butter with the bread instead of olive oil."

Despite the somber reason for their meeting, he found himself smiling at her zest for fatty food. Their drinks arrived and Evan clicked martini glasses with her saying, "To good, fatty, greasy, calorie-infused Italian food."

The comment made Aurora break up with a giggle and it warmed him to see her laugh.

"So, here's what I'm thinking, Evan. There are several major art showings at the gallery, each one scheduled at the end of the month. That will take four months to manage. The gallery crew will re-hang each new show and take down the old ones. Can I showcase the artwork you finished before your vacation?"

"Of course. I have them at the condo. I'll get them to you."

"Belinda will handle the catering, wine, and the invitations to be sent out automatically from the computerized list. What I want you to do is help with the publicity. Can you be available on the reception nights, greet patrons, new guests, and introduce them to the featured artist? I'd suggest we have your new work shown in the last month since I've featured your older work for a long time. How does that sound to you?"

"Sure, sure, I can do that. Belinda's a gem and she's easy to work with."

"If I'm feeling up to it, I may stop in, but I've been told these opiate drugs have serious side effects, and if I look like a refugee waif, I don't intend to appear and have people speculating about my being anorexic."

"Understood. Does Belinda know you're sick?"

"Yes. I told her. Besides telling you, Belinda and my parents, I haven't told anyone. Oh, of course, Delfine called Kelly. Sorry about that. You know my mother. She had to call your mom."

"Should you be drinking with the drugs you are on?"

"No, of course not. Stop being a cop. I'm going to die anyway."

"Yes, but I don't want you dropping dead in this restaurant. You're scaring me."

"I'll sip plenty of water. Stop worrying about me."

Evan rubbed the back of his neck in frustration, realizing it was her decision.

"So, tell me about—what's her name, Denyse?"

"Danielle," he corrected her, wondering if she really forgot or was being spiteful. She told me how she met you, Aurora, so I know you already have a great deal of information about her. She teaches English and other subjects at a private school, and comes from a close family. Her father owns the largest yachting company in Nice."

"Good catch, Evan. Fancy life and all that money."

"Wasn't like that, Aurora. When I met her, I thought she lived in a hamlet on a farm."

Aurora pursed her lips and raised one eyebrow. "Now that's a hoot. You're not exactly the plaid shirt stuffed under overhauls farm-boy type, are you?"

Evan let the comment go and took a long swig of his drink, summoned the waiter and ordered another martini, an expensive bottle of Castello dei Rampolla, a dense vibrant wine, and two glasses of ice water for Aurora.

"Do you plan to marry her?" Aurora glared at Evan.

The question struck him like a deliberate bolt of lightning. He didn't want to hurt Aurora, especially in her emotional state, but he was done lying about his feelings.

"I don't know when, but yes. We have things to work out."

"Things not exactly perfect?"

"It's not that, Aurora. She wants children and you know how I've struggled with Ashley's death."

"Huge understatement, Evan. That's when I met you. Without me, you'd still be sitting in art class without a gun, no longer a cop and with no purpose in life."

"Aurora!"

"Sorry. It hurts, Evan. I thought—I planned for us to get married someday."

"I know. I did too." He stared at her and sighed.

Evan's phone rang with a loud musical tone, forcing other patrons to glance with disapproval in his direction. He looked at his phone with a quizzical frown. It was Sheriff Cosley, of all people. "Excuse me. I am going to take this call outside. It's my former boss in California."

Aurora frowned at Evan, miffed and took a swig of her drink.

Evan answered the call, asked Bob to wait a minute while he excused himself, and left the table.

"What's up, Bob? I haven't heard from you in a long time."

"I hope I didn't catch you in the middle of something, but the cold case about your sister and the robbery resurfaced again with a real twist."

Evan's skin paled and his pulse quickened. "What do you mean?" he said with one finger in his ear to drown out the bleeping horns and traffic.

"LAPD called me with something unbelievable. The man who flew the helicopter during the bank robbery was dying of emphysema in a hospital in Southern California and wanted to do a dying deathbed declaration."

"What? Speak a little louder. It's noisy here."

"This repentant guy claims he flew the copter during the bank robbery. His conscience was riddled with guilt because he admitted he got a hefty sum of money for flying the copter, but he never signed up for murder."

"Holy shit! Did you get the declaration in writing?"

"Yes, I have it in the office, but the detective in charge in LA actually taped the declaration statement, which as you know, can be used in evidence and is not hearsay."

"Unbelievable. Can I talk to the guy?"

"Nope, sorry. He died. But he did give me the names of the two guys who hired him."

Evan started shaking, and his breathing became rapid and weak. "I need to sit down. Just a minute." He looked for a quiet place to sit down but there wasn't anything available. He walked next door and stood in the space between the two buildings grateful to be in the shade.

'You still there?"

"Yeah. At a restaurant with Aurora—long story. What were the names of the two guys?"

"Jed and Ted Reddiger. Sound familiar?" Bob wondered.

"Yeah. Those are the first names of the guys the bartender at Purple Place mentioned. Do you know how I can find these two assholes?" Evan blurted out and could feel his face flush with anger.

"Ted died shortly after the robbery shooting. Apparently he was hit in the leg and bled out—must have hit an artery," Bob said.

"Where did Ted and Jed meet this pilot?"

"In the Army," Bob coughed to clear his throat.

"What was the pilot's name?"

"Rusty Chamberlain. He owned a charter copter business in Manteca."

"How did Rusty get to a hospital in Southern California? Evan coughed.

"No idea."

"Did he say where Ted and Jed were from, because I tried to find Jed in Southern CA, as you know, with no luck." Evan began to pace nervously up and down the walkway rubbing his chin as he remembered fuzzy details about his call to Columbia Yachting when he tried to learn if Ryan Coltrane worked there, but was told instead it was Jed Reddiger who had worked there and left without notice. Evan forced himself to refocus on what Bob was telling him.

"Originally from Kentucky. He didn't know much about either of them, but something about their having a rotten, abusive childhood."

Evan rubbed his nose, trying to assimilate this information. "Did Rusty say what Jed and Ted looked like?"

"Yes. Medium height, muscular build, both with reddish blonde hair."

"Anything else?"

"Ted wasn't the only one shot. Jed was hit in the shoulder, but the bullet went through, so Rusty flew him to Manteca, patched him up."

"You're kidding, right?"

"No, he was a medic in the Army."

"Oh, of course he was. I can't believe all of this. What happened to Ted?"

"They buried him in a field in the outskirts of Manteca. We have a probable location and are tracking the area."

"Any family?"

"None. Get this. Rusty said Ted killed their father."

"Shit! My nerves are on edge. I haven't had time to think about this since I left St. Paul. I'm in the middle of dinner."

"Sorry to interrupt you. Do you want to call me back?"

Evan glanced at his watch, wondering how long he'd been on the phone. "Maybe later after I finish eating. I'm just curious about something. Did Rusty say where Jed planned to go with the money he got from the robbery?"

"Not specifically, but he planned to buy a yacht, sail around the south of France, and get a new identity. Ted was the one who shot the people in the bank, and it all went wrong. They planned to be in and out of bank, grab the money and fly out in the copter waiting in the open field. Unfortunately, someone lunged at Ted, the gun went off, people started screaming and a bank employee pushed the alarm. Ted then starting firing in a panic. All hell just broke loose."

Evans hands were clammy. Sweat dripped down his back from shock and the stifling heat of Tribeca. "Gotta run, Bob. I'll call you in a few days. I need to sort this all out."

"Take care, buddy. I hope this helps in some way. I know you want to avenge Ashley's death, find her killers, and bring them to justice. Vindication is a powerful motivation in solving crimes. I can put you back on the force if you want me to. Jed can't get away with this."

"Agreed. Let me think about it. I'm stuck in New York for several months."

"Sure. Take the time you need. I'm here when you need me." Bob clicked off his phone.

Evan was numb with information overload. If he wasn't stressed enough about Aurora's situation he was now faced with new evidence about the men who committed the robbery. For much of the time he spent with Danielle, he was distracted about Armond's murder. Recuperating at the DuBois estate gave him the respite he needed to recover from the scuba diving accident and deepen his love for Danielle. Thinking about who killed Ashley and the other the people in the bank robbery several years ago took a back seat to living in the present. He wiped the back of his neck, rattled with facing the possibility of finding justice for his sister.

Evan walked back to their table. Aurora had a pissed look on her face, creamy garlic on her chin, gulping food down like it was her last meal. Evan's dinner sat there cold.

"What the hell was so important that you left me sitting here so long?" Aurora stabbed her fork in the last of her shrimp capellini, wiped her chin and glared at Evan.

"Sheriff Cosley has a strong lead. All this time I've believed I'd never know who murdered Ashley, and now I've got exactly what I need."

"But, Evan. You're no longer a cop."

"Once a cop, always a cop. Until Ashley's death is vindicated, mentally I'll be a cop for the rest of my life if that's what it takes."

Aurora nodded, seeing the person she met years ago in the same raw emotional state again. "Do you want to have the waiter bring you a different entrée? Your sea scallops have gone cold."

"I want something with meat, and two pasta dishes to go, since I have no food in the condo."

Evan glanced past Aurora, as if she were not there, and drank the rest of his martini in a single gulp and then poured himself a glass of Castello.

"You're not going to renege on me, are you?"

"No. I promised I'd help you with the gallery. Solving Ashley's murder will have to wait."

After Evan finished eating, he called a cab for Aurora and one for himself.

"Thanks for dinner, Evan. It was exactly what I needed. I'm stuffed."

"My pleasure. This isn't easy for me, Aurora." He slid his arm around her waist. "When do you have to go into hospice?

I hate to ask, but am wondering how long you can be up and around?"

"Not for another week," she grimaced. "Maybe longer. Depends on how I feel."

Evan hugged her goodbye, opened the taxi door and helped her get settled. "Talk to you soon. Bye, Aurora."

She waved from the cab as it wove through the jumble of traffic.

CHAPTER 40

Evan and Danielle

It was late when he got home from Scalini's, but waited a couple of hours to call Danielle. He stood at the window gazing at the city lights. Evan's head was spinning. His life had become overwhelmingly complicated in a matter of days. He thought breaking up with Aurora would be the hardest thing he would have to do, and then he was blindsided by her cancer coming back. If that wasn't enough, she wanted him to manage the gallery showings for the next four months.

He had art school exams next week and he hadn't started to study or complete his final semester design project. His head was woozy from the combination of martinis and wine, but also from the shocking, unexpected information from Sheriff Cosley. He had given up hope of expecting a call where a new, critical piece of evidence would come to light— evidence so rattling it put him back to where he was in 2011. Ashley's death was raw again, as if it just happened, with the pictures of her corpse wrapped in a bloodstained sheet at Mercy Hospital in Folsom front and center in his mind.

He hung his head in the kitchen sink, turned on the cold water and splashed it on his face before dialing Danielle.

"Evan! I'm so glad you called. I tried earlier, but got a busy signal. Should I call you on your home phone or cell?"

"My cell is best. I'm not likely to be at home much."

"You okay? You sound funny."

"I'm a little drunk, to put it mildly." He sat in a soft black leather club chair kicked off his loafers and put his feet up on the coffee table.

"How's school?"

"Great. I have twelve students, five girls and seven boys. I've finished my lesson plans and I think they will learn English quickly. Strange. I live in France and rarely speak French anymore unless I'm in shops or restaurants. You take your exams next week, right?" Danielle inquired.

"Yes. I haven't studied. There's so much going on I need to tell you about."

Evan hesitated, took a breath, rubbed a mild cramp in the arch of his foot and wondered if this would be the end of their relationship if he didn't communicate his situation properly.

"Let me take the phone outside on the patio. Weather's great here," Danielle said. "I really miss you."

"Me too. I think you need to sit down. I have something very frustrating to tell you and don't even know where to begin," Evan said in a cracked voice. He coughed to clear it up.

"You're scaring me. What's wrong?" Danielle's voice sounded frightened.

"It's Aurora. Her cancer is back. I don't know if you knew she had cancer?"

"No, I didn't. Is it serious?"

"Very. She's not expected to live more than three or four months."

"Evan, that's terrible! Can't they do something to help her?"

"Her cancer is so advanced, in multiple organs"—his voice broke into a restrained sob. "I feel terrible about what she's going through."

"Does she have family who can help her through this?"

"Her mom and dad live on Long Island. They've been in close touch with her oncologist. Her cancer is very late stage. There's nothing that can be done, and Aurora doesn't want to go through any experimental treatment because, at best, she'd only live maybe another month. She's already so thin, and, uh—frail."

"You've seen her?" Danielle's voice went up an octave, tinged with incredulity.

"Yes, she came over. I'm sorry about how that sounds, but she's a wreck and needs me to run the gallery for a period of time until she can find someone to buy it."

"Oh! How long will that take?"

"I don't know. Maybe a few months." Evan shifted nervously in his chair.

"You're still putting your condo on the market, though, right?"

"I don't think I should do that until—well, until—"

"Until what?" Danielle sounded frustrated.

"Until after she dies." Evan heard his own words and it made him cringe.

"I'm shocked. I know you have history with her and she's the one who launched your career in New York. Do you still love her?"

"I'm not in love with her, but I will always love her in a way that has nothing to do with you."

"I feel like she's stuck between us. Are you sure she's really sick and not using this to her advantage?"

Evan flinched. "She's gaunt. Her skin is hanging on her bones like an emaciated skeleton. She really has terminal cancer."

"I'm so sorry, Evan, for what I just said. What can I do?"

"Can you give me time to help her with the gallery openings? There are four more events, and by then hopefully we can find a new owner."

"Are the events coming up this month?"

"I wish. No, they are spread out over the next four months at the end of each month."

Evan could hear Danielle breathing, but she wasn't saying anything.

"You still there?" Evan rubbed his temple to relieve the pressure throbbing in his head.

"I'm here. Shaken by the news. I'm realizing you won't be moving here for at least four months. That's heartbreaking. I'm really upset."

"Me too. I never expected this. Please trust me. I love you. If there's any way I could get out of this, I would. She said I owe her, and that I can move after she's gone."

"Of course. I think I understand. You have a life there. I know you want to help. Is there anything else I should know?"

"Oddly enough I got a call from Sheriff Cosley, my former boss, while I was at dinner. He had new information about Ashley's case. They found the person who flew the helicopter during the robbery. He died, but just before he did, he called the police in Los Angeles to make a dying declaration. I learned a lot about the two brothers who hired him to fly the copter. I need to sort this all out."

"You sound so far away, Evan."

"I'm here, Danielle. There's no place I'd rather be than in St. Paul with you. Besides Ashley's death, this is the hardest thing I have ever gone through. I'm devastated to be stuck here in New York. It's not where I want to be."

"I believe you. I just miss you terribly—I'm afraid of losing you."

"That won't happen. I promise on my life, that won't happen."

"Okay." Danielle let out a huge sigh and he could hear her sniffling.

"How are your parents? Everyone doing all right?"

"Mom's stable, weak, but doing as well as expected. By the way, Lena wanted me to tell you she thought she was a brat for treating you so badly. She likes you a lot."

"Good to hear. I wish I'd had more time to spend with her and the rest of your family."

"They feel the same. Oh, I wanted to tell you something odd that happened with a yachting rental customer."

"Oh, how so?"

"This Iranian-looking guy and his friend came into the office and wanted to pay cash for renting one of our larger yachts. He insisted on paying fifty-five thousand for the week, and dad said it was only fifty. The customer was adamant Ryan had told them it was fifty-five, was rather irate and demanded to pay in cash. The customer did not want to use a credit card, and dad was flummoxed about how to handle the transaction."

"Hummn. That's bizarre. I wonder if he got the amount wrong?"

"Well, you know my father. Honest to the penny. He was suspicious, but accepted the entire fifty-five grand and extended the charter for two additional days. He's talked to Lucas about it because he didn't want to confront Ryan. I'm a little worried about all of this."

"Have you heard any more about the investigation of Armond's death?"

"Not much. The police couldn't find any suspects. Armond didn't seem to have any enemies. Even Armond's younger brother, Giles, said everyone liked and respected Armond. However, Giles never liked Ryan but wouldn't say why he felt that way."

"Did they ever find out whose blood was on the carpet in Ryan's office?"

"I hadn't heard. Do you want me to ask?"

"No. Let it go for now. I've got so much on my mind. I can't get involved with Armond's case. If they haven't resolved it by the time I move to St. Paul, I'll see what I can do when I'm there."

"You putting on your badge again?"

"Maybe. I'm not sure mentally I ever took it off."

"I love you whether you are an artist or a cop or both."

"Your love means everything to me and is the only thing that will get me through this."

"Call me tomorrow?"

"I promise, and I don't break my promises." Evan stood and shook out a leg that had fallen asleep. The moon poked through his windowpanes, casting a crosshatch pattern on the concrete floor.

"Love you." Danielle closed the conversation.

"Love you more." He clicked off his phone.

Evan went to the kitchen to put the two Scalini entrees in the refrigerator, glad for some extra food. Tomorrow he'd study for his exam, but tonight he'd do absolutely nothing but watch the Mets and fret over the swirling facts in his head about Ted and Jed, Aurora, Ryan—talk about overload.

CHAPTER 41

Danielle and Marie

Marie wandered into the kitchen for an ice tea and saw Danielle sitting cross-legged on the sofa with her head in her hands.

"You okay, honey?"

"No. I'm not okay." She moved over and motioned for her mom to sit beside her. "I got a disturbing call from Evan."

Marie's eyes widened. "Tell me about it."

"I'm in shock, as if I've been hit in the chest with a baseball bat. Evan's not able to move here right now and might not be able to move for four months."

"That's not what I expected. I thought he was going to put his condo on the market when he finished his exams." Marie said and adjusted the sofa pillows behind her back.

"It's Aurora. She has cancer. Whatever she had before has returned, and worst of all, she's not expected to live because they can't do anything to help her."

Marie's eyes widened. "Mon Dieu! That's terrible. How long does she have?"

"Maybe three or four months, which is why Evan is staying to help her run the art gallery until she can find a new buyer."

"Oh, honey. I'm so sorry." She blinked her eyes and shook her head.

"It's one of the reasons I love him so much, mama. He's a good guy who wants to do the right thing. He has history with Aurora and was in love with her before he met me."

"This has to be very, very hard on Evan," Marie sighed and reached out a hand to soothe her daughter's shoulder.

"It is. He's a wreck. Not to mention he got a call from the Sheriff he worked for in El Dorado Hills or something, when he was a cop. He learned new information about the robbery and Ashley's killer."

Marie bit her lower lip contemplating what she could say to her daughter that might be helpful. "If he can resolve his sister's crime, I think it would lift a tremendous burden from his shoulders. Your life together would be free of this unresolved angst he carries with him—a sadness I detected whenever I talked with him."

"You're right, as always, mama. I'm afraid I'm going to lose him. What if he never returns to St. Paul?"

"He loves you, Danielle. What are three or four months? Women lose men to war for long periods of deployment. They never know if their husbands, sons or daughters will ever return."

"That's true. I don't want to be selfish, and in my heart I understand his motive and sense of responsibility. I applaud it, but I miss him desperately."

"Come here, honey. Let me hug you. I promise you it will all work out."

Danielle let her mother cradle her in her arms, as if she were a small child again, never too old for her mother's comfort and understanding.

"Thanks for listening. I need to work on my lesson plans. Anything you want me to fix for dinner, mama?"

"I thought we'd have croissants with chicken salad, and maybe some fruit," Marie smiled.

"Sounds good. I'll set the table for everyone. Papa said he'd be home around six. " Danielle set plates and flatware on the table, then turned toward her mother who was chopping grapes and pecans. "By the way, I told Evan about the unusual confrontation with that customer who insisted on paying for the yacht rental in cash. I hope that's okay?"

"I don't see why not. It's never happened before and quite odd that someone insisted on not only paying in cash, but refused to accept the standard price for the rental. Ryan wouldn't have made a mistake. The customer must have heard the price incorrectly."

"I'm not sure, mama. I've given Ryan the benefit of the doubt despite Evan's concerns that there's something dark about him—something hidden. He's been papa's partner for a couple of years, and up to now, there's been no reason to be suspicious or concerned. It makes me uncomfortable to worry about him. The whole thing with Armond's murder was tragic and remains unsolved. This has been such a difficult time for all of us. I miss having Evan here because he makes me feel safe."

"Have you talked to Ryan lately?" Marie tilted her head to the side and looked over her shoulder while she sliced croissants and filled them with chicken salad.

"He called me the other day. He didn't know Evan had left. When I told him, he seemed rather pleased and wondered if we could go to dinner."

"What did you say?" Marie raised her eyebrows.

'I told him no, that I was sorry, but I had fallen in love with Evan and wouldn't be going out with him any more. I told him Evan was going to move here."

"What did he say?" Marie set small snippets of red and green grapes next to each croissant.

"He said 'damn'. That's exactly what he said."

Marie started to chuckle. "I'm not at all surprised."

"I want to shower and change clothes for dinner. Be back in a half hour or so."

"Okay, see you later dear."

Danielle went to her room, scampering up the stairs two at a time. When she got to the top step, she felt dizzy and grabbed the railing to steady her balance. For a minute she thought she might faint. She righted herself and proceeded to her bedroom shaking her head about the nonsense of being dizzy. A blue blouse and white jeans appealed to her.

She took a quick shower, dried her hair and slathered on coconut oil scented body cream. Her bra fit tightly so she loosened the clasp notch a bit and started to pull on her jeans. Although she had worn them a month ago, they were unpleasantly snug and she tugged at the zipper to close it. "Darn," she said to herself and looked in the mirror. "I seem to be gaining weight. That's unusual. Maybe too many dishes of ice cream before bedtime. I'd better stop it or Evan will return to a fat woman he won't want to marry."

Danielle slipped on white sandals and proceeded downstairs anxious for dinner where she promised herself she'd only eat one croissant.

Gaspard drove up the driveway a half-hour later than expected. The rest of the family was already gathered at the kitchen table laughing and picking at the sprigs of grapes garnishing the croissants. "Papa, good to see you. How was your day?" Danielle said and tucked her wet hair behind her ears.

"Good, good." He smiled at her and put his briefcase on the floor next to the table nudging Thor to move over. "Plenty of customers this time of year. We've redone the website and the advertising has paid off. I've been thinking of taking on another crew member to help with the charters."

"Lena, how do you like working in the office?" Danielle asked.

"It's interesting. I've helped design the new brochures. Mostly, I enjoy meeting the customers when they come in and explaining the different yachting options. Some customers only want a sailboat; others prefer an inboard."

Marie acknowledged how pleased she was Gaspard had asked Lena to be part of the business. For the first time in years, Lena seemed to have newly found confidence about who she was—a sense of accomplishment. She'd even stopped dying her hair weird shades of purple and softened her makeup.

Conversation flowed freely about the day's events and the challenges at the yachting firm, as well as Danielle's new students. The hospital had kept Chloe very busy and she announced she was considering becoming a surgical nurse.

Unexpectedly, Danielle grabbed the top of the table to steady herself. All conversation stopped to stare at her. "Are you okay?" Chloe asked.

Danielle's head spun and waves of nausea overcame her. "I think I'm going to be sick." She bolted up from the kitchen table and ran to the bathroom just getting to the commode in time to upchuck her dinner. Her face was flushed and skin felt clammy. She ran a washcloth under cold water and dabbed at her pink flushed cheeks.

"You okay in there?" Chloe's voice resonated concern for his sister.

"I'm not sure. I lost dinner." Embarrassed, Danielle opened the door. "Check my forehead. Do you think I have the flu or something?"

"You don't seem to be running a temperature—in fact you're shivering."

"I'd better lie down upstairs until this passes. Can you walk me to my room?"

"Sure." Chloe put her arm around Danielle and walked her down the hall to the stairs. "I hate to ask, but did you have your period this month?"

Danielle glared at her sister. "No, not yet. But, you know I'm not regular."

"Do you think you could be pregnant?" Chloe hesitated.

"Oh, Chloe. That's possible. But I can't—I mean I don't want to be pregnant. I was only intimate with Evan once."

"Well, sis, all it takes is once. Did you use protection?"

"Evan did, of course."

Chloe raised her forehead, sighed and patted her protectively on the back. "Maybe you do have the flu."

She then helped Danielle get settled in her room, brought her a glass of water and opened the window for fresh air. "Can I get you anything else?"

"No, I'm fine. Just close the door and let me rest awhile."

After Chloe left, Danielle put her hands to her face and started to cry because her memory of the torn condom was now very vivid.

CHAPTER 42

Gaspard and Lucas

Lucas took a break from managing his lavender business and headed over to the outdoor seafood restaurant where Gaspard waited to meet with him. Lucas could sense some urgency in his father's voice, but didn't know what it was about.

"Glad you could make it." Gaspard said. "Thanks for coming. Beer, fish and chips?"

"Sure. Sounds good."

"Gotta make a pit stop. Be right back." Gaspard walked down the hallway.

The hostess showed Lucas to a table on the deck overlooking the sea. Waves stretched on to the beach and then retreated taking half-built sandcastles with them. Dogs ran freely ahead of owners loping through the water, chasing balls and sticks. Bronzed, suntan oil-slathered bodies sat in beach chairs sipping drinks with tiny umbrellas. Tourists and residents snoozed on blankets or frolicked in the water. Surfers paddled out in the deep, lulling on their boards, chatting and hoping for a big wave to crest and ride.

Lucas never got tired of the sea and brushed his black curly hair out of his eyes.

Gaspard returned and sat down to join Lucas.

"What's up, dad?" Lucas stared at his father.

"I wanted to talk to you about Ryan."

"Oh?" Lucas' eyebrows knitted together and he folded his hands on the wood table.

Gapsard described the bizarre event where the customer insisted on paying more than five grand above the standard price for renting the yacht, adamant that Ryan told him the price.

"Don't clients usually pay after the charter, not before?"

"Often that's the case. This guy seemed perturbed on principle alone—wanted pay in cash, and to pay upfront. Different cultures have different preferences."

"Do you think the customer got it wrong?" Lucas asked.

"No. I wish I did, but customers don't want to pay more, they want to pay less. The customer's insistence on paying fifty-five grand instead of the standard fifty for that yacht made me suspicious. Also, he said Ryan specifically told him the amount was fifty-five grand.

"Why would Ryan up the price?"

"Exactly!" Gaspard said and sipped the cold beer's froth at the top of the glass.

Lucas stared at his father's furrowed brow and could see that he was upset.

The waitress arrived with baskets of freshly grilled cod piled on top of garlic fries and set them on the table.

Lucas chose his words carefully. "Is there something going on with Ryan?"

"Maybe." Gaspard grabbed a handful of fries and popped one in his mouth.

"Like what?" Lucas gave him a quizzical look and swatted at a fly.

"First there's Armond's murder—a terrible tragedy. The investigations were grueling and Ryan seemed to be a suspect, but there was no proof he was involved. At the time I was aghast the police would even consider Ryan's involvement— my business partner. Incredulous! Lately I started thinking about the accident Ryan had in his office—the mess in the carpet from the painting that fell off the wall when he supposedly stumbled into it and all the broken glass from the shattered coffee table. Unlike Ryan to be so damn clumsy. Don't you think? Dammit! I think he lied to me." Gaspard scowled and pounded his fist on the table. He looked at Lucas and noticed he had startled his son, who didn't look anything like him, but instead resembled Marie with his fine bone structure and small frame.

Lucas stiffened. His eyes widened, attentive to his father's anger.

"I see. Why didn't you tell me your concerns before now?"

"I don't know. Gave Ryan 'benefit of the doubt' consideration. But something doesn't ring true. He's been my partner for several years. I couldn't have asked for someone with a better knowledge of yachting, mechanics and salesmanship. He's made us a lot of money."

"I agree. I don't pay much attention to what's going on with you and Ryan because I've got my own business to manage, but I understand your concerns. For what it's worth, Ryan was never someone I could get close to. We just sort of stayed out of each other's way, and it annoyed me that he was interested in Danielle. Sometimes I'd even see him sneak away with Lena on our boat outings."

"That galls me. Danielle and Ryan dated. I know that. She can take care of herself, but Lena only wanted what Danielle had. Silly, stupid sister jealously."

Lucas nodded, dipped a fry in tartar sauce and took a swig of beer out of the bottle.

"Don't think he's interested in her," Gaspard said. "He may flirt and tease, but he's not sleeping with her. If he was, I'd want to kill him."

"Dad!" Lucas put down his beer and glared at his father.

"Well, not kill him, but beat the crap out of him."

"So, what can I do?" Lucas put his elbows on the table and folded his hands under his chin.

"I want you to follow Ryan. I know this is a lot to ask."

"Seriously? But, I have a job. I can't be following Ryan around."

"Not during the daytime, but perhaps a couple of nights during the week and on the weekend. I'm suspicious about what Ryan's doing after hours. As soon as Armond was killed, Ryan was more than willing to pitch in and manage the accounting—handle the books. I gave him Armond's password because he asked."

"Do you think he's grifting?"

"Could be. If he's charging more than he should for the charters, I wonder where the extra money's going. It's not showing up on the books because I checked the computer spreadsheets." Gaspard stabbed a chunk of fish with his fork.

"Did you confront him about the recent customer wanting to pay fifty-five grand? Lucas picked up his napkin to wipe tartar sauce off his chin.

"No. I wanted to see what was booked. I logged on to Ryan's computer at night after he left. The amount posted was only fifty grand. Ryan doesn't know the client paid me $55K.

"So, what was he planning to do with the extra five grand? It makes no sense. You're paying him a substantial salary. Why would he be stealing from you?" Lucas stared at his father in disbelief.

"Gambling is one possibility. Monte Carlo's just up the coast. Another might be drugs. What if he's using or running drugs at night?"

"Are you serious?" Lucas rolled his eyes and his mouth went agape.

"It's just a suspicion. I checked out the fleet recently when Ryan went home for the day. All of the large yachts and sailboats were clean. Exhausting search. Drugs could be anywhere. Couldn't find a thing except on the dive boat he used with Evan. There were traces of white powder on the bathroom floor."

"Maybe Evan was doing drugs."

"Doubt it. Evan's not the type and he'd never be so stupid as to ask Ryan to get coke or heroin for him."

The waitress came to the table and inquired if they wanted another beer. Both men sat in silence not wanting to have their conversation overheard. Gaspard nodded. She agreed to get two more beers and went to the bar.

"Have you ever seen Ryan high?" Lucas stared at his father.

"No evidence whatsoever. He's anything but hyper. No dilated pupils. No traces of powder around his nose. However, he could be injecting drugs. Or maybe he's found a buyer and distributor."

"If Ryan's running drugs, where's he getting them from?"

"Good question. That's what I want you to find out. This coast is a natural target for drugs cartels. I might be way off base about my suspicions about Ryan."

The waitress brought the two beers. "Will there be anything else?" she asked.

"No. We're good. Just the check." Gaspard smiled.

Lucas twisted his lip. "Where were we?"

"My thought was that you could follow him—camp in your car outside his apartment in Nice. See if he goes anywhere late at night. Maybe he heads to the marina dock. If he does, take out a skiff and follow him, but stay a decent distance behind him and don't turn on night beams. If he sees you, you'd have no reason for being out in the same water."

Lucas contemplated all of this while chomping on the last chunks of fish and fries.

"Of course, I'll help, but I feel like I could be in real danger if he's a murderer."

"I agree," Gaspard said. He pulled a small leather satchel out from under the table. "That's why I'm giving you this gun."

"Jesus, dad, you're serious!"

"It's mine. I took it from the house. If we're robbed, I'll be screwed, and will have to beat the shit out of the intruder." Gaspard blurted out a hearty laugh. "Of course, Thor would be angry with me for doing his job."

"Glad you can find some humor in all of this," Lucas said while squeezing the tip of his nose in nervous tension. "I guess I'll have to go shopping," Lucas added.

"For what?" Gaspard wondered.

"Clandestine clothing. A black hoodie, dark glasses and binoculars." Lucas said with one eyebrow raised trying to be humorous.

"Damn good idea!" Gaspard stood and slapped Lucas on the back. "That's my son."

CHAPTER 43

Lucas

Lucas never expected to be sitting in his car late at night parked about a half block from Ryan's apartment. He knew where Ryan lived, and was grateful for the abundance of leafy trees and shrubs obscuring his car. Even with his dark sunglasses on, he still had a good view of Ryan's driveway. With the hoodie draped around his head, he struggled to stay awake to watch for Ryan's BMW.

He munched on a donut and sipped hot coffee while watching other apartment residents either driving in or out of the building. There was no sign of Ryan.

A glance in the rearview mirror showed a couple walking toward his car, mere meters from him. The gun made him nervous, so he tucked it in the empty bag and stuffed in under the front car seat. He pushed the seat back and ducked down beside the dash. Sweat began to trickle down his neck. How did cops manage a stakeout? He heard footsteps and a cane tapping the sidewalk. He held his breath. The couple laughed and passed his car without incident. When they were out of sight, he started the engine to open the windows. It was unbearably stifling in a fleece hoodie in late summer with a muggy dampness hanging in the air like wet laundry.

Layers of clouds drifted in front of the waxing moon. In the darkness he could not see his coffee cup and accidentally knocked it over. Warm coffee spilled over his jeans between his legs as if he had just peed. "Damn!" he muttered. He grabbed paper napkins covered with powdered sugar, dabbing the area between his legs and wiped the seat.

It was nearly one in the morning with no sign of Ryan. Maybe Gaspard had it all wrong. On the other hand, maybe it would take a couple of stakeouts before he managed to snag Ryan coming or going. For that matter, he didn't even know if Ryan was at home. What if he was out gambling? He pondered Gaspard's concerns and wondered how his dad had actually met Ryan. He made a mental note to ask him before his head drooped and slid against the window in slumber.

"Hey! You can't sleep out here." The elderly man scolded him like a child and tapped his cane at the window. "When we can't sleep we go for a walk. Scat. Get out of here, you homeless swine."

Lucas sat upright and saw the man glaring at him with obvious disgust while an old, startled, woman clutched the man's other arm. A car drove past them down the street and entered the apartment building's garage complex, but Lucas couldn't check to see who was driving because of the current altercation. Was that Ryan?

"Sorry, sorry. Dozed off." Lucas raised a hand to shield his face.

The man huffed at him and whacked his cane on his bumper.

"I'm going, I'm going. Stop banging my car!"

Lucas started the car and turned on the air conditioning. The couple continued walking to their destination. How long he'd been sleeping he had no idea. A quick glance at his watch indicated it was almost two. He didn't want to be perceived as a vagrant. It was time to get the heck out of there. If someone called the police, he'd have no explanation as to why he was there and he didn't want the police finding him with a gun.

If Gaspard insisted, maybe he'd try this again, but in his father's Mercedes. Perception was everything. Why not wear a lightweight suit and sit in the car and do email on his phone? At least he wouldn't raise suspicion about being a thief simply by his grunge clothing and older model car. However, he decided he'd keep the dark glasses.

He slapped his face to force sleep away while he drove home with the air conditioning on full blast. An embarrassing, rather nerve-wracking, wasted evening without results. He wanted to believe he'd catch Ryan leaving the building and have a chance to follow him. The idea of the chase sounded good. On the other hand, had he been required to follow Ryan on the chance he was going to the marina, the actual reality of tailing him was so scary it made his muscles twitch.

He reached home, opened the gates and drove up the driveway. Having sublet his apartment, he was glad he had recently moved back home. Without making a sound, he quietly found his way to his old bedroom, anxious to get take off his wet jeans. He set the paper bag on the dresser, peered inside at the Luger lightly dusted with powdered sugar, rolled up the bag and buried it under clothing it in the back of his dresser drawer.

Dawn would not crack through his window shades for a couple of hours. He crawled into bed grateful to catch some sleep before going to work. He thought about the car that drove past him and entered the garage while the elderly man was ranting. Was that Ryan? Darn that old couple. Now he'd never know. He shook his head in frustration. In minutes he was dead asleep.

CHAPTER 44

Evan

Despite all the chaos in his life, Evan managed to trudge through his final exams. He completed his final project based on the design of the Milwaukee Art Museum, an architectural masterpiece by Spanish architect Santiago Calatrava, someone Evan had admired for years. The museum, noted for its movable Quadracci Pavilion, contained a 217-foot wingspan brise soleil that opened like a massive winged bird and closed at night or during inclement weather. Evan had visited there on a vacation a few years back, became captivated by the architecture and studied Santiago's projects. The thirty-five thousand works in the museum's collection on four floors encompassed art from the 15th century to the present, including work by Wisconsin native Georgia O'Keefe. But his favorite works were Fragonard, Rodin, Degas, Monet and Pissarro.

His final project required him to construct an addition to the museum, add a dining pavilion overlooking Lake Michigan and to create three design boards using India ink, Prisma markers and a tri-color fabric scheme. It took him nearly a month to draw the sketches and map out a to-scale rendering of the addition. When he completed the design boards, he was dumbstruck by his own talent. For someone who started school at Parsons without a sliver of known talent, he had discovered he could not only draw, but had a passion for architecture and design. Now graduating with an A.S. degree in Art History, he was befuddled with what he would do with that degree, much less his life.

Graduation, itself, was surreal. Aurora was unable to attend because she felt weak and tired. Her mother, Delfine, drove in from Long Island to spend time with her daughter. Danielle wasn't there—the only person he really wanted by his side. Evan's parents, Kelly and Baxter, flew in for the event, stayed at the Sheraton and took him to dinner after graduation. Kelly continued to offer herbal suggestions for Aurora's medical condition, as if she didn't want to concede to the reality of her impending death, and because she was afraid her demise would destroy Evan. Baxter was supportive, but concerned about Evan's probable move to St. Paul and future ability to earn a living.

After his parents returned to California, he retreated to his condo feeling desolate and anxious for a chat with Danielle. Because of the time difference, he waited until she'd be awake to reach her. To pass time, he made a pot of coffee, read the paper and listened to the news. He punched in her number on his cell.

"Evan! I'm so glad you called. I thought about you all day and wondered how your graduation went. I'm so proud of you."

"I appreciate that. I should feel elated, but I'm sort of numb and really tired."

"Of course you are. You've been under tremendous strain. What can I do?"

"Well, actually I thought of something *we* should do. Do you know what Skype is?"

"No, sorry. Should I?"

"It's a camera app that can be enabled on your computer. I have one on mine and then when we call each other, we can chat and see one another, as if we were in the same room together."

"Oh? That's really fascinating. I don't know much about computer technology. Kids in my classes know tons more than I do. Maybe Lucas could set that up for me. Dad has a computer in his office here at home, and I'm sure he'd let me use it. I can't believe you could actually see me when we talk!"

"It's pretty neat. I should have thought of that before. What's happening in your world?"

"Can you hold on a minute? My toast just popped up."

"Sure." Evan kicked off his slippers and rubbed his feet waiting for her to get back to their conversation. He could hear dishes clanking and the whistle of a teapot. Here he was in New York wishing he could have breakfast with her. A small pleasure to share a meal with the person he loved was one of those blessings he took for granted—especially now when he couldn't do these simple things with her.

"I'm worried about mama. Her doctor wants to install a pacemaker. He feels it will bring more oxygen to her blood and improve her strength."

"Is she feeling okay?" Evan asked with a worried tone in his voice.

"She's still in need of oxygen at times at night, and is weak. She tires easily and I'm constantly worried. I help her every morning, but with school now, I have to get up an hour earlier to ready her before I head to class."

"When would they want to hospitalize her for the procedure?"

"Hopefully next week," Danielle said in a frail voice.

"Don't worry, hon. I'm sure the doctor wouldn't recommend this if he didn't feel it would really be beneficial."

"Chloe thinks it's necessary and is very supportive of the idea. She hopes mama will be able to do without the oxygen."

"It sounds as if surgery could be helpful. Everything else okay?"

"Thor misses you. He paces around the yard and the guesthouse looking for you. He mopes. So do the kids. All three of your paintings are hanging in their rooms. Josh and Valentin keep asking me when you will be back, and I've told them it will take a couple of months. They're in school, and so are Amber and Juliette.

Valentin has a special tutor for his dyslexia, and we hope this will really help him this year."

"How's Gaspard? Anything new going on in the yachting business?"

"No. Not much. Ryan's been fully booked with clients, and papa is working too many hours. He seems rather agitated these days, but I don't know why."

"And Chloe?"

"She's been accepted for surgical nursing training."

"Hey, that's great. I'm happy for her. Tell her congrats for me. Next time I get bit by an eel, she can stitch me up herself." Evan laughed.

"Oh, sure. What a wacky sense of humor you have. You know how your diving incident scared me to death."

"Scared the crap out of me as well. I'm happy to stay out of the water for a long time, I promise. You sound a little pre-occupied. Is everything okay?"

"I'm fine, Evan. Just a little tired."

"Call you tomorrow. Let me know when you have the Skype device set up."

"I will. Seeing you will help. I just want to snuggle in your arms. I keep concentrating on the last days with you here in St. Paul and our time together in the guesthouse. Every night when I go to sleep I close my eyes and relive your kissing me," she sighed.

"And, I do the same. I remember your perfume—the soft touch of your skin—and a whole lot more. This is what gives me hope for the future."

"How's Aurora doing?" Danielle asked, the inflection and tone of her voice implied genuine concern.

"Not well. Of course she wanted to be at my graduation, but wasn't up to it. She's deteriorating quickly. It's hard for me to see her in this weakened condition. I've started organizing the upcoming art gallery showing, with her assistant, Belinda, and there's a lot I have to do to get ready for the event."

"As much as I want you here, I respect you for wanting to help make things as easy as possible for her." Danielle said.

"Just taking it day by day. I'm praying she won't suffer in agony. She's planning on going into hospice next week."

"Oh, I didn't remember this was happening so fast."

"Cancer seems to have its own schedule. They are upping her pain meds, but if they give her too much, it will hasten her death."

"I'm sorry, Evan. Really. I disliked her when I met her, especially under the circumstances, but knowing how much I love you, I can better appreciate how much she loved you too. I don't hate her for loving you or for the things she said to me. I feel sorry for her because she's dying. It's so sad. She won't have the life she had planned."

Evan could feel his throat constricting and emotions getting the better of him. He cleared this throat. "You have no idea how much this means to me, Danielle. Your kind heart is what drew me to you in the first place."

"Uh huh. Sure, that and my cute butt."

"Well, I didn't say it was only your heart."

They both laughed and Evan hung up the phone, grateful for their conversation but nonetheless, he still felt like he was standing on Jell-O.

CHAPTER 45

Danielle

Danielle woke early to help her mother with her routine. Now that school had begun, Danielle needed extra time with her mother before attending to her own lesson preparation. She crawled out of bed and had that uncomfortable woozy feeling again making her wonder if, in fact, she might be pregnant. Certainly, the smell of food made the idea of eating unappealing. She walked toward her shower, flipped on the water and noticed small spots of blood on the tile floor. With a huge sigh of relief, she raised her head toward the ceiling and thanked God for not making her pregnant. She grabbed some feminine protection, set it on the counter, and continued her morning bathing. After dressing she went to check on her mother.

Marie was struggling with breathing. The lack of necessary oxygen to her brain and muscles sapped her strength. Surely the pacemaker would help, but the idea of surgery terrified her. "Do you think I really should go through with this?" she asked Danielle, hoping for a different answer.

"Chloe highly recommends it. The doctor said it would alleviate your breathing difficulty, and reduce the swelling in your ankles. It will be okay, mama, don't worry." Danielle reached over and gave her mother a warm embrace of comfort.

"What can I fix you for breakfast, mama?"

"How about French toast with some syrup and berries."

"I'll be happy to make that for you. Let's get you showered and dressed first."

After they finished the morning routine, they headed to the kitchen, arm in arm, to help steady Marie's walking.

Danielle opened the refrigerator to get eggs, but had to turn her head away since the odors from the refrigerator made her stomach flip. She held on to the refrigerator door handle to steady herself. If she had her period, why did the smell of food make her nauseated? Perhaps it was the power of suggestion and just thinking about being pregnant. Marie glanced at Danielle and set her cranberry juice on the table. "Are you okay? You look pale."

"I'm fine mama. It might have been a bit of food poisoning. Don't worry, it will pass."

Danielle couldn't figure out what to eat because she wasn't hungry, but knew she couldn't manage a day at school with nothing in her stomach. She poured herself some dry cereal, added a bit of milk and sat at the kitchen table with her mother.

"How is Evan doing?" Marie inquired while pouring blueberry syrup on her fried egg-dipped French toast.

"Things are pretty hectic at the gallery, but he's through with school and did very well on his final examination projects. His parents flew in from California to be at his graduation."

"How nice. I hope to meet them someday," Marie said. "They must be very proud of their son."

"Evan told me one of his professors touted him at graduation for being so successful in the art world, even before he graduated. He's the envy of many students who only wish they could follow in his footsteps and achieve that kind fame.

Danielle then explained to her mother how the Skype app would work and how excited she was at the prospect of seeing Evan's face when they talked. She managed to down her cereal in small bites. After a deep breath, she felt like this meager breakfast would stay in her stomach. Thor was nudging her in the side of her leg, so she put down her bowl and let him lick up the last of the milk.

Marie continued to stare at her daughter, trying to discern what was different about her. Sullen one moment, elated the next. Perhaps normal for someone absent from the person she deeply loved. However, she felt Danielle was somehow distracted, as if she had something else on her mind, but decided not to pry, knowing Danielle would tell her in good time when she was ready.

After a quick hug and kiss atop her mother's head, Danielle scurried to the garage and got in her car, suddenly mindful that she'd forgotten her tote bag. She ran back to the house, lumbered up the stairs to her dressing table, gathered her bag and headed down the stairs, only to have miserable nausea overcome her again. She paused, fanning herself with her hand and touched her fingertips to her forehead. Her stomach cramped making her bend over to the point of forcing her to sit on the stairs while the room spun around her head.

Marie caught a glimpse of her daughter sitting on the stairs. "You're not at all well, darling. I'm not sure you should be going to school today. Should I call and ask them for a substitute?"

"No, mama. It's just my time of the month and I've got cramps. If I stopped doing things every time I had to deal with this annoying womanly episode, I'd never get anything done."

Marie smiled at her and did her best to restrain her concern. "Sometimes, we make quite a pair, don't we?"

Danielle laughed, hugged Marie one more time and left the house for school. She was looking forward to meeting her new students. It gave her such pleasure to to teach children and help them learn English. Not only was it gratifying to do something she was good at, it helped her miss Evan a bit less.

Hours later, near lunch time, Danielle felt so tired she thought she might have to sit in her car and take a short nap. She felt bloated and her breasts hurt—all signs of dealing with being a woman. Perhaps a quick nap would be a good idea. She grabbed a tuna sandwich, some potato chips and a diet soda from the school cafeteria and went to her car to have quiet lunch.

As soon as she opened the sandwich, the very smell of the tuna was ghastly. She felt the gag reflex, steadied her throat and forced herself to take slow, deep breaths. She quickly rewrapped the sandwich, opened the bag of potato chips and munched on those, downed with the soda. It was hard to concentrate. Her brain felt like tangles of glue. She decided to curl up for fifteen minutes and take a quick nap. Perhaps that would help. Because there was a nice breeze, she rolled down the windows a bit and then locked the car.

The sound of sirens frightened her awake, and an ambulance driver banging on the window confused her. Where was she? What was happening?"

"Can you open the door, sil vous plait?"

Danielle sat up, confused and noticed bloodstains on her skirt, which terrified her. She opened the door in a daze and glanced at her watch. She'd been asleep in the car for five hours. It was nearly four-thirty and she was horrified at her behavior. Where did her students think she had gone?

The ambulance attendant helped her out of the car and when she tried to stand, she merely saw flashes of light and then blacked out.

When she awoke, she was at the hospital in a private room with Chloe by her side, holding her hand.

"How did I end up here?" Danielle asked, unaware of being transported to the hospital.

"Apparently you went to your car and fell asleep for several hours. Your students were concerned because you did not return after lunch, so they contacted the school authorities and sent them looking for you. They checked other classrooms, the library and the grounds, but they couldn't find you. Mrs. Habersham, who is in charge of your school, said it was not like you to wander off. They were worried you'd been kidnapped or worse. She suggested looking for your car and she spotted it in the parking lot, peered inside and noticed you were asleep, pale as a white lily. She called to you and tried opening the door, but couldn't rouse you, so she called an ambulance."

"Oh, for heaven's sake. I'm so embarrassed. I don't know what's wrong with me. I remember now. I'm dealing with that female thing—got it this morning and felt like death. My stomach cramps were terrible. They're usually not this bad."

"We're running some tests, but I have my suspicions," Chloe said.

"Well, at least I'm not pregnant," Danielle stated emphatically. "I really have to go to the bathroom—my bladder is about to burst."

"Let me help you. I don't want you falling. You've fainted once already today."

"I did? I don't remember that at all."

"Trust me. You were limp like over-cooked noodles. I've washed the blood out of your skirt as best as I could."

Danielle leaned on Chloe's arm and made her way to the bathroom. When she finished, she was glad to have an empty bladder. There wasn't any more blood on her toilet tissue, which didn't make sense to her because by now she'd have regular flow. She let Chloe help her back to bed and had her raise the bed behind her head.

"I'm not in Nice at your hospital, am I? Danielle furrowed her brow.

"No. Mrs. Habersham called mama, who called me. I drove over from the hospital in Nice to be with you. There are plenty of nurses there to cover for me."

"Oh, no. Mama knows?"

"Danielle, you can't hide anything from her. You know mama. She has a sixth sense about her children. She knew you weren't well this morning, and she's very concerned about you."

"I didn't mean to be a bother. I'm sure it's just food poisoning or something."

"Do you feel like eating?"

"I'm famished. I couldn't eat much this morning, and I suppose that contributed to my fainting. How stupid of me."

"I'm going to get an IV going for you to balance your electrolytes, and then order you some broth. In the meantime, I want you to drink plenty of water," Chloe said and handed her a filled glass.

Danielle dutifully sipped water, set the empty glass down on the nightstand and bunched up her pillow to make her head more comfortable. Her eyes were glazed with fear.

"It's okay, Danielle. Whatever the situation is, we'll deal with it."

"I can't believe I'm pregnant—I mean, I don't want to be pregnant. Evan doesn't want children."

"Are you sure? He seemed to enjoy our family so much while he was staying with us."

"He might want a child one day, but I promised him I'd give him plenty of time to think about it. He hasn't even moved here yet and he would think I trapped him."

"Did you?" Chloe asked with her index finger on her chin while her eyebrows rose.

Before Danielle could answer, the duty nurse opened the door with a cart.

"Here's your broth," the nurse said and wheeled the tray's cart over her bed so she could eat.

"If I want a hamburger, can I have that too?" Danielle asked. "I'm surprisingly hungry enough to devour meat."

"After we finish some tests, we'll see. You're running a slight temperature. Are you cold?"

"Chilled. Can you bring me another blanket?" Danielle pulled the thin bed blanket under her chin.

"Of course," the nurse said. "I'll bring you a warm one," then she turned and left the room.

As if Chloe didn't miss a beat, she poked Danielle lightly in the arm for an answer.

"No, I didn't trap him. There was a tear in the condom. I saw it on the floor when I was putting the covers back on the bed, but I didn't tell Evan. We only had sex once, well, twice in the same day. I didn't want to alarm him about the tear in the condom, so I didn't mention it."

Chloe rubbed her forehead, and shook her head with her eyes narrowly focused on Danielle whose freckles stood out like scattered spots on a fawn. Her brown eyes pleaded for a different outcome—anything other than having a baby.

"I've gotta' run, sis. I'll tell mama and papa that you are doing well, and for them not to worry."

"I feel terrible. Mama's facing surgery and here I am in the hospital. It's all my fault. I love Evan so much. I wasn't thinking. I thought we did everything to be safe, and now this. It's not fair."

"Sometimes we have no control over what's fair, but we can gain strength from how we deal with it. Remember, no matter what, you're not alone in this. I'm here to support you and help you."

"I love you, Chloe." Danielle reached out her hand to her sister.

"Love you, too, Danielle." Chloe took Danielle's hand in both of hers and gave it a squeeze."I'll see you tomorrow. Dr. Bendick is your physician. He's nice. Said he'd stop by later tonight on his rounds. Call me if you want to talk."

Chloe got up, waived goodbye to Danielle and left the room.

Danielle glanced out the window and started chewing on the inside of her lip. This couldn't be happening. She made a mental note to call Mrs. Habersham in the morning and ask her to get a substitute, and to thank her for coming to her rescue.

After finishing her soup and a hamburger, courtesy of her attentive nurse, Danielle nodded off. Dr. Bendick stopped by, but Danielle was asleep and he decided not to wake her. The news of her condition could wait until morning.

CHAPTER 46

Gaspard and Lucas

The morning after Lucas' failed attempt at clandestine surveillance, Gaspard called him at his office anxious to learn how the evening went.

"Dad? Give me a second. I'll go outside." Lucas took his cell phone and went to the patio for privacy. He stared at his lavender production fields in full bloom with bees buzzing from flower to flower, creating a frenzy of collecting nectar. Lucas found a wooden bench in the gravel courtyard and sat down with a sullen look on his face.

"Dad, I'm not sure I'm cut out for this. I lingered there in the dark, as far back as I could on the street so I could see Ryan's driveway. It was bloody hot in the car—spilled coffee all over myself and then had to sit there in wet pants. Stunk."

Gaspard laughed but tried to do so in a manner that wasn't punitive.

"Did you see Ryan?"

"Nada. Didn't know if he was home. Please, if I do this again, you'll have to call him at home phone first. Make up some concern about a problem at the office. Then, if he's at home, call me on my cell and at least we'll both know where he is."

"Agreed. Good plan. Smart thinking. Sorry I sent you on a stakeout without knowing his whereabouts."

"The worst of it was having the gun on the floor. I stuffed it in a paper bag, but it terrified me. Then, this elderly couple walked past the car and I had to slide down on the seat to hide, and thought I'd stop breathing. Have you considered hiring a private detective? Someone trained? I suck at this."

"I had," Gaspard responded. "But, I don't want to risk getting another person involved. Calls can be traced. I don't

218

want to go to the police because they have their own suspicions about Ryan. If I mention I'm concerned about drugs or stolen money, it will feed into their investigation. It gives Ryan motive."

"You mean for Armond's murder?" Lucas spat out the words and rubbed his forehead.

"Maybe Armond found out Ryan was somehow involved with drugs. It would make sense, as ludicrous as it sounds. I'm not raising a flag to the police. If I tell them what I'm thinking, it will only confirm what's already on their mind."

"Do you think they might be trailing Ryan at night?"

"Maybe. They've not conveyed this to me. Could you manage to do at least one more stakeout?"

"Dad, do I have to? I'm so busy at work right now. We're getting ready to harvest for the season. Perfume needs to be made, soap, and many other products. You know this. I'm swamped."

"Yes, of course. If you work late, like 1:00 in the morning, it would be perfect timing. You could head over to Ryan's."

"Dad, I need to sleep at night. I was a zombie at work after being at the stakeout.

"Son, please. I need your help. You can sleep the rest of your life."

Gaspard could hear Lucas kicking pebbles with his shoe during a moment of silence.

Lucas finally said, "If you insist, I'll do it. I'm wearing decent duds and I'm taking your car. You drive mine to work. Didn't enjoy that codger smacking his cane on my car or being called a pig."

"Understood. I don't want you in danger, so please take the gun."

"I don't think anything's going to happen. Ryan's been your partner now for sometime, and he's done nothing but help you run the best charter yachting business in the Côte. I can't understand why he'd put himself at risk, and our company as well. After all, it's his company too."

"That's what causes me the most angst. Imagine what it's like for me to work with him and have these unsettling thoughts? It's given me heartburn more than once." Gaspard rubbed his chest in sympathy for the bile gurgling in his stomach.

"I'm sure it's hard to work with someone you don't trust. If I didn't trust my employees, I couldn't work with them. Once someone breaks my trust, it's nearly impossible to get it back," Lucas added.

"I'm trying to give him the benefit of the doubt, but I'm not stupid either. I built this business into what it is. Ryan has helped, but I'll be damned if anyone takes me for a fool."

"Understood. Dad, hang on. I've gotta take another call."

Gaspard grabbed a bottle of whiskey with one hand, cradled the phone between his shoulder and his ear and poured himself a drink, then settled in a chair in his library. He stirred the ice cubes with his finger and waited for Lucas to respond.

"Okay. I'll try another surveillance later tonight. I'll go home, have dinner, get the Luger and put it in my briefcase. Does mama know about this?"

"No, and don't tell her. She's under enough stress with this pacemaker thing. I'm not going to upset her. She'd never let me put you in this position, but I can't do it myself. Too many people would recognize me. If Ryan saw me outside his apartment complex in the middle of the night, he'd be wary. I'd be forced to confront him. What would I say? I don't have any evidence to back up my suspicions."

"True." Lucas sucked in saliva over his teeth.

"Don't want to do that. He'd deny everything. Then he'd stop doing whatever he's doing and we'd never know what's going on. If he put the company at risk, I need to know about it."

"All right. Makes sense." Lucas sighed in defeat. "I'll report back tomorrow morning."

"I'm thinking," Gaspard sipped his drink and paused. "On the off chance you do see Ryan and tail him, call me. If he's headed to the Marina, I can be out of bed in no time and meet you there."

"What will you tell mama, if she asks?"

"Don't know. I'll make something up about forgetting to lock the front door at work."

Lucas clicked off his phone, shook his head in disbelief, and went back to his office. He thought about how persuasive his father could be. As much as he hated the idea of another stakeout, he didn't want to let his father down.

CHAPTER 47

Danielle and Chloe

Danielle tried to rub her eyes and realized one arm was hooked up to an IV. Where was she? For a moment, she'd forgotten. The smell of antiseptic was overwhelming. She glanced at her watch sitting on the nightstand. It was eight in the morning. Had she slept that soundly? Then she remembered everything, including the night nurse giving her a mild sedative.

She rubbed sleep out of her eye with her free hand. With a deft maneuver, she managed to untangle herself from the IV and swing her legs off the side of bed, grateful the railing was down. Besides having a full bladder, she was still wobbly and decided to call for a nurse. She stood up and held on to the IV pole in something less than a nightgown, shamefully open at the back. Her exposed derriere made her blush.

The door swung open. "Ah, you're up," the nurse said. "Let me help you so you don't fall. I'm Claudine."

Danielle smiled. She recalled a movie star with that name from watching old movies years ago.

As soon as Danielle finished in the bathroom, Claudine guided her back to bed and took her vitals. "Fever's down. That's good, but it's not gone."

"Do you know what's wrong with me?" Danielle stared at the nurse's rosy cheeks and the smile lines around her pale blue eyes.

"No, I'm sorry. Dr. Bendick's making rounds. He'll be here shortly. How are you feeling?"

"Unsteady, weak. I've never been sick like this before."

"Your sister, I'm sorry, I've forgotten her name, said she would call your school to arrange for a substitute teacher."

Danielle cringed and closed her eyes. "Chloe. She's a nurse."

"That's wonderful. Does she live at home with you?"

"Yes. There's so much going on right now. My mother's having pacemaker surgery. Lousy time for me to be in the hospital causing everyone all this distress."

"Don't be so hard on yourself." Claudine hooked up another bag of IV fluid and adjusted the flow.

The door swung open. Chloe burst in with a bouquet of peach and yellow roses. "Morning, Danielle. How are you feeling?"

"Weak, but better. Concerned because I'm still spotting. Ate a burger before bedtime and it stayed in my stomach. I slept well, due to a sleeping pill of some sort."

"Morning, ladies." Dr. Bendick appeared in the doorway with his wire-rimmed glasses perched on the edge of his nose and a stethoscope around his neck. His wavy brown hair tinged with strands of grey made him look scholarly.

Chloe moved out of the way, put the vase of flowers on the windowsill and took a seat.

"Do you know what's wrong with me?" Danielle bit her lip.

Dr. Bendick pulled up a chair and sat next to the bed and motioned for Claudine to leave the room. He moved his glasses further up his nose with his finger and flipped through a set of X-rays. "You don't need to worry," he patted her arm. "You had a ruptured ovarian cyst." The taciturn doctor set the X-rays on the bed and didn't offer more information.

Chloe leaned forward and slapped the top of her thigh. "That explains everything— the abdominal pain, cramps and bleeding."

"Well, not exactly," Dr. Bendick noted.

"Do I need surgery?" Danielle pulled the sheet tighter to her chest.

"No. The cyst will shrivel and pass on its own. We were worried you might have an ectopic pregnancy where the fertilized egg becomes attached to the fallopian tube instead of the uterine lining. That's not your case, so you don't need surgery."

"Thank God!" Danielle turned her head and smiled at Chloe. "See? I'm going to be okay."

"Yes," said Dr. Bendick. "You should have a normal pregnancy."

"What?" Her jaw dropped. Danielle glared at Dr. Bendick.

"You're pregnant. If you take it easy, everything should be fine." Dr. Bendick's glasses slid back to the tip of his nose. His right hand fingered his stethoscope in a matter-of-fact way while he looked at her with his dark brown eyes and waited for her to say something.

Danielle's face remained frozen. Her vocal cords were stuck in disbelief.

Chloe put her fingers to her lips and bit back words that once spoken could hurt her relationship with her sister. She stared at Dr. Bendick waiting for him to break the tension. Finally, he reached over and grabbed the X-rays.

"I'll come back and check on you a little later. Eat something if you're hungry. I want you to stay here a few more days until you get your strength back." Dr. Bendick stood, checked Danielle's chart on his mini laptop, nodded and walked toward the door. "Better stay off your feet for a few days," he said in a cautionary tone. He then gave a slight finger wave to both women and left the room.

Chloe got up from the chair against the wall and took the seat next to Danielle's bed. She reached for her sister's hand. "It's going to be okay."

Danielle said nothing, heaved a sigh and shook her head. She stared at her feet and twisted the sheet in her hands.

Chloe waited and let air hang in silence to fill the gaps in their conversation.

Finally, Danielle blurted out in a strident tone. "I can't tell Evan!"

"Why not?" Chloe soothed her sister's frustration by caressing her forearm with the tips of her fingers.

"He doesn't want children, remember? He'll think I did this on purpose."

"You're thinking for him—you don't know what he'd say."

"I'm worried he'll never leave New York. I promised him I'd give him time to consider having a family." Danielle sat up and pulled her knees up to her chest.

"Well, this gives him about eight months." Chloe pushed out her bottom lip and raised her eyebrows. "You know, you don't have to go through with this. You didn't plan it. You're already in the hospital. You could take care of it."

"It's not an *it*. It's a growing baby." Danielle snapped at Chloe.

"Of course. I didn't mean to sound harsh. There's no need to throw your future away."

Chloe let her hand slide away from Danielle's arm and could see tears starting to brim in her sister's eyes. "Take some time to think about it. If you're so afraid Evan won't leave New York because you're pregnant, then maybe you don't want this baby now. You can always decide to have children later—when he's ready."

Danielle's chest started to heave but she held back her emotions. She refused to submit to a torrent of tears. At the moment she felt more rage than sadness, partly at her sister, but mostly at her own reckless behavior.

"Chloe, I love and respect you. I know you're talking to me as a nurse and not as my sister. I'll think about all of this. However, I love Evan. This baby is part of him. Whether he decides he could love me, this child is a risk I'm willing to take. However, I don't intend to tell him."

"What?" Chloe stood and put her hands on her hips. Her face registered a blank stare of frustration.

"I'm not telling Evan just yet. With all that's gone on here, I could lose the baby. If that happens, it's God's will."

"I think that's a mistake—not telling Evan." Chloe frowned and pursed her lips tightly in frustration. "It's your decision. Just take care of yourself. I'll let you rest now. By the way, everything's fine at school. Your sub started today and can be there as long as needed." Chloe picked up her purse and started toward the door.

"Chloe?" Danielle's face registered fear.

"Yes?"

"Don't you dare tell mama about the baby. You hear me?"

"Okay, okay. I'll let you do that. We'll get mama through her surgery. You decide when to tell her."

"Thanks for the flowers, sis." Danielle tried to manage a slight smile.

Chloe nodded, turned and walked out the door.

CHAPTER 48

Lucas

Lucas found a different spot to park the Mercedes. He had a good view of Ryan's garage entrance through the front windshield. A dimly lit frosted glass light post stood at the corner; his rearview mirror reflected the street scene behind him. If that elderly couple walked the sidewalks at night, they'd likely show up again, and he was not going to have another encounter with them.

He glanced at his watch, noted it was past midnight, adjusted his sunglasses, and waited. The gradient tint in his glasses allowed him to see well enough at night, and although he wished he didn't have to wear them, he couldn't risk being recognized. Thunder rumbled in the distance with flashes of heat lightning. It felt like rain. The linen suit he sat in felt damp. Determined to stay awake, he now wished he hadn't had so many cups of coffee. The briefcase sat on the seat next to him with the gun stuffed in a bubble-wrap mailing envelope tucked under a newspaper.

His phone pinged. Startled, he took it out of his breast pocket. Gaspard had sent him a text. *Ryan home. Asked him to cover for me at work. Taking Marie to the hospital tomorrow. Good excuse. U okay?*

Lucas texted back. *Good here. Watching. Nothing yet. Text U later.*

Before he put the phone back in his pocket he noticed the battery level was low so he turned it off. He wished he'd remembered to charge his phone at work. He settled in, sank down in the leather seat and waited. Thunder moved closer and rain spotted the windshield. He started the engine to roll up the windows and humidity engulfed him. The car felt like a coffin. He opened the briefcase, took out the newspaper and fanned himself. The coach light outside Ryan's garage gave off an amber glow in the distance, a faint light in the darkness. Rain clouds hid the moon.

What started as a drizzle turned into pelting rain. Lucas' bladder bulged in discomfort. Where did guys on a stakeout pee? He thought about getting out of the car to relieve himself but dreaded getting soaked.

A car came up the street from the rear. He glanced in the rearview mirror and held his breath. The car drove past and paid no attention to him. Probably couldn't see him because of the rain. He shifted in his seat and leaned into the headrest. Minutes seemed like hours with nothing to do but observe.

His thoughts wandered from problems at work to a girl he liked, but had no time to pursue. He hoped his mother would be better after the operation. Concerns about his father fretting over Ryan bothered him. Knowing Danielle was still in the hospital with a recent medical scare was a lot to deal with. At least he'd recently moved back home—that was a good thing. It gave him more time to spend with his younger siblings. He thought of how dutifully Chloe had stepped in to take care of mom in Danielle's absence. Another quick glance at his watch. One-thirty. Time moved slowly when he had nothing to do but think—and wait. He set the newspaper on the passenger seat with the briefcase. When he looked up he saw the garage door opening. A car was coming out.

His pulse quickened. He thought, *Let it be Ryan. No, please don't let it* be...

Rain came down in sheets, the wind blowing and slapping water sideways. He grabbed the newspaper as a foil and took off his glasses because he couldn't see a damn thing. The BMW edged closer to him. Despite the rain, he cupped his hand around the left side of his face and caught a glimpse of the driver through his windshield. Oh my god, it was Ryan. *"Damn!"* he said under his breath and clenched his teeth, frustrated he'd have to follow Ryan.

He waited a few minutes before starting the engine and then turned the car around so quickly he nearly knocked over a trashcan. The wipers were on full tilt when he got to the corner. Which way had Ryan turned? A flash of lightning illuminated the road. He caught sight of the BMW after another car passed. Ryan was heading up the coast. Intermittent lightning and blurred red taillights made it difficult to follow Ryan's car from a safe distance. Not many cars on the road because of the storm. Sand blew across the highway splattering the windshield. The wipers scraped and groaned slapping sand back and forth. Lucas gripped the steering wheel with determination coupled with fear. Where was Ryan going? Oh hell, he was heading to the marina.

He stayed at a safe distance and let Ryan pull into the parking lot. Sweat drizzled down his neck and adrenalin raced through his body. He pulled in alongside a storage shed where he could still see Ryan's car. He watched him get out with a slicker over his head and run to the dock.

Lucas waited. He knew he'd have to follow him. "Shit!" He had to pee so badly it hurt. "Hells bells," he grumbled and sat there, bladder muscles clenched so tightly they might burst.

Ryan got into a recognizable X250 skiff, started the motor and headed out to one of the larger yachts. Lucas watched from a distance and waited. Whitecap angry waves were rolling in, slamming into the bow of Ryan's skiff, but Ryan still motored ahead out to sea.

Lucas got out of the car, peed on the spot and let the warm liquid run down his pants. Searching for a secluded location to relieve his bladder was not an option. Urine soaked pants were the least of his problems. What about the gun? "Stupid briefcase," he said to himself. "Not carrying a briefcase and nowhere to put the gun." He left it in the car, locked it and headed toward the pier with his hand cupped around his forehead in an attempt to shield his eyes from the rain.

Now soaked, he ran down the pier, found a skiff and started the motor. It chugged and spit, but started. Lucas was grateful the harbormaster at this marina left motors on the skiffs for owners to get to their boats after hours. In the distance, he saw Ryan's skiff reach the yacht. He heard the yacht's engine rumble and then the yacht started to pull away.

Lucas took off his jacket, threw it on the floor of the boat. He brushed rain from his dripping curly hair and hunkered down in the skiff. The storm had lessened. Lightning now flashed in the distance as the storm moved inland. He left the beam lights off and followed the yacht at a safe distance staying out of the wake. A rogue wave bounced off the bow. It flipped him forward into the control panel and he banged his head hard on the steering wheel. It knocked him off balance and sent him backwards to the floor while the skiff motored on its own, bumping and bouncing waves in the sea. Winded, he crawled back up, grabbed the wheel and steadied the skiff. His clothes were covered in mud and water. He reached up with one hand and felt a throbbing lump on his head. Drops of blood slid down the side of his face washed with rain and trickled into his mouth. How big a gash? Stitches? No time to think about that now.

His heart pounded in wild thumps. Then Ryan's yacht stopped. Lucas shut off his motor and waited. The boat tossed around like a buoy with a broken anchor. Why had Ryan stopped? Lucas sat on the seat, held the steering wheel and waited. What was that in the distance next to Ryan's yacht? A whale breeching? Something monstrous was rising out of the water! Lucas strained to see what was happening and wished he'd brought binoculars. What the hell? Merde! It was a strange looking submarine.

He watched it surface, but just to the deck level. It was enormous. He heard voices but couldn't understand the words. A flashlight beamed from the sub to the yacht. Something tossed—a box or a bag. Then the sub started to submerge into the deep as if it was never there in the first place. Lucas heard the yacht's engines start. Ryan was moving the yacht. What to do now?

Lucas' whole body shook, soaking-wet cold and terrified. If Ryan turned the yacht in his direction, he might see him lurking in the water. Good time to silently pray. *Please, God. Make him turn the yacht around and move away from me. I can't start the engine—he'll hear me, then see me...or worse, he'll run into me. Shit! This can't be happening. Sucks, sucks. Nothing to do but wait.*

The yacht moved out to sea a bit further, made a wide arc in a different direction and headed back to shore. The wake moved a cascade of waves toward the skiff. Lucas sat motionless, lulling from side to side, waiting. He shivered violently. The yacht was now a good distance away from him. He calculated they had been several kilometers out—maybe more.

Fog drifted across the water obscuring the lights on the shore. Lucas patted his head wound. It felt crusty but didn't seem to be bleeding. Gaspard would be shocked, and probably angry, to hear about all of this. He reached for his cell phone. No battery. In the rush, he'd forgotten he'd turned it off. Although he'd promised to call Gaspard if he spotted Ryan heading to the marina, there wasn't time. He hoped his father would understand. Time to go home.

He tried to start the engine. It turned over, sputtered but didn't start. He tried it again—nothing. The skiff's fuel gauge light was on. He was out of gas. What now? The boat was floating aimlessly, rocking to and fro. The tide would bring him closer to shore. He'd have to wait until morning—until someone else saw him. He picked up his wet jacket, slapped it against the side of the boat like a madman until much of the water dissipated. He curled up on a seat cushion, threw the jacket over his chest and stared at the engulfing fog. He'd miss work. He couldn't call in. No one knew where he was. He was never doing a stakeout again, ever.

CHAPTER 49

Gaspard

Something was wrong. He felt it. Terrible dread—a sense of overwhelming guilt. He shouldn't have sent Lucas on a stakeout—not once, but twice. Why hadn't Lucas called him last night? One way or the other, a call would have been nice. *"No, I didn't see Ryan" or "I'm tailing him..."* What had happened?

It was almost five in the morning and Lucas wasn't home. Gaspard stood in the kitchen, nerves rattled, sipping a freshly made cup of coffee. Grey skies added to his inner gloom. He paced the floor barefoot not sure what to think. Chloe would be getting up soon to help Marie ready herself. Today, of all days, Marie had to have surgery. If only the surgery were tomorrow—he could bolt from the house and drive over to Ryan's. Was the Mercedes still parked outside somewhere near Ryan's apartment? Where the hell was Lucas?

Gaspard tried not to have terrible thoughts—Lucas hurt somewhere. Chills filled his body despite the warmth of the hot coffee in his mouth.

He'd tried calling Lucas on his cell. No response now and nothing last night. Gaspard feared the worst—Lucas might be dead.

Chloe entered the kitchen dressed for work. "Morning, Chloe." Gaspard managed a weak smile.

"Hi dad. Everything okay?" You look frazzled.

"Ah—worried about the surgery today."

"She'll be fine. Simple procedure." Chloe poured herself a cup of coffee.

"What time's the operation?" Gaspard turned toward her.

"Eleven." Chloe stared at the wall clock. "I'll come by the hospital in St. Paul this afternoon. Another nurse is covering my shift at the hospital in Nice.

"Great." Gaspard nodded and grabbed a croissant.

I'll get mom ready." Chloe grabbed a peach and took a bite.

"How's she doing?" Gaspard absently slathered jam on a croissant.

"Nervous. Scared."

"Take good care of her." Gaspard put his hand on her shoulder.

"Of course, dad. Don't worry."

Chloe left the room. The absence of noise and complete silence forced Gaspard back to reality. Unable to eat the croissant, he decided to shower and dress. He heard his phone buzzing in the bedroom—the other room he'd slept in for over a year so that Marie could rest comfortably. The gurgling of oxygen tubes kept him awake, and his snoring bothered her. His bare feet slapped against the floor tiles as he ran to his phone.

"Hello?"

"It's Jack. We've got your son."

"What? Where?"

"Did my Maritime Gendarmerie run this morning and found him."

"Gaspard felt his throat constrict in panic. "Where was he?"

"In a skiff. Not far from the marina. Ran out of gas."

"Is he—?"

"He's fine. Cold, annoyed, embarrassed."

"Can I talk to him?" Gaspard let out a sigh of relief and sank down on the side of the bed.

"Daaad?" His strained voice broke.

"You okay?"

'Yeah. Fine. Pissed."

"Where are you?"

"Marina. Car's here. I'm coming home. I'll explain everything."

Gaspard clicked off his phone. He sat on the edge of the bed, hung his head and thanked God. Lucas was alive. He didn't feel less guilty, but he was grateful.

Sometimes one got a second chance after doing something stupid. He was never going to put Lucas in danger again.

CHAPTER 50

Evan

He dialed Danielle's number a second time—no answer. What the heck? Had she lost her phone? Two days without talking to her. It made him nervous. He had Chloe's number and decided to try that.

"Chloe?" He pulled at his earlobe.

"Oh, hi Evan. How are you?"

"I can't reach Danielle. Her phone is off or something."

"Uh…let me take this call outside."

"Did I catch you at a bad time?"

"No. Just getting mama ready. Hang on a minute."

Chloe excused herself, set Marie in a chair and went outside. "Danielle's in the hospital," she said, her voice barely above a whisper.

"What?" Evan felt his heart skip a beat.

"She, um, had an ovarian cyst burst. She's fine. Should be home tomorrow."

Evan tried to take in the information about Danielle. He felt as if someone had siphoned the blood from his veins.

"Here's the number at the hospital. You can call her there. She's in room 105."

"Thanks, Chloe. " Evan clicked off his phone and sat there numb.

The very idea of Danielle being in the hospital was overwhelming. The long-distance aspect of their relationship was difficult enough. With her facing medical issues, he felt helpless. More than anything, he wanted to comfort her—be with her—hold her. He felt his world was collapsing around him, like quicksand sucking at his feet, then his waist, moving up his neck making it hard to breathe.

Aurora had a very bad day and was struggling in hospice. She missed the art gallery showing, which she had hoped she could attend. Emaciated now, she couldn't eat, and couldn't swallow without excruciating pain. So many machines hooked up to her, monitoring her pain medication, her nutrition, her breathing.

He'd spent much of the day with her yesterday—reading a book, filling her in on the details of the gallery showing and watching her sleep. Even in her sleep, she groaned in agony. Most likely she wouldn't last the month. Watching a vibrant, spunky, determined woman evaporate before his eyes was anguish he'd never experienced—a feeling of complete and utter helplessness. Aurora's parents rented a furnished apartment close to the hospital so they could be with her every day. For that, he could be thankful.

Drexel, Aurora's father, took a leave of absence from his company. Delfine, devastated by her daughter's illness, put her psychiatric practice on hold, grateful to have had a renowned business partner to handle her patients. Seeing Aurora's intense suffering made thinking about Danielle being in the hospital even worse.

Evan had not expected to learn more about Aurora's parents under these devastating circumstances. It was odd, in a way, to spend time with them in the hospital, reminiscing about Aurora's childhood, their vacations during the summers on Long Island when she was young, how much she enjoyed swimming and playing with their dogs. It was as if he learned more about her from her parents than he ever knew while dating her. He knew about her love of art, but didn't know she liked country music, nor did he know she was a sci-fi movie fan. Much of their dating centered around activities he liked. He'd assumed she enjoyed classical music because he'd taken her to the symphony on several occasions. Since she had a cat, he thought she didn't like dogs. Listening to Delfine describe Aurora's childhood was insightful and painful at the same time. He never knew she was petrified of heights, nor was he aware she hated broccoli. How often had he fixed that vegetable for her when he made her dinner at his condo? She never complained. He thought people hated brussel sprouts.

A person he loved, who he didn't know as well as he thought, was slipping away. Perhaps had he not met Danielle, his life would have been different. Either way, he'd be in the same place now, dealing with her impending death. He felt guilty about not marrying her—what stopped him? He wasn't sure. Marriage didn't seem important. Being on the rising artist success circuit, all the publicity, all the drama, the parties—it consumed him. They'd been happy with each other. Life was simple, wildly exciting and fulfilling. Flashbacks of their colorful life flooded him while he watched her in the hospital, while he tried to sleep at night—eyes closed reliving their time together. To his surprise, when he broke down, the tears were about letting her go. Someone he had loved was dying and there was nothing he could do about it. Dying was part of life. He hated it—hated Ashley dying, and now Aurora.

CHAPTER 51

Gaspard

Lucas spent half the morning explaining the events of the previous evening. Gaspard listened intently to Lucas' story, yelled at him periodically about not calling him when he started tailing Ryan and was bewildered to find out about the submarine. Although Gaspard rarely swore, he'd let out a string of words in French. He was more than upset—angry he'd put his son in danger and galled by whatever Ryan was doing. The gash in Lucas' head made him cringe; he'd have to come up with a plausible explanation to tell Marie.

It was now obvious Ryan was involved with drugs. What else could have been in those packages tossed from the submarine to the yacht? In other countries Gaspard had heard of subs running drugs, but he never thought of sub transport in the Côte—and certainly, he never thought Ryan, his partner, the person he trusted, would deceive him. What drove someone to take such risks? Did Ryan not think he'd be caught? Gaspard shook his head thinking about people who ended up in prison. Most criminals in prison didn't expect to get caught. Were those who did end up in the slammer careless? Fearless? Maybe they were just desperate.

Gaspard had his car washed on the way to the hospital. Sand was everywhere...under the wipers, on the grill, under the hood. What a night Lucas must have had in the storm. Gaspard shuddered at the thought, then decided he'd visit Danielle first, then Marie. How odd both his wife and daughter would be in the hospital at the same time. Life was strange. At least Marie didn't see Lucas' head wound.

He watched Chloe earlier this morning help Marie to her car—her breathing labored, her strength minimal. They drove away. He considered Marie might not return home—that wasn't likely because Chloe said it was a *simple* surgery. Nothing to worry about. *Simple* was not supposed to end in death.

Gaspard was a worrier—he accepted his flaw. He felt if he worried himself into a frenzy, things would turn out okay. Something about his own mother's way of telling him that was how she handled life. If one didn't worry, one was not prepared for disaster. When you worried, you considered the worst. You expected things to go wrong. It was a way of cushioning yourself against the inevitable. Things you could not control.

Danielle worried him too. He knew how much she wanted to be with her students. He had raised her to be different—less afraid of life than he was at her age. She'd be okay. She had to be. Her whole life was ahead of her. How could he not worry about two women he deeply loved? His thoughts shifted to Lucas, his son, willing to play detective and put himself at risk. What if Ryan was a murderer? Drugs were probably the reason Armond was murdered, but how would he prove it?

He remembered the day he first met Ryan. He was at the marina. Ryan was coming in with his yacht at the same time he was mooring *Belle Chloe.* They admired each other's yachts and struck up a conversation that led to lunch and a partnership. Ryan had been living up the coast, closer to Monte Carlo, but wanted to join a yachting company. Said he'd worked in yachting for years in California, was a mechanic, raced sailboats and liked the marketing side of the business. Odd as it was, Gaspard recalled he had been thinking of expanding and adding a partner. He'd been so busy with clients and the day-to-day operations of running the company, he'd had little time to do any marketing.

In retrospect now, he wondered if Ryan had overheard yacht club gossip. Others knew he was looking for a partner. The fact that Ryan was willing to add his own yacht to the fleet and put one-hundred grand into the business made the deal seem too good to be true. He was struck by Ryan's good looks and laid-back personality, his knowledge of yachting and zest for making Gaspard Yachting the largest in the Côte. Should he have checked references? Sure. Hindsight. However, the day they became business partners all that mattered to him was his own life had suddenly become easier.

As Gaspard drove to the hospital, he thought of Evan and wished he were here. Danielle had shared, in confidence, that Evan had been a cop, and his sister had been killed. A tragedy so horrible, it made Gaspard wince to think about it. Perhaps he'd call Evan—bounce a few things off of him. After all, Evan had spent time with Ryan. They had scuba dived together, which had not gone well for Evan, but Ryan had saved his life. Odd to think about this dichotomy—a business partner who could have killed Armond and yet saved Evan. What kind of person did that? Didn't make sense. Giving Ryan the benefit of the doubt gnawed at him, made his stomach knot, his head throb, and made him very angry. How could someone be so duplicitous?

CHAPTER 52
Three Month's Later

Aurora passed away earlier than expected. Her parents hoped she would have more time, and so did Evan, but it was not to be.

In the end, she was barely conscious and slipped away peacefully. Evan was by her bedside, along with her parents. He attended the church funeral and burial ceremony with his parents who flew out from California, stayed with Evan for a few days and then returned home. Evan was surprised when asked by Aurora's attorney to attend the reading of her Will. To his amazement, she had given him part of the proceeds from the gallery sale. She had written a secret letter to Evan, before she became deathly ill, and had contacted a gallery in St. Paul. They agreed to show Evan's work, which stunned him. Her final words to Evan were about how much she loved him, wished him happiness with his art and his life with Danielle.

For months after her death, Evan was not himself. He moped. He drank. He ate junk food. He put one foot in front of the other, walked the streets late at night, and bided his time until he could move to St. Paul.

Evan's condo went on the market after Aurora's last gallery showing. Because his condo was attractively priced, he received several over-market offers.

Danielle had recovered from her medical scare, returned to school and was delighted with her students. Her frequent Skype chats with Evan resulted in his finding a two-bedroom house, in St. Paul, with a lease option to purchase. He hired a moving firm, packed and crated his personal belongings and had his paintings sent to St. Paul, temporarily housed in storage there.

Marie's pacemaker surgery was so successful she no longer required assistance in the morning. She'd even taken up yoga and found a friend to join her on walks around the hills in their neighborhood. With plenty of natural oxygen carring red blood cells to her muscles, she was stronger. Her skin color, according to Danielle, was no longer pallid. It was as if Marie had been given a reason to try everything new. Not burdened with having her children care for her, she got up mornings, whipped up pancakes, eggs and bacon for her family, then downed fruit and yogurt for herself. She joined a book club, gardened and did things she used to do when she was much younger. It took at least a month for Danielle to stop asking if her mother was really up to doing all of this herself.

All was well, except for issues with Ryan. Evan learned from Danielle what Lucas had gone through tailing Ryan. Gaspard had called Evan to bounce his concerns off someone who understood his frustration and ask for his help. He ultimately decided, based on Evan's advice, to wait until he moved to St. Paul to deal with Ryan. In the meantime, Ryan acted as if nothing was wrong, continued working and added clients to the business. He had many successful charters and no further incidents of bizarre over-payments.

Gaspard found it unnerving and challenging to work with Ryan daily, disturbed and suspicious about Ryan's clandestine drug activities. The only thing keeping Gaspard sane was his belief in Evan's detective skills for how they would deal with Ryan. It was a plan he could wait for, however agonizing it was not to pursue this immediately. Ryan had made no inappropriate entries in the computer ledger spreadsheets, so Gaspard watched and waited for a slip-up—something he could observe directly. He believed someone who had something to hide eventually made a mistake.

CHAPTER 53

Evan and Danielle

"Do you want me to pick you up at the airport?" Danielle asked with her phone on speaker, volume up high. Her phone sat on her dresser while she brushed out her hair in her mirror.

"No, sweetie. I'll rent a car. Going to need to buy one shortly anyway."

"Can't even believe you're going to be here—living here." Danielle said with as much enthusiasm as a giddy child. She sprayed a bit of cologne behind her ears and wrists.

"It's been so long since I've held you." Evan said.

"I should warn you—I've, uh, put on a little weight. Sort of chunky around the middle from all the food I ate while you were gone," Danielle sighed and gently patted her abdomen, now alive with a growing baby.

"Me too. All the stress from Aurora's death—and the move, it's been exhausting, but this will be everything I've waited for. We'll be so good together."

"Love you. Call me when you get in. Just drive to my house. I'll be here."

"Know the way—can't wait. This is really happening."

Danielle clicked off her phone. Evan would be there shortly. She stood in front of the door's full-length mirror and raised her gauzy tunic, enough camouflage to cover her pregnancy. How long could she keep this a secret? Since she wasn't showing more than a rounder tummy and fuller face, she intended to tell him about the baby—just not yet. She felt good now—no morning sickness. Eating for two, she gobbled up everything that appealed to her.

Dr. Bendick referred her to a skilled OB/GYN, who recommended vitamins, moderate exercise and plenty of fresh veggies and fruit. She'd taken up swimming on a regular basis and had acquired a golden bronze tan. A pair of trendy baggy cargo pants went well with her flowing top, seemingly concealing her secret. Even her mother didn't know of Danielle's pregnancy, courtesy of loose fitting clothing and a ruffle skirted bathing suit when she swam. Only Chloe, who remained her trustworthy sister, knew her secret.

Danielle picked at the inside of her thumb until it was raw. Nerves. Giddy nerves. Worried nerves. She knew she'd have to tell Evan when the time was right. When would that be? Too rattled to read or watch TV, she grabbed homemade tea from the refrigerator, added ice cubes topped with a slice of lemon and decided to sit on the veranda and wait for Evan.

Marie finished doing laps in the pool and shouted to Danielle from the pool's edge. "Hey. Do you think I should make something for Evan to eat when he gets here? Or, do you want to go out?"

"I want to go out, mama. Haven't seen him in so long. Don't bother with food, okay? And, I probably won't be home tonight."

"Sure. I understand." Marie dipped under the water and continued a slow, deliberate stroke barely making waves in the pool.

The unmistakable sounds of the gates opening and tires crunching on gravel made Danielle bolt from her chair. The glass of ice tea spilled onto the grass. She heard Evan turn off the ignition. He shut the car door and spotted Danielle, now running toward him with her arms outstretched.

He ran to her. They embraced, kissed long lingering wet deep-tongue kisses, hands everywhere—unabashed groping while time stopped for them. Both were filled with long-suppressed emotions. Evan gently placed his hands on her shoulders and looked into her tear-filled eyes. His were the same. Time had passed, but their love hadn't changed— intense and tender at the same time.

He caressed the side of her face and brushed her auburn sun-streaked hair off of her forehead.

She looked up at him with all the courage she could muster. "Evan—I'm, uh"—she couldn't find the words, "so damn in love with you."

He patted her on the butt, and put his arm around her waist as they walked up the path. On the way to the front door, they stopped at the patio. He saw someone swimming in the pool he did not recognize. When Marie raised her head, Evan's mouth dropped.

"I know," Danielle said. "Can you believe it?"

"Not the same Marie I left, that's for sure," Evan shook his head. "Remind me when I'm old to get a pacemaker," he joked, laughing as he said it.

Danielle slapped him on the back in jest. "You're not getting old. I won't let you."

Marie climbed out of the pool, wrapped a towel around her waist, tucked it in and walked toward Evan with her arms extended in the same manner Danielle had greeted him. "You're finally here, Evan. I'm so glad to see you," she said, hugged him and kissed him on both cheeks. "Oh, sorry. Did I get you all wet?"

"It's okay. You look fantastic. I can't believe you are the same person."

"I feel like my old self—well, older yes, but like I did in my youth. I'm still on medication and watch my salt intake."

Marie removed the towel from her lean body and patted her head with it, drying off droplets of water. "How was your flight? Tell me everything that's happened. God, it's good to see you." Marie's enthusiasm resembled a giddy teenager.

They found chairs and settled down enjoying the late afternoon sun. Danielle went inside to get more ice tea. Marie and Evan talked like friends they had become—a bond between a mother and the person her daughter loved. Danielle returned with three ice teas on a tray and a basket of chips.

"Hungry?" Danielle said.

"Starved." Evan smiled and winked at her and grabbed an ice tea.

"Looks like you put on a few pounds," Marie said, then wished she hadn't implied he was fat, which he wasn't.

"True. Stress and bad eating habits." Evan winked and glanced at Danielle. "You look great—strong, healthy," Danielle added.

"I still run. Missed running here on the beach."

Evan sipped his tea and reached for Danielle's hand. She closed her fingers around his hand and gave them a squeeze. "New York ain't the same when you want to run on a sandy beach with palm trees."

"Danielle's put on a little weight too. I'm sure you noticed. I supposed we all eat too much pizza around here, not to mention late night ice cream before bed." Marie stared at her daughter waiting for a response she hoped to provoke.

Danielle shot her mother a disapproving glance. "What's the problem with a few extra pounds? More to love." She stirred her ice tea with her spoon trying to make light of her mother's comment.

Ever the gentlemen, Evan said, "I hadn't noticed."

They munched on herb and garlic chips, caught up on the status of his rental house and new art gallery showing. Thor, who must have been asleep somewhere in the house, spotted Evan and ran to him with happy howling, tail wagging as if motorized on Energizer batteries. Evan got on the ground, rolled with Thor, rubbed his ears and stomach. Thor wiggled like a child, thrilled to see someone he had grown fond of and missed. "Funny," he said. "I used to be terrified of this dog."

"He scares a lot of people," Marie said. "That's the point, though. This is the dog I want for protection. He keeps away any intruders."

"He's trained, right?" Evan asked.

"Yes. He'd attack a stranger who tried to break in—and, he'll attack on command."

"I'm glad you have the protection," Evan offered. "It's a crazy world we live in. We lost our sense of freedom after 9-11."

Marie nodded. "You two going out for dinner, right?"

"I want to spend some alone time with my guy, mama."

"Of course. Lovely temperature. Have a wonderful time."

Danielle got up, hugged her mom. Then Evan did the same and waved goodbye as they walked to his rental car.

"God, she looks good! I can see why your father fell in love with her."

"I know," Danielle said. "It's like she's ten years younger."

On the drive to the restaurant, Danielle confided how different her life was now that her mother was doing so well. She admitted she'd felt a bit lost not having her daily caregiver routine, not being needed. Of course, she was thrilled with her mother's improvement. However, she confessed to Evan how taking care of her mom had become an obsession—a reason to be useful and necessary. It never occurred to Danielle when her mother was frail to focus on her own needs, like a spa treatment, or going out with girlfriends. Now, these simple pleasures, including reading novels and being a girl's soccer coach at school completely changed her outlook on life. She told Evan she began to enjoy freedom from being a caretaker.

"How's Lena?" Evan glanced at Danielle.

"Oh, glad you asked. She redecorated our yacht business lobby—enjoyed it so much she's planning on enrolling in Interior Design school in Nice. Best of all, she's found a new boyfriend, an architecture student from Spain. Never seen her happier."

They drove to one of Danielle's favorite restaurants outside the ramparts. La Colombe d'Or was legendary for artists and celebrities. Danielle liked its romantic setting, with a lovely terrace overlooking the valley. In the 1950's, one could encounter Yves Montand and Simone Signoret, who were married in St. Paul. It was not unusual then to dine with Chagall, Calder and Braque. Danielle told Evan the restaurant was built in 1920, called Chez Robinson. Artists decorated the walls. The façade was assembled with stones from an old castle in Aix-en-Provence. The architect, Jacques Couelle, designed a fireplace with the hand imprints of the people who helped build it.

Danielle's hair was piled atop her head in a bun with wispy tendrils cascading across her cheeks. She reminded Evan of Audrey Hepburn in *Breakfast At Tiffany's*, without the cigarette holder, elbow-length haute couture gloves and wide-brimmed hat. Irresistible, nothetheless—Danielle was a woman to cherish and protect.

Their waiter seated them outside on the terrace under a canopy of olive trees. Patrons chatted and laughed, ate and drank wine while waiters carried cuisine to their tables sending wafts of delectable entreés to tempt the palate.

"What do you feel like eating?" Evan said to Danielle as he reached across the table to hold her hand.

Danielle watched a waiter carrying a platter of crudités, grilled peppers in olive oil and stuffed baby vegetables. Aromas of blended scents filled her nostrils.

"If they have duck confit on the menu tonight, I would like that."

Evan scanned the menu and couldn't decide what he wanted—maybe poulet roti with fresh peaches in Calvados sauce. "Would you like me to order a bottle of wine—Pinot Grigio?" He peered at her over the wine menu waiting for a reply.

"Uh—why don't you order whatever you'd prefer. I want something I can guzzle—lemonade please, if you don't mind." Danielle shot him a forced smile.

They placed their orders and enjoyed a basket of bread and baked Provençal tomatoes as a starter. Evan sighed, looked up at the night sky and shrugged his shoulders. "I can't even believe I'm here—going to *live* here. Sort of feels unreal."

"It's real," Danielle said. "Tough couple of months for both of us."

"The worst. I'm glad it's over. Everything that tied me to Tribeca is now finished—gone." Evan wrinkled his forehead thinking of his past life there.

"Do you miss it? What about your friends—the entire art community?"

Evan took a sip of his white wine. "I'll begin again. Fresh starts cleanse the soul. This is where I want to be—here in St. Paul with you, the woman I love."

"Your friends must have been shocked when you left Tribeca."

"Jealous, is more like it. Who wouldn't want to be here?"

The evening air was pleasant with a cool breeze. Danielle pulled a wrap around her shoulders and drank her lemonade. Evan talked non-stop, exceptionally enthusiastic about the new art gallery soon to be showing his work.

"Which gallery is representing you?" Danielle asked, while she stirred the lemon slices around in her drink.

"Bogena. It's outside the ramparts. Do you know it?"

"I've heard the name—run by a woman, right?"

"Yes, Bogena Gidrol. Expanded the gallery in 2013—old building renovated and close to the Maeght. I like her philosophy of radical contemporary showings."

"You're radical?" Danielle laughed, trying to be funny.

"My work is. Her gallery plays host to other art forms—music and literature. She likes to showcase international artists. Seems thrilled I've moved here. I think we're a good fit."

"You staying at the same hotel?"

"Yes. The Le Mas De Pierre. When I first met you, I couldn't sleep. All I could think about was what it would be like if you were naked—I mean—"

"You wanted to sleep with me so soon after you met me?"

"Silly woman." He shot her an enticing grin. "Then and now. Do we have to order dessert?" Evan took the napkin from his lap, folded it with nervous tension and set it on the table.

Danielle slid her toe up Evan's leg and looked him in the eye with a wink. "I'm not the least bit hungry for dessert."

Evan grinned, motioned for the check, paid the bill and helped Danielle with her chair. He put his hand on the small of her back and guided her through the terrace. "Would you like to walk a bit?"

"No, Evan. Walking is not what I had in mind."

CHAPTER 54

Evan

Evan awoke in his hotel with Danielle cuddled against his chest facing him. His right arm was wrapped around her bare shoulder. One of her legs was entwined with his. Her hair fell across her face, eyes shut by impossibly long eyelashes. Her full lips were slightly parted. He had never seen her look more radiant. Something about her seemed to glow even without makeup. It was this naturalness about her he liked the best—the unpretentious, intelligent, kind-hearted caring person who also happened to be drop-dead gorgeous, and was in love with him.

The *Do Not Disturb* sign was on the outside door latch, so sleeping in remained uninterrupted. With Marie healthy, Danielle was no longer consumed with responsibility for getting her mother ready in the morning. It was the weekend and Danielle didn't have school to contend with. They could luxuriate in between expensive sheets and eat breakfast in bed, ordered the night before. What time was it? He took a quick glace at his watch. Breakfast wouldn't be arriving for another hour. Now relaxed, he watched her stretch and turn over on her side. Still asleep, she had nuzzled into him. She felt natural there—as if they had always been in love.

He thought of getting the movers to uncrate his belongings and move them into his rental. Some of his paintings would go directly to the gallery. All of this mental commotion could wait another day. He rolled on to his back and put his arm across his forehead keeping one arm under Danielle's head.

Sooner or later he would have to tell her he was planning to meet with her father to talk about Ryan, but for now, he planned to keep it a secret. Evan wondered if Ryan knew he was in St. Paul. There was no way around this—it could become an ugly situation. When Evan asked Danielle to send him an iPhone photo of Ryan from one of their family yachting outings, it was the one thing Evan needed to confirm one of his worst suspicions.

Evan had faxed the photo to Columbia Yachting, then called asking if the guy in the photo was, in fact, Jed Reddiger. The owner confirmed Jed's face and was still pissed at him for leaving so abruptly. The day Evan made this fateful call to Columbia was the day all of Evan's pent up frustration exploded. He had spit out a string of swear words through clenched his teeth, and threw a beer bottle at his condo window, shattering the glass. He was shocked at his impetuous behavior, but he wanted to strangle Ryan—beat the shit out of him. It was hard to admit, he wanted to kill him. Being stuck in New York and dealing with Aurora's death kept him from doing something to Ryan he would have regretted—not because he didn't want to kill Ryan, but because there was no specific plan to convict him and it wasn't just about revenge for Ashley. Other people died that day during the bank robbery. They all deserved justice.

Knowing that Ryan, or his brother, Ted, killed Ashley was enough for long-sought revenge, but he wanted more than revenge—he wanted justice. Evan recognized his boiling rage bordered on violence. However, there was a better way—a well-crafted plan. Evan still had suspicions about Ryan's involvement in Armond's murder. During his upcoming conversation with Gaspard, Evan was determined to convince him how they could jointly work with the police in Nice. Ryan wasn't going down for one murder—the bastard was going down for several—Ashley, plus those innocent people who died that day, and Armond. All Evan needed was proof. Seeking justice burned inside of him like an abscess about to rupture.

Evan recalled what Gaspard had told him about the shocking night with the submarine and Lucas, poor guy, tailing Ryan. Whatever Ryan was up to it was definitely stealth and involved drugs. Evan didn't know if it was coke, heroine or meth—not that the specific drug mattered, but he wanted to find out if Ryan was dealing or transporting. Something else he could add to Ryan's long rap sheet once he was convicted.

Evan also wanted to investigate evidence stored with the police department in Nice, since it was still an open case. Something about Armond's clothing when he was found in the dumpster kept gnawing at him—a feeling about blood found on the clothing. The missing shoe found near Armond's home was more than a coincidence. He was convinced Armond had been murdered at home— all he had to do was prove it. Every day he had to wait to act on his plan was like chewing nails and then swallowing them.

Evan decided to let Danielle awaken when she was ready and not bother her today with all of this. One day soon, yes, but not today. Today was a bubble of bliss to savor, to cherish. He snuggled tighter against her back, her breast exposed where the sheet fell in a fold under her arm. He didn't remember her breasts being so full and he started to respond to her again, helpless to the nakedness of her body.

She yawned, untangled herself from Evan, stretched and rubbed her eyes. "Morning," she said in a warm, drowsy voice.

"Hey, sleepyhead." Evan grinned at her, stroked her hair and forced himself to relax his urge to pull her on top of him.

"I was thinking you might want to stay in the guesthouse until you move in."

"Appreciate the offer, but there are too many little people running about. I like the privacy we have here in the hotel. That okay with you?"

"Sure. What's on your mind?" She grinned and stroked his inner thigh.

"You needed to ask?"

"I mean, after that?"

"Gotta run to my rental—pick up the key."

"Is it furnished?"

"Modestly. That's an understatement. But it has a bed and the basics."

Danielle laughed. "It had better come with a bed."

CHAPTER 55

Danielle

Now back home, Danielle fretted about not telling Evan the night before she was pregnant, but couldn't find the words. When they awoke, she couldn't ruin the moment either. He had told her he liked her ample breasts and attributed their new fullness to her weight gain. Her stomach was a bit round, but not so that you could tell it was from a baby growing—she looked like she had put on ten pounds, and he was such a gentleman, he didn't mention it.

She recalled Chloe going out with a guy last year who was a fitness nut—demanded she eat healthy, bike with him, and workout at his health club. At first, it was fun. Then it became a chore. He ridiculed her if she put on weight—refused to let her eat dessert when they dined out. After six months of trying to please him, she cut him loose. Nothing worse than dating someone who demands and expects physical perfection and doesn't see you for the person you really are.

Evan made her feel loved, appreciated and grounded. She didn't worry about what she wore or whether she had makeup on. However, this secret she carried would reveal itself sooner than she would have liked. It tormented her to think he would not want the baby—and then, maybe he wouldn't want her. Of course, he said many times that he loved her. She could feel that he did, but giving him a child was such a relationship breaker for him—especially when he hadn't had time to consider his emotions or acceptance of having a family. She'd hoped, in time, they'd marry and decide on a family later. Then, life sent her a curve ball. She touched her belly, patted it tenderly, talking to the baby as if the growing embryo could hear her. Was it a girl? She hoped so. Perhaps if it was a boy,

Evan would be more accepting of her pregnancy—the idea of a son—*his* son gave her hope.

Telling Evan about her pregnancy wasn't the only thing she dreaded. How would she tell Marie? Her mother would be upset, and maybe even angry with her. Of course, she'd worry about her daughter's health. Danielle suspected her mother would demand she tell Evan immediately—she was too frightened to tell him just yet.

The longer she waited to tell Evan, the harder it was not to confide in her mother. Danielle admitted she felt both exhilarated and scared at the same time, recognizing these negative emotions might not be good for the baby.

She dressed in a bright hot pink and black ankle-length floral skirt, grateful for the stretch elastic in the waist. A matching pink top seemed to brighten her face. She twisted her hair into a ponytail, sprayed on a bit of perfume, put on a black beaded necklace, donned her daisy sandals and scampered down the stairs.

"Hi dear," Marie said, smiling at her daughter from the kitchen table. The French doors were wide open. A soft breeze moved the yellow daffodils in a blue and white ceramic vase back and forth in a little dance.

"Morning, mama. Such a beautiful day." Danielle gave her mother a warm hug.

"Yes, it is. Do you have any plans? Marie glanced up at her daughter. "You look wonderful."

"Not really. Evan's getting his furniture out of storage— moving in. He said his new place is furnished, but only the basics."

"He could have stayed here." Marie said and picked up her gilded porcelain cup, sipped her herbal tea and set it down gently on the saucer.

"I know, mama. He, um, wanted privacy—didn't want to bother us again."

Marie smiled and didn't say anything. She dipped her fork into her quiche.

"He must be thrilled his work will be shown in one of our galleries," she said wiggling her fork in the quiche. "Which gallery again?"

"Bogena's." Danielle turned toward the sink and began washing last night's dishes.

"Ah! Great gallery—very modern. Should be just right for Evan's work from what you told me. Do you plan to move in with him?" Marie raised both eyebrows and placed her elbow on the table with one finger under her chin.

Danielle did a half-turn toward her mother. "Haven't thought about it. Maybe when he's settled. I want him to have his own space."

"Wise thinking. I raised a smart, good girl." Marie bit her upper lip and narrowed her eyes. "We're close and you tell me everything, right?"

Danielle could feel her face flush. She turned and faced the sink, adjusted the faucet sprayer and choked out a reply. "Of course." She faced her mother and put her hand on her hip in defense. "I've always told you everything, sooner or later, right?"

Marie gave her a stilted smile, sipped more tea and changed the subject. "Does Ryan know Evan's back in town?"

"I don't know. Maybe. If Dad told him, then probably." Danielle nodded and continued washing dishes.

"Knowing Lena, she's already told him. It would be something she couldn't wait to impart."

Danielle shook the dishwater off her hands, dried them in a towel and turned toward her mother. "Why should Lena care?"

"She doesn't. Likes the drama of it all."

"Why? What's she saying?" Danielle flinched and pulled at her necklace.

"Not much. Said Ryan's not at all happy that Evan's back."

Danielle sat in the ladder-back chair next to her mother. "Why should he care? We're no longer dating. Besides, Lena says he's got a girlfriend—someone he met in the bar at the Negresco."

"I'm not sure why Evan's being here should bother Ryan. I've asked your dad, but he doesn't want to talk about it."

"Mama, you're worrying about nothing." Danielle rose from her chair, threw both arms around her mother's shoulders and kissed her on the top of head. "Have a good day. I have some errands to run. See you later."

Danielle walked to her car, perplexed about the conversation with her mother. Something reminded her when Evan was still in New York, he'd asked for a photo of Ryan, which she had emailed to him. What was that all about?"

CHAPTER 56

Evan

The movers delivered Evan's furniture, wished him good luck, and left with their large truck wheels scattering gravel from the driveway onto the slightly overgrown front lawn.

His new temporary home on a hillside hamlet was crowded, dusty and filled with boxes. Somehow the Internet photos made the rooms look a bit more spacious. Furniture that fit properly in his large condo in Tribeca was oversized in his new residence and bulged into doorways. He looked forward to sleeping in his own bed, assembled courtesy of the movers, and putting the double bed that came with the furnished rental in the guest room.

He wondered if he could paint in this dimly lit environment. Perhaps he'd have to consider painting plein air, in the backyard. Or maybe the gallery would allow him to create new pieces there. He made a mental note to check with Bogena.

Some of his smaller paintings, still crated, stood against the peeling plaster walls. A jute rug peeked out atop the knotty plank floor as if it were begging to have the boxes removed.

The kitchen was adequate, except for the refrigerator reminiscent of the first apartment he had in college—slightly wider than his own girth. It would hold beer and leftover pizza—he'd survive. A combo washer-dryer stood in the corner of the kitchen. He'd have clean underwear. How lucky could I guy get? Two small bedrooms, one with café curtains dangled on an askew curtain rod missing a bracket. A drafty breeze threatened to send the curtains collapsing to the floor. Both bedrooms, on opposite sides of the narrow hallway, lacked closets, but had decent windows—one with a bench seat under the window ledge. Curved iron candle-bulb sconces lit the textured plaster hallway walls that led to a modest bath with a shower not much larger than the refrigerator. The house was charming, but oh so tiny. He felt like he was living in a dollhouse and he was Gulliver.

He moved boxes off the furnished rental sofa, upholstered in a dark green paisley print, something more at home in England than France, and smacked the haze on the cushion hard making it release a fluff of dust. He sneezed and waved the flying particles from his face and shook the fuzz out of his hair. The wooden floor creaked under his feet and made him feel as if the floorboards might give out.

The sofa was surprisingly comfortable, albeit ugly. He hoped to give it back to the rental company and use his own leather sofa standing on its side in the corner along with his favorite matching club chair. Despite the chaos of moving, and the small quaintness of his new living quarters, he felt grounded. St. Paul was where he wanted to be.

Side-latched arched wood widows faced the front yard. From the living room, he could see a massive palm tree, assorted shrubs, roses and a fountain with a stone-cast alabaster bird spurting water from its mouth into a floral-shaped dish. Neighbors were several meters away, not encroaching on his privacy. He stood, opened a window, closed his eyes and drank in fresh Mediterranean air. This was the right decision. A new life awaited him—a life with Danielle, the woman he deeply loved.

Before he could concentrate on his future he had to have a strategic plan for ensnaring Ryan, something he could not do without informing the French police involved with the case. Sheriff Bob Cosley, his former boss from El Dorado Hills, had been on Evan's mind. He'd been a great boss and good friend who supported him through his depression after Ashley died. Thanks to Bob, he'd recently learned the names of the two brothers who robbed the bank in El Dorado Hills. Would Bob help him now?

Twilight lingered with a purple tint turning the sky shades of deep violet and dark blue. He stared out the living room window. No longer content to sit in the dark, Evan used his phone as a flashlight, and looked for an electrical socket to plug in a lamp. There was an outlet behind the sofa. He plugged it in, pulled on the chain and a bulb slightly brighter than a large candle lit up. Evan dialed Bob on his cell phone and took a deep breath.

"Bob? Evan here."

"Hey bud. Good to hear from you. Where's here?"

"I've already moved into my new manse, complete with running water."

"You in St. Paul already?"

"Yeah. Found a rental—a two-bedroom bargain. How's Kathy?" Evan pushed a box away from the sofa, kicked off his loafers and put his feet on top of a box he used as a temporary coffee table.

"She's great. Busy considering buying more art from Joey Cattone, our favorite local artist up here—our home is full of her stunning paintings. If you come visit, you have to meet Joey and see her work."

"Speaking of visits, I was thinking you have to take a vacation. I really need your help. This is something that can't be done over the phone. Do you think you could fly here for a week or two?"

"When were you thinking?"

"As soon as possible. There's proof Ryan Coltrane is, in fact, Jed Reddiger."

"No shit! How did you put that together?" Bob's voice rose an octave.

"Had Danielle send me a photo from one of their yachting outings."

"Not following this." Bob hesitated, then coughed to clear his throat.

"Remember when I tried to contact Columbia Yachting?"

"Yeah. The ruse about you being the rich uncle—"

"Clever idea that didn't work at the time." Evan crossed his ankles and pushed off a sock with his big toe.

"Remind me again."

"Back then, I thought Ryan Coltrane worked at Columbia—didn't know Jed and Ted Reddiger committed the robbery until you told me about the guy who made the dying declaration. Didn't know Ryan *was* Jed until I faxed a photo of Ryan to the owner at Columbia. He confirmed the guy in the photo was Jed."

"Did you let on that you knew he was involved in a robbery?"

"God, no. I'm no longer on the force—I'm so bent on killing the guy, but damn happy to send him to prison for life." Evan balled his fist and banged it on the cardboard box. Peanuts flew out of a dish and scattered across the rug.

Bob hesitated. "The whole extradition thing is going to be complicated."

"He won't have to be extradited. I want to prove he killed Armond Fouquet."

"Sorry, who?" Bob's voice strained.

"I'll explain everything when you get here. Please, Bob. I've never asked for a favor. I really need this—if not for me, then do it for Ashley's sake and everyone who died that day." Evan could hear Bob sucking his teeth. "You still there?"

"Yeah. Thinking."

"Think palm trees, warm air, salty breezes..." Evan pushed the other sock off his foot. "What's better than the Riviera?"

"Sounds inviting. I'll talk to Kathy and let you know."

"Thanks, Bob." Evan clicked off his phone, uncrossed his legs and stood on a patch of carpeting with his bare feet. He made a mental note to get a new rug for the living room. Jute rugs felt like dried hairy dead animals.

His stomach rumbled. Time to get something to eat from a nearby restaurant, pick up some groceries and then unpack some boxes before sleeping in his bed, with or without sheets. Evan had no idea where the movers packed his stuff. He hadn't a clue how to run the French washer/dryer. Danielle would have to teach him. He consoled himself realizing he could live weeks with one tee shirt, loafers and one pair of shorts, but he'd have to find his packed underwear.

Evan did a quick glance around his new, dusty digs. If Bob agreed to come to St. Paul, he'd have to get a cleaning lady in to tidy up and get rid of the dust and cobwebs. He grabbed his baseball cap, slipped his bare feet into his loafers and headed out, now hopeful Bob would agree to visit.

CHAPTER 57

Ryan

Ryan ran a wet comb through his hair and slicked it back on the sides. He looked like a spitting image of Jordan Rodgers, Aaron Rodgers' pro-football brother. Sometimes yachting clients from America asked him if he was, in fact, Jordan. He'd roll his eyes and tell them he'd never played football in his life. Now getting ready to go out for the evening, he tucked his crisply tailored black shirt into his trousers. The mirror reflected someone he was pleased with—tan, sun-bleached hair, physically fit. He swiped a bit of cologne on each side of his clean-shaven face. A night out dancing and partying was what he needed.

He drove to Les Trois Diables, noted for their wild dance club atmosphere and DJ parties. It was one of Nice's best and longest running clubs. The night was clear and cool without being damp.

Things were going so well. He'd increased yachting clients by ten-percent this year alone, with many customers intending to repeat business next year or recommend their friends to Gaspard Yachting. However, he'd lived long enough to know when things went well, they didn't last.

Gillian Esposito was waiting for him at their favorite bistro table, and he wanted to spend time with her, his recent girlfriend and partner in his secret life. He had a stash of coke in the car to give to her—something he'd stored at his home for a client who requested it, then managed instead to bring his own recreational drugs on a yachting outing.

Gillian hung out at the Negresco bar in Nice where they'd met over drinks and crowded hot body dancing. Their sexual tension escalated to a frenzy of desire. She invited him to her place so they could explore one another. It led to an agreement for her to buy the drugs he said he had. He made sure she wasn't a DEA agent—not only wasn't she wearing a wire, she wasn't wearing a bra or panties.

They had X-rated sex most of the night. Afterwards, he insisted on checking her house for 'bugs', which he didn't find. Her passport and driver's license indicated she lived in Nice. She told him she lived there much of her adult life, and simply enjoyed recreational coke, as did many of her friends. She was disappointed to learn he didn't do coke, but understood his migraine issues. With the preventative medicine he often took, he didn't need or want any other drugs in his system.

The fact that he made a profit selling coke to her was a financial perk. She didn't need much of a stash, and he didn't either. The kilos he got the other night from his submarine dealer would last both of them a long time—plenty for her, and enough for any future yachting clients who requested recreational drugs.

Life with her was exciting and easy. Having a girlfriend who walked the edgy, wild side of life was fun, and he liked that about her. Gillian had a body he could never tire of. By comparison, Danielle was merely a distant, unclaimed prize. Although Danielle was pretty, to him, she was a schoolteacher—attractive, yes, but probably way too inhibited for his tastes. When they had dated in the past, he found her friendly, but tentative. Gillian, from Colombia, was anything but inhibited.

Ryan rubbed his neck, turned off the engine, sat in his BMW and let the breeze blow through his hair as he looked up at the stars. Life was damn near perfect except for one, relentless, miserable thing. Evan had returned. Where was he living? Lena would tell him if he asked her. Somehow when Evan left to go back to Tribeca, he thought Evan wouldn't return to St. Paul. Didn't the guy have a life there? He bounced his knee up and down in the car, fighting off nervous tension.

An earlier plan to make Danielle fall in love with him didn't work out. Evan got in the way—had to take a vacation, had to end up here of all places.

Night owls were arriving at the club—women in tight, glittery short dresses followed by buffed men hungry for a one-night stand. Music blared through the doorway when patrons entered the club. A bouncer, straight out of the *Sopranos*, stood at the doorway. Several other bouncers mingled inside the club, ensuring violence did not break out.

Ryan slicked back his hair with spittle, and decided he'd deal with Evan, the displaced artist, the former cop, some other time. Tonight was not the time for anxious fear or plotting. He chewed the inside of his lower lip, biting hard until he drew blood—a bad habit he acquired as a child.

He remembered saving Evan's life—a regret now coming back to haunt him. Stupid Evan—panic-stricken, inept scuba-diving Evan nearly cost him his own life. Ryan sat there thinking he should have let Evan drown—should have run over him with the dive boat. It could have been a believable accident.

He opened the car door, slid out and stood on the pavement in his expensive, black leather Italian shoes, not quite ready to enter the club. To release pent up tension, he tilted his head from shoulder to shoulder until his neck cracked. He popped the trunk and threw a towel over the duffle bag stashed with coke, shut the trunk and began to walk to the front door. Without turning, he clicked the door of his car locked. The music vibrated against his chest masking his own heartbeat. He welcomed the anticipated taste of Vodka, Grey Goose preferred, but more than alcohol, he welcomed the uninhibited taste of Gillian's flesh.

CHAPTER 58

Evan

Bob agreed to help Evan with whatever plan Evan had in mind. Who would have thought three days ago, he'd be arriving? Evan picked him up from the airport and drove him to his house. They chatted about Bob's life, his work and marriage.

Bob and Kathy were happy and Evan wanted that for himself.

"Here we are," Evan said as he pulled up the driveway.

"No garage?" Bob noted.

"Not often available here. Weather's good—don't need it, although it would have been nice for storage. Let's get your luggage."

Bob stood, rubbed his twitching eye, a recently diagnosed vitamin deficiency. "Nice place." He mouthed a wide smile to avoid his shock. This was not the villa he'd expected.

"Wait until you see the inside," Evan joked. "It's much, much worse."

Bob ducked entering the doorway to avoid hitting his head on the arched doorframe, which made him feel like he was entering hobbit land—tiny rooms that looked like something out of a *Lord of The Rings* movie.

"Let me show you the guest room." Evan led the way down the hall.

Bob sauntered behind Evan, with his flip-flops catching on a rumple in the carpet runner.

"Here you go." Evan said. "Vacation paradise, don't you think?"

Bob laughed. "Not what I was expecting. It's so fancy. Fit for a king."

"So much for arranging this rental in a hurry, but the location's good."

"Closet?" Bob asked, looking around the room and bending over as if a closet might appear from under the bed.

"No, sorry. Have to buy an armoire. For now, just throw stuff on the chair."

Bob rolled his eyes, not so much about not having a closet, but one look at the bed and he knew his tall frame would mean his feet would be hanging off the double bed. "House have a bathroom?" Bob teased. "Or, is there an outhouse for that?"

"Did I forget to mention there's no bathroom?" Evan kept a straight face and watched Bob's forehead pinch. "Just joking. John's at the end of the hall."

Bob walked a few steps to the bathroom, stuck his head in the doorway, and broke up in hysterics. He was laughing so hard he couldn't talk.

"What's so damn funny?" Evan put his hand on his hip and tilted his head in an effort to understand Bob's hysteria.

"The shower! That little thing? I'll never fit. I'm going to stink the entire time I'm here."

Evan started to laugh, and now both men were doubled up with laughter.

"Move, move out of the bathroom," Evan said and reached under the vanity cabinet and threw several washcloths at Bob, who caught one on the fly.

"This a towel?" Bob snorted, bent over and grabbed his stomach.

"Stop it. My bladder is going to burst." Evan said and slithered past Bob who was holding a washcloth by his fingertips and pushed him out the doorway. He closed the door intent on having the last laugh. "Learn to sponge bath. You're a smart man. I'll even provide soap."

Later, Bob and Evan shared a pizza, picked up from a local restaurant, and spent the evening talking over beers. Evan had been successful in getting the paisley sofa returned, and his leather couch and club chair now filled the living room space.

Boxes still served as lamp stands, and a coffee table. The kitchen had a small breakfast table with a leaf for expansion and two chairs with mismatched threadbare cushions.

"So, tell me about this guy, Armond, something?" Bob said and gulped down a large piece of pizza while holding up the end with his fingers so the vegetables wouldn't topple off.

Evan told him the saga of Armond being murdered, found in an alley dumpster near his home, in a restaurant district.

"Where are the police in the investigation?" Bob swiped tomato sauce from his chin with his finger.

"Good question. Gaspard didn't want to involve the police, which is why he had Lucas do the stakeout."

"Poor kid. Could have been killed." Bob used a toothpick to unlodge a fennel seed from between his teeth.

"If I'd been here, I'd have done it. Gaspard couldn't risk it himself—too easy to recognize."

"So, what are you thinking?" Bob slouched back in the leather sofa, and dangled one long leg off the side arm.

"Armond's murder could have happened at his home. I want to know what the police found when they searched his house."

"What are they looking for?"

"Good question. When I overheard the interrogation with the detective in Ryan's office, there was this shoe thing— something about a missing shoe being found at Armond's home."

"A shoe? Sorry, not following." Bob frowned.

"Neighbor's dog found Armond's shoe near his property. When the police found Armond's body in the dumpster one shoe was missing."

"Oh, that's interesting." Bob rubbed his forehead, thinking.

"I need you to work with Gaspard and the two investigators, since I can't."

"How am I supposed to appear on the scene now? I'm not part of this case."

"But you are!" Evan shot Bob a serious glance. "We can't prove Ryan shot Ashley—he wore a mask and so did his brother, Ted. Ryan could say Ted shot Ashley, and now Ted's dead. Can't even prove who shot the people in the bank—all circumstantial evidence. But, we can prove they committed armed robbery in El Dorado Hills that killed people."

"Yeah—that's a California crime. Has nothing to do with Armond."

"But it does, if we're smart. If Ryan killed him, he can go down for that murder. He'll rot in prison in Nice. Not exactly the justice I wanted for Ashley and everyone else killed that day, but if we share our information with the police here in Nice about the duplicity—Ryan having an alias—he's not who he says he is and he was involved with another robbery and murder. I think we can get them to work with us."

"Good point. What do you want?"

"Get Armond's clothing taken out of evidence. Ask the police to check the DNA. The bloodstains are probably Armond's, but they might also be Ryan's."

"How?" Bob squinted at Evan and took a swig of beer.

"Don't know how. I'm thinking Ryan and Armond had a fight in Ryan's office. The whole charade of a broken coffee table, shattered glass everywhere, Ryan's split lip—none of that ever made sense to me."

Bob twisted his lip, pondering the information and set his gangly leg back on the floor and leaned forward. "If they had a fight in Ryan's office, he didn't kill him there, did he? How'd the body get to the dumpster?"

"Here's what I think. Makes perfect sense if the ruckus happened at the office—maybe late at night and Ryan followed Armond home."

"So, he killed him at home and then hauled the body to the dumpster?"

"Is that so far fetched?" Evan stammered, paused and began to crack his knuckles.

Bob got up, paced around the room. "Wanna another beer?"

"Sure. Bring two." Evan said. "Bottle opener's in the drawer to the right of the sink." Evan fidgeted with a cramp in the arch of his foot and tried to rub it out.

Bob was so much taller than the refrigerator and maneuvered around the dollhouse without complaint, now seriously concerned about the complexity of the double murder cases involving one suspect. "I need to talk to Gaspard and want you part of that conversation."

"Agreed. Also, I don't want Lucas or Danielle involved. Lucas already knows too much." Evan folded his arms across his chest. "Gaspard can indicate he's working with the police if questioned by his family—they expect that. They know Ryan was a suspect, but nothing came of it, so Gaspard's family believes Ryan's in the clear about Armond's murder. Lucas knows Ryan's involved with drugs. He may know his dad thinks Ryan might be involved with Armond's murder, but Lucas knows nothing about Ryan's bank robbery."

"Let's talk more tomorrow," Bob suggested. "I'm beat."

"Me too. I've been a wreck worrying. See you in the morning."

Bob rose from the sofa, stretched his long legs and threw his shoulders back to loosen kinks. "Nice temperature for sleeping."

"Yeah, tropical. Use the fan in your room, if you want. Don't have air conditioning."

"I'm so surprised," Bob yawned, turned and walked toward the bedroom but headed into the john. Evan waited in his room for the toilet to flush, the joy of sharing a bathroom with a guest. After Bob's bedroom door closed, Evan crept across the squeaking floor to the bathroom. He ran water into the sink, brushed his teeth, splashed cold water on his face and wiped it with a washcloth. He'd provide Bob with a real towel in the morning. The guy would be overjoyed with the luxury of something as long as his torso.

Evan found it impossible to sleep. He put his arms behind his head on the pillow and stared at the ceiling. The room was bright, almost like daybreak because the curtain hung lopsided at the open window letting in the glow of the moon along with night air. He thought about Danielle. She had an event at school, so he'd told her he'd call her in the morning. She knew Bob was visiting and looked forward to meeting him. It rankled him not to be able to discuss his plan with her—the real reason Bob was really here, but for her own safety she couldn't know about this.

Ryan had been part of a murder once, and probably twice—that made him a dangerous criminal—possibly a sociopath, who walked the earth without concern or remorse for what he'd done. Didn't he have any guilt? How did he live with himself? He wondered what had happened to Ryan to turn him into a criminal.

Hours passed and Evan was still fretting. Ryan was a monster who deserved everything horrible that would happen to him in prison. But first, Evan had to build a solid case against him. With Bob's help, he was hopeful he'd be able to get the evidence he needed. He pulled the pillow over his head to block out the moon's rays and finally nodded off thinking about Danielle.

CHAPTER 59

Evan, Gaspard and Bob

Evan had contacted Gaspard to set up a critical meeting about Ryan, and Gaspard suggested he take them out on one of the unscheduled fleet yachts for privacy. Ryan had already taken clients out on a sailboat to Cap Ferrat for a visit to Beatrice de Rothschild's villa and gardens. It was mid-morning and Ryan wasn't expected to return at the marina until late afternoon. To be safe, Gaspard planned to take Evan and Bob in the opposite direction toward Cannes.

Gaspard waited on the marina dock for Evan and his guest. Not entirely sure why they were meeting, he put on a blue and white captain's hat, white trousers and a navy and white print shirt. Evan spotted him on the dock and waved his hand in a friendly hello. The two men greeted one another with warm hugs, and then Evan introduced Gaspard to Bob.

"Good to meet you," Gaspard said. *Belle Juliette* is ready to go. Bob smiled and shook Gaspard's hand and stepped into the tender. The harbormaster recognized Evan, asked about his foot, and then took all three men to the yacht.

They boarded the yacht and went to the upper deck. Gaspard offered them cold beverages and chips before going to the bridge to start the engine. Bob and Evan wandered the deck, looked at the vistas, then settled on the aft deck's blue cushions.

Bob drank his cola and grabbed a handful of chips. "Now, this is living," he said with his hand cupped over his forehead to shield his eyes from the glare of the sun in a cloudless sky. The sea was calm as the yacht roared toward their destination. Seagulls followed the wake, rode the air currents, swooped and peered into the water looking for fish.

"How many yachts does Gaspard have?" Bob asked.

Evan wrinkled his forehead. "I'm not really sure—I never asked. Shortly after I met Danielle, Gaspard took us out on the *Belle Chloe,* a yacht much larger than this."

"Much larger? Seriously?" Bob's eyes widened.

"Biggest yacht I've ever seen."

"I no longer dislike your small abode," Bob chuckled.

Evan laughed. "You sleep okay? If you're uncomfortable I can get you a good hotel room."

"It's fine. Really. I'm here on business. By the way, thanks for the towels."

"You noticed?"

"Yup, used two. Put my hands above my head, squeezed the shampoo, turned on the water and stood in one place. New way to shower without moving."

"I knew you could adapt." Evan shot Bob a wide grin.

"Today being on the water with this skyline makes up for it."

Gaspard shut off the engine, left the bridge to join Evan and Bob. "So, tell me what's so critical about this meeting." He sat and took off his cap and put both hands together with his elbows resting on his knees. He leaned forward.

"I want to be honest about everything, but this will be hard for you to hear, Gaspard," Evan said. He could feel trepidation creep up his spine.

"Go ahead." Gaspard's wrinkled forehead registered concern.

"Bob was my boss when I was in California. He is a Sheriff in El Dorado Hills where I used to work as a cop."

"Oh," Gaspard said with raised eyebrows. "What does this have to do with Ryan?"

Evan explained the entire incident that took place in 2011, the horrific tragedy of losing his sister, the bank robbery and subsequent deaths. He watched Gaspard's face grow grim, but continued the unbelievable story of how the case went cold, then surfaced with the conversation from the bartender at the Purple Place with the two guys who were looking to rent a copter.

A number of times, Evan rubbed his hands together reliving this nightmare that refused to go away, took deep breaths and continued on with the story. Bob remained silent until Evan asked him to talk about the phone call from the Los Angeles Police Department alerting Bob to the guy who was dying and made a final declaration before his death about being the man who flew the copter.

Gaspard listened intently but had a quizzical look on his face. "I'm still not sure I understand what this had to do with Ryan?"

Evan shifted in his seat and took a deep breath, knowing what he was about to say would be painful for Gaspard to hear.

"Ryan Coltrane is an alias. His real name is Jed Reddiger. He and his brother, Ted, who is now dead, committed the robbery and murder in El Dorado Hills. One of those two brothers killed Ashley, but I can't prove who did it. I shot one brother in the shoulder, the other in the leg, but they wore masks. Couldn't see their faces."

Gaspard's normally ruddy face went pale. He was shaken by the information and clutched his hand to his chest.

"Are you all right?" Evan asked, worried Gaspard might be having a heart attack.

Gaspard nodded. "I'm shocked. Didn't expect this." He took his hand off his chest and clasped his hands together. "All this time, I've doubted Ryan because of Armond's murder. And now I learn this bastard, my partner, is responsible for this other horrific crime."

Bob put his cola on the teak coffee table. "I'd like to summarize what I think has gone on here."

Gaspard leaned back on the seat cushion. "Go ahead."

"Evan told me how he overheard the interrogation with Detective, Nicholas was it?"

"No, Nichols," Evan corrected and focused on Bob.

Bob continued. "Detective Nichols suspected Ryan might have been involved with Armond's murder. Where are they in their investigation?"

"Not sure," Gaspard said. "So much went on with Danielle's hospitalization, and then Marie's surgery, I've not pushed the police."

"But you suspected Ryan?" Evan waited.

"Yes. It's why I sent Lucas on a stakeout—well, two. Now there's the drug thing. Has Evan told you about that, Bob?"

Bob glanced at Evan and nodded. "He's transporting drugs or involved with them in some way. Gives possible motive for murder if the police knew this."

Gaspard stood, turned his back to his guests and stared at the sea. "I've purposely kept the police out of this because I wasn't sure—wanted proof."

Bob and Evan waited patiently while Gaspard digested this unsettling information.

Gaspard turned toward Bob and Evan with his lower jaw jutted out. His face was red with rage. "Can we arrest Ryan?"

Bob held up a hand to Evan so he could speak first. "We could, but much of what we have is circumstantial evidence— not the conviction we would want."

"I don't understand," Gaspard sat back down and slumped.

"It's complicated," Bob said. "Our laws would require him to be extradited to California to stand trial for the robbery and murder which took place there, but I can't prove Ryan shot anyone—I can prove he was part of the robbery, a felony, but he'd get maybe ten years for robbery with a firearm, twenty if we could prove he killed Ashley and people in the bank— which we can't. Could have been his brother, Ted. Ryan would get twenty-five years to life only if we could prove *he* committed a felony and murder."

Gaspard shifted in his seat and rubbed his forehead. "I need a drink. Anyone else want one?"

"Sure." Evan said. Bob indicated he'd stay with soda.

Gaspard went to the bar, poured scotch into two glasses and returned to the seating area.

Bob continued the conversation. "I believe we can prove Ryan killed Armond. If we can do that, he'd be arraigned in Nice, prosecuted here, convicted and sent to prison."

"How do we do this—prove he killed Armond?" Gaspard scowled.

Bob pointed at himself. "Let me work with the detectives in charge of the investigation. Evan wants Armond's clothing from the murder analyzed for DNA. He thinks a fight broke out in Ryan's office—probably about drugs, which could be the motive."

Gaspard rubbed the stubble on his chin with his thumb and index finger while he contemplated this plan. "If we can prove he killed Armond, you'd be okay with that, Evan?"

"Yes. Has to be absolute proof. If it is, then he can rot in prison here—I can live with that—justice for Ashley and those killed that day, and justice for Armond's family."

Bob leaned forward. "I have a plan for how we would handle Ryan's conviction, if it comes to that, in El Dorado Hills. Those families deserve to know who committed the crime—even if it's to say it's the 'Reddiger brothers'—let me worry about how we give that to the press."

Gaspard sat quietly sipping his scotch and nodding his head. He chewed on his thumb, leaned forward and looked at Evan and Bob. "How do you say, in America? Let's roll!"

Gaspard, Bob and Evan clicked their glasses and raised them towards the sky. The hunt had begun.

CHAPTER 60

Ryan

After a successful day sailing with customers up the coast to Cap Ferrat, Ryan headed back to his office. He wanted to tell Gaspard the good news. Today's customers planned to return next year for a vacation sail to Monaco, however Gaspard was nowhere to be found.

He searched for Lena. She was in her office on the phone busily explaining chartering options to a potential customer. He sat in a chair in her office, picked up a recent yachting magazine and thumbed through it, patiently waiting to niggle information out of her, one way or another about where Evan was staying. Lena hung up the phone, turned her chair around from her desk and glanced up at Ryan.

"Hey you. What's up?" Lena twirled a pen between her fingers.

"You should have come with us today."

"That right? Why?"

"Good looking guys, wealthy as hell, enjoying traveling the Riviera."

"Two guys? You think I want *that* experience?" She held up a limp wrist.

"Not gay, just rich." Ryan moved and sat in the chair across from her desk.

"Rich, I can do. Ask me next time." She gave Ryan a conciliatory smile.

"So, I hear Evan's back in town." Ryan probed.

"Yeah. Rented a house in St. Paul."

"Danielle staying there with him?" Ryan grabbed some hard candy from the dish on her desk and peeled off a wrapper, popped one in his mouth and waited.

"No. Evan just moved in."

"Haven't seen Evan since his accident. Give me his address and I'll stop by, say hello."

"Have to call Danielle. She has it—I'll get back to you."

Ryan stood. "Thanks. I'll be in my office."

"How's your girlfriend?" Lena crossed her arms and leaned back in her chair.

Ryan moved his hands in the shape of an hourglass. "Hot. Smokin' hot."

Lena picked up a hard candy from the dish, threw it at Ryan, who ducked. The errant candy flew over his shoulder.

"Think about anything besides sex?" She teased.

"Not much." Ryan laughed, picked up the candy from the floor and tossed it at her. It landed in her coffee cup, splattering liquid on her desk."

"Out, out," she flipped her wrist at him, showing him the door.

Ryan spent about twenty minutes in his office entering the latest financials. It was a helluva month. High season lured tourists to spend their money on yacht rentals—tourists from Turkey, Dubai, Indonesia, Germany, and even England where warm water diving and spectacular weather for sailing was unheard of. Almost two-hundred fifty-thousand in profit so far this month was bound to be a record breaker.

His phone rang. "That was quick, Lena."

"Got a pencil?" she asked.

Ryan wrote down Evan's address on a small pad of paper, tore it off and stuck it in his pocket. "Thanks, Lena."

"No problem. You going over there tonight?"

"Doubt it. Taking Gillian to dinner. Do you know where your dad is?"

"No, sorry. He left in a hurry this morning."

Ryan finished up for the day, while waiting for Gaspard to return. It was late afternoon before he heard the familiar throaty voice talking on his cell phone. Ryan pushed his chair away from his desk and walked towards Gaspard's office. The door was closed. He knocked.

"Yeah? Who is it?" Gaspard's voice sounded impatient.

"Me. Bad time?" Ryan waited in the hallway.

"Uh—fine, come on in."

Ryan opened the door, stuck his head in and noticed Gaspard abruptly ended the call. He glanced up at Ryan with a startled expression.

"Everything okay?" Ryan asked, his eyes hiding the suspicion in his brain.

"Sure. Just stuff at home." Gaspard blurted out and tapped a pen on his desktop.

Ryan sat down on Gaspard's sofa and filled him in on the day's activities and financial gain. He watched Gaspard nod, but his eyes darted around the room as if he were miles away. He'd fidget with his coffee cup and kept rubbing his elbow. Ryan sensed he was uncomfortable. It was obvious Gaspard was not in the mood to converse. Ryan didn't know what to make of it, so he decided something went amok at home, scratched the back of his head and said he's see his boss tomorrow. "You take some clients out today?" Ryan threw Gaspard one last bone trying to assess where he'd been.

"Uh—no. Needed time on the water. Took *Belle Juliette* out. Helped clear my head."

Ryan nodded, sighed and stared at Gaspard. Was he telling the truth?

"See ya' tomorrow." Ryan turned and started to leave. "Door closed?"

"Yeah, please." Gaspard shot an arrow stare at Ryan and forced a taut smile.

For the first time in a long while, Ryan felt uneasy. Gaspard seemed *off,* but he had mentioned there was some problem at home. Paranoia was setting in again and he blamed this on Evan's return. Ryan drove home to relax, take a swim in the pool in his apartment complex and snatch a nap before taking

Gillian out to dinner. After his date with Gillian, when it was dark, he planned to take a drive and find out where Evan lived.

Dinner with Gillian was fun—a trendy new restaurant with upscale sushi. She kept wiggling her toe, rubbing against his leg under the table, hinting for what she hoped would entice him to her place. After dinner, he walked her to his car, caressed the small of her back and begged off intimacy. They stood there in a loose embrace swaying to music from a nearby bar. He said, "I'm beat. Spent the day on the water—always tires me out. Catch you next time and make up for it?"

Gillian shrugged her shoulders, pressed her body next to him and ran her finger across his bottom lip. "You'd better," she said and squeezed his buttock. "You know what you're missing." She moved her hand between his legs.

He kissed her with both of his hands on her face, pressing his bulging erection into her thigh. "Damn right." He smiled, winked at her. "I'm taking you home before I change my mind." When they got to her residence, he kissed her again in front of her apartment building. "I'll call you."

She winked at him, sighed in mock disappointment, and then turned around. He watched her leave, her perfectly formed derriere swaying from side to side as she walked up the steps to her apartment.

He got in the car, looked at the address on the piece of paper from his pocket. Gillian could wait. He had other things on his mind. As he drove down the coast, he mused at how naïve Lena was. Getting information out of her was effortless.

He wound his way up the ancient village. Hairpin turns forced him to move along with caution to the summit. The air thinned and became crisp as he climbed higher deftly avoiding an occasional goat. Stone houses, perched on the hillsides, huddled together as if to strengthen against a landslide. Low, hand-built craggy abutments clung to the side of the hills preventing him from skidding off the road to an untimely death. The sensibility of living in Nice held greater appeal to him—flatter terrain, streetlights, cafes and on-going night activity. Hamlet living never appealed to him.

Gravel spit sideways under his tires. He flicked on his bright night beams and continued driving. His navigation system indicated he was approaching the address. A small house stood on a corner plateau with a large palm tree in the front yard. He had arrived. What would he do now? He wasn't sure. He parked out front with the engine running and turned off his headlights. Almost ten, but lights were still on in the house.

He shut off the engine and watched, craning his neck between the steering wheel and windshield. He sat in the dark and wished he had a cigarette, a bad habit he'd tried to kick. He picked at his gums waiting for a glimpse of Evan. Someone walked past the window. Evan? No, wait—this guy was tall, not Evan. Who the hell was this? Then he spotted Evan. The two men were talking—an animated conversation, possibly an argument?

Ryan became agitated. His mind raced trying to make sense of why Evan, who just moved in, would have a male visitor late at night? Hell, he didn't even know anyone in town besides Danielle's family. What the—? He started the car, left the lights off, drove past Evan's house, made a turn in another driveway and began the drive down the hillside.

He'd have to check with Lena. Maybe she knew who this other guy was. Then he had a bizarre thought. Maybe Evan swung both ways. Did Danielle have a clue? In an odd way, he found Evan's possible bi-sexual preference amusing. He recalled Danielle had dumped him shortly after Evan arrived here the first time from New York. Thwarted his plans for marrying her and inheriting all of Gaspard Yachting when the old man croaked. Maybe karma was paying attention.

After a narrow, u-shaped turn, he turned on his high beams and continued down the hillside barely missing a stray cat wandering in the night with a small mouse tucked in its jaws.

He drove to his apartment, entered the garage, shut off the car and walked to the elevator. The doors opened and a couple got out, an elderly man and woman he recognized but didn't know. He nodded at them, got in the elevator and rode to his floor. His interaction with Gaspard in the afternoon still bothered him. He wondered where Gaspard had gone alone on *Belle Juliette*—he'd check with the harbormaster in the morning.

He knew what was coming—the familiar private display of flickering lights, like flashbulbs going off, signaling a threatening migraine. Fearful tension brought on these damn migraines. He could work his ass off all day and never get an aura, or anything resembling the arrival of a migraine, but send in fear and his brain circuitry misfired.

Ryan dug his fingernails into his palm. He knew exactly why his head hurt and had a mental conversation with himself. *Evan's recent arrival, now here only a week and he's already crawled into my head, banging musical symbols, pounding drums and making me nauseous; signals to take not one, but two preventatives. Evan's fault. Gaspard's fault.* He gritted his teeth and walked to his bedroom, downed the medication with a huge glass of water and shut off the lights. Darkness was salvation until the medication took hold. If it didn't, he'd feel like killing someone.

CHAPTER 61

Evan, Bob and Danielle

Evan had arranged a dinner reservation at a popular seafood restaurant for Danielle to meet Bob. There was no way Evan could keep Bob's visit a secret, and no reason why his former boss couldn't be on vacation.

Danielle entered the restaurant, glanced around the bar area and caught Evan's hand-wave. She wore a white flowing skirt, and a ruffled, off-the-shoulder blouse. As always, she looked stunning.

Bob stood to greet her and shook her small hand. "It's great to meet you—I've heard wonderful things about you."

Danielle grasped his hand, thanked him and moved to Evan. She placed her hand on the back of his neck and gave him a quick kiss.

"Want drinks first, or just head to the table?" Evan asked.

"Whatever you want," Danielle said. "Sticky hot tonight— I just want water. On second thought, give me a cola, with ice, please."

They ordered drinks and the hostess seated them at a table next to the veranda.

"How do you like St. Paul?" Danielle said and twirled the ice cube in her drink with a straw. She thought both Evan and Bob looked like tourists in tropical print shirts and shorts.

"Great, so far." Bob grinned.

"Did you fit on Evan's guest bed? Now that I've seen you, I can't imagine..."

"No, I don't fit, but it doesn't keep me from sleeping."

"Bob calls it a hobbit house." Evan mused.

"Hobbit, what?" Danielle looked to Evan and Bob for an explanation.

"They were little people in the land of—never mind. Can we just agree it's small and temporary?" Evan hoped to change the subject.

"How long will you be staying?" Danielle asked sipping liquid through her straw until it gurgled at the bottom of the glass.

"Maybe two weeks—depends on my work schedule in California."

Evan signaled the waiter to bring Danielle another Coca Cola, and a vodka tonic for Bob, while he continued pouring a refresher from a regional bottle of Bordeaux.

They chatted about Danielle's family, her students, Lucas' lavender business, and Evan's new gallery exhibition scheduled later in September. Bob admitted he was more than impressed with Evan's art success in New York. Danielle had many questions about California and was surprised to learn crops were grown there to feed the world.

She knew the state was impossibly long, had several major cities, such as Los Angeles, San Francisco and the capital, Sacramento, but she was unaware of the vast geographical changes—from the Cascades and Sierras to the Pacific Ocean. The idea of cold water for swimming in California coastal waters made her face wrinkle in pouty amazement, since she was certain the ocean should be a great deal warmer in San Diego than it was in San Francisco. By the time Bob and Evan were finished describing the Golden Gate Bridge, Pacific Heights with its mansions, and the charm of Sausalito, Danielle was begging Evan for a visit.

Dinner arrived and three hungry people enjoyed soupe au pistou, heavily flavored with garlic, ratatouille with plenty of eggplant, zucchini, tomatoes and herbs and fresh white fish. Danielle gobbled up her lobster, drizzled with butter, as if she had not eaten in a week, and then shocked Bob and Evan by asking what was for dessert. After finishing a blueberry gateau topped with ice cream, Danielle sat back in delight and smiled at Evan and Bob. "It's a lovely night—best time of year—a bit humid, but no Mistral, no major storms. I was thinking, I should have my father take you out on one of our yachts, Bob."

Bob coughed, swallowed hard and immediately took a sip of his vodka. He glanced at Evan with raised eyebrows, pleading to take the pressure off him for an honest response. Evan rubbed his chin and smiled while his heart skipped a beat with a split second to either lie or tell the truth. "I did take Bob for a drive up the coast to the marina. Your dad was there and offered to take us out."

"Oh!" Danielle frowned. "He didn't mention it. Where did you go?"

"Just toward Cannes so Bob could see the Riviera from a distance."

"Beautiful, isn't it?" Danielle said, seemingly satisfied.

"Vacation paradise," Bob noted.

They left the restaurant and walked Danielle to her car. "I'll call you tomorrow," Evan said to Danielle as he stood hugging her with his hands clasped together around the lower part of her back until she moved away.

"Great to meet you, Bob. Enjoy your vacation with Evan." Danielle waved to both men and got in her car and drove away.

Bob stood there with a toothpick between his teeth. "Awkward?"

"Understatement." Evan said while they walked to his car. "I wanted to tell her what's going on. Damn hard not to."

"I'll contact Detective Nichols tomorrow," Bob said. "The sooner we get this plan moving, the easier it will be on you."

"My gut tells me none of this is going to be easy," Evan sighed, got into his car with Bob and drove home.

CHAPTER 62

Evan, Bob and Gaspard

Bob and Evan carefully reviewed the plan to convince Detectives Nichols and Wilkes to pursue Armond's murder with new details about Ryan's alias, transportation of drugs, and additional information gleaned from Rusty's dying declaration. They arrived at the Nice police department headquarters where both detectives worked and had agreed to meet with Gaspard, Evan and Bob.

Gaspard was waiting in the noisy lobby already bustling with activity. Bob went to the reception desk and announced their arrival to the clerk, turned and sat down in a wooden chair next to Evan and Gaspard. All three men sat stoically in the lobby waiting for Detective Nichols or Wilkes, hopefully both, to greet them. Evan asked Bob if he was nervous and he said he wasn't. Gaspard picked up a newspaper, folded it in half on his knee and began reading. He looked up at the sound of rapid footsteps.

A small man with dark buzz cut hair and beady black eyes walked toward Gaspard and held out his hand. "Good to see you. You're looking well." Detective Nichols said.

Gaspard stood to shake Detective Nichols hand. The detective turned toward Evan. "I remember your face, but tell me your name again."

"Evan. Evan Wentworth. Danielle is my—um, well, fiancé."

Bob stood and extended his hand. "Sheriff Robert Cosley."

"Come gentlemen. Please follow me." Detective Nichols walked briskly in front of them down a long corridor of interior offices with frosted glass windows. Dark wooden doors led to an interrogation room with a metal table and two chairs. A ceiling fan wobbled an annoying hum. "Please sit," Nichols pointed his finger at the two chairs. "I'll get three more. Detective Wilkes will join us."

Nichols returned with Wilkes, each dragging chairs across the linoleum floor. Evan sat down next to Bob and Gaspard. "Would you like coffee?" Wilkes offered. He forced a pleasant smile making his bushy grey eyebrows and trim mustache tilt upward.

"No, water would be fine." Wilkes nodded and left the room, closing the door behind him.

"Where are you from again, Sheriff Cosley?" Detective Nichols probed.

"Call me Bob. Northern California—El Dorado Hills."

"Ah, yes—near the Pacific coast. " Nichols pursed his lips and nodded to acknowledge Bob's comment. He clicked his pen and worked it in a circle on his notepad in an attempt to get the ink to flow.

Detective Wilkes arrived with five bottles of water cradled to his chest and shut the door with the back of his foot. It slammed hard making the glass rattle. He placed the water bottles on the table and sat next to Detective Nichols.

"So, why are we here today?" Nichols said in an abrupt tone.

Bob looked at Evan. "May I proceed?" Evan nodded.

Both detectives listened to the tragedy that took place in El Dorado Hills in 2011. Bob explained Evan's six-year old sister was killed in the armed robbery. Both detectives' faces turned glum as they glanced at one another.

Evan put his elbows on the table and rested his head on his hands, once again listening to the story that tugged at his heart making him suffer in silent anguish. Bob continued the story. Other people died that day besides Ashley, Evan's little sister.

"How much did the robbers get away with?" Wilkes asked.

"Too much! Local casino transferred their cash to the bank for three nights. Had a fire in their vault room and needed a quick remodel. Obviously, someone tipped off the robbers. Small banks rarely have much cash on hand.

"Batards se sont enfuis avec beaucoup d'argent!" Gaspard exclaimed in French, unable to keep his frustration in check. He glanced at both detectives who were staring at him in surprise. He rubbed his nose in embarrassment at his temerity and decided to remain quiet.

The detectives listened intently as Bob continued to explain why the case had gone cold for months—then shared how clues were unearthed from the Purple Place restaurant and bar when two guys wanted to rent a copter before the robbery—a bartender who overheard the conversation but didn't pay attention at the time. Bob explained how he was contacted by the LAPD. Subsequently Evan also learned about the dying declaration from Rusty Chamberlain, who flew the copter. To clear his conscience, Rusty fingered the brothers who committed the robbery—Jed and Ted Reddiger.

"What does that have to do with Armond?" Detective Nichols frowned in frustration and began cracking his knuckles.

Evan spoke up. "I talked to Ryan Coltrane on a yachting outing with Gaspard shortly after Armond was murdered. He told me he had worked for Columbia Yachting in Southern California. Although something about Ryan irked me when I first met him, I had no idea who he was."

"Was?" Detective Wilkes sipped his water and stared at Evan.

"Ryan Coltrane is, in fact, Jed Reddiger. His brother, Ted, died shortly after the robbery and was buried somewhere outside of Manteca, in the woods near Rusty's charter copter business. When Rusty indicated Jed was planning on buying a yacht and heading to the south of France, every suspicion I had about Ryan made sense."

"What does all of this have to do with Armond's murder?" Detective Nichols was tolerant, but from the strained expression on his face, it was obvious he was frustrated.

Evan continued. "I was in the restroom at Gaspard Yachting the day you interrogated Ryan. I overhead some of your concerns about blood fibers in the carpet, and the missing shoe."

Detective Nichols stared at Evan but said nothing.

Bob took over the conversation. "Because we now know Ryan Coltrane is Jed Reddiger, we know he committed the robbery in El Dorado Hills, but we can't prove he shot anyone, least of all Ashley. They wore masks. Evan shot one of the robbers in the leg, most likely Ted, and the other robber under his shoulder. Ryan has a wound under his shoulder blade, disguised by a tattoo on the front and back of his torso—all circumstantial bits of evidence. We can prove he was there, but if he were arraigned in California, to stand trial and be convicted, at best he'd only get a felony conviction for armed robbery since we can't prove murder."

"Let me understand this," Detective Nichols said, nervously tapping his pen on the top of his pad. "What makes you think Ryan killed Armond?"

Evan shifted in his chair and leaned forward. "You think he's guilty and so do we. Something I picked up from the tone of your voice during the interrogation."

Nichols put the tip of his pen in his mouth, but just sat there not saying anything.

Gaspard pushed his chair back and stood. He cupped his fist to his chest and coughed. "I tried to ignore my suspicions about Ryan until my son, Lucas, followed him to the marina and watched Ryan sidle up to a submarine supplier in the middle of the night while someone from the sub tossed packages to Ryan on his yacht. This was shocking for me to accept—my partner involved with drugs. But, to learn from Evan and Bob that Ryan committed a crime in Northern California made me intent on finding out for myself if this man, my partner, had been duplicitous about everything from the beginning. I was too ashamed and angry to get you involved because I had hoped I was wrong about my own suspicions."

Detectives Nichols and Wilkes turned to each other not sure who should speak next. Wilkes continued. "What do you want from us?"

Bob pushed his chair back and stood, leaned forward with both hands on the table. "First, we want Armond's clothing, if still in evidence, tested for Ryan's DNA. Check the blood spatters on his shirt. If a fight took place in Ryan's office, perhaps over drugs, then it's possible Ryan's blood is on Armond's shirt. Remember, Ryan claimed he got a split lip from a fall in his office—shattered glass everywhere."

Nichols said, "I didn't buy that story."

Gaspard let out a sigh and began rubbing his thumb bent inside his closed hand.

"Did you test the blood stains in the carpet?" Bob said and stood back, both arms now crossed on his chest. "If we can prove, with your help, that Ryan killed Armond, we'd like to have him arraigned and tried here in France and not extradited back to California."

"I see," Detective Nichols twisted his lip. "He'd end up in prison here for murder. By the way, the blood on the carpet in Ryan's office was his."

"How many years?" Evan asked.

"Well, if convicted with irrefutable evidence, twenty to life. Since you can prove armed robbery in California for another unresolved crime, it would help the case against him."

"Did you search Armond's house after the murder?" Bob asked.

"Yes, of course," Nichols said. "Nothing disturbed. No fingerprints. Found an odd piece of rubber by the toe kick near the sink cabinet in the kitchen. We thought it came from something under the sink, but there was nothing like this rubber material in the kitchen."

Evan interrupted. "Do you have it in evidence? Can I see it—please?"

Nichols instructed Wilkes to get the evidence from the shelves in storage in the basement. "How long will the DNA test take?" Evan asked.

"Couple of weeks—maybe less if I can get Captain Bouchamp to press to get it done faster. Ryan's blood is already on the carpet fibers, so it shouldn't take too long to see if the blood on Armond's shirt is a match."

Wilkes returned with a clear plastic bag containing an odd piece of rubber. He placed the closed bag on the table. Evan picked it up, studied it carefully by turning the plastic bag toward the window. It appeared to be a thumb-shaped fragment of black neoprene rubber like the material used in diving wetsuits.

Evan bit back his thoughts and set the bag back on the table. Gaspard picked up the bag and held it up. "I want to check the gear on one of our boats used specifically for diving. It looks like wetsuit material."

"We'll come with you," Nichols said.

"No! Better you don't come along. Ryan won't be suspicious if I check the dive boat. I can do it off hours when our clients are not using it and Ryan's gone home for the day."

Detective Nichols finally stood. "I agree with your plan and will move on this as quickly as possible, provided you agree we work together."

"Agreed." Bob smiled and shook both detectives hands.

"You have a license to carry, I assume?" Nichols said to Bob.

"Of course." Bob nodded.

"Do you have a gun with you?" Nichols asked.

Bob shook his head. "Didn't know about this plan until I came to France and talked to Evan."

"I'll arrange to get one to you. Ryan or Jed, whomever, is a dangerous criminal."

"Tell me something I don't already know," Gaspard said. His face flushed, filled with tension—they saw the angst in his eyes.

"Don't be too hard on yourself, Gaspard." Evan said. "This guy's a pro. He slithers through life without retribution for what he's done. That's about to end."

"I should have known better." Gaspard hung his head.

"Sociopath's don't advertise. He's probably done a lot of terrible things we'll never know about."

"We'll be in touch," Detective Nichols said. "Let me walk you out."

Wilkes remained in the interrogation room making notes, and Nichols walked his three visitors to the lobby and bid them good day. He thought to himself that all three men were involved with Ryan in different ways—all seeking truth, vengeance and justice.

Gaspard shook Bob and Evan's hand and said he'd check the dive boat's wetsuit gear and get back to them as soon as possible, then turned and went to his car.

"Meeting went better than I thought it would," Bob looked at Evan.

"As long as this scumbag goes down hard, I'm okay. I couldn't have done this without you, Bob."

"We both needed to solve this crime. I never would have anticipated this case would take me to St. Paul and Nice," Bob said.

"Neither did I." Evan agreed and slapped Bob with a friendly gesture on his back.

"What do you make of the neoprene?" Bob asked.

"Ryan took me diving—nearly lost my heel to a Moray."

"A what?" Bob scrunched his nose upwards.

"Never mind. Long story. But if there were no fingerprints on Armond's body, and he was strangled, then maybe Ryan—I have to stop calling this asshole by that name—Jed, strangled him with diving gloves."

"Clumsy, no?"

"Not if you wanted to silence someone at the same time you were choking them. You could smother a face with a glove like that and not be able to breathe."

"You've read too many crime novels," Bob mused.

CHAPTER 63

Ryan

Ryan drove to work the next day after a disturbing evening doing much of nothing sitting in the dark outside of Evan's home. Who was the man he'd seen in the living room? He'd ask Lena as soon as he arrived at the office.

A customer from Greece with his mother, his wife, their six children and an entourage of support staff were scheduled for a trip to Eze, a picturesque village atop a jagged mountain with a vast view of the Riviera. A summer storm had passed. Palm trees still shook in the wind. Whitecaps rolled and broke. It would be choppy out there today. Perhaps he'd take his own yacht, *Southern Cross*, named after Crosby, Stills and Nash— the song, years ago, made him determined to have a yacht of his own. The *Southern Cross* was fast, and cut through rougher seas very well.

He noticed Gaspard's car in the parking lot, grabbed his leather folio and got out of his car.

"Hey, Nicole."

"Morning, Ryan. Your customer will be here in a half-hour. Called and said traffic was horrific."

"Where are they staying?"

"Monte Carlo."

"Lena in yet?" Ryan thumbed through the booking calendar on the counter.

"Yeah. She's in the back. Marie baked a peach pie for us. Hope there's a piece left for you."

Ryan hoisted his folio under his arm, walked into his office and tossed it on his desk.

"Want pie?" Lena stood against the doorframe with her hand palm-side up balancing a plate with a piece of pie and a melting scoop of ice cream dripping off the side on to the carpet. "Oh, sorry," she said and lapped up the ice cream melting off her plate with her fingers.

"Sure, thanks," Ryan said and took the plate from her hand. "Got a minute?"

"Yeah. What's up?" Lena positioned her leg under herself and sat in a chair dangling her silver leather sandal on the toe of her other foot.

"Who's the guy staying with Evan?" Ryan asked as nonchalantly as if he were checking on the weather.

"Danielle said he's Evan's boss, or former boss or something from California. Didn't catch his name."

"Is he an artist?" Ryan spun around in his chair, fiddling in his credenza drawer for plastic utensils. "Ah! Found some." He turned toward Lena, dipped a spoon into the soft ice cream, scooping it up along with a piece of pie.

"Don't know. Want me to ask?"

"No. No problem." Ryan chewed on a sliver of piecrust and mumbled. "God, she makes good pie."

"My mom's the best cook, as you know. She's feeling so good these days, she's cooking all the time."

Ryan's phone rang. "Yes, Nicole?"

"Mr. and Mrs. Abuldusa and their family are here."

"Thanks for the pie. You're the best." Ryan got up, left a smidgen of pie on the plate and went to greet his customers.

They agreed to follow him to the marina because there was no way they'd all fit in one car. As it was, they'd rented an SUV and packed themselves into it with small children sitting on various laps, hands plastered against the window, poking and tickling each other.

They arrived at the marina. Pierre, the harbormaster, greeted Ryan, smiled at his customers and bent forward to shake the hands of the children who were squealing with excitement.

"Which yacht are you taking out today?" Pierre asked.

"Mine. Take us to the *Southern Cross.*"

Pierre nodded. "Thought you might want to take the *Juliette* out—your partner, Evan and his friend took her for a jaunt the other day."

Ryan stood there as if he'd been struck by lightning. Gaspard had told him—lied to him—that he'd taken *Juliette* out by himself. He gritted his teeth and forced a smile. "Let's take two tender trips to the yacht so everyone won't be so cramped."

The rest of the morning and afternoon went well, but it was as if Ryan were in the netherworld. He kept thinking about Evan, and his guest. Why would Gaspard take them out? Of course, if he was Evan's former boss, Evan would want to impress him. Then it dawned on him. Evan's friend could be a cop. Ryan's skin prickled despite the heat and salt spray from the yacht. The peach pie didn't sit well in his stomach.

He stayed on the yacht while his clients toured Eze, something he'd seen and done many times. It took two trips in his Zodiac to get the entire entourage, a security guard toting a gun strapped under his jacket, Mrs. Abuldusa's maid and children's caretaker from the yacht to shore. Ryan thought of how difficult it would be to be so wealthy or prominent that one had to travel with security.

Unsettled, he wandered around the deck watching the waves undulate toward shore. He rarely drank with customers, but today he'd break that rule—he needed a drink. The bar was heavily stocked, and he chose bourbon, found a shady spot to sit on deck and look at Eze towering up the hillside from a distance.

He chewed on the inside of his cheek, soothing it with booze, alternately numbing it and biting on the flesh. Many times he convinced himself Evan could not possibly have been there the day of the robbery. Even if Evan was there that day, Evan couldn't prove anything. No one saw him, or his brother, Ted. A day gone wrong, but a wealthy heist nonetheless. He winced remembering Ted getting shot in the leg and then rubbed his own shoulder wound in sympathy.

Poor Ted. Worked at Red Hawk Casino. Knew about the fire and movement of the cash to the bank during the remodel. Such a good plan—three days where the casino's cash would be at the bank. They'd watched the Brinks truck enter the bank the night before. They'd considered a night robbery, but alarms made it difficult, if not impossible. So, they decided on a morning heist.

Everything was so well orchestrated and yet it turned into a disastrous robbery gone wrong. Worst of all, Ted lost it in the bank—killed those people, as if everything horrible in his childhood boiled up and he exploded. Ted's violence was always just below the surface. Ryan missed Ted, his tough, but broken brother—the only person who would ever understand what they went through as kids.

Ryan slugged back the rest of his bourbon, got up and filled the glass halfway.

Time to figure out what was going on with Evan. Ryan rubbed his chin back and forth considering possibilities. Suppose Evan's friend is a cop and he was there that day, or worse, they were both there that day. Could they have found out Ted and I were involved in the robbery? Impossible! Our faces were covered. No fingerprints. We got away clean. Weeks later, the news media stopped covering the story because there were no suspects.

Ryan crossed his feet at the ankles and put them up on an ottoman. Wind blew decorative pillows off seating, scattering them on the deck. Ryan ignored them and thought of Rusty instead. Old Rusty, partner in crime copter pilot who promised, with a lump of cash, never to tell. Ryan made a mental note to call Rusty. If Rusty hadn't talked, there is no way anyone could trace the robbery back to him.

Maybe, however, this wasn't about the California robbery. What if it was about Armond? Had the police found something? If they could prove he murdered Armond, he'd be going to prison—locked up, maybe on death row—in solitary. Not happening, he sighed. Never, ever going in a hole again. Once in a lifetime was enough. He had a flashback of the dark storm shelter where he was kept as a child with his brother. He blinked the horrific image to the back of his brain.

While the yacht drifted and tugged at the anchor, he dozed in the shade until the glass slipped out of his hand. It crashed to the deck and skittered across the floor. The noise jolted Ryan back to realty. A quick glance at his watch reminded him his clients would return soon.

He stretched out on the cushy curved lounge and decided it was time—time to go to plan B, the plan he hoped to never use. Time to move his funds to another offshore account, again. Time to buy explosives. Time to get the hell out while he was still alive.

CHAPTER 64

Evan and Danielle

While waiting for DNA evidence to be tested by the Nice police, Bob decided to tour Cannes for the day. He headed out early intent on finding a piece of jewelry for his wife, Kathy, as a gift when he returned to California.

Evan enjoyed the peace and quiet of having his rental house to himself, but longed for some alone time with Danielle. She agreed to meet him at his house to hang out and talk about the future. It was warm and he felt comfortable without a shirt. He heard the knock on the front door. The jute carpeting poked his bare feet so he slipped into his loafers and went to greet her.

"Hey, babe." He pulled her inside and shut the door, kissing her and nudging her toward the sofa where he reached under her blouse, fondled her breasts and kissed her neck. "Wait one second." He dropped his shorts and quickly put on a condom. She smiled and waited in anticipation. Then her lips found his and they both were so aroused with passion it felt like the first time they made love—the anxiety, the all-consuming desire dispelling any doubt that they both needed this. She dropped her skirt and panties, and hoisted herself on top of him, eager to please him, desperate to feel him inside of her. She tossed her tank top on the floor while he unhooked her bra. He smothered himself in her full breasts and could barely contain himself, but he did until both bodies were in a heated rhythm of ecstasy. When their passion subsided, they remained entwined in a soft embrace and let their breathing fill the air.

Contented, and finally awake, Danielle carefully slid off of Evan, naked and self-conscious of her slightly rounded abdomen. She reached for the afghan and draped it on top of her stomach. "That's what I call a real welcome," she teased.

"You've worn me out, but I so needed you. Bob's a great guest, but sleeping alone and thinking about you made me nuts."

"When will he be back?" Danielle asked while retrieving her clothing.

"Sometime later today. He said to do whatever we wanted—he's enjoying being a tourist."

"So, what do you have planned?" Danielle asked, and donned her bra and tank top.

"Can we talk about our future?" Evan asked, sitting naked on the sofa.

Danielle's eyes brightened. She moved next to him, put her legs across his lap, and then immediately shifted the afghan to hide her stomach.

"I thought we'd look at houses. Where do you want to live?"

She twisted her mouth in consideration of the possibilities. "Cannes is too expensive and Nice, although a bustling city, it is too commercial. I'd like to stay in St. Paul—be close to my family."

Evan nodded, not really expecting her to say something different. Her family meant everything to her—her parents, her siblings—it was like breathing to her, a necessary part of her existence.

"I was thinking," she ran her fingers through his dark, wavy hair, "that you'd want to be somewhat close to the gallery, and I could still be close to school."

"Exactly what I thought. Let's look at properties online and see what's available." Evan reached for his laptop on the coffee table and scrolled through real estate properties. Danielle nestled in closer to him. He brought up listings for properties in St. Paul and together they looked at homes on the market.

"Oh, I love this one," she beamed and then put her hand to her lips. "What about price? I know you are just starting out here as an artist in St. Paul and I don't want something too expensive."

"Not to worry. Aurora left me a considerable sum from the sale of the gallery. My parents set up a trust for me long ago, which I won't need for years to come. Money's not an issue."

"I had no idea Aurora left you money!" Danielle seemed shocked and slightly irritated.

"It was in her Will as a gift of appreciation for my staying with her until the end, and helping with the last art showings."

Danielle nodded, trying to take in the surprising information. The tone of her voice softened. "I think I understand. It was a nice gesture."

Evan and Danielle browsed through properties until Danielle gasped at one she was very attracted to.

"How many bedrooms?" she asked.

Evan craned his neck trying to read the small print. "Um, let me see. Three chambers. Will that work for you?"

"Yes. One for us, one for guests and one for the baby."

And there it was—the word *baby*, hanging in the air—a word unable to be retracted. Danielle hung her head, as if ashamed of what she had said, hoping he would think she meant in the future.

"What did you just say?" He backed away from her and could see her face had drained of color.

"Evan, I don't know how to say this—so I'll just say it. I'm pregnant."

Chills traveled up Evan's spine and he acted as if he didn't hear her correctly.

"What do you mean—you're pregnant?" His face was devoid of emotion and Danielle couldn't tell if he was upset or perhaps even angry with her. Evan rubbed his nose, trying to assimilate what she had just said to him. His brain fired off conflicting emotions."How long have you known?" he said in a snippy tone as if she were on a witness stand.

Tears brimmed and began trickling down her cheeks. She bit her lip and barely uttered, "I found out right after you left for New York. I was in the hospital for a ruptured cyst. I'd been bleeding and didn't know what the problem was. Then the doctor told me my pregnancy would be normal. I was shocked—with the bleeding I was sure I wasn't pregnant."

Evan got up from the sofa, grabbed his shorts and put them on. "You should have told me right away. Why didn't you?" His voice conveyed annoyance and hurt.

Danielle's tears flowed in fear. She sniffled, "I knew you were caring for Aurora—didn't want to burden you," she choked out words in between breaths. "I was afraid—afraid you wouldn't want me."

"What?" He glowered at her. "How could you say that?" His loud voice was harsh.

"Don't yell at me, Evan."

He shook his head. "You should have told me. We promised not to have secrets from one another."

"I know. I'm so sorry." She sat there shaking, wiping tears off her chin.

"Don't you love me enough to want to share something like this—my child, *our* child?" He gave her a look of incredulity.

"Of course! It broke my heart not to tell you. I was afraid you'd think I trapped you."

"Why?" He stood, staring at her. "We used protection. How did this happen?"

"I found a torn condom on the floor when we made love in the guest house, but didn't say anything—it was our first time together. I was really hoping this wouldn't happen." Danielle's face was flushed, spotty and she was starting to hiccup.

"Does anyone else know?" Evan asked her, still standing in the middle of the floor with his hands on his hips.

"Only Chloe." Danielle whispered.

"Christ! Your sister knows, but I didn't? Why did you tell her?"

"She was in my hospital room the day my doctor gave me the news."

He looked at her, saw her suffering in anguish, but couldn't bring himself to comfort her in his befuddled state.

"You want me to go?" She said, frightened to utter those words.

Evan turned, looked out the window and paused —"I think it would be a good idea." With such finality, he knew he'd crushed her spirit. He listened to her sobbing with his back to her.

She picked up her skirt, slipped it on, grabbed her purse and walked toward the front door. She thought about turning around to plead with him, but she didn't. She slammed the door in frustration because she was terribly upset with herself, however she was more than devastated because Evan was angry with her.

He ran to the front door and yelled, "Wait!"

She was already in her car looking over her shoulder backing out of the driveway and didn't see him. She sobbed on the way home. What had she done?

CHAPTER 65

Danielle and Marie

Marie was curled up on the sofa with a book in the living room when the front door slammed. She recognized the unmistakable sounds of the daughter she knew so well—the one who hiccupped and sniffled at the same time. "In here, honey,"she said.

Danielle hiccupped her way into the living room, looking defeated, blotch-faced, again, in the middle of some sort of crisis carrying a full box of tissues. She sat down next to her mother and blew her nose.

"Tell me what happened." Marie reached and put her arm around Danielle's shoulder.

"It's all my fault. I'm—I mean, I'm, uh—"

"You're pregnant, aren't you?"

Danielle looked at her mother, nodded and the waterfall of tears started again.

Marie sat quietly, rubbing Danielle's back and neck in an effort to console her.

This was not the time for recriminations, reprimands or blame—it was simply time to be a mother.

"I told Evan." Danielle blurted out the words and wiped her eyes.

"Let me guess," Marie said. "It didn't go well."

Danielle nodded and let her head drop forward. She shrugged her shoulders. Marie waited patiently for her daughter to find her own courage to speak whatever guilt she needed to expunge.

"I should have told him sooner—but with the ruptured cyst, I didn't think I was pregnant. Dr. Bendick surprised me when he told me the pregnancy would be normal. I mean—

Evan and I used protection. This shouldn't have happened, but the condom tore."

"Oh, honey. I know you didn't plan this."

"Evan's angry. I don't think he'll forgive me. I should have told you, but I felt I had to tell him first."

"You should have told him as soon as you knew. He would have wanted to be there for you."

"But, he had Aurora's illness and death to contend with. I couldn't burden him with the thought of a baby. Chloe asked me to consider whether I wanted to keep it, and I told her I wouldn't have an abortion."

"Chloe knew?" Marie's jaw dropped. Danielle looked at her mother and could see the hurt in her eyes.

"I'm so sorry, mama. I should have told you sooner, but I found out right before your operation and didn't want to worry you—and I was scared." Danielle's doe eyes pleaded for acceptance and understanding. "When did you guess?"

"Probably when you were sick that night at dinner. After your hospitalization, you began to put on weight, not to mention how much you were eating!"

Chloe burst into the room, still in her scrubs. "What's going on in here?"

Danielle pointed to her abdomen and wiped her nose with a damp wad of tissue. "Please don't tell Dad, or Lucas, and certainly not Lena. I don't want this all over the office."

Marie spoke up. "I respect your privacy and won't tell Lucas or Lena, but I insist on telling your father. He has a right to know. I don't want to hurt our marriage by keeping something this important a secret."

Danielle sighed. Her shoulders slumped in defeat, but she nodded her approval.

The three women talked about Evan's reaction and both Marie and Chloe decided Evan was in shock—rightfully so, and to give him time to accept the situation.

"I'm not sure he'll forgive me." Danielle said.

Thor waddled into the room, sensitive to Danielle's tears and put his head in her lap. She cuddled Thor with her arms, kissed him on the head and rubbed the back of his ears.

"Just think," Marie's face lit up. "In a few months I'm going to be a grandmother."

"What if Evan won't want me, won't marry me?"

"Then we will be here for you—we're family and nothing can change that."

"I love him so much. I didn't want to cause anyone pain."

Marie patted her daughter on the knee. "Honey, you didn't do this alone—remember that. Evan needs to think this through. He loves you deeply. We've all seen that. Give him time."

Chloe chimed in. "I agree. He's barely settled here. I'm sure he has a lot on his mind."

The three women spent the rest of the late afternoon talking about Lena's new boy friend, the architecture student on scholarship from Spain, and Lucas' new girlfriend from work, Alyssa. Marie was thrilled Lucas had added several seasonal workers to help with the lavender business now that soap and perfume production would be expanding overseas. Chloe shared that her surgical nursing studies were going well, but she anticipated the exams were going to be very tough.

Gaspard walked in the back door, heard the conversation coming from the living room and planted himself in the archway. "What's going on in here?"

All three women gave him the 'go away' hand signal. He left, shaking his head and muttering, "Another female powwow—never ends around here."

CHAPTER 66

Evan

After Danielle left, Evan sank into despair. He hadn't wanted to hurt her the way he did. The stress of fretting about Ryan, having Bob there as a guest and co-conspirator to figure out how to work with the Nice police had taken a lot of emotional energy out of him. Lately, if he wasn't thinking about Danielle, he was anxious about Ryan and the anticipated results from the DNA. As lousy as today had gone, he was grateful Bob went touring on his own. Evan considered himself mentally tough, however after today he realized he wasn't as astute or considerate about a woman's feelings as he should be.

Danielle's thoughtless slip about her pregnancy wasn't done with malice or willful neglect. When she learned she was pregnant, she was consumed with her own medical issues and was worried about her mother's surgery. He sipped a bottle of beer playing the conversation over again in his head feeling like an insensitive schmuck.

He also knew he had explained to her more than once his concerns about having a family. How he wished now he had told her he *did* want children with her—and that he loved her so completely an early pregnancy wouldn't change his feelings. Instead, he had sent her away broken-hearted and it ripped at his insides.

He wished he could have been the one to decide when they would have have children. Stubborn, righteous control was such a dangerous trait. He had been more concerned about his own feelings than hers—and what a burden it must have been for her to hide this from him out of fear he'd leave her. He wished he could take it all back—wished he had not accused her and instead reached out and held her and told her he loved her.

He walked into the kitchen, opened the refrigerator and scanned the shelves for something to eat. Leftover pizza looked appealing, but there was no microwave to heat it up. Could he fry pizza on the stove? How did the oven work? No sooner did he put the pizza on the counter when he heard a car in the driveway.

Bob walked in carrying a roasted canard, green beans, potatoes and a six-pack of beer.

"Lifesaver." Evan blurted out. "Was about to try frying leftover pizza."

"I noticed you didn't have much food in the house, so I thought I'd pick up something easy to eat." Bob set the food down on the counter.

"Oh! I see you got a TV." Bob popped off the beer bottle cap.

"Couldn't stand it any longer. Not much I absorb in French, but CNN is everywhere. Makes me feel connected to the world." Evan forced himself to carry on a conversation as if nothing was wrong.

"Have a DVD player?" Bob chewed on a crispy duck thigh.

"Yeah. It's in a box in the bedroom. You can help me hook it up and we can watch some oldies."

"Like?"

"How about '*No Way Out*' with Hackman and Costner?"

"Great movie. Sure." Bob grabbed a plate, helped himself to a glop of mashed potatoes and green beans. He sat at the kitchen table waiting.

Evan returned with the DVD player and a box of DVD's. "Boys night in?"

"Sounds good." Bob said between devouring dinner. "How was your day? You seem a little somber."

"Shitty. Absolutely shitty. Danielle's pregnant. Just found out and I handled it badly."

"Oh! That's a surprise." Bob fumbled for words.

"That I handled it badly?"

"No, dope head. That she's pregnant. I don't know what to say."

"I shouldn't have let her leave the house the way I did, punishing her. I feel like a jerk."

"Need something to cheer you up?" Bob held out a duck breast to Evan.

Evan grabbed the duck and took a bite. "Pretty good. Better get a plate. I'll join you."

Bob waited for Evan to heap food on his plate, sit down at the table and finish a swig of beer. "I've got news I think will cheer you up."

Evan frowned. "So what could possibly be good news?"

"DNA results are back. Blood on Armond's shirt was his, of course, and Ryan's."

Evan bolted up from the table and knocked his plate on the floor. "No shit?"

"Did you know Armond's neck was snapped?"

"What? No. Gives me chills."

"Captain Bouchamp is as anxious to get this case solved as we are."

"Ryan's going down—that no good scumbag." Evan said, with his hands visibly shaking. He bent over and started scraping up mashed potatoes off the kitchen floor.

"Gotta call Gaspard. Have to tell him right now when he's at home and not at the office."

"Finish your dinner," Bob said, "Then you can call him."

"Can't eat." Evan put his head into his hands and openly wept—raw emotions spilling out. Frustrating emotions about snubbing Danielle. Pent up emotions about justice being served after so many years—finally an end to all of this, which for so long seemed to have no clues and no end in sight.

Bob sat there watching Evan, knowing exactly what he was going through now that Ryan could be arrested. This would be a case he could also finally put to rest.

Evan composed himself and looked directly at Bob— someone he didn't need to hide his emotions from. He'd seen him at his worst after Ashley died, and knew how much solving this case meant to him. Finally, a win-win for both of them.

Bob picked up his beer bottle and held it in the air. "As Gaspard said, let's roll."

CHAPTER 67

Evan and Gaspard

Later that night Evan reached Gaspard on his mobile at home. After he explained the results of the DNA testing, Gaspard bellowed out a string of expletives, and Evan could hear Gaspard bang something—maybe his fist on his desk. "Hold on a minute—let me shut the door to my office."

Evan heard a door close, waited and chewed on his thumbnail.

"I didn't want to believe he could do something like this—actually kill Armond. And then to learn he was involved with a robbery and murder before we became partners—serious lack of character judgment on my part. He seemed so congenial when I met him. I failed and let down Armond's family. God, I hate this. I have to stop beating myself up. Why did Ryan kill him?"

Evan offered support. "Until he's arrested, assuming we'll get a confession, we'll never know the exact reasons. I suspect Armond confronted him about his grifting and Ryan panicked."

A moment of silence and then Evan switched the subject. "By the way, did you have a chance to check the wetsuits?"

"Took awhile to look through the dive suits—nothing missing there, but I did find a pair of gloves in Ryan's duffle bag with a slice of neoprene missing from one of the thumbs."

"Why am I not surprised," Evan blurted out. "Will have to take the gloves to Detective Nichols and see if the missing slice matches the piece of neoprene in evidence. Did Armond scuba dive?"

"Hell no. Hated the water. Never learned to swim. Why?"

"Wanted to be sure there was no reason for a piece of neoprene to be in Armond's kitchen."

"What's next?" Gaspard wondered.

"I've talked to Bob, who's been in touch with Captain Bouchamp. They're ready to arrest Ryan tomorrow."

"The sooner the better."

"Have you told Marie what's going on?" Evan walked to his kitchen window and stared at the weeds growing in his backyard.

"No. All the women in my family talk to each other, and I didn't want Lena knowing about this. I haven't even told Lucas."

"Good. I'll talk to Detective Nichols and see if we can make the arrest tomorrow. Do you want to do this at the office?"

Gaspard didn't answer.

"You still there?"

"Yeah. Thinking. I hate to do it at the office, but I want to see his face when he's arrested."

When does he usually come in?"

"First thing—around eight-thirty. If he has clients scheduled, it's usually not until late morning."

"Okay. Will confirm with Nichols and plan to be there tomorrow morning around nine."

"Bob coming?"

"You'd better believe it."

Evan ended the call and slumped into the sofa. He needed to go for a long run—anything to get the lactic acid out of his muscles. Besides being tense like a guitar string strung too tight, he was riddled with guilt over not having called Danielle. He wanted to apologize, but couldn't find the right words. Worst of all, he couldn't even think about being a father and having a child in his life right now. Ryan's upcoming arrest was consuming all his time and mental energy. He wanted to tell Danielle about what was going on with Ryan, but couldn't. Now, he faced the same guilt about keeping secrets. Would she understand? Or, perhaps they had both blown the prospects for a lasting future together because trust had been shattered.

Bob was hiking around the neighborhood and was expected back in an hour, then Evan would fill him in on the plan for tomorrow. Maybe he'd convince Bob to take a long run on the beach with him. Evan knew if he didn't run, he'd never be able to sleep no matter how many sheep he'd try to count. He finished a beer and decided to change into his running attire. While he was undressing, he wondered about how much evidence had been in Ryan's trunk before he had it redone—the convenient story about having spilled wine—he'd thought of everything. All Evan's years as a cop, one thing always rang true—sooner or later the murderer always made a mistake.

CHAPTER 68

Ryan

The dynamite was securely wrapped and stuffed in his duffle bag in the trunk.

He'd thought long and hard about what needed to be done. It had been a tedious day at the office with numerous month-end financial reports to be filed.

Gaspard had avoided him, and instead spent much of the day in his office talking with the design firm Lena had contacted to give them a bid about remodeling the kitchen. Before Gaspard left for the day, he stopped by Ryan's office.

"You going to remodel the kitchen?" Ryan smiled and raised his eyebrows trying to show some enthusiasm for what was going on at the office.

Gaspard twisted his lip. "Probably. Haven't decided whether it's worth the money, but Lena wants the experience so she can add it to her resume."

"Oh, right. Forgot she intends to go to design school. Hadn't thought about that."

"You'll be in tomorrow?" Gaspard's brow furrowed making him look older than his years.

"Why are you asking?" Ryan shifted in his chair.

"We can go over the financials. I need to see what kind of month we've had."

"They're pretty much finished. I can leave them on your desk."

"If you wish. Worn out. Gout's bothering my toe again. Just want to go home and get off my feet," Gaspard said and shifted his weight to his good foot.

"Didn't know you suffered from gout?" Ryan's eyes widened.

"Yep. Damn pain in the ass, like some people. Comes from eating too much meat." Gaspard turned, gave a piercing look to Ryan and left the office.

Ryan sat in his office, tilted back his chair and put his feet up on his desk. He had no doubt about what had to be done. Gaspard's odd behavior confirmed his suspicions. Was kind of a shame, actually, because Ryan admitted to himself that his partner had been a good boss, and he hated to proceed with what he now had to do. He liked the guy, dammit. He wished he didn't because it would be so much easier.

Everyone had left for the day, except Lena because he had asked her to stay. She innocently wandered into his office with a pad of paper and a pen stuck behind her ear—a new habit she'd picked up, thinking it looked authoritative for someone aspiring to be a designer.

"So, what did you want to discuss?" She sat down in a chair across from his desk.

"I was thinking of redecorating my apartment and wondered if you'd consider doing it for me."

"What? You're kidding, right?" Her face lit up with enthusiastic curiosity.

"No. I'm sick of the blues and orange that came with the apartment. The owner said I can repaint and I need new furniture. Hate the non-descript stuff I bought—was thinking of mid-century modern like this photo in the magazine here."

"Oh, that's stunning. I love it. I could do that—um, uh, would you actually pay me?"

"Silly girl. Of course. Can we talk about it over dinner?"

"When, now?"

"Pick your favorite restaurant. I'll drive. After dinner I'll take you to my apartment."

"That works for me. I'll get my purse. Can we eat lobster? I'm so in the mood."

They left her car in the parking lot and drove along the coast to a trendy restaurant, Les Pecheurs, specializing in seafood. The restaurant was very crowded, but they were seated at an intimate small table in a corner and ordered their entrees.

Lena talked with animated hands as she described various patterns in fabric she thought he might like. "How about off-white, silver and black?" She gushed, waiting for approval.

"Very sophisticated." Ryan smiled and sipped his wine.

"I would paint the walls light mauve or grey."

"Sounds nice." He bit into a chunk of bread.

"I'm so pleased you think I'm good enough to do this—I really don't have much experience except for what I've done at the office. You're so thoughtful to give me a real design opportunity. You'd be my first client."

"I think you've earned it. You're talented."

Their orders arrived on large platters. The waiter set them on the table.

She sipped her Chablis, while drizzling more butter on her lobster. "Thanks. I like working at the office, but it's not a passion. I can't wait to go to design school."

"How's Gillian?" Lena asked.

"Couldn't be better." He cracked a lobster claw and removed the meat.

"How's your new boyfriend—an architecture student or something?"

"Yes. He's fun—we have a lot in common. Comes from a large family too."

"Is it serious?" Ryan finished his wine and set his glass on the table.

She pursed her lips and pondered his question. "Not sure—too soon to tell."

They finished dinner and he walked her to his car. The sun dipped below the horizon and the sky flooded with a rainbow of deep hues of magenta, pink and cyan. Other than the waves rolling in slowly with the tide, it was dead still. She continued chatting about an older movie she had seen on television with Nicole Kidman, *Dead Calm.*

"I remember that movie," Ryan said. "Crazy person ends up on their sailboat and tries to kill her."

"Yeah, and she knows enough about sailing to save her life."

"How about you? Do you know much about boating?"

"Ha! You'd think I would, given my father's company, but until recently, I didn't pay too much attention unless someone was bringing me a cocktail on our yacht. That's my dad's arena—and yours."

"You swim?"

"If I have too. Hate getting my hair wet—messes with my dye job. Why do you ask?"

"Just curious. No reason."

Ryan drove into his apartment garage. They got out and walked to the elevator. "You know," Lena said, "I used to dream about this."

"About what?" Ryan turned toward her in the elevator.

"About us. I had such a crush on you, but I knew you wanted Danielle."

"I'm flattered." The elevator doors opened and Ryan led her down the hall to his apartment. He turned the key, walked in and turned on the light.

"Oh," she said. "This *is* rather gaudy, isn't it?"

"Ya' think?" Ryan rolled his eyes.

"Can I take some photos?" She reached in her purse for her iPhone.

"Sure. Take all you want. How about some wine?"

"Do you have a measuring tape? I'd like to get some idea of the size of this room."

"I'll see if I can find one. Let me pour you some wine first. Red ok?"

"Yeah, sure." She wandered over to the windows, crossed her arms and stared at the night sky. "Pretty view from here."

"I like it," he said and dropped the powder into her glass of Cabernet, stirred it with his finger and wiped it off on a wet paper towel.

He walked toward her. "Here's to my new digs." He smiled a deliberate infectious charming smile and handed her wine in an opaque royal blue goblet.

She turned toward him, took her glass and drank a big gulp.

"Do you think I should keep the drapes?" He pointed at the windows.

"God no. They're horrible." She drank all of her wine and yawned.

"What do you suggest?"

"Blinds or automated shades—or, um—sorry, I'm feeling odd—drowsy."

"Let me get you a refill. I want to discuss the carpeting. Maybe a rug instead?"

She rubbed her eyes in an attempt to focus, and let him pour more wine into her glass. Hoping to appear courteous, she finished the wine in two large gulps.

"Mind if I just sit for a minute on your sofa? I need to put my head down. I hope I'm not going to be sick, but the room is spinning—"

The glass fell from her hand as she slumped into the sofa. Her head fell back at an odd angle, making her look like a porcelain doll whose rubber band had snapped in the neck.

He took the syringe out of his pocket and injected it into her arm. She didn't even flinch. This part of his plan went well. She'd be out for several hours. He picked up her glass, took it to the sink, then rinsed it out with hot water and wiped it of any fingerprints—not that it mattered. For once, it didn't matter at all.

CHAPTER 69

Gaspard, Evan, Bob and the Police

Gaspard dressed in such a hurry, he forgot his belt. His regular work shoes hurt his big toe, so he donned a pair of old deck shoes and forced his sore foot inside. Marie ran into the kitchen in a tizzy, waving her arms as if she had just seen a giant spider.

"Lena didn't come home last night!" she wailed, putting her hand to her chest.

"What? Did she call?" Gaspard rubbed his forehead.

"No, she didn't call. I checked her room and she didn't sleep in her bed."

"Maybe she stayed with her boyfriend?" Gaspard shrugged his shoulders.

"It's not like her. She always calls," Marie said defensively.

"I'm sure something came up. She was at the office last night when I left. Did you try her cell phone?"

"Of course! It just goes to voicemail." Marie paced the floor.

"When she shows up for work, I'll have her call you, okay? Don't worry so much—she's not a kid anymore."

Gaspard planted a kiss on Marie's forehead, rubbed Thor between the ears and was nearly knocked over by Valentin and Juliette chasing each other through the kitchen. Amber followed, the older child, trying to get them to settle down.

Danielle wandered in, still in her PJ's and rubbed sleep out of her eyes. "What's going on? Mom, you look distraught."

"Lena didn't come home last night." Marie crossed her arms and rubbed them trying to find comfort.

"Oh? Well, it must be a boyfriend issue, don't you think?" Danielle said and started to pour herself a cup of coffee.

"Should you be drinking that?" Marie winced.

"It's just coffee!" Danielle scoffed at her mother.

"No! It's caffeine. It's not good for you."

Gaspard looked at Marie. "What's wrong with caffeine?"

Danielle shot her mother an annoyed, pinch-faced glance, and shook her head. "Dad, you're limping. What's wrong?"

"Damn gout again." He set his peanut buttered toast on a dish and turned toward the coffee pot on the counter. Valentin and Juliette ran through the kitchen again, with Thor chasing at their heels. Thor stopped at the table, sniffed and snitched a slice of toast and ran off.

"Merde, Thor!" He shook an angry finger at the dog, then kissed Marie on the cheek. "Gotta run," Gaspard said. "It's a madhouse here."

Lucas walked through the doorway tucking his shirt into his slacks. "Morning. I noticed Lena's car isn't in the driveway. Didn't she come home last night?"

"Don't ask." Danielle said. "Bad morning around here."

Gaspard could hardly concentrate on driving to the office. His nerves felt stuck in his chest like a knotted ball of twine. Sweat beaded on his forehead. He gingerly pushed the gas pedal down, trying hard not to put pressure on his gouty toe. He wiped the sweat from his brow onto his slacks. This was going to be a day like no other—as much as he was determined to see Ryan in handcuffs, he was distraught that it had come to this. He pulled into the parking lot and glanced at his watch—only 8:30—a half hour before the police would arrive. He grabbed his briefcase and shut the car door, then stood frozen in place. Lena's car was still in the parking lot. Chills went through his body and his heart clenched as if he'd been stuck with an ice pick.

Lena, the late sleeper, was never early for work. Why was Lena's car still in the parking lot? Did someone pick her up? Maybe her boyfriend took her out last night. He walked to her car, peered in the window and saw nothing unusual. Of all days, he didn't need this—plenty to worry about without wondering where his daughter was. Not like her to be late for work either—what the hell was going on today?

Nicole greeted him with her usual cheery voice. "Morning, Gaspard. You're limping."

"Yes, gout. Hurts like hell. Have you seen Lena?" he snapped, obviously agitated.

"No. She hasn't come in yet. Why do you ask?" Nicole cocked her head.

"Her car is in the parking lot. Did she mention going out with someone last night?"

"Not that I know of. When I left, I think she was still in her office."

"Christ. Where's Ryan?" He ran his hand through his hair until it stood up in an odd way making him look as frazzled as he felt.

"Haven't seen him either this morning." Nicole glanced at the schedule to see if a client was expected. "Ryan left an email message saying he couldn't take the client out this afternoon, and asked if you would do it."

"What the—? Unbelievable!"

Gaspard limped to his office, doing his best to avoid pressure on his foot. His face was now flushed from a combination of nerves, anger and a sore toe. Where the hell was Ryan? He heard cars arrive in the parking lot, sirens blaring—three separate cars. He peered out of his office window and spotted Detectives Nichols, Wilkes and Captain Bouchamp. Evan and Bob drove in following them with a screech of tires as they stopped abruptly.

Gaspard hobbled out of his office, past Nicole whose eyes were fixated on the drama in the parking lot. "What's going on?" she said in an alarmed voice.

"Don't ask." Gaspard huffed and lumbered toward the front door waving his hands as if the sky was falling. In a gruff voice, he yelled back to Nicole. "Ask one of the crew to handle the charter today."

"All set?" Detective Nichols asked when he saw Gaspard on the steps.

"He's not here!" Gaspard panted as he hobbled toward them.

"What do you mean he's not here? You mean he's late?" Evan said.

"He didn't come to work today—doesn't plan to come to work. I don't know what's going on!"

Evan put a hand on Gaspard's shoulder. "You okay?"

"No. Dammit. I'm not okay. Lena is missing! Her car is here in the parking lot and she didn't come home last night—and now Ryan's not coming to work—and I feel dizzy."

"Here, sit down in my car," Evan offered. Bob assisted Gaspard to the front seat.

"Give me Ryan's address and we'll go to his residence."

"I think its, um, 4112, no 1442—crap. I'm too upset to remember. Nicole has it. My receptionist will give it to you."

Detective Wilkes went inside the building.

Gaspard was breathing like he'd run a half-marathon. "Can someone get me some water?"

Bob ran inside and asked for water—Nicole pointed down the hall. "There's a refrigerator with water in there. What's going on?"

"Don't ask." Bob said and ran down the hall.

Bob returned with two bottles of water and gave one to Gaspard, who guzzled it down like he'd been parched in the desert for days. Bob held out the other bottle to the police, who shook their heads, so he kept it for himself.

"You think Ryan's at home?" Detective Nichols asked.

Evan piped up. "Doubt it. I think we've got a runner."

Gaspard spit out a gulp of water. "A runner? You mean he's fled?"

Evan sighed. "He may have decided it was time to disappear. It wouldn't surprise me. He's crafty—definitely not stupid. I think he's played us."

"I've got the address," Wilkes said. "Let's drive over there—you all coming?"

"Hell, yes!" Evan said and scrambled into the car with Bob and Gaspard.

Bob tore out of the parking lot following the police, their sirens blaring in the singsong sound French police cars make. Evan slammed his fist against the passenger window and scared Bob. "He may be at home," Bob said trying to be optimistic.

"Fat chance. If you were Ryan, would you be there?" Evan sniped.

"No—if I were Ryan, I would have been long gone. What I can't figure out, is how he knew we were coming for him today?"

"Maybe he didn't. Might have had other plans."

They arrived at Ryan's apartment building. Detective Wilkes agreed to stay on the street in the police car with Gaspard in case Ryan was home and might make a run for it.

Detective Nichols went up the back stairwell while Evan and Bob took the elevator. When all three men reached Ryan's apartment door, they knocked and waited in panicked silence. Nichols drew his gun. "Doesn't appear to be home."

"We could knock it down," Evan whispered.

"Don't have a search warrant," Bob grimaced.

"So?" Evan said. "Not letting that stop me now." He heaved his foot into the door, while Bob side-armed his shoulder into it for a full-force impact. It burst open, sending Evan to the floor. Nichols stood with his mouth agape in the hallway shaking his head, while Evan righted himself.

An elderly woman yelled down the hall from her partially opened apartment door, "Merde! What's going on?"

Nichols peered into the hallway and waved her back. "Police matter. Stay inside." He shouted.

The white-haired woman gasped and her eyes widened in alarm, but she dutifully closed her door.

Bob entered the apartment and went to Ryan's bedroom while Evan followed.

"He's not slept here—bed's made," Bob said.

"Shit! Closet's empty except for a couple of business suits. Safe's open—no passports or drugs. Check the bathroom," Evan hissed.

Bob opened the medicine cabinet above the sink. "Nothing in here, as if I expected to find anything."

Evan slumped against the bathroom door in frustration.

"He's run—dammit! I knew it." Evan said, shaking his head in anger.

"Where the hell do you think he is?" Bob asked.

Nichols holstered his gun. "I would guess he's on a plane or TGV train. We can check manifests and passport control to see if he planned to leave the country."

"Doubtful he's using his real name," Evan suggested. "All we have is a description of what he looks like."

The three men assembled in the hallway. Evan stared at the broken hinges on the slightly closed door, rolled his eyes and said, "Tsk. Yeah, I'll pay for it."

"Need to check with the neighbors—see if anyone saw anything. Let's check with the lady down the hall." Nichols grabbed a small pad of paper and a pen from his shirt pocket.

They knocked on several other doors, but no one answered. When they reached the old woman's apartment, they knocked. "Police—please open up. We'd like to talk to you."

The door opened and they faced a curious, elderly man in baggy pants and a cardigan sweater. He smelled of liniment, leaned on his cane and cupped his hand behind his ear. "What's the problem?"

"You speak English? Good." Nichols said loudly and introduced himself. "We're looking for Ryan Coltrane in apartment 306. Do you know him?"

"No. Don't know him, but see him around occasionally."

"Did you happen to see him today?" Nichols started writing with his pen.

"Not today, but we—my wife and I, we like to take late night walks—helps us to sleep."

"Yes, and?" Nichols pressed.

"Saw him yesterday with a woman. They were walking down the hall to his apartment."

Evan interrupted Nichols train of thought. "What did she look like?"

"Hard to say—didn't see her face. Small woman—dark hair."

Evan looked at Bob, who didn't say a word. "Anything else you can remember about her—what she was wearing, perhaps?"

"Dark slacks and a printed top—not good with colors, so I can't say."

The wife appeared in the doorway poking her head next to her husband's shoulder to gaze at the police. With pursed lips she added. "Her top was green and black, and she had on silver sandals."

Nichols jotted the information down on his pad. "Anything else you can think of?"

"When we got back from our walk, he was backing out of the garage on to the driveway," the man said.

"Oh!" Evan piped up. "About what time was that?"

The wife chimed in, "We usually walk around one or two in the morning—don't look at me like that—when you get old, you'll understand. Sleep is a precious, elusive thing."

"Yes, ma'am." Evan nodded. "What time did see you him?"

"Oh, not just him. Saw her too, but she was asleep against the car window—poor thing. Probably kept her out too late."

Evan felt blood drain from his face, like a ghost had just entered the room and dropped the temperature a few degrees. He shivered.

Bob glanced at Evan's pale countenance. "You okay?"

Evan shook his head. "Gut feeling—it might have been Lena."

"Who's Lena?" Nichols asked.

"Gaspard's missing daughter. She didn't come home last night."

Nichols finished getting the names of the couple and their phone number. He jotted the apartment number on his pad and said, "If you see either of them, would you call me immediately." He handed them his card. "Oh, and please tell the apartment manager we'll pay for the damages to the door."

Evan and Bob followed Nichols to the elevator. They checked the parking garage for Ryan's car—it wasn't there.

Wilkes stood next to the squad car, impatiently leaning on the hood for support while Gaspard slouched in the front seat, gently rubbing the top of his foot. He took one look at Evan as he approached the car and knew something was terribly wrong. "What took so long?" Gaspard huffed out his displeasure. "My foot is killing me."

"Ryan's not home," Evan said. "And, it doesn't look like he stayed the night. Closet and safe are cleaned out and so is the medicine cabinet."

"So, he's on the run?" Gaspard stammered. "I don't believe this!"

Evan spoke in a low tone and kept his voice carefully modulated. "You said Lena didn't come home last night. Do you remember what she was wearing?"

"Why are you asking?" Gaspard settled back into the car seat and peered through the partially open window at Evan, Bob and the two detectives.

"An elderly couple who live in the building saw Ryan with a woman last night."

Gaspard rubbed his eyebrow. "Well, that doesn't surprise me."

"Please," Evan pleaded with Gaspard. "Think about what Lena wore to the office the last time you saw her."

"I dunno. What do women wear? Pants, some sort of colorful top—what she usually wears. Sheesh, I can't believe you're asking me this."

"What kind of shoes?"

"Are you serious?" Gaspard snorted in frustration. "Same sandals she always wears to work—metallic silver."

Evan grabbed the roof of the car with both hands and looked directly at Gaspard. "I wish I could tell you something else, but it's what the couple upstairs said the woman with Ryan was wearing."

Gaspard leaned forward and began breathing heavily. "Ryan has Lena?" He looked up at Evan, pleading for a different answer.

Bob interrupted. "We don't know that for sure, but apparently the woman in Ryan's car was asleep last night when Ryan pulled out of the parking garage."

Everyone became silent watching Gaspard absorb the information. He put both of his hands to his head. "Do you think he kidnapped her?" His voice croaked out in sort of an animalistic howl before he banged his fists on the dashboard. "Damn murdering sonofabitch—now he's added kidnapping to his repertoire? Why Lena? He has no interest in her—never had. Makes no sense."

"I think he might use her as leverage."

"For what?" Gaspard said, shrugging his shoulders in disbelief.

"Maybe a ransom," Bob added.

"Let's head back to the station. We'll check the airports and train stations. "How old is your daughter?" Detective Nichols asked.

"Which one? I have five!" Gaspard said, purposely defiant.

"Sorry, Lena." Nichols added.

"She's just—his eyes brimmed—she's only eighteen. If he hurts her, I'll kill him myself."

They headed back to the station, exhausted and weary. It had been a frustrating day. Bob and Evan followed behind Nichols, Wilkes and Gaspard.

Evan held on to the steering wheel as if he were in a high performance racecar. His knuckles turned white and he ground his teeth. Bob broke the silence. "Where would Ryan go?"

"I hate being in Ryan's damn head. How the hell do I know?"

Bob nodded. "Well, if you had to guess?"

"For the life of me, I can't figure out why he'd kidnap Lena—as if his rap sheet isn't already going to be long enough? This is just plain stupid."

"Agreed. But, where would he go—or where would you go if you were him?"

"Bad question." Evan shot Bob an ugly glance. "I'd fly out of the country to some remote place where I'd never be found."

Both baffled, they rode in silence the rest of the way to the police station.

Evan briefly thought of Danielle—needed to apologize, but the present danger overshadowed every unspoken emotion he'd hoped to resolve by now. He missed her, and it bothered him that they hadn't had a chance to talk. With all this chaos, there was no way he could deal with his personal life.

They arrived at the station. Wilkes helped Gaspard out of the car and assisted him up the front steps of the building. "Let's go into my office," Nichols said and led them down the hall. "Restrooms are beyond the drinking fountain. If anyone is hungry, we've got a vending machine in the kitchen— nothing fancy. Sandwiches, chips, candy bars. Here's some change if you need it. Help yourselves."

Bob, Evan and Gaspard hit the restroom, as did the detectives, for an awkward silent moment of relief. Then they headed to the kitchen. "I could go for some chips or something," Bob said. Evan nodded.

The vending machine was nearly empty, but supplied necessary snacks.

Evan sat in Nichols office and bit into a chocolate crunch bar. Gaspard returned with a soda and some chips he didn't feel like eating. He offered them to Bob who changed his mind and shook his head. Gaspard no sooner sat down when his cell pinged. He put in his pass code and started reading the text message. He suddenly bolted up, oblivious to his pained toe and knocked over his soda.

"It's Ryan. He has Lena!" He showed Evan the text message.

"By now you know I'm gone, but where? Yes, I have your daughter. I'll tell you where you can find her in two hours."

A chill went down Evan's spine as he realized Ryan didn't ask for a ransom. Worst of all, he implied Gaspard could find her in two hours, but he didn't say if she was alive. What the hell was he doing?

Gaspard looked at Evan. "I have to call Marie. By now she's worried herself into a frenzy. It's late, and she has no idea what's happened today. I'm afraid I'll destroy her with what we now know. I hate to call her on her cell—she'd notice the fear and agitation in my voice."

"Can you call Lucas instead?" Evan suggested. "If you reach him you could tell him she's with Ryan. It's a white lie—a terrible lie, but at least she won't come undone. Don't tell her what Ryan's email said. Tell her Ryan said he'd call in a couple of hours. Marie might assume they hung out together, and that she'd even spent the night with him—which is disgustingly true in the worst sense."

"Perhaps I should do that. If I don't call, she'll be frantic about Lena and me as well. I'm usually home by now."

"Have Lucas tell her you're out with me and that you'll be home later."

Gaspard gave Evan a weak smile. "You're rather good at making up lies."

"Comes with the job of being a cop—can't always tell the exact truth."

Gaspard thought the better of it, and called Lucas. He didn't reach him, but left a voice mail that Lena was with Ryan and to tell Marie not to worry, and he was out with Evan and would be home late. He reluctantly munched on chips and the second soda Nichols got for him.

There was nothing to do but wait for two hours, which passed slowly like a drip line in ICU. Wilkes and Nichols were busy calling airports and train stations. Bob had nodded off in a chair with his head against the wall. Evan stared into space with a look of incredulity that hung around him like a shroud. The night cleaning crew sloshed water on the tiles, vacuumed floors and emptied wastebaskets, making the din of noise the only distraction from tension.

Nichols walked into his office, his shoes squeaking on the wet floor and announced there was nothing on the flight manifests for Nice, Marseille or Paris. They checked the train station, and no one at the ticket counters recognized the photos supplied by the police. Gaspard had provided a photo of his daughter, and the police already had several photos of Ryan.

Evan stood, nerves so on edge he wished he could go for a run. "Anyone have a cigarette?" Nichols nodded and pulled a pack from his desk drawer and offered him a pocket lighter. Bob looked at Evan. "Didn't know you smoked."

"I don't." Evan said and walked out of the room with a lit cigarette.

CHAPTER 70

Ryan and Lena

So far, things had gone as planned. He'd managed to carry Lena in her drugged condition, down the back stairs of his apartment complex without notice. She slept slumped against the car window and didn't awaken. If she did, he was prepared to give her another injection to knock her out.

His duffle bag contained what he needed—some tee shirts, shorts, and, of course, his medicine. His passport was stuffed into his jeans. He tossed rope, duct tape, dynamite, and a container of gasoline, a torch and a high-beam flashlight in the duffle bag.

He glanced at his watch while driving—almost 10:00. He had two more hours before he'd text Gaspard on Lena's whereabouts. Since he didn't show up for work, he assumed by now Gaspard had contacted the police.

The air was thick, with stifling humidity, but at least the indigo sea was calm. A partial waxing moon cast a flood of light on the rolling waves as he drove along the coast. A touch of melancholy flittered through him as he realized how much he'd miss the Côte. Worst of all, he'd miss Gillian. Breaking up with her was traumatic, and she didn't deserve to be dumped. He couldn't recall anyone slapping him so hard— except for his father's beatings. The sting of flesh on his face brought back memories he stuffed in a remote part of his brain. He accepted her slap, but never deserved his father's drunken abuse. Before she slapped him, she stood in shock when he told her he felt sex with her was phenomenal, but she was not the type to be the mother of his children. Couldn't get much more creative than that.

He passed a few cars on the way to the marina and drove into the parking lot where he purposely parked his car in a visible space close to the pier. Lena stirred and moaned. "Where am I?" she sat up in the car, dazed and groggy.

"I'm taking you to my yacht. Can you walk?"

"Humm—not sure. I can—um, talk, I mean walk." She fumbled for words and then started to giggle. Her eyes closed again and her head tilted sideways against the headrest.

"I'll help you. Just sit here for a minute."

He got his duffle bag, heavy as it was, out of the trunk and opened the passenger door. Although she was wobbly, he managed to get her upright and put his arm around her waist, with one of her arms behind his neck. He had to lift her a bit as they walked. She stumbled. Her sandal broke and came loose. He stared at it and decided it was perfect to leave it in the parking lot.

"Where are we going?" she mumbled and slumped. Her knees buckled.

"On a little trip."

He realized once he got her into a skiff, he'd have to drug her again if she became resistant. For now, she was in lala land where drug addicts wander.

She was a small person, nearly dead weight, and she made him struggle with getting her into a skiff, but he managed. He tossed his duffle bag on a cushion in the back. He'd told the harbormaster a couple of hours ago which skiff he'd be using. It was the responsibility of yacht owners to refuel the skiffs, but not everyone was cooperative, and tonight there could be no slip-ups.

Lena flopped against the skiff seat, with her arms limp like a rag doll as he motored to the *Southern Cross* in the moonlight. He heard the familiar sound of a motor before he saw the other boat. Another skiff was returning to the marina. The man noticed Ryan and waved to him. Ryan waved back hoping the guy would continue on, but no—he slowed down.

"Everything okay there?" he yelled out from his skiff.

"Yeah, wife's fine. We partied too much. She's drunk as a skunk."

"Ahhh, been there."

"She can sleep it off on the yacht. She'll feel worse in the morning," Ryan laughed trying to make a joke.

The man nodded, revved up his engine and continued toward the skiff slips.

Ryan took a deep breath. "Damn easy lie," he muttered into the wind as his hair blew across his face. *Exactly what I had planned to say if anyone saw me with her in this condition. I can be so damn clever.* The smile on his face was psychotic, devious and determined—like Robert DiNero in *Cape Fear*.

He approached the *Southern Cross*, sidled up to the ladder, picked up Lena, hoisted her small frame over his shoulder and maneuvered to his yacht.

He placed her on the bed in his sleeping chamber and went back for his duffle bag.

When he returned, he glanced at the clock on his nightstand—nearly 11:00. Perfect timing. He opened his duffle bag and took out the duct tape. He'd have an hour to complete his plan.

Lena opened her glassy eyes and stared around the room—she'd seen it before, but nothing made sense to her right now. Her hands and feet were taped, and she couldn't move her lips because there was some sort of cloth and tape across her face. She tried rolling off the bed by bringing her knees to her chest, but instead managed to hit her head on the nightstand. She fell directly onto the floor and winced out a muffled cry of pain. Footsteps made her glance up at him.

"No, no, honey. No place to go." Ryan picked her off the floor and set her back on the bed. She glared at him in panic, and uttered guttural screams through the cloth and tape across her mouth.

What he had to say to her was very important—he'd thought about it for days. "I'm not going to hurt you. I like you, Lena. But I have to do this. There are things about me you don't know, and I can't face life anymore. I will set you free because you don't deserve to die.

I've already contacted Gaspard, and I've told him where to pick you up. I'm going to put you in my Zodiac with a high-beam flashlight taped to your chest. Sorry, but I have to keep your hands tied to the flashlight."

She stared at him in horror and disbelief. Then she tried swatting him with her tied hands. He ducked and her hands missed his face. Her voice groaned out of her body like a wounded animal, and it rankled him to listen to the pathetic sounds.

"Stop it!" he screamed at her. "I said I won't hurt you, but I'm going to have to give you another injection so you remain calm. Whatever you do, stay in the Zodiac. Your life depends upon it. Got that?"

She nodded. Tears ran down her cheeks and her chest was heaving short bursts of air in and out through her nose.

"One more thing. I have to tie you up to the bed so you don't try to go anywhere. I need to calculate something, but I'll be back shortly."

He was pretty sure he heard her grunt out "asshole" while he tied her up.

CHAPTER 71

Gaspard, Evan, Bob and the Police

The last ten minutes dragged on as if each minute was an hour. Gaspard paced on his good foot, digging his other heel into the floor to keep his gout toe pointed upwards. Somehow fear had replaced pain. Evan sat in a chair next to Bob, who was asleep against the wall. Nichols and Wilkes came and went, talking on the phone trying to locate Ryan and Lena's whereabouts. Evan sipped black coffee in attempt to stay alert.

Gaspard's phone pinged. He fumbled for the phone and it dropped to the floor. He couldn't bend over to pick it up, so Evan rushed to pick up the phone and placed it in Gaspard's shaking hands. He looked anxious, relieved, terrified and angry—as if he couldn't decide which emotion to project. "It's a text from Ryan," he blurted out so loudly it woke Bob up.

"Do you want me to read it?" Evan offered.

"No. This is my daughter—I have to read it."

"I've decided not to keep your daughter. You can find her in my Zodiac at these latitude and longitude coordinates. She will be groggy because I've given her a drug to make her sleep. Her hands are taped to a high-beam flashlight in an upright position so you will be able to spot the Zodiac. I suggest you drive out to the marina and pick her up before she freezes to death. Please understand I didn't want to do any of this—but it's necessary."

Gaspard's knees buckled and Evan caught him before he hit the floor. Bob rose to assist Evan and both men helped Gaspard to a chair. He hung his head and began to weep. Fear engulfed him and he was unable to speak. Evan knelt on the floor and put a hand on Gaspard's knee. "Hang in there— she'll be okay. He said he hasn't harmed her."

"I know. I'm overcome with gratitude, but I'm mad as hell."

"Okay, then. Let's go get her, and then, let's go get him."

Nichols tossed Bob a gun and a holster supplied with bullets. Bob strapped it on.

"Two cars?" Evan said.

"Yes. We'll lead and turn on the sirens. Just follow. There is no speed limit under these circumstances."

They drove at high speed down the coast road, passing a few cars, and staying in the fast lane. A light fog wafted in sheets across the highway, leaving nothing but muted visibility and intermittent patches of clear driving. Evan stayed close behind the police car, driving like a maniac. Out of nowhere, something slapped against the windshield and Evan swerved the car to avoid hitting it. Bob yelled, "You just hit a beach ball!"

"Damn!" Evan said and swerved again nearly hitting an oncoming car. Gaspard said, "Kids leave them on the beach. In a storm, I've even seen an umbrella fly across the highway."

"As if our nerves are not on pure adrenalin, as it is." Evan let out a huge sigh and put his foot on the gas to catch up to the police car.

They arrived at the marina, peeling into the parking lot and drove as close to the pier as possible. Everyone got out of their cars and headed toward the skiff area.

Gaspard glanced down and noticed a metallic sandal on the pavement. He bent to pick it up. "It's Lena's. I'm going to kill the guy myself."

Evan let Gaspard's anger go. "What boat do we take?"

"Let's take the dive boat. It's not only faster than the *Belle Chloe* and the *Juliette*, but it has the flattest flip-down aft so that we can get the Zodiac and Lena on board."

"You feel well enough to skipper?" Evan asked.

"Damn right. There's also a rifle on board." Gaspard hobbled along oblivious to his painful toe. "That's Ryan's car—there, in the parking lot by the pier."

"How will we spot her?" Nichols asked.

"I've got the coordinates—I'll plug them in, and we'll head out in that direction. It's only slightly on an angle from the shoreline—about a mile out.

Everyone piled into the skiff, tightly sitting against one another. They bounced along at break-neck speed until they approached the dive boat.

Bob got out of the skiff first, and helped Gaspard board the dive boat. Everyone else followed in rapid succession.

Gaspard turned on the lights in the bridge and started the engine. "Evan, can you go down to the storage area? There's a closet. It has a rifle, a blow horn and a telescope. We're going to need that to spot the Zodiac."

Evan scampered down the deck to the lower quarters. Nichols, Wilkes and Bob braced themselves for a rough ride. Waves crested with white caps as the tide came in.

The dive boat picked up speed and hummed along, with occasional slap-bobbing wave thrusts. Evan set the rifle and blow horn under a cushion next to Gaspard. "Gun loaded?" Evan asked.

"Always. Sometimes unsavory characters try to rob dive boats—especially during high-tourist season."

"What can I do?" Evan asked.

"Take the telescope to the front of the bridge here and see if you can spot anything."

Evan picked up the telescope and worked to get it to focus properly.

Above the roar of the engine, Gaspard said. "Where the hell do you think Ryan is going?"

"Damned if I know." Evan yelled to make his voice heard. "We'll pick up Lena first—see if she's ok. Then find Ryan. He's out there somewhere."

Bob yelled to Nichols. "Should you call the Coast Guard?"

"Already have. Their boats are the fastest on the Côte."

Bob nodded, smiled and held on to the railing for dear life as the dive boat smashed into waves, throwing up sprays of water soaking everyone.

Wilkes tried to stand, grabbed the railing already seasick from the bouncy ride and heaved the contents of his recent vending sandwich over the side. Nichols looked at him and scratched his head. "You don't look well."

"Hate boats," he said.

Gaspard had turned the bow's spotlight on. It spread a beam across the water for a short distance. Clouds and misty fog obscured the moon's rays. Only intermittent glimpses of light illuminated the ebony sea.

"There! Out there!" Evan shouted. "I see the beam."

Gaspard throttled up the engine and moved ahead in that direction.

As they came upon the large raft, he slowed, however the boat's wake made the Zodiac bob around in circles. "Get me the spotlight!" Gaspard yelled.

Evan fetched the light and directed it toward the Zodiac. He couldn't see Lena. For a moment, he thought this was all a ruse. What if she wasn't out there?

He crawled to the railing, wrapped his legs around it and pointed the beam directly into the Zodiac. "There! She's in the front of the boat."

Gaspard stopped the engine. Evan and Bob ran to the rear dive lift as Gaspard let the dive boat drift in the Zodiac's direction. "I'll jump in," Evan said. He took off his shirt and kicked his shoes aside and dove into the water.

His lungs burst with air when he surfaced. The water was icy cold this far from shore. He swam to the Zodiac and reached the rubber boat. The curvature of the boat's side was inflated, rounded and above his head. He tried to hoist himself into the boat, but couldn't get enough thrust to pivot himself over the edge. He swam back to the dive boat.

"Gotta get closer," he yelled to Gaspard. Bob pulled Evan out of the water.

Gaspard yelled back. "There's a rope in the side hatch here. Tie it around this cushion and then toss it into the Zodiac. You can pull yourself toward it. When you're close enough, you can jump in—but do it close to her or you'll catapult her out of the boat."

Evan tied a decent criss-cross knot around the cushion and gave it a heave toward the Zodiac. It missed and settled into the water. "Crap," he said and pulled the rope toward himself. The wet cushion was now heavier, but the knot held. He wrapped his arms around the cushion, squeezed it a bit, and gave it a discus throw. It landed in the Zodiac. Wilkes and Nichols cheered! Evan pulled the rope toward him, slowly and deliberately. He spotted Lena. Her mouth was taped and she didn't appear to be breathing. Water had settled into the bottom of the boat. Christ, had she drowned?

Evan stood on the edge of the dive boat's platform, waited and then jumped in a side roll into the Zodiac so he'd be able to grab hold of Lena when he landed.

He hit the bottom of the boat with a splat on his back, rolled toward Lena and yelled, "Put the spotlight on her."

She was wet and shivering, which meant she was alive. He peeled the duct tape off her face, tossed the cloth and yelled for a knife. "Anyone got something I can cut this duct tape with? She's wadded up like a mummy."

Gaspard yelled to Evan. "Is she alive?"

"Yes, she's breathing. Pull the line in and let's get her on board."

Hauling Lena aboard the dive boat proved to be easier than Evan imagined. If they had taken a different boat, or a luxury yacht, they never would have been able to manage this maneuver. Bob assisted Evan with cutting off the duct tape and makeshift cradle for the flashlight. He turned it off. "Someone get me some blankets. She may be going into shock. We don't know what drugs he's given her, and she's ice cold."

Gaspard got to his knees and reached for his daughter, grabbed her and picked her limp body up in his arms. He bit his lip to hold back tears. Nichols said the Coast Guard was on the way and would be there shortly.

"Let's go get Ryan," Evan said. "Give me that gun."

"No. Lena's health is more important—I want to take her back—take her to the hospital."

Evan felt his stomach knot. This was his only chance to get Ryan—he'd waited three years for this moment, and now it was slipping out of his grasp.

This was his future father-in-law. There was no way to win this argument, and Danielle would never forgive him if Lena died because he insisted on going after Ryan.

Bob hovered and said, "I hear the Coast Guard. Can't they take Lena to the hospital?"

Gaspard was silent. "I want Ryan as much as you all do—maybe more—but I can't leave my daughter at a time like this. I need to protect her—do everything to save her life."

His words gave Evan a chilling flashback—the very words about protecting the person he loved, his sister, Ashley before she died. It was his responsibility. He couldn't protect her. Shaken, he sat on the deck defeated. Bob put a hand on Evan's shoulder, knowing exactly what he was feeling.

The Coast Guard arrived and Wilkes explained the situation. "We'll take Lena and Gaspard to the hospital," the coast guard skipper offered. "Our boats are much faster." Gaspard nodded. Evan grabbed the telescope and positioned it out to sea, looking for Ryan. "Do you think he took his own boat?"

Gaspard nodded. "Let me look." He took the telescope and fingered the lens. The moon was now bright across the water, like a deliberate pathway to the end of the earth. "I see his boat—it's the Southern Cross—doesn't seem to be moving very fast," Gaspard said and handed the telescope to Evan whose nerves were jittery and raw.

"I see him now," he said in angst and set the telescope down. "Damn! He's not that far away." He groaned in agonizing frustration.

Then they all felt it before they saw it—a deep underwater rumble. The sky lit up with an explosion into a giant mushroom cloud. Several consecutive explosions followed. From a distance the sky was a ball of black smoke, red and yellow fire, with shards of fiberglass floating through the air, then crashing back into the sea.

Evan stood on the deck in disbelief, knotted his fists and screamed "No, no, no!" He dropped to his knees in a mournful wail of defeat.

The Coast Guard men watched in shock and momentarily lost focus on Lena. Bob numbly watched the explosion at a complete loss for words. "Let's go," the Coast Guard driver said. "We'll check on the mess tomorrow morning and get it cleaned up."

Evan sat on the deck not moving. "Come on Evan," Bob said. "Ryan had his reasons. I'm sorry this isn't the justice you wanted. It's not what I wanted either."

"I needed him to rot in prison." Evan spat out, trying not to break down.

"We don't always get what we want," Bob said to offer comfort and compassion. "But, it is over—it's really over."

Evan let Bob pull him up from the deck and stood on wobbly knees shivering.

One of the Coast Guard guys climbed aboard the dive boat and offered to bring it back to the marina since Gaspard was leaving with Lena for the hospital. He was already on the phone talking to Marie, who would meet them at the hospital. Chloe was not on duty, so she agreed to drive her mother, now completely beside herself with worry.

Evan, soaking wet, shivering violently and filled with grief, slumped against the cushions. He watched the fireball lift into the atmosphere with a cloud of smoke as if Krakatoa had erupted.

CHAPTER 72

Evan, Bob and Gaspard

The Coast Guard arranged an ambulance for Lena. She was taken with Gaspard to the local hospital in Nice, the same hospital where Chloe worked and where Evan had recovered from his decompression sickness and eel bite. Evan drove with Bob in eerie silence to the hospital. When they reached admitting, they tried to speak to the doctor who was treating her, but were told they would have to wait in the lobby. No sooner had they seated themselves when Marie, Chloe and Danielle ran in. Lucas followed, putting his keys in his pants—obviously having driven his mother and two sisters. They walked past Evan and Bob, as if they didn't see them—stressed and emotionally fractured, intently focused on seeing Lena.

Evan called out to Danielle. She raised a hand and shook her head, "Not now," she whimpered and followed the attending nurse down the hall. Evan slumped back into his seat, shivering in wet clothing. Images of Ashley fighting for her life scuttled through his mind like flashbulbs going off. "Let me get you a blanket," Bob said, got up and asked the emergency staff to assist. They sat and waited. "Want some coffee?" Bob said. Evan nodded and hung his head in his hands, elbows balanced on his knees.

Time passed in slow motion despite the hectic activity in the hospital ER lobby. Eventually Gaspard returned and sat next to Evan and Bob. "How is she?" Evan asked, as he sipped hot coffee and pulled the blanket tighter around his shoulders.

"She's unconscious. They ran a toxicology screen on her. Looks like he gave her something called GHB. They think she'll be all right and have given her an antidote."

Both Bob and Evan knew what GHB was and shook their heads. Gamma Hydroxybutyrate, a central nervous system depressant, often abused by young adults at parties and all-night dance raves— frequently placed in alcohol or combined with alcohol. "Explains why she's unconscious," Evan said.

"Odorless and colorless it's often a date-rape drug," Bob said, then wished he hadn't. He changed his commentary. "It can make the user sluggish and disoriented. Sometimes users have amnesia and can't remember what's happened to them. High doses of GHB result in profound sedation."

Gaspard's pallor had not improved. He settled into a waiting room chair next to Evan and Bob. "They have her on a ventilator, which I don't understand."

Bob said, "It's to keep the airways open. The good news is the drug has a short half-life—something like thirty to sixty minutes."

"You seem to know a lot about drugs," Gaspard said.

"Suppose so. Comes with the job. Can't tell you how many kids we take to the ER with drug abuse."

"How's Marie doing?" Evan asked and took several sips of coffee. The blanket around his shoulders made him look homeless, especially with his disheveled hair.

Gaspard put a hand on Evan's shoulder. "Marie's a wreck. You saved Lena's life, you know."

"I wish I could have prevented this—I'm just glad we found her in time."

"What happens now?" Gaspard asked.

"Coast Guard and police will file the necessary reports and get in touch with Armond's brother, Giles. Painful as it will be to discuss this, Giles needs closure about what happened to his brother—he deserves to know who killed Armond."

Detective Nichols walked toward them. "We're done here for the night. We'll check on how Lena is doing in the morning. The nurse who examined her said she hadn't been raped."

Gaspard bit his lips together, nodding without saying anything.

"I suspect this explosion will be all over the news and newspapers tomorrow—we'll have to talk to the media and put out a statement tonight," Nicholas noted.

"Would you copy me on that?" Bob asked.

"Of course," Nichols agreed.

Bob said, "I have to head back home tomorrow. I'll craft a press release and send it to you first, and copy you, Evan."

"Gaspard, I'd like to see Lena before we leave," Evan said.

"Not possible. Too many people in the room already—half of them in tears—better to stop by tomorrow."

"You going to stay?" Evan glanced at Gaspard.

"Yes, sure. I'll drive everyone home in Marie's car."

"Tell Danielle I love her." Evan looked at Gaspard, who seemed to have aged a lot in a short period of time.

"Of course. I'll talk to you tomorrow."

Bob shook Gaspard's hand. "Thank you for all of your help, Bob."

"I'm glad I was able to be here."

Evan wrapped his arms around his future father-in-law and clung to him, as if holding him would somehow make things better. The blanket slipped to the floor. Evan picked up the blanket, waved goodnight to Nichols and Gapard and then walked toward the front door with Bob.

Evan drove, because Bob had no idea how to get to Evan's house from Nice.

"You okay?" Bob asked after not hearing a word out of Evan for quite awhile.

"No. Second worst day of my life—not okay."

Bob understood and knew Evan would need time to adjust to being pulled emotionally in so many directions—his past flooded back to him, Lena's dramatic rescue and precarious health, his strained relationship with Danielle and now Ryan's death—more than enough to send any man over the edge.

Although Evan was mute on the way home, suddenly he turned to Bob.

"I have to talk to Lena when she's awake—have to interview her and understand what Ryan said to her. How did he get her to his apartment? I have so many unanswered questions."

"Let's hope she remembers what happened to her. Sometimes that's a good thing—other times, not so much." Bob glanced out the window at the waves rolling across the sand, knowing it was the last time he'd see the Côte.

CHAPTER 73

Evan

Bob left on an early flight. The empty house seemed deathly quiet except for a woodpecker hammering for termites on the underside of an eave. Evan had no appetite. He felt like he was getting a cold since his head throbbed and his nose was stuffed up. Not surprising given the amount of time he spent in the water rescuing Lena. His left arm hurt at the rotator cuff, something he didn't even notice last night with all the commotion. Perhaps his sideways flip into the Zodiac strained a ligament. He gingerly moved it around in circles trying to assess if anything was torn.

He hadn't shaved and knew he looked like hell. It reminded him of the days when he was in a deep depression and not caring a hoot about his appearance. His cell phone rang bringing him back to the present. He glanced down to see who the caller was, surprised to see it was Danielle.

"Evan? It's me. Lena's awake. She wants to talk to you."

"I want to talk to her too. How is she doing?" he straightened up and tried to get the kink out of his neck from sleeping in an awkward postion.

"Better. Dad told me what you did—how you dove into the sea and how hard it was to get into the raft. I don't know how you managed to land in the Zodiac so they could pull her into the dive boat. Are you okay? You sound terrible."

Evan coughed and tried to clear his throat. "Think I'm getting a cold."

"Not surprised. I should make you some soup."

"You at home?" he asked.

"No, I'm at the hospital. Want me to stay?"

"Would you please? I need to talk to Lena, but I really need to talk to you."

"Of course. I'll wait for you. About how long?"

"Be there in less than an hour. Have to clean up. I look like hell."

She clicked off her phone and the dial tone rang in his ear. He decided to shower and shave even though lifting his arm hurt. He sniffed the tee shirt he'd slept in. It smelled like seaweed. He pinched his nose in disgust and chose fresh clothing.

On the way to the hospital, he pondered the events of last night and mulled over the questions he would ask Lena. He wasn't sure whether Danielle should be in the room while he questioned her sister. Danielle didn't mention anything about Ryan on the phone. Surely she must have known he blew himself up and undoubtedly it was too difficult to talk about. He realized the office staff at Gaspard Yachting must be reeling with shock—Armond was murdered and now, Gaspard's partner had blown himself up. What a terrible time for all of them.

Evan tried to shake off his guilt. So many layers of guilt he wasn't sure which layer to peel off first—certainly not forgiving Danielle for being pregnant with his child—that was huge; not telling her about the plan to snare Ryan and learning who Ryan really was would deeply upset her. Evan wondered if she would ever trust him again.

The sky was ominous with massive grey clouds tumbling around in different directions as if a major storm was heading toward the coast. Drizzle splattered the windshield. He turned on his wipers and headlights. The vision of the beach ball smacking across his windshield last night made him shudder. It could have ended badly—he could have hit an oncoming car—both he and Bob could have been killed. He had a sudden realization that when it wasn't time to die, you didn't die—it was that simple—the whole mystery about a master plan you couldn't change the hour in which you were going to die.

His mother, Kelly, believed those things and often told him God knew every hair on your head, which never made sense to him since so many men went bald—then what? How would God recognize you? However, when he thought about the turn of events yesterday, he wondered what God thought about someone who chose their own hour of death. Ryan ended his. Why? He could have flown to another country and disappeared. Why would he kill himself?

He drove into the hospital parking lot with a mental list of questions to ask Lena. Hopefully she could shed light on some of the missing puzzle pieces. It would not make him feel better, but at least he might understand Ryan's motive.

An attending nurse was leaving Lena's room when Evan approached the door. He poked his head in and noticed Lena looked like life had re-entered her frail body. Her skin was deathly pale, but she was eagerly sipping some liquid with a straw. Danielle was asleep in a chair. "Hey there?" Evan said and woke Danielle up. She rubbed her eyes and stood, seemingly unsure about how to greet Evan, so she moved to one side of the bed closer to the window. Lena gave a weak wave and told Evan to sit down.

"Can I hug you?" he said.

"Sure, just not too hard. I ache everywhere."

"You had a really rough time. I'm sorry for what you went through," Evan said and fluffed her hair a bit.

"Dad told me what you did. I owe you my life," she said as tears welled up in her dark eyes.

"Do you feel up to answering some questions?" Evan pulled the chair up next to her bed.

"I'll try. Not sure what I can remember. My head hurts and my brain feels, well, drugged. I've been told what I was on. Tried drugs a couple of times with guys I dated. The day after gave me a horrid hangover, so I stopped doing drugs."

"Smart girl." Evan nodded. "I've run across a lot of kids who have died taking GHB and god knows what else they combine with it—as if kids can't have a good time without it. Some guys use it as a date rape drug because they know women won't remember what's happened to them."

"I prefer to enjoy my sex," she said, laughing. Her words cracked Evan and Danielle up, lightening the mood.

"I see you haven't lost your sense of humor." Evan smiled. "What can you tell me about how you ended up in Ryan's apartment?"

"Well—let me think. I was at work and so was he. Oh! I remember now. We started talking about his apartment—he wanted me to redecorate it. He offered to take me to dinner."

"Where did you eat?"

"Can't remember. Probably Les Pecheurs. I think I had lobster or some seafood."

"How did you get to his apartment?"

"He drove—we left my car in the parking lot at work—oh my god, it's still there!"

Danielle piped up. "Not to worry. Lucas drove it home."

"I feel so stupid. He duped me into thinking he really wanted my design help." Lena shifted positions in bed and stuffed another pillow behind her head.

"What happened at his apartment?" Evan turned on his cell to video record.

"Um—nothing much. We had wine and talked about the colors he wanted for his, um, what was it—oh, removing the drapes—blinds would have looked so much better."

"And?"

"That's all I remember. I felt dizzy. I think I passed out."

"How did you get to Ryan's boat?"

Lena hesitated while tears trickled down her pale face. "I—uh, I don't remember," she drifted off looking out the window, her voice sounding weak and tiny. Her face scrunched into a scowl. "Next thing I'm tied up on his yacht. He taped my mouth shut."

Evan could still see the marks on the side of her face. "I'm sorry he did that to you. Did he say why he did it?"

"Let me think—uh," she paused, blew her nose and said nothing. Evan waited. Danielle didn't interrupt.

"Oh! Now I recall. Fuzzy bits of his saying something about not wanting to hurt me."

"Good. What else?"

"Um, I'm not sure. My head does not feel like it's on my body—I hate this," she sniffled and grabbed some more tissues.

"You've had a traumatic experience—take your time."

Danielle shifted around in her chair, but kept quiet. Evan glanced at her and noticed how exhausted she looked. He could imagine the strain this had put on her and her family.

"You know what he said to me?" Lena wailed out a mournful sigh. "He said he couldn't face life—didn't want to live anymore or something like that. He said I didn't deserve to die." She pulled her pillow up over her head and put it into her face and broke down in painful sobs. She paused and removed the pillow. "I liked Ryan," she choked out—"maybe thought I loved him at one point. I can't believe he's dead."

Evan shut off his phone and sat in silence with Lena and Danielle. There was nothing more to say. Danielle's face was pinched and tears were flowing down her cheeks. All of this was too much for her to bear—so much had happened to this family and he could see how deeply Danielle loved her sister. Lena's anguish was her anguish—they shared in their joys and sorrows. He remembered Danielle had told him awhile ago that sister jealousy was a phase Lena had matured out of, leaving her vulnerable and open to finding love on her own. Lena no longer needed or wanted whatever Danielle had. Their differences complemented one another, gave them strength and appreciation for their unique gifts. He looked at both women and could see the bond they shared.

"How 'bout if I stop by tomorrow?" Evan asked and stood to leave.

"I'd like that," Lena sniffled and composed herself.

"Can we talk soon?" Danielle looked at Evan with her eyes pleading for his touch.

Evan walked over to her and put his arms around her, held her tightly and kissed her on the forehead. "Of course. Please know that I love you. I'm really sorry."

Danielle nodded and released herself from Evan, her lips trembling, but managed a small smile—a smile of hope.

Evan left the room, and Danielle moved to the chair closer to her sister.

"What's happened with you and Evan? Is everything okay?"

"I think it will be. I have something to tell you—it's a long story," Danielle said.

Lena reached for her sister's hand and gave it a gentle squeeze. "I'm not going anywhere."

CHAPTER 74

Evan and Danielle

The next day Detective Nichols contacted Gaspard and told him the Maritime Gendarmerie investigated the explosion and found a tennis shoe floating on a piece of debris. There was no evidence of a body, nor did they expect to find one since the explosion would have decimated Ryan. Nichols said Captain Bouchamp intended to close the matter and said a copy of the news release would be forthcoming shortly. He indicated he'd be sending it to Sheriff Cosley as well.

Evan, ever curious, went to the marina. Intent on seeing the remains of the disaster for himself in daylight, he borrowed a skiff from the harbormaster and motored out to the wreckage. The white-hot sun in a cloudless sky felt good on his cold-stuffed head. As he approached the wreckage, he saw heaps of fragmented metal, wood, fiberglass and chunks of deck furniture floating aimlessly in the sea while the Coast Guard worked with a salvage crew to clean it up. Fuel slick was everywhere, reflecting the sunlight with a greasy film that would remain for days. Evan knew exactly what he was looking for—a body, or what was left of a body floating amongst the debris, but there was none. He wasn't sure his stomach could stand the sight of a partial limb—he turned the skiff around and headed back to the marina.

The wind whipped through his hair while sea spray splattered his shorts. He decided he'd put off the conversation long enough. When he docked at the marina he dialed Danielle's phone number.

"Evan. Where are you?"

"Marina. I'm finished here. How's Lena?"

"Much better. She's coming home today. Mama's at a friend's house now, but will pick Lena up around four."

"Such good news."

"Dad's going to close down the company for a few days— Nicole and the staff, especially the crew that worked with Ryan are so upset about his death. "

Evan moored the skiff into its spot, got out and nodded to Pierre in the distance. "Understandable Gaspard would shut down the company. It's been an impossible time of tragedy." Evan stood on one foot and shook water out of his shoe.

"You doing anything now?" Evan wondered.

"I'm at the house. Valentin is here, but everyone else is gone. Do you want to come over?"

"I do. How about in about thirty minutes, okay?

"Yeah, great. See you then."

Evan drove to St. Paul, enjoying the ride on the way to Danielle's home. It seemed so long ago when he first met her—the woman who changed his life—the woman he deeply loved and had let down. He hoped he'd find the right words to convey his feelings.

He'd already called Kelly, his mother, who was so emotional when he told her Danielle was pregnant. Kelly said she had not thought of being a grandmother—didn't expect it to happen. The idea of a baby being part of her life in the future was a gift from God she didn't expect. Both Baxter and Kelly were shocked to hear the turn of events regarding Gaspard's partner. To learn that Ryan was actually Jed Reddiger, who had committed the robbery in El Dorado Hills, was unsettling, and yet provided necessary closure. Evan explained a news release would be forthcoming soon from Sheriff Cosley, who'd been exceptionally helpful in solving this case. Kelly had mentioned she felt the victims who died that day had families who deserved to know who had been responsible for their loved one's deaths.

To cheer his parents up a bit, Evan told them he hoped to be able to bring Danielle home soon for a visit.

As he rounded the corner to her property, he saw Danielle standing by the gate. She wore a pale blue halter dress. A wide-brimmed straw hat sat atop her head with blue grosgrain streamers trailing down to her shoulders—he could have sworn it was the same hat she wore when he first met her.

He parked his car just inside the gate. She walked over to greet him. "I've got a nasty cold," he said apologetically with his arms outstretched.

"I don't care," she said and let her body melt into his embrace. Her hat toppled to the ground. He reached for it, grabbed it by the brim and handed it to her.

She beamed. "I think you've done this before."

"Same hat, right?"

"Uh-huh. Thought it would bring me good luck," she said.

"Somewhere private we can talk?" Evan glanced toward the guesthouse.

"Sure. Valentin's working on his math homework. His dyslexia is so much better. He's going over to a friend's house this afternoon."

Evan put his arm around Danielle's back and heard the familiar barking before he saw Thor, who bounded down the pathway, jumped up and put his paws on Evan's shoulders.

"Hey, boy." Evan rubbed Thor's back while fluffing the thick hair around his neck and ears. Thor howled a happy 'thank you' in dog-speak and slapped his tail into Evan's thigh, then playfully nipped at the heels of his shoe while he walked with Danielle.

She opened the door to the guesthouse. Thor wanted to come in. "No, Thor. Go play," Danielle insisted. Thor plopped down on the patio, extending his front paws and lowering his head with a dejected pout. He refused to move.

Evan looked around the room remembering everything that had happened there—his recovery from his heel surgery, and his intimate moments with Danielle—so intense it led to her pregnancy.

"How's the baby?" he blurted out.

For the first time, she unabashedly lifted her dress showing him her growing abdomen. "Really good. Doctor says everything is fine." She immediately put down her dress as if to hide the uncomfortable elephant in the room.

"When is the baby due?" Evan sat on the bed and motioned for her to sit next to him.

"Less than five months." She cupped her hands around her baby-bump and restrained the conflicted smile of excitement she wished she could show him.

"I have a lot I need to say," Evan put his hand on her shoulder. "It's my fault."

"No, no. Evan, it's no one's fault."

He shifted on the bed toward her. "I don't mean the baby. I acted selfishly when you told me—the shock overwhelmed me. I'm deeply sorry I hurt you when I should have comforted you."

"I understand." She stroked the side of his face with her fingertips. "I shouldn't have kept it a secret."

"I've been afraid for years." He paused and bit his lips. "I didn't want kids in my life because I felt I couldn't protect them. Before Ashley died I was always in control—sure of myself—tough on the inside and out. As a cop, I had to be. It hardened me to some extent because otherwise things I saw ripped me raw."

Danielle nodded and put her hands in her lap but didn't take her focus from his face.

"Everything that's happened to me this past year has shaken my façade, the protection I put up to avoid dealing with the angst and burden I managed to carry around—blame was an easy out. As long as I felt guilty, I was doing the penance I thought was expected of me."

"Being raised Catholic," she said, "I understand the guilt and penance thing. You know, my dad is a lot like that. He suffers and self-flagellates well past when he should just let it go."

"I think the longer we do the guilt trip, the more we assume God will forgive us, which is ridiculous," Evan said.

"God doesn't carry a grudge." Danielle slid sideways on the bed and leaned on her elbow.

"I don't want to live my life in fear," Evan said. "I want this baby—*our* baby."

Danielle sat up and her hands flittered back and forth in front of her face like a hummingbird. "I, uh, can't talk right now," she managed to squeak out.

"Then don't talk." He took both of her hands in his and kissed them, then kissed her forehead. She lifted herself to her knees and threw her arms around him.

"Evan, I love you so much. Please kiss me."

"I don't want to give you or the baby my cold," he protested and instead kissed her forehead.

"Can we just cuddle?" She pleaded and rubbed his back taking in the scent uniquely his.

"That we can do." He pulled her next to him and they spooned. "What do you think your dad will do now that he has to run the company by himself?"

"Claude, the head crewmaster, asked if he could take over Ryan's client duties. He's a terrific mechanic and has been with papa for years. After what's happened, papa wants to manage the financials himself."

"I'm really glad to hear that."

"Have you told your dad about the baby?" Evan asked, feeling horribly responsible for getting her pregnant.

"I didn't, but mama did. He's thrilled. From the size of our family, you can tell he loves babies. However, they had quite an argument when she found out he'd put Lucas in jeopardy on those stakeouts."

"Oh, you know about that?" He rubbed her arm.

"Not much stays a secret in this family. Once someone starts yelling in the house, everyone knows what's going on. By the way, I told Lena yesterday I was pregnant."

"Oh?" Evan could feel himself flush. "What did she say?"

"She's so happy for us. Obviously she has a lot on her mind, but the idea of having a baby around cheered her up— gave her something to look forward to. By the way, Evan, I have something to ask you."

He took a deep breath, wondering what she was about to say.

"Why didn't you tell me you and Bob were going after Ryan?"

He turned her over on her side so he could see her face. "I didn't want to keep it a secret from you—but I couldn't put you in danger. Think about what's happened to Lena. It could have been you!"

She twisted her lips to the side of her face carefully considering what he just said.

"Are you going to do this cop stuff when we are married?"

"Hell, no. I'm so done with this. I want to get back to my art. The dark, somber work I did in the past reflected my grief. Now, I feel like my work is going to burst on the canvas with vibrant color. The gallery owner is waiting for me to contact her to arrange an exhibit. Obviously I couldn't tell her what had been going on. She thinks I'm still settling in."

"You know you avoided my mentioning getting married?"

"Speaking of that—I'd marry you tomorrow, but I'm concerned about your family. I respect them deeply and don't want to rush or offend them in anyway."

"I've been thinking, if it's okay with you, let's wait to get married until after the baby is born," Danielle suggested.

"Oh! Well, I hadn't thought of that. But considering the recent events, a wedding now is bad timing. It feels wrong for your family to be planning a wedding when they are feeling the impact of Ryan's death."

"Let's wait," Danielle said. "At least six months—besides, I want a flat stomach in my wedding dress," she giggled.

"It will be winter here by then," he said.

"I'll wear something with white fur on the cuffs of the sleeves. We can go somewhere warm for our honeymoon."

"Where would you like to go?" he said with a quizzical expression on his face.

"How about Majorca? I've always wanted to visit that island off Spain."

"Sounds great. Whatever you want. The very thought of giving up frigid, icy, snowy winters in New York isn't going to bother me one bit."

"I'm chilly," she said and snuggled into his arm. Thor pawed at the glass on the door. "Dog's gotten very attached to you. Remember how terrified you were of him when we first met?"

"Who me? Terrified? You must be mistaken."

She laughed and kissed him on the cheek.

"What are you doing tomorrow?" he smoothed tendrils off of her forehead.

"Why?"

"Thought you'd like to see the house I bought for us."

"The what?" she bolted up in bed and put her hand to her mouth.

Evan explained he had put a down payment on the house she'd fallen in love with—the one with the dusty blue shutters looking like it was straight out of Aix-en-Provence. He'd arranged to break his lease on his rental for a small fee. As it was, the rental company had another tenant lined up.

Thor kept pawing at the door until Evan let him in. He immediately jumped up on the bed and started licking Evan's face. "I assume you want a dog?" she said.

"Baby first, dog later."

They snuggled like a married couple, Thor at their feet snoring, as they dozed off. Later, the setting sun poked through the glass and woke Evan up. Danielle stirred.

"You know," he said. "I figured out why Ryan kidnapped Lena—kept her and then put her in a raft—it was as if he wanted us to see him—needed us to see his yacht explode. I'm not sure he's dead."

"Evan! Stop it. Just stop being a cop. He's dead! With what we've been through, my family needs him to be dead. Promise me you'll let this go?"

He sighed deeply and turned over on his back. "I'll try."

EPILOGUE

It was cold and inky dark floating in the water. He'd flapped around at the surface a safe distance from the yacht in his BC. He'd dropped the tank he needed to dive deeply after he spilled gasoline below deck, lit the dynamite fuses and jumped in the water. As he watched the explosion in the dark, he felt a sense of exhilaration and regret. He loved that boat.

The submarine spotted his flickering flashlight, then picked up him at the exact coordinates he'd specified. Hours later, his skin was still blue even after they peeled off his wetsuit. He had tucked a waterproof plastic container of his meds and a few other critical items he needed into his wetsuit zip pockets. For now, he rested on a tiny hammock while the sub ping-pinged its way through the depths.

Two weeks later he awoke on his new sailboat in Majorca with a different identity and a new passport, courtesy of the sub drug runners. He'd not yet adjusted to wearing glasses or seeing himself in the mirror with bleached blonde hair. The mustache and facial scruff would grow out in time, making him unrecognizable. The telltale tattoo wound would need a lot of new color added to it for camouflage.

Originally, he planned to buy another yacht with the money from his offshore accounts and settle into an apartment on the coast. Then he saw the boat for sale and couldn't resist it. *Slipped Away,* was the perfect name for a sailboat that fit his new life. Nick Fontaine would live on his boat and sail at will. Majorca held great promise for yet another new life.

THE END

ACKNOWLEDGMENTS

To Michele, June, Linda and Tarra—my critique partners for a year who also became beta readers and helped me evolve into a better writer, more comfortable in my own skin. I want to thank, Terry, my sister-in-law, who has been such an enthusiastic cheerleader for both of my novels. I am also indebted to Mary and Afton for their eagle eyes for content and line editing. Special thanks to Lee Lofland for his expert police procedural advice, and Sheriff Robert Cosley for allowing me to create him as a character in this novel. Thanks also go to Lisa for her insight. I am grateful for Patty G. Henderson, owner of Boulevard Photografica, for her creativity and exceptional cover design. I am indebted to my formatter, Rob Preece, with his tremendous knowledge and skills. Once again, my husband, Jim, deserves credit for listening to the story as the chapters unfolded always asking the right questions. Your support means everything to me.

Many authors write romantic suspense where robberies, murders and unpleasant things occur. However, those of us who believe in justice focus on the importance of solving crimes and preventing them. Grief, no matter what the reason, is never easy, and difficult to deal with. For anyone who has suffered the loss of a loved one, especially that of a child, this book was written for you.

REQUEST FOR REVIEWS

If you enjoyed this story, I would appreciate a positive review on Amazon.com and Goodreads under books, DANGEROUS DUPLICITY. Reviews remind authors what our readers value and enjoy, as well as keeping us motivated to continue writing. It takes a tremendous amount of time to research a novel, draft and redraft 100,000 words into a compelling story. I write because it's challenging and I enjoy it. If someone else enjoys my novels and short stories, I'm thrilled! Thank you for purchasing my work. Partial proceeds go to to the Cystic Fibrosis Foundation and St. Jude's Hospital for children.

PRAISE FOR DANGEROUS DUPLICITY

DANGEROUS DUPLICITY is a tightly written, contemporary romantic suspense that we've come to expect from author Sherry Joyce—and she does not disappoint in this, her second novel. There are more twists in this fast-paced murder mystery than the actual death-defying hairpin turns on the towering hills above the seaside in St.-Paul-de-Vence. Whether onboard multi-million dollar yachts in the Riviera or diving under the sea, this adventure will take you on a wild ride with its intricate plot and memorable characters as they grapple with tragedy, grief, difficult decisions and the ultimate redeeming power of love.

...T.T. Thomas, Author, Mistress of Mogador

Sherry Joyce is a gifted storyteller, one of those writers who can keep you reading, reading, reading. DANGEROUS DUPLICITY, a story with twists, turns, dangers and lies that will keep you intrigued from the first gunshot to the last explosion.

...Michele Drier, Author of the Amy Hobbes Mysteries and Kandensky Vampire Chronicles

Well-written deceit has the power to lure me through novels as DANGEROUS DUPLICITY did when it grabbed me by the throat from the opening pages and introduced me to a bounty of fascinating individuals coming up against dangers of a subtle, yet deadly sort. It was hard to put the book down. I was so engrossed in Sherry Joyce's artful portrayal of the villian, as well as the protagonist when they confront one another through her well-constructed plots. An absorbing read!

...June Gillam, Author of the Hillary Broome Novels

AUTHOR BIO

Sherry Joyce is the author of two contemporary romantic suspense novels, THE DORDOGNE DECEPTION and DANGEROUS DUPLICITY. Two of her short stories, were recently published. COZUMEL CALAMATY was published in Our Dance With Words/A Collection of Fine Writing, by Northern California Publishers and Authors. MURDER BY CONCLUSION was published by Sisters In Crime's 2016 Capitol Crimes Anthology.

She also owns Sherry Joyce Creative Writing Services, assisting luxury home market real estate agents, and has written extensively for several years for BEHIND THE GATES, a local magazine. She is a guest feature writer for THE HILLS LIVING.

As owner of SJ Designs Interiors, she was published in GENTRY MAGAZINE, CALIFORNIA REMODELER, NATIONAL KITCHEN AND BATH, and a college textbook on interior design. She won Best Peninsula Interior Designer, two years in a row. An artist, she is a Board Director for the El Dorado Arts Council, is a member of the California Writer's Club/Sacrament, Sisters In Crime, Sacramento, Northern California Publishers and Authors and Women's National Book Association, San Francisco.

Happily retired in 2000 as a Vice President of Human Resources with worldwide responsibility for several high-tech firms in the Bay Area, she now lives in El Dorado Hills with her husband and two West Highland Terriers.

LEARN MORE ABOUT THE AUTHOR

WEBSITE: www.http://sherryjoyce.com

Other novels: THE DORDOGNE DECEPTION

Published short stories:
COZUMEL CALAMITY, Northern California Publishers and Authors, 'Our Dance With Words' – a collection of fine writing, MURDER BY CONCLUSION, Sisters In Crime/Sacramento Chapter, Capitol Crimes/Anthology

BOOK CLUB QUESTIONS AND DISCUSSION TOPICS FOR DANGEROUS DUPLICITY

Why does Evan Wentworth have such a difficult time with his sister's death? Does grief have timetable? How is loss different for each person?

When Evan meets Aurora Banfield, is he ready for a lasting relationship? If so, why or why not?

Why is it so easy for Evan to be caught up in the art world?

How had Danielle DuBois defined her life while caring for her mother?

When her mother improves, how does this affect Danielle's life?

Should Gaspard have put his son, Lucas, in danger? Were his reasons justified?

When Evan meets Danielle, how is his relationship with her different from his relationship with Aurora?

When Evan explains his reasons for not wanting children of his own, how does meeting Danielle's siblings affect his decision to have or not have a child of his own someday?

What causes Aurora to behave in a despicable way when she first meets Danielle?

Do you think justice is always necessary to move on? If there is no justice, what happens to the individual carrying the anger or rage?

What motivated Ryan to commit the robbery in El Dorado Hills? Was he a heartless killer? How did his upbringing affect his decisions about right and wrong? If he was a sociopath, why did he save Evan's life?

Should Danielle have told her mother she was pregnant? How did keeping her secret affect her relationship with Evan? Should she have told him sooner?

What about Danielle's family resonated with you? Did you feel they were close? Did they keep secrets out of loyalty or to protect those they loved?

Did the book have a surprising ending for you? If so, why or why not?

www.ingramcontent.com/pod-product-compliance
Lightning Source LLC
Chambersburg PA
CBHW030810260626
47169CB00001B/271